Sins of the Father

A Barrett Women novel

By Fleur Blüm

Fleur Blüm is a Melbourne-based writer, performer and musician.

Her blog can be found at https://fleurblum.com/blog

Also by Fleur Blüm:

Sophie's Path: A choose your own romance adventure

Discovering the Franklins

My Mother's Secret

Singular Focus

The Mother's Fault: a Barrett Women novel

First edition 2022

Copyright © 2022 Fleur Blüm
ISBN 978-0-6483654-5-7

Editor: Annie Seaton
Cover Design: Charmaine Ross

Published by Fleur Blüm, Melbourne, Australia

For all the women and girls out there who have had difficult experiences and come out the other side.

1. Goodbye Daddy

1985

Janine Barrett was too hot in her black dress. Her mother, Vicky, had made her wear stockings even though it was the middle of February, the hottest month of the year.

'I won't have you looking like a tramp at your own father's funeral,' she'd said.

Janine had crossed her arms and put on her best pouty face, but in the end, she'd given up. Mum had bought her the new dress for the occasion. Shiny black polyester, off the shoulder with a big bow across the boobs rustled as she walked. She was surprised her mother had allowed it, the dress was tight-fitting and only came to mid-thigh.

They hadn't had much time to get things ready; Vicky was in full crisis mode and didn't care much what Janine was doing. Unless it included 'slutting around'.

As if she was innocent at my age, Janine thought as she sat in the hot chapel beside her mother. She wasn't listening to the droning voice of the minister. He must have been even hotter than her in all that getup.

Her father's coffin was closed. One side of the chapel was filled with men in uniform. If they hadn't all been Dad's pals she might have found them attractive. Janine loved uniforms. But on closer inspection they were all salt and pepper haired with bulging bellies.

The booklet in her hand had a photo of her father, taken when he'd been promoted to sergeant. Even on the other side of forty, still handsome, with broad shoulders she'd always loved riding as a child. When he was home that was.

The job in the army meant he was away from the family for most of the year. He'd be placed on some project or other around Australia, sometimes in the Pacific. 'Godforsaken deserts and bug-infested jungles' he'd called them.

Her mother never allowed them to visit him. She didn't care for any of it. Janine wasn't really sure why they had married at all sometimes. She'd always wanted to see what her dad did to experience the challenges and meet the natives he always spoke about. *No chance of that now.*

Janine was surprised she didn't feel particularly sad. She'd cried a little when her mother had broken the news, but mostly she felt numb. Maybe it would have sunk in better if she'd been allowed to look in the coffin, but the army guys said she'd better not see it. Something about bloating and discolouration.

It was patronising—just because she was a girl. She wasn't a child anymore and he didn't get shot or anything. Her mother didn't want to see him.

Her dad, big strong man that he was, had died of pneumonia. In the desert, somewhere out the back of nowhere in the Northern Territory doing secret army stuff, and he'd stood on a rusty nail. His tetanus shots weren't up to date, and the army doctor had run out. While they'd trying to treat him, he developed pneumonia and drowned in his own fluids.

Her mother snuffled into a hanky. She hadn't stopped crying in the three days since they'd found out. It had to be for show; her parents were hardly close.

Bill, her dad, had only been home one month out of every six, sometimes all at once, sometimes only a week before he was sent off somewhere else. He always brought Janine a present.

'You're my special girl,' he'd say, and kiss her.

At the front of the chapel, the minister clutched the pulpit. He swayed slightly, Janine narrowed her eyes.

I bet he's drunk. Her mother would often have several glasses of wine with dinner, before dinner, and after.

'Bill would have been proud to see his daughter growing into a woman. I'm sure he will be watching over her as she develops. I'll call on her now to read from Corinthians.'

Janine stood, the back of her legs damp with sweat as she walked the short distance to the pulpit. She'd practised the passage repeating it over and over to herself to make her father proud.

They weren't a religious family, her father had believed in God, they went to church at Christmas, Easter and for special occasions. This was the first time Janine had spoken to a congregation.

She cleared her throat. '*I declare to you, brothers and sisters, that flesh and blood cannot inherit the kingdom of God, nor does the perishable inherit the imperishable,*' she said.

The celebrant nudged her and pointed up. She swallowed and tried again, louder this time.

'*Listen, I tell you a mystery: We will not all sleep, but we will all be changed— in a flash, in the twinkling of an eye, at the last trumpet. For the trumpet will sound, the dead will be raised imperishable, and we will be changed. For the perishable must clothe itself with the imperishable, and the mortal with immortality. When the perishable has been clothed with the imperishable, and the mortal with immortality.*'

Janine's hands were trembling as she read. She grabbed the sides of the pulpit, just as the minister had, and swayed a little.

'You're doing fine,' he whispered.

'*Then the saying that is written will come true: Death has been swallowed up in victory. Where, O death, is your victory? Where, O death, is your sting? The sting of death is sin, and the power of sin is the law. But thanks be to God! He gives us the victory through our Lord Jesus Christ.*'

She staggered back to her seat on legs made from jelly. She'd done a good job, heads in the crowd nodded, and she felt a silly urge to grin. She pushed it down and set her mouth in a stony line.

Grownups don't grin at funerals. Her father would have understood she was pleased and relieved, and her mother would use it later.

As she sat down, her mother dabbed her eyes with a sodden handkerchief and replaced her hands in her lap.

Several of the men in uniform on the other side of the chapel spoke. Her father's superior spoke of how he was a credit to the army, how he had been a committed soldier for twenty-five years and that he would be sorely missed. *I bet he says that every time someone dies.*

A man, about the same age, and whose face was weathered and sunken from long working in the sun, stood at the front and told stories of how he and Bill had played pranks on the new recruits, created rapport with the locals, and always left their mark on the people they had helped.

Janine was both fascinated and bored hearing about her father's life. Still, the sadness didn't come.

Finally, it was her mother's turn. Janine had offered to help her mother write the eulogy but had been told to keep her fat nose out of it.

'I met Bill through my brother; they were both in the cadets and he thought we'd get on. He was right, of course, we got on like a house on fire. I had hoped—' she broke off to blow her nose with a honk.

'I had hoped that we would grow old together. That when he finally finished gallivanting around saving the world, we would find a little cottage and keep bees.'

Janine stifled a snigger. Her mother in a cottage with bees? She was a rigidly reputable woman with champagne taste. She liked nice things and used them to feel superior to others. Retirement spending every day with Bill? She was clearly delusional. Whenever he was home for a month straight, they were bickering and hounding each other within a fortnight. Her mother nagged incessantly; she'd had no idea how to give Dad what he needed.

'Bill was a good man, a good provider, and when he was with us on leave, a great help around the house.

'Now all we have of him are memories. Our daughter will always be a reminder of the man I've now lost. Along with all the half-finished projects in the shed!' There was a smattering of laughter, and the men in uniform nodded.

The service ended with a hymn. Some rubbish the minister had chosen. Her mother didn't sing, she said it was undignified. The sweltering chapel filled with the droning of fifty men who would rather do anything else.

Outside was much cooler, a late afternoon breeze swept past Janine. The sweat collected inside her dress had soaked through her knickers and strapless bra was chilly against her skin. She followed her mother back to the car.

'How did I do, Mum?' she asked.

'What?'

Janine jogged a few steps in her teetering black stilettos to catch up. 'The reading, how did I do?'

'You weren't a complete embarrassment. Stiff as a board and barely audible, but we can't do much about it now.'

Janine's smile faded. She should have known better than to expect praise from her mother, but maybe this day, of all days might have been the exception.

*   *   *

The wake was held at their family home in Camberwell, a large, single-storey, cream, weatherboard Edwardian house. Her father's parents lived in a similar house around the corner and it had been his idea to buy there. Her mother constantly complained about the snobs in the area.

Her grandparents had insisted on having the wake catered, and the black-clad staff were waiting outside the house when they arrived.

'You're here. I thought someone would have let you in already. Keep the canapés coming and stay out of my way,' Vicky barked at the closest.

The woman, in her forties, dark hair pulled back in a severe bun, held a clipboard and looked to be in charge. She widened her eyes slightly, then nodded and started giving instructions to the staff.

Her mother poured herself a glass of red wine as soon as she walked in the door.

'Do I have to be at this party?' Janine asked. She was tired and watching the coffin be lowered into the ground had released some of the sadness she'd pushed down.

'Yes. You will not humiliate me,' Vicky stared out the kitchen window. 'Go put on some perfume or something, you smell like a pig.'

'Can I have some wine?'

'No. You're fifteen.'

'You never let me do anything,' Janine whined. 'It's Dad's bloody wake. Can't I just have one glass?'

'Let her have one, Vicky, it can't do any harm.' Her father's mother, Claire, had let herself in behind them.

'Fine. It's on you if she does anything stupid,' Vicky said. She refilled her glass and stalked off toward her bedroom.

'Don't mind her, she's had a hard day too.' Her paternal grandmother was Janine's favourite. The one who spoiled her, she barely saw her mother's parents.

'She's so mean.'

'I know, sweetheart. Don't let it get to you, eh?' Claire put her plump hand on her shoulder. 'Have some of this.'

She poured out a glass of red wine and held it out to Janine. 'Sip it dear, like a lady. Make it last.'

Her grandmother wore thick glasses, her grey hair was cut short against her head, and she was almost as round as she was tall. It was grandma who brought chicken soup when they were sick, and gave Janine secret chocolate. Her mother wouldn't keep any kind of junk food in the house.

It wasn't Janine's first taste of wine, but it was her first whole glass. She used to steal a little when her mother was nodding off on the couch and drink it furtively in the kitchen. She'd never had enough to get drunk, and wondered what it would feel like to have to hold onto something to stand upright.

Guests started arriving in dribs and drabs. Everyone who had been in the chapel, and at the cemetery, of course, as well as a number of her mother's friends who had had to be left off the guest list to fit all her father's army buddies.

Only once the wine was being sent around with the wait staff, and the smell of the hot nibbles wafted through the house, did her mother made her appearance. She'd redone her makeup and changed into a floor length gown of deep navy shot through with flecks of silver. Janine thought it looked like she'd tried to wear the night sky, although looking glamorous at your husband's funeral was tacky.

*   *   *

Janine nursed her glass of wine; her grandmother had topped the glass up a couple of times. 'It's still only one glass if you top up before you finish,' she said.

Janine's cheeks were flushed, the tight dress and thick black stockings felt suffocating. It was nearly midnight when she stood up and moved quietly towards her bedroom.

'Where do you think you're going, you little slut?' her mother whispered at her elbow, appearing out of nowhere. She was quite drunk now; her teeth and lips had turned purple from the wine and rage burned in her eyes.

'I'm going to bed, Mum, it's late and no one is talking to me.'

'More important to be entertained constantly than to show any kind of respect?' Vicky's words were blurred at the edges.

'No. I'm just—it's boring and I'm tired.'

'You think you're tired? Twenty-seven years with your father and now I have to make conversation with the men who made him the way he was, you think you're tired?'

'I'm sorry.'

'You will be sorry. What do you think they'd do if I told them what you get up to, eh?' Vicky had hold of her elbow, her fingers digging in and tingles ran down her forearm.

'I'm sorry.' Janine looked down at the floor. She'd never seen her mother this bad before. She had no idea what she was supposed to say.

'I know you about you and your father. Don't think I didn't see how you looked at him.'

Janine looked at her mother's face. 'You knew?'

'Of course, I knew. I knew every hole your father ever poked and he wasn't picky.' Her breath stank of sour wine. 'A word in the ear of the right people and no boy will ever come near you.'

'He told me I was his special girl.' Janine's eyes stung with tears.

'You weren't special. Get out of my sight.'

She released Janine's arm and walked away. She barely swayed if you didn't look too closely.

Janine ran to her room, slammed the door and lay face down on her bed. He'd said what they did was special, it was pure. All those nights he'd come into her bedroom, the camping trips.

Her mother had known. She'd known it was wrong and had never done anything about it. She thought Janine had seduced him. Everything he'd said was a lie. Everything her mother had done was out of spite and jealousy.

Janine's hands trembled with rage. If it was so bad, telling anyone would make them hate her, why had her mother let it go on? She didn't know anything about keeping a man happy and now he was gone she deserved to be left alone with her wine and diets.

Janine decided it was time to leave home, there was nothing tying her there now. She got up, stripped off her dress, sticky from a long sweaty day, and peeled off her tights.

She slipped on her thin cotton nightie and lay on top of the bed. It was too hot to have even a sheet over her. In the dark, she planned her escape. She couldn't stay with her grandparents; as liberal as her grandma might seem she wouldn't abide having her stay. She didn't have a job and couldn't leave school until she was sixteen. Maybe Gerry, who hated being called Geraldine and was Janine's best friend, would let her stay for a while. A few of the other girls at school might let her stay over. Maybe she could set up a sort of roster. She could tell each of the parents that her mother had to go away for work, now that her father was dead. Janine guessed she might be able to get away with a week at a time.

She would leave all her school things in her locker, then she'd only need to carry some clothes and a couple school uniforms. She drifted off to sleep going over everything she might need to take with her.

2. A New Man

When Janine arrived at Gerry's house after school on Monday, Gerry's mother was welcoming and understanding.

'Your poor mother must be having a terrible time. Of course, you can stay a few days,' she said.

On Wednesday, when Janine and Gerry got home from school, Gerry's mother was waiting for them at the orange Laminex table with her hands folded across her chest.

'Janine. Your mother says you ran away from home and she's been mad with worry.'

Janine looked at her feet.

'You lied to me, both of you. And your mother, who's been through quite enough already, has been worried sick. You made me a part of your deceit, Janine.'

When Gerry's mum was angry, she used your name a lot.

'And Geraldine.'

Gerry flinched next to her.

'I'm very disappointed in you. I didn't raise a liar.'

'You don't understand what her mum's really like. She's a total bitch and doesn't even care about her.'

'How dare you? I spent half an hour trying to stop Vicky from crying. Janine, sweetie, I know you're in pain, losing your father must be very difficult, but there's no use lashing out. Go back to your mum. Comfort each other. It will all be alright in time.' Gerry's mother stood up, uncrossed her arms and hugged Janine tightly. It seemed like it had been years since anyone had hugged her like that.

'I'm sorry.' Janine started to cry. Gerry's mother held her, swaying gently, and stroked her hair until she was cried out. Deep inside her anger at own mother burned brightly, but her experiment had failed. There was too much work lying to everyone, worrying about where she was going to sleep, and whether she would have anything to eat.

It's only a few months. When I'm sixteen I can get leave school, get a job and be rid of her.

*   *   *

Gerry and her mother dropped Janine home in time for dinner. They didn't stay, and she couldn't blame them. Vicky was a mess. Her eyes were swollen and red, and she constantly blew her nose.

Janine didn't trust the tears, but she'd made a deal with herself to stay for the moment.

Gerry and her mum waved goodbye as they drove off. Then Vicky grabbed Janine's arm and dragged her inside. She slammed the front door closed and slapped her hard across the face.

'After everything I gave up to care for you, you ungrateful little shit.'

Janine was shocked by the blow. Her mother hadn't hit her since she was a child. Her eyes were strangely glazed and she was surprised Gerry and her mother hadn't smelled the stale wine on her. Perhaps they had, but didn't want to make a scene.

'Next time I'll call the police. You can't just run off. I own you, and you will do as you're told.' She tightened the grip around Janine's arm.

'You're hurting me,' Janine said.

'Good.'

They stood staring at each other for a long time, perhaps it was only seconds. Janine's hatred sat in a hard ball in her stomach. If she hadn't promised herself she'd stay she would have fled. She would sleep on the streets if she needed to.

'Can you let go of my arm please, Mother?'

'Go to your room. You will not bring shame on this family.'

Janine picked up her bulging backpack and trudged to her room. Her belly rumbled but there would be no dinner for her today.

*   *   *

Janine and her mum developed a routine of barely speaking to each other. Janine would come home from school and go straight to her room. Vicky would knock when dinner was ready and they would eat in front of the television.

It was approaching the June school holidays and Janine wasn't looking forward to having to spend days with her mother, wordlessly needling each other.

'Gerry said I can stay with her for the holidays.'

'What does her mother say?' Vicky didn't look at her.

'She said it was fine as long as you agreed.'

'I see.' She took a sip of her wine, her eyes fixed on the television. 'Are you asking me or telling me?'

Janine wasn't sure what her mother wanted to hear.

'From your tone and the fact it wasn't a question, I could be forgiven for thinking otherwise. Are you finished?' She reached for Janine's plate, although it wasn't finished. She started to say something but decided against it.

'I guess.' Janine watched the plate of partially eaten rissoles and veg disappear.

'Go do your homework,' Vicky said. She sat at the kitchen counter and turned up the volume on the TV.

Neither of them said anything more about it for three days. Janine was determined to wait her mother out.

'When are you leaving to stay with that whore?' Vicky asked. She leaned against the frame of Janine's bedroom door, her stance casual, but her eyes were full of malice.

'If you mean Gerry, the plan is to go straight to hers on the last day of school.'

Her mother made a harrumphing sound in her throat and strutted away.

I'll take that as permission. In a little over a week, she'd be free.

*   *   *

Gerry knew a crowd of older kids, friends of her older brother. Some of them had cars. The two girls had been invited to a party of the last day of school. The house was in Canterbury, a slightly less wealthy suburb close by.

Gerry's brother Tom had invited them, one of his mate's had the house to himself while his parents were out of town and they had taken the opportunity to have a party. Everyone he'd ever met was invited, and those people had invited a bunch of people, and so on; everyone who was anyone would be there according to Gerry.

Tom drove them all there, he'd bought two slabs of VB and would get through all forty-eight cans himself or give them away. His car was a cherry red 1984 Holden Commodore he'd told Janine at least three times. Black plastic louvres on the rear window and the side panels had a silver stripe which he'd paid good money for.

Unlike his sister, who was short, curvy with permed auburn hair, Tom was tall and broad-shouldered with luscious brown hair. Janine wasn't sure how he got it to maintain that level of boost throughout the night, he looked like he'd taken lessons from Farrah Fawcett.

'Stop it,' Gerry said, elbowing her in the ribs as they got out of the car.

'What?'

'Ogling my brother, it's so gross and you're totally not his type anyway.'

'Sorry. I can't help it.'

'Well … help it.' Gerry walked after her brother towards the house, her hips swaying under the bulky blue folds of her dress. Janine wore the black dress she'd worn to the funeral, this time without stockings, and with a cute boxy white jacket. Though it was mild for June, she shivered.

The girls had spent a long time doing their makeup before they left the house. They wanted to look older. To be cool. Gerry had electric blue eye-shadow to match her dress, while Janine went with yellow and orange eye-shadow to match her earrings; they both wore pink lipstick.

The house was another large Edwardian with a wrap-around veranda and coloured-glass panels in the windows at the front of the house. The lawn at the front was well-manicured, but there were no plants or flowers to break it up.

Inside everything was stark black and white minimalist style; the couch, the kitchen, the art on the walls. Furniture in the lounge had been pushed back to make a dance floor, in one corner was a DJ with two decks and boxes full of vinyl records.

Tom took the beers into the bathroom and pushed a dozen cans into the ice in the salmon pink bathtub. Janine that she didn't know anyone here apart from Gerry, and a wave of panic sent fizzles of energy though her. She folded her hands up under her armpits for comfort.

'Come out the back and meet some people. The party won't get going for a while yet,' Tom said.

The girls followed him outside, where a few groups of men stood smoking and talking. Tom thrust a can of VB into each of their hands and gave them a look Janine interpreted to mean "be cool".

Tom offered her a cigarette, and she took it. She'd smoked a handful of times before, enough not to choke and make a fool of herself.

'The DJ is spinning some decent tracks,' Tom said.

'Yeah, totally,' Janine said, she didn't know most of them. She'd never really been interested in music and her mother wouldn't let her use the stereo or have a radio in her room.

'Oh my God, I love this song. Come dance with me!' Gerry grabbed Janine's hand and pulled her back into the house.

'What is it?'

'Oh. My. God. I can't believe you don't know WHAM! They're only the biggest thing.'

Clearly others at the party agreed with Gerry and the previously bare lounge room was crowded. As Janine bopped along, she noticed an older man leaning against the wall, smoking, watching her. He wore all black, tight pants tucked into huge army boots, a dress shirt opened halfway to his navel, and a tailored black jacket. More noticeable though, were his eyes. Janine had never seen a man wearing eyeliner before and she was immediately intrigued. His hair was teased and stood out from his head at wild angles.

'Someone thinks he's Robert Smith,' Gerry whispered in her ear.

Startled, Janine took a step back. 'What?'

'I saw you checking him out. Don't tell me you don't know The Cure either? You're hopeless.'

Janine did know The Cure, not for their music, but for the posters on the walls of Tom's bedroom. They stayed on the dance floor for a few more songs Janine didn't know.

'I'm thirsty,' Gerry announced and pulled her to the bathroom for more beer.

'Let's go sit out the back. Maybe your admirer will come talk to you.' Gerry gave an exaggerated wink.

'He's not my admirer.' Janine wished he would be. She wanted to know who this man was, so mysterious, so cool.

They found two recently-vacated chairs. The party was getting busy and the girls sat with their beers. Janine watched the French doors for the man in black, Gerry had fallen into conversation with a boy sitting next to her. He didn't look much older than them, and had terrible acne covering what would otherwise have been a beautiful face.

She sipped her beer, now she was onto her second one, it didn't taste quite so bad.

She looked away from the doors to pull at the hem of her dress, her legs were covered in goose bumps. When she looked up again, the man in black was standing in front of her, towering over her. Looking up at him made Janine feel funny, hot and as though she might be sick. It could have been the beer, but she suspected it was him.

'I'm John.' He held out his hand towards her. She shook it, trying not to show how nervous he made her.

'Hi John. I'm Gerry, my rude friend is Janine.' Gerry elbowed her in the ribs, and she dropped his hand.

'Sorry, I'm Janine.'

'I haven't seen you around before. Who do you know here?'

Gerry shot her a warning look. 'We came with Tom, over there.' She pointed.

'Ah, yes, Tom's a good sort. Seems to know a lot of people.' He was talking to Gerry, but he hadn't taken his eyes off Janine.

Gerry was making faces at her she didn't understand for several silent moments.

'I have to go talk to Tom,' she said, standing. 'You can have my seat if you like.'

'Thank you.' John watched Gerry walk away. Janine hoped he didn't catch the eyebrow movements she was making as she turned away.

'I'm—I don't go to many parties,' Janine said.

'I had rather guessed that.' John smiled. He seemed catlike and hungry; she was both intrigued and afraid.

'Sorry.'

'No need to apologise. A young lady such as yourself might be making her first foray into parties of this sort.' He held her gaze, his half-lidded eyes trapped her where she was. She giggled and her cheeks flushed.

'How old are you anyway? Eighteen?'

She giggled again.

'Sixteen?'

He was much older than she was, she didn't want him to dismiss her as a useless frippery as soon as he learned how old she was.

'I'll be seventeen next month,' she lied.

'Ah, lovely.' He frowned slightly, perhaps he didn't believe her. 'A pleasure to meet you. You certainly look older than you are.'

'Thanks. I really like your outfit. I've never seen anyone dress like that.'

'Really? It's quite popular among certain crowds.'

'I'm not really allowed to go out much.'

'Of course. Your parents will want you to focus on your schooling.'

'Yeah, Mum won't let me do anything now Dad's dead.'

John reached over and took Janine's hand. 'I'm so sorry to hear. Losing a parent is awful. And for someone as pretty as you to be sad, I wish I could do something to make you smile.'

His black-ringed eyes watched her closely. She knew she should pull her hand away; it wasn't wise to let a man flirt with her so openly, but she didn't want to.

His cigarette was getting towards the end and he pulled it from his lips, let it fall to the group and stamped on it. 'Can I offer you one?'

'Thank you,' she said. He handed her the cigarette and leaned over to light it for her. It was very romantic, having this man pay her such attention.

'I really like your dress. For someone who says she doesn't get out much, you have wonderful taste.'

'Don't tease me.'

'I'm not, I mean it.'

Janine watched Gerry from across the backyard. She was talking to Tom, their heads close together. When Gerry saw her looking, she nodded her head vigorously and gave her two thumbs up. Tom winked at her. It seemed they approved of this new admirer.

'Let's dance,' he said, breaking into her thoughts.

'I'm not a very good dancer.'

'No need to be modest.' He took her hand, and led her back into the house. The music had changed mood a little and the dance floor was packed with people. When the song changed to *I wanna know what love is,* one of the few that Janine recognised, John spun her around into a slow dance hold. In her high heels she was almost as tall as he was. He slipped his arm around her waist and held her firmly. He felt hot against her, his body warmth radiating through her dress. Up close she realised how handsome he was. Her mind spun with thoughts of how she would stuff this up and he would lose interest.

As the song finished and the DJ started the next one, John dipped her and kissed her. She was so surprised she nearly fell over, but his strong arms held her.

When he stood her up again she was wobbly.

'Let's sit down, I'll get you another drink,' he said. Instead of heading out to the back yard, John took her down the hallway towards the front of the house. He opened one of the doors to reveal a dark bedroom and flicked on the lights.

'Have a seat, I'll be right back.'

3. The Morning After

Janine looked around the room. The bed was covered in shiny blue satin sheets, pine framed with a large, smooth headboard. The rest of the room was empty except for a pile of milk crates which served as a wardrobe and a pile of clothes on the floor.

She wondered whose bedroom it was, and why John had brought her here, and if he was planning to seduce her. It was thrilling and a little scary.

John walked back into the room, his black boots clumping across the wooden floor. 'I got us a nightcap,' he said, handing her a small glass of what looked like water. She took it and the distinct odour of rum reached her nose.

'Drink up.'

She took a sip and it burned a little on the way down. He sat down next to her, and she had to shuffle her bum back on the bed so she wouldn't slide off.

'I think you're hot, Janine. I'm sure you know that.' John put his hand around her shoulder, Janine giggled, her cheeks burning with the attention of this hot older man.

'I know you're a good girl, you wouldn't ever have been alone with a man before.'

Janine shook her head.

Her father didn't count.

'Now, we can stop at any time, if you feel uncomfortable just say the word and we'll go back out to the party.'

'Okay.'

John put his other hand on her knee, his thumb stroking her thigh. 'Do you like that?'

She nodded, finished the rum and put the glass on the floor next to her feet.

'Why don't you lie back?'

'Whose room is this?' she asked.

'It's okay, we can use it.'

Janine lay back on the bed, looking at the cracks and the overly floral ceiling rose above the naked lightbulb.

John's hand moved up her thigh, gently squeezing. He lay propped on one elbow next to her and stared at her face. She closed her eyes and turned away.

'I want to look at you, you're very beautiful Janine.'

She turned back to him. He was so commanding, his jaw was set and strong, and he smelled like patchouli and spicy aftershave. He leaned over her and kissed her; a chaste peck on the lips. She let out a sigh and opened her lips.

He kissed her deeply, as though he wanted to consume her. Heat grew between her thighs, and her underpants started to be wet and sticky. She arched her back, pushing her breasts towards him.

'You're a natural,' he crooned in her ear. 'I want you to touch me now.' He took her hand and placed it over his pants. She felt the hot bulge twitch as she touched it.

He looked into her eyes with an intensity that might have scared her if he hadn't been so handsome. It was intoxicating to have someone as sophisticated as John paying her attention, as though she were a grown woman. He opened his pants and she felt his naked cock. It was smooth and hard and bigger than she expected.

'Mmm, that feels so good.' He rolled onto his back as she continued to stroke and rub him.

'Do you think you would like to put it in your mouth?'

She'd done it before a few times, but she didn't know if it would be the same with John. 'Uh...'

He smiled. 'That's okay, just use your hands.'

'No, I want to,' she said. She sat up and wriggled down the bed, flicking her long blonde hair out of the way, taking him into her mouth. She worked her hand on the shaft and put the tip in her mouth.

'You dirty girl, where did you learn to do that?' he murmured.

Janine kept up a steady rhythm, she knew that you couldn't stop when a man was aroused. You could really injure him, according to Gerry.

It didn't take her long to make him come. He jerked but was silent. She crawled up the bed and lay next to him. After a while he buckled his pants.

'Roll over, I want to hold you.'

They lay together, her knickers were hot and soaked with her arousal, until she heard him start to snore. She wished she could get up and turn off the light, but didn't want to break the embrace. He was so beautiful, so mature, and he'd chosen *her*. She hoped he liked what she'd done, although she guessed he had.

Then the door burst open and a young man she vaguely recognised from the party stumbled in.

'Who the fuck are you?' he asked.

'Sorry, friend. We were just having a little lie down. No offence meant.' John sprang up from the bed, his voice calm and authoritative.

'Who are you and what are you doing in my room?' the man said.

'I'm John, this is Janine. We'll just go back out into the party and leave you in peace.'

'You think you can just fuck some slut on my bed?' He was clearly drunk, he smelled of beer and swayed unsteadily.

'Now, I don't want any trouble. We'll just go, and everything will be alright.'

Janine was still sitting on the bed, unable to speak. She stood, pulling her dress down where it had ridden up, and picked up her shoes.

'I'm really sorry,' she said.

'Who's talking to you, slut?' the man said.

'That's no way to talk to a lady, friend,' John said.

'She's no lady.'

'Come on.' John took her hand and they went back into the party. Thankfully the man didn't follow, and she was relieved; the idea of a fight filled her with terror.

Back in the lounge room the music still pumped full blast although the crowd on the dancefloor had thinned. She looked around for Gerry, or Tom, but she couldn't see them anywhere.

'I can't see my friends.' Her voice wobbled and betrayed her panic.

'We'll have another look around.'

They made another circuit of the party, but couldn't find any sign of Gerry, or anyone else she knew.

'Oh God. How am I going to get home? My mother thinks I'm at Gerry's place I can't call her, and Gerry's left me here—what am I gonna do?' Her words tumbled over each other.

'It's okay. You can come to my place. Give your friend a call in the morning and it will all be alright.' John held her shoulders and spoke firmly to her. She felt instantly better knowing that he would take care of her. He'd made the decision, and everything would be okay.

'Thank you.' She looked up into his face and she knew she was falling for him.

Her tall, dark stranger.

*   *   *

The next morning Janine smiled as she woke up in a bed beside John. They'd taken a taxi to Kew where he had a small two-bedroom unit, but he lived on his own.

His bedroom was stylish and black—the bed, the sheets, the wardrobe, all the clothes peeking out of the huge built-in robe. He'd slept next to her and hadn't tried anything. Janine was grateful he hadn't pushed, as hot as he was, she wasn't sure she was ready to take that next step with him; it was supposed to be special, only with someone you really love.

He slept in only boxers, so she could take her time looking him over. Under his long sleeves and tight black pants, he had a thick covering of dark hair. Even the backs of his hands were hairy. They were also much broader and more calloused that she remembered.

Sleeping, he looked younger. The deep lines between his eyebrows smoothed out and the brooding glamour of last night was replaced with a more innocent beauty. She smiled and snuggled herself into his side.

By the time John woke up it was well into the morning and Janine had started to think he would sleep all day. Her tummy rumbled loudly.

'Morning, sleepy,' she said.

He grunted in response and shuffled to the toilet. He pissed for a very long time, then she heard him open and close some cupboards and clean his teeth.

'Sorry, I never feel very sociable until I've done my morning routine.'

'That's okay. Should I go?' she said, he had made no move to come back to bed and she was suddenly unsure of herself.

'No, I was just looking at you.' He pulled on a black dressing gown. 'I'm going make coffee, and I think you should call your friend. I hope she's not worried about you.'

Janine's stomach lurched as she remembered why she was there. How could Gerry have left her there? It was so unlike her.

'You're right, I'd better give her a call. Do you mind?' She looked towards the black phone mounted on the wall next to the bed.

'Go ahead.'

She waited for him to leave, heading back towards the kitchen before she picked up the receiver.

'Hello?' Gerry's mother answered the phone.

'Uh, hi, is Gerry there?'

'Is that you, Janine?' she asked.

'Yeah.'

'I thought we were having you to stay last night.'

'Oh, uh, no, Mum changed her mind last minute. I'm coming over this afternoon. Is Gerry there?'

'Sure, Gerry! Phone.'

Janine wondered why Gerry's mum never covered the receiver when she shouted to her daughter. It was the same every time she called.

'I've got it, Mum,' Gerry said, there was a click as she picked up the extension in her bedroom.

'Right.'

The girls both listened for her mother putting down the receiver in the lounge before they said anything.

'Hi,' Janine said.

'Hi.'

'Where did you go last night?'

'Where did I go? Where did you go? That tall dude said you were staying with him so we split. I can't believe you would ditch me for some guy!' Gerry sounded more pleased than angry.

'Really?'

'Yeah, just after you disappeared into that bedroom!'

Janine could almost see her eyebrows wriggling in excitement as she said it. 'He set it up so I'd have to go home with him.' Janine couldn't help grinning.

'Well, older guys do have all the moves. So did you do it?'

'What? No. Of course not.'

'Seriously? You stayed over with him and you didn't do anything?'

Janine dropped her voice to a whisper, 'I never said we didn't do anything.'

'Janine, your coffee is getting cold,' John called from the other room.

'Thanks. Be there in a minute,' she said. 'Gerry, I gotta go, but I'll tell you all about it later today. I told your mum that my mum said I couldn't come till today, so back me up yeah? See you soon.'

'Okay, bye.'

Janine hung up. She looked around the room for her dress and jacket, she hadn't brought anything else with her. John had loaned her a T-shirt to sleep in, it was huge on her and came halfway down her thighs, but she didn't think she should walk around his house in it. She wriggled into the dress, it seemed to be harder to zip than last night, and slipped her jacket on. It was very cold and she wished she had slippers or shoes that weren't ridiculously high-heeled.

John was leaning against the bench in the kitchen cradling his mug between his hands.

'You got dressed.' He sounded disappointed.

'Yeah, I can't stay long.' Janine put one foot on the other, trying vainly to keep the cold lino away from her toes.

'Here,' he said, he held out a cup of steaming coffee to her.

'Thanks.' It was very strong and black. She didn't usually drink coffee, but she thought it would be rude to refuse. It was smooth and bitter with a lot of sugar.

'Gerry said you told them I was going home with you. That's why she left.' She took another sip of the sickly coffee and waited.

'You've uncovered my plot.'

She looked up and he was smiling at her, the same catlike grin.

'I had rather hoped you would want to come home with me, all the signs were there, and if you had the right motivation, you'd be more inclined to accept.'

'But, didn't Gerry ask? Like I've only just met you.'

'I know her brother, he said I'd keep you safe, and I have.'

A shiver ran along Janine's body as the chill in the air started to get to her. 'I guess.'

'I know I shouldn't have lied to you, but I really like you.'

Janine didn't get chased by boys, let alone men. She was slim and blonde—well, blondish—but she wasn't anything special. Her mother had told her over and over what a plain girl she was. Her father said she was the prettiest thing he'd ever seen, but he was biased. It felt nice to be pursued. A handsome older man lies to her so he could spend more time with her.

'Okay, but don't do it again.'

He tried to look sheepish, but the catlike grin undermined it. 'Scout's honour.'

John made them toast for breakfast, though he had barely anything in the cupboards. The coffee, Janine discovered was two teaspoons of instant coffee powder with two teaspoons of sugar and boiling water. He made her a second cup with their toast and by the end of it she felt as though her heart might pound its way out of her ribcage and skitter across the floor.

'Well, we'd better get you to Gerry's before she starts to worry for real,' he said.

John's car was long and black, like a station wagon but somehow not like a station wagon.

'It used to be a hearse,' he said when she stared. 'I got it cheap from a friend. Also, I think it's pretty cool. Back when I was in a band all the gear would fit in and then some.'

'You were in a band?' she asked.

'We could have made it big, but that's a story for another time. Hop in.'

4. My House, My Rules

Janine and John saw each other a few times a week for a while before her mother showed any interest in the person she was spending so much time with. By mid-September, they had been dating for three months and Janine was completely smitten.

'Mum's being a total pain in the arse. She says she won't let me go out with you anymore unless you come have dinner with her,' she said one night on the phone.

'I don't do meeting parents. I mean, your mother will probably think I'm a total creep because of my age,' John said.

'You're not a creep.'

'I know you think so, baby. Listen if it's going to be too hard, then maybe I should just stop seeing you.'

'What? You don't mean that. We're soulmates. I could come out even if she says I can't. What's the worst she could do?'

'Exactly, baby, you know what's best. I have to go, I'll see you tomorrow night.'

'I love you,' she said.

'I know.'

She'd gone against her mother's wishes a few times since her father died, they were fighting much more now he wasn't coming back, but this was a different thing all together. She'd never snuck out before and didn't know how her mother would react. Probably scream, and call her every name she could think of. Maybe even slap her, it wouldn't be the first time.

*   *   *

The next weekend Janine told her mother she was staying with a school friend, Libby, for a sleepover and she spent the night with John. They'd been having sex for some time now and Janine wondered if she should get some birth control pills. When she brought it up with John, he said he couldn't have children.

On Sunday she arrived home around two o'clock. She'd taken John shopping so when there was food in the house for her to cook. Though not the greatest cook she could do the basics and liked to take care of him.

'Where have you been?' her mother asked as soon as she walked in the door.

'I was with Libby. You know that.'

'I didn't like the look on your face when you told me so I called Libby's mother.'

'Oh.' Janine felt the heat rising up her cheeks.

'Yes. She said that you weren't there, so I called Gerry, I thought maybe I got the names mixed up. She said you were with Libby, so you're getting her to lie for you too.'

Janine said nothing. This was the moment she'd dreaded. The easiest thing to do was let her mother's anger wash over her until she was done, then try to fix it.

'Where have you been? Off fucking your boyfriend no doubt? Like the whore you are,' her mother's voice was getting louder. 'Nothing to say for yourself then? I hope he gives you the clap.'

Her mother stood in the hallway, her arms folded across her petite body. Janine waited for something else, but it seemed her mother was done. She tried to go around and into the house.

'Oh no.' Vicky put out her hand and put it on Janine's chest. 'You don't think you're coming into my house, do you? A lying, no good slut like you?'

'What are you talking about?'

'You are no longer my daughter. I've put up with you for months, tried to tell myself you were grieving, losing your father must have been hard, but now I see you do what you want. You have no respect for me or the sacrifices I make to keep a roof over your head.'

'Come on Mum, I haven't been that bad.'

'No? You lie to me constantly. This boy you've been seeing, I know what he's after. And knowing you, you've done nothing to stop him. When you're broke, kicked out of school and pregnant don't come running to me.'

Janine tried to take another step and her mother pushed her back.

'I mean it Janine. Leave and don't come back.'

She was astounded. It had been a rough seven months but she had never expected this. The hatred in her mother's eyes was so intense she felt dizzy.

'You can't. I—where am I supposed to go?'

'That's not my problem.'

'Shit.' Janine felt the straps of her bag digging into her hand, she tried to relax her grip. 'Can I get some of my stuff then. I need my school stuff and clothes and—'

'You should have thought about that before.'

'You're unbelievable,' Janine said.

It's no use trying to talk to her. She turned around and walked away from the front door.

'And you can leave your key too. I don't want you sneaking back here.'

'Fine.' Janine pulled her key out of her pocket and threw it at her mother.

Janine walked down the street to the phone box and called Gerry and told her what had happened. She thought she should be more upset, but somehow it didn't seem real. Her mother would come around eventually.

*   *   *

For two days she let her mother cool down. Vicky would be back around six o'clock on a Tuesday after bridge, and she knocked on the door about fifteen minutes later.

'What do you want?' Vicky stood in the doorway, her eyes full of hatred.

'I'm sorry. I know I've been a nightmare to live with these last few months.' Janine's first strategy was to grovel.

'Yes. You have. Is that all?'

'Uh... I wanted to come home. I hoped you might have changed your mind.'

'I haven't. And I won't. I'm no longer a mother, I have no child.'

Janine clenched her teeth. *What a load of shit!* She'd just been biding her time till she could get rid of me. Ever since Dad died and she didn't have to keep me around to make sure his money kept coming in.

'I mean it, Mum, I'm sorry, I learned my lesson. Please?'

'Go back to your boyfriend.' Vicky stepped back and moved to close the door.

'Can I get my school stuff then? What use is it to you? It's just cluttering up your house.'

There was a flicker of emotion across her mother's face, it would be too much for Janine to hope it might be remorse.

'Fine. Get your things and go.' She opened the door a crack and Janine slid through. Her room was exactly as she'd left it. Her things were everywhere. *I'm not going to be able to carry all this with me, it'll have to be the bare essentials.*

She packed her school things, textbooks and notepads into her schoolbag, she put her uniforms and as many clothes as she could fit into the old suitcase from under her bed. She would have to leave everything else behind.

The two bags seemed so small; she was leaving so much of her life here in this room. She dragged her things to the bus stop and waited, it was too far to walk to Gerry's with her bags. Gerry's brother, Tom, would have come to pick her up if she asked, or even John, but it was something she needed to do alone.

*　　　*　　　*

Gerry's mother looked at the bags when she walked in and shook her head.

'Janine, darling, I love seeing you, but you can't live here.'

She explained the fight to Gerry's mother, who was sympathetic and insisted Vicky would have softened by now.

'Mum says she's not changing her mind.'

'What about your grandparents?'

Janine looked down. Claire was pleasant but a meddler. 'It's okay, I'll sort something out. Can I crash here till the weekend?'

Gerry's mother clutched her hands together. 'I don't like it, but you can stay. Until the weekend.'

'I promise.' Janine smiled her most winning smile and took all her worldly possessions into Gerry's room.

Gerry was lying on her stomach on the bed, her head resting in her hands, reading her biology textbook

'She didn't back down then?' she asked, folding down the page and closing the book.

'Nope.' Janine dropped her school bag with a thump and sat down on the floor. She rested her head against the door of the wardrobe. *How did it get to this?*

'She must really hate me.'

'I'm sure she doesn't hate you.' Gerry didn't sound very convincing.

47

Janine eyes stung and tears streamed silently down her face.

'I'm sorry, hun.' Gerry sat next to her and pulled Janine onto the bed with her.

'What am I gonna do?'

'I don't know. Call John. He had a hand in getting you into this mess, and he's a lot older, maybe he should do something to get you out of it.'

Janine didn't want to ask John. She hadn't spoken to him since Sunday. Part of her expected that he would say no, or immediately break up with her, she was never sure of how he would react to things. She wasn't ready to lose him, not today.

'Go on, he's a good guy.' Gerry offered her the phone. 'I'm going to watch TV with Mum.'

Janine sat, staring at the phone for ten minutes before feeling calm enough to call.

'Hello,' John's dark, silky voice answered.

'It's me.'

'You sound funny, are you alright?'

'No.' Janine started crying again.

'What's happened? Do you need to come over?' John's voice was full of alarm.

'No, it's okay. It's just…' Somehow she couldn't say the words out loud.

'What is it? It's okay, it can't be that bad.'

'Mum's kicked me out.'

'Oh.' There was a long silence. 'I thought this might be coming.'

'Really? I had no idea. I thought she was joking, or that she'd change her mind after a couple of days to think about it.'

'In my experience, mums don't do these things lightly. I think you'd better come stay with me for a while.'

'Are you sure? Isn't that a bit... I dunno, soon?'

'Do you love me, baby?'

'Yes, of course I do.'

'So, it's fine.' John sounded so calm and assured.

'You're right, of course. It's fine.'

'Where are you now? Should I come get you?'

'I'm at Gerry's. I'll come on the weekend.'

'You sure?'

'I'm sure. I have some assignments I need to get done and with all the stuff with Mum it might be better if I'm not distracted by a handsome man.'

'Are you flirting with me, Janine?'

'I might be.'

'What are you wearing?' he asked, his voice low and gravelly. One of John's favourite games when they were apart was flirting with her down the phone. Describing what he was going to do to her next time he saw her in explicit detail. Janine wasn't as experienced at dirty talk as he was, but she played along. At least she was smiling again by the time she hung up the phone.

5. A Grown Woman

Janine moved in with John that weekend. The commute to school was longer, and she didn't get to sit with Gerry on the bus anymore.

The end of the year was approaching fast and with it came her birthday. She didn't want to ask John to host a party, worried he'd say no, and anyway, only her close friends knew she'd moved.

'You have to do something though, my love, it's your sweet sixteenth.' John stood behind her as she turned chops in the pan trying not to get fat on her school uniform. He would have eaten chops with boiled veggies and mashed potato every night of the week if it were up to him.

'I don't want to make a big deal of it. It's fine really.'

John's hand, which had been rubbing circles on her upper back, stopped. 'Is there something you're not telling me?'

'No, it's nothing.'

'Hhmm.'

'I have a lot of homework and with everything I do around the house I hardly get through it. I just think having a party will be too much.'

'What does it matter if you're leaving school this year?'

She hadn't told him about wanting to finish. 'I thought I might stay on next for year eleven next year, even do my year twelve. There's not much available for a person who hasn't finished high school.' She turned the stove-top off and served the dinner.

'You know I only have year ten. It's never held me back.' John ran a bricklaying business he'd taken over from his old boss when he'd retired. He'd been running it for three years and considered himself an expert.

'I didn't mean anything by it.'

'And we talked about how I was paying for you to live here, how you needed to contribute. It's not fair for you to ask me to pay for your rent and food and bills and everything else for another two years. I'm not your father.'

They sat down at the chipped Laminex table. Janine was silent as John chewed and later was quiet doing the dishes, listening to the television in the other room.

She stuck her head around the corner of the kitchen. John was engrossed in his show, so Janine went into the bedroom to call Gerry.

'John wants me to leave school,' she blurted as soon as Gerry came on the line.

'Oh, shit.'

'Yeah.'

'I guess you're not paying rent or anything.'

'I know. I feel bad. Couldn't I just get a parttime job? Saturdays or something, that would help.'

'When would you get your homework done? It's going to get worse from here. You barely keep up as it is. I'm always letting you borrow my answers.' Gerry wasn't angry, but it was true Janine copied off her constantly.

'I know. John's probably right, I can get by with year ten. Maybe I'm not smart enough to do year twelve.'

'I'll miss you.'

Janine twirled the phone cord around her fingers, she saw Gerry every day. They had most classes together and lunchtime. 'You have to promise to still be my best friend.'

'Who am I going to talk to?'

'You'll just have to come visit me at work, keep me up to date with stuff that's happening. It won't be so bad.' Janine already hated the idea of work. She had no skills; she couldn't use a typewriter or a computer, could cook passably well, but nothing special, and she hated talking to strangers.

'I hope you're right. Anyway, I gotta go, Mum wants the phone. See you tomorrow.'

Janine hung up and sat on the big bed in John's bedroom. She hadn't ever thought of it as their room, it was filled with his things. When she had a job, she would be able to buy herself some new clothes, and maybe some records. John wasn't as stingy with the stereo as her mother had been.

'Did Gerry have any ideas about your birthday?' John asked, walking into the room.

'Uh, no.' She was startled from her thoughts.

'I know you're scared about getting a job, but you'll be fine. What about I take you out for a nice meal for your birthday? Something real fancy.'

'Okay, that would be nice.'

John sat with her on the bed, put one arm around her shoulder and pulled her to him. She sank into his embrace and knew he was right.

He dropped his hand to her thigh and moved it up her leg, under her school uniform. She wasn't particularly in the mood, her world seemed to be changing so quickly, but John had his needs. These days at least he didn't take long to get what he wanted from her, and while he was sleeping afterwards, she would be able to do her biology homework. She lay back and thought about what jobs she might be able to do.

*   *   *

Janine managed to leave at the end of year ten with a passing grade. She tried a number of different jobs she'd found in the local newspaper. First the door-to-door makeup sales job, she only lasted two weeks because it was a commission-based salary and she didn't sell one product. John said she wasn't assertive enough.

Then a chicken and chip shop. The owner was a sleazy, rotund man who only employed women. He said because they all worked so closely together any men would get ideas about the girls.

He put her on for a trial, at half pay, for six weeks which he extended to eight weeks. Then instead of putting her on a proper salary, he fired her; something about it not working out, but John said he was dodgy.

She tried leaflet distributing but with the walking and the summer heat she was exhausted by the time she got home, and John told her she had to give it up.

By the end of February John had found her a job answering the phones for a mate of his who ran a plumbing business. Her boss was an enormous Greek man named George. He was a little older than John, in his late forties, and had a plump Greek wife and two equally enormous, baby-faced sons who also worked in the company. Most of the staff were related to George in some way, his wife Elena, helped with the books, and his cousin was a partner. The apprentices were friends of the family and constantly flirted with Janine. She didn't tell John about that.

The wage wasn't much but better than her other attempts and she knew she had to stick with it. John got her the job and had asked her to cover half the rent and bills now she was working. He earned much more than she did but she used half the house, half the electricity and the rest. She never ate half the food though; John was a very good eater. Since they'd met almost a year before, he'd gained quite a bit of weight. The skinny Robert Smith character was being replaced by a demanding, flabby grump. But Janine loved him, and liked to look after him.

*   *   *

'What's up your arse?' John asked her from the couch one night. Janine was at the sink washing the dishes.

'Nothing.'

'Don't nothing me. You've been in a sulk for days. I mean I just assumed you were on your rag but you're not, are you?'

Janine took her hands out of the soapy water, turned around and leaned back on the sink. 'No. I haven't had a period for about six weeks. I'm starting to worry I'm pregnant.'

'Yeah, right. Pull the other one.' John drew his brows together in a frown.

'I'm serious. I know you said you were sterile, but I'm really worried.'

'Have you been fucking someone else?'

'No, of course not. How could you think that?' Janine clenched her teeth, what a thing to accuse her of. Her hands were pruney from the hot water, she rubbed them together and walked into the lounge room. John was facing the TV and didn't look at her when he spoke.

'Then you're not pregnant, are you?'

'I guess not.' She hovered behind his shoulder, she wanted him to be comforting, to take her in his arms and tell her he had always wanted a baby and they would be a family. She would need to see the doctor for a pregnancy test, perhaps she could drop in on her way home.

'What are you doing standing there like a ghost?' John sighed and turned to face her. She half expected him to yell at her.

'What would you do if I was, y'know, pregnant?'

'You'd have to get rid of it. I don't want kids. But it would be a miracle if you were. I'm shooting blanks, even got tested one time and they said my swimmers were defective.'

'Of course.' Janine's heart sank. She wasn't ready to be a mother, not by a long shot, but she had never considered having an abortion. Where did you go for one anyway? They were illegal and she didn't know anyone who'd had one. At least, no one who had admitted it.

She went back to the dishes and put her hands into the lukewarm water. Her period was pretty regular; it had certainly never been two weeks late before. John wasn't interested in helping her with the problem.

Once she'd washed, dried and put away their dishes, and made the sandwiches for tomorrow's lunch, Janine went into the bedroom to lie down. John stayed in the lounge room watching *Prisoner: Cell Block H.* She wasn't particularly interested in the show, but John insisted the women's prison drama would produce a girl-on-girl kiss at some point.

As she lay on her back on top of the bed cover, Janine put her hands over her lower belly. If there was a life in there, how could she kill it? On the other hand, she was only sixteen, and if John didn't want a family, would that mean he would throw her out? She couldn't be homeless. After what happened with her mother, she never wanted to be treated that way again. She would do everything she could to keep John happy, even if it meant killing the life that was growing inside her.

*　　　*　　　*

Janine didn't have a local doctor in Kew, where she and John lived, and she hadn't been back to her family GP since she left home. Elena suggested someone near her office when she asked. Thankfully, Elena didn't have any follow-up questions.

She sat in the doctors' office twisting her hands in her lap. She didn't think she had any urine for a sample and hoped she could produce some when the moment came.

The doctor was a short, round, red-faced man in his fifties. Kind but brisk.

'Fill this, at least to the line, then come back,' he said, holding a specimen jar.

Janine managed to squeeze out enough to fill the jar to the line and only got a little on her hand. In his office the doctor took her sample and left the room. As she waited for him to return, she looked around at the wood panelled walls, the maroon fabric chair, the dark grey carpet tiles on the floor.

The wait seemed interminable, but the doctor finally returned.

'Congratulations. You're pregnant.' His face did not reflect his words.

'Oh.'

'Take these and read them. You'll need to come back for a check-up in two weeks.' He handed her a selection of brochures for pregnant women.

She took them. 'Okay.' She walked out of the room in a daze and nearly forgot to pay.

*   *   *

She was pregnant. The trip home seemed like the longest forty minutes of her life.

'John? Are you home?' she called as she let herself in.

'Dunny.'

'I'm pregnant.'

'For fucks' sake. Didn't I just tell you not to worry about it?' John walked into the lounge; he shoulders hunched and his head thrust forward like a bull.

'I know, but I went to the doctor today. I'm definitely pregnant.'

He opened and closed his mouth several times, various emotions passed over his face in quick succession before anger settled back into place. 'Shit.'

She waited for the tirade to start, hugging herself for her for comfort.

'You'll have to get rid of it.'

'Are you—there's no way you would want to be a dad?'

'I've never wanted to be a dad. This shouldn't even be possible.'

'I'm not sleeping with anyone else I swear.' She shrank back, sure he would start shouting now.

'You pathetic whore, I know you're not. I keep my eye on you, I know where you are every minute of the day. If you were dumb enough to cheat, I'd know, and I'd have thrown you out on your ear.'

Janine was shaking, rooted to the spot.

'Jesus, would you get out of the way?' He walked past her back to the lounge.

*   *   *

The next day at work Janine worried about an abortion. She'd heard people talking about coat hangers and backyard clinics and was afraid. They wouldn't use actual coat hangers, she hoped. It would hurt, maybe she'd be damaged, what if this was only chance to have a baby? Her mind was spiralling, and she didn't have anyone she could call on to help her.

Since moving in with John, she'd let her school friendships slide. They had nothing in common now and it seemed like such an effort to call them up.

Gerry had called her a few times, they'd talked about who was doing what at school, who was dating who, but it was tedious. Janine had other stuff to worry about now, like whether she had enough money to pay her share of the bills, what to cook for dinner, making sure she kept the boss happy and keep her job, and her boyfriend happy enough to keep her around. But she was lost, confused and alone.

When she arrived home, she started on the dinner; sausages and mashed potato. It didn't need much preparation, but she stayed in the kitchen anyway. A phone was mounted on the wall near the doorway that linked the kitchen to the lounge. It was a small house, but John had installed three phone handsets so he could talk wherever he was. He spent a lot of time on the phone to people with weird names.

Gerry's mother answered. 'Hello?'

'Oh, hi. It's Janine. Is Gerry there?'

'Janine? My goodness, we haven't heard from you in, oh, it has to be months. What have you been doing with yourself?'

Janine's heart was racing, and her hands were unsteady on the phone, 'I've just been working, you know how it is.'

'You're not at school anymore, is that wise?'

'I didn't have much choice. Can I speak to Gerry please?'

'Of course. I'm sorry, I didn't mean to pry. I'll get her for you.'

She heard her put down the handset and listened to high heeled footsteps, then some muffled voices.

'Janine? Is that really you?' Gerry sounded breathless.

'Yeah. Hi.'

'So...'

The silence down the phone was crushing. Janine wished she hadn't called.

'I need your help,' Janine said finally.

'With what? This sounds exciting.'

Janine hesitated. What if her friend didn't want to help? 'I'm pregnant, and John wants me to get rid of it.'

'Holy shi . . .ivers.'

'I didn't know who else to call.'

'I'm so glad you did. I miss you.'

The lump in Janine's throat threatened to choke her, and she blinked back tears. 'I'm sorry.'

'Never mind that now. What are you gonna do?'

'John says he knows what to do but, how can I?'

Gerry's voice dropped to a whisper. 'You can't have it though, if he doesn't want it.'

'I know. Everything's gone to shit.'

Gerry giggled softly at the swear word. She remembered why she'd thought Gerry was childish.

'I heard that one of the girls in year twelve had one last year. I can ask around for you?'

'Was she okay?' Janine asked.

'I guess so. No one knew at the time, it started going around the school like, three months later when her best friend started blabbing about how much of a slut she was.'

Janine was silent.

'You know I'd never do that to you. You're my best friend. Even if you do ignore me for months at a time.'

Janine sighed. 'Thank you.'

Now that she'd told someone she trusted a weight lifted from her shoulders. 'Enough about that. Tell me the goss.'

Janine listened to Gerry talk about the people at school, a world she was no longer a part of, but it was soothing to hear about what counted as drama back at school. While Gerry talked, Janine turned the sausages and prodded the potatoes with a fork. They needed a few more minutes. She smiled, maybe everything would be alright.

She heard keys in the door, and turned to see John walking in. She waved from the kitchen, still nodding occasionally to the stories Gerry was telling her.

'Where's tea?' John yelled from the bedroom.

'Five more minutes, honey,' she called back. 'I have to go, I need to get his dinner on the table, or he'll be grumpy.'

'Right, sure. Don't leave it so long next time, okay?' Gerry said.

'I promise.' Janine put the phone back in its cradle.

6. Working Nine to Five

Janine had the abortion in a room at the back of a nondescript, slightly decrepit terrace house in Carlton. It had been dark and smelled of fear, bleach and mould. John had refused to come, Gerry had school, so she was alone.

It took two tram rides and a ten-minute walk to get home afterwards. She shook with fatigue and the aftereffects of adrenalin when she walked in the door and made it to the couch before she collapsed. The doctor had warned her she may experience side effects, including pain and bleeding, and had given her a supply of morphine and Valium. He said she could come back if she needed more medication, for a price.

She'd put a maxi pad in her knickers before she left Carlton. As she lay on her back on the couch, she felt the sodden, heavy pad against her flesh. *It's probably soaked through; I'll get up in a minute and change it.* She took another morphine tablet and let her eyes closed.

*   *   *

She must have fallen asleep because she woke with a start to the sound of John's keys in the door. Outside it was already dark, and the bright green VCR clock showed it was after six.

'Hi,' she said weakly, trying to sit up. She felt a sharp, shooting pain travelling from deep in her bowels and down her legs as she moved.

'You been lying there all day, have you?' John's face was flushed, he must have had a few beers before he got home. 'Where's my tea?'

Janine sat very still, when she moved the sharp pain flared up, but if she kept still, it seemed better. Her skin felt cold and sweaty all at once.

'I'm sorry love, I haven't made anything, I'm not feeling so flash.'

'What am I gonna eat then?' John down on the couch heavily, the jolt of his weight sent the searing pains through her abdomen again.

'Order a pizza, hun. I'll pay.' She couldn't afford it, John had refused to pay for the abortion, but it wouldn't help anything if she started a fight.

John grunted and reached for the phone; he knew the number for the pizza place without having to look it up.

Janine took a deep breath, which created another small ripple of pain, and tried to stand up. She needed more painkillers and to lie down. John would watch TV for a while, sometimes he even fell asleep on the couch. She hoped that would happen tonight.

When she stood up she realised that she had bled onto the couch. She felt the colour drain from her face and the world tilted a little on its axis. John followed her gaze to the spot, about the size of an apple, which had spread onto the blue fabric of the couch.

'What the fuck, Janine?' John jumped up from the couch immediately, grabbing her arm.

'I'm sorry, I'll clean it up.'

A look of recognition flickered across his face. 'You had it done today?'

'Yes.'

'And that's why you feel sick? Why you didn't have my dinner ready?'

'Yes.'

'Jesus you're disgusting. First you get knocked up by God knows who, and then you bleed all over my fucking couch.' The fingers on her arm were digging in painfully. She closed her eyes briefly trying to get her bearings.

'It was your baby, John. I just need to rest; I'll clean this up tomorrow and I'm sure I'll be back to normal by then.'

'You better be. What's the use of keeping you around if you can't do anything?' John looked at her face, and he softened his grip. 'I'm sorry, baby, I don't mean to yell. You know how I get when I haven't eaten. Go grab a towel to put over that, and I'll come get you when the pizza is here.'

Janine was so relieved she almost fell over. His hand on her arm was all that was keeping her upright. Walking was painful, but she brought back a dark brown towel to put over the stain and shuffled to the bathroom. She peeled off her blood-soaked pants and knickers. She was tempted to throw the whole mess out, but she couldn't afford to buy new pants.

She washed herself gently with a flannel, put on a clean pair of knickers, a fresh pad, and some old clothes and put herself in bed.

*   *   *

Her first morning back at work on Thursday, more than a week after the procedure, she had her last morphine tablet the night before and by lunch time she was sweating, her heart raced and she was sure she was dying. She didn't understand what was happening.

'Are you feeling alright, love? You don't look well,' Elena said, handing her a cup of tea with far too much sugar in it.

'I'm okay.'

'Do you need anything, *koukla*? I have some painkillers if you need.'

Janine had told the office that she'd had her appendix out. 'Maybe that would be good. I've run out of the stuff the doctor gave me.'

'They never give you enough, stingy bastards.' Elena winked at her and went to her handbag. She fished around in it for a little while before withdrawing a small fabric wallet with a triumphant look on her face.

'Here we are. Have a little oxy. That oughta take the edge off. You should go get some more tablets though, if you're still in a lot of pain.'

Janine didn't know if she was in pain, she couldn't think at all, but the offer of drugs had released some tension she hadn't realised she had been holding.

*   *   *

Once the tablet had kicked in, Janine floated through the rest of the day without a care in the world.

'What was that tablet you gave me? I'll have to get the doctor to give me some,' She asked Elena as she was leaving for the night.

'Oxycodone, love. It's the best stuff for pain. You need to be careful who you ask, try my doctor.' She fished around in her handbag again and handed Janine a business card. 'It's a bit further than the local place you went to last time, but they give you what you need.'

'Thank you. I mean it.'

'No worries, hunny, you'd do the same for me.' Elena turned and walked out of the office, her stiletto heels clicking down the corridor. Janine had always thought she was pathetic, her ample body stuffed into tiny leopard print outfits and perfume so strong it made Janine sneeze, but this maternal side was something Janine hadn't seen before. She made a mental note to be nicer to Elena from now on.

*   *   *

Janine's work was boring; she typed up orders and invoices, she typed letters George recorded on a small tape recorder. She would watch through the glass wall of his office pacing up and down talking into it. *He thinks he's so important*.

They didn't pay her very well, and with all the bills and rent at home she never had much of her pay check left over for anything nice. Now she and Elena were on better terms Janine had started dreaming of getting herself better clothes and having nice hair like she did.

If I didn't dress like a schoolgirl pretending to be an office worker, I'd get more respect. She looked down at her blouse and skirt, both purchased in the opportunity shop around the corner and refastened her top button. It always popped open. *I should get rid of it. George doesn't need any more excuses to look down my top.*

Janine hadn't been to the doctor that Elena recommended. She wanted to save it for emergencies, but she was struggling without the painkillers. The abortion had been a little over two weeks ago, but there was still a constant dull pain in her abdomen and some light bleeding. John wasn't happy she was still 'closed for business'.

'I need to fuck something. Your mouth is fine for a change, but it's not the same. Maybe I'll try the back passage.' He'd winked at her, but she shuddered. The only time they'd tried anal sex it had hurt so much she'd cried into the pillow.

'I'll be right soon, baby, I'm sure,' she'd said.

'Oi, Janine, come in here,' George yelled from his office.

She stood up and tried not to wince. It caught her by surprise every time she stood up or twisted in a certain way a fiery hot poker of pain ran through her. She sucked her breath through her teeth as it left as quickly as it had come.

'What can I do for you?' Janine leaned on the door frame of George's office.

'Come in, I need to show you something.'

Janine walked over to the desk; it was always covered in papers with his scrawled handwriting all over them.

'Sit down, sit down,' he waved his meaty hand towards the two seats in front of his desk. Janine sat carefully, hoping that the pain would only be mild. She was wrong, but she kept her face as bland as possible.

George's expression was serious, the smile that seemed to live permanently on his lips was gone. 'I found this in the stationary cupboard. I believe it belongs to you.'

He handed her a glossy-looking calendar. Janine didn't understand, she reached forward to take it and flipping open the first page she realised it was pornography. January was a thin, busty blonde lying on a stack of hay bales. Nude, her knees splayed apart, her breasts and vulva on full display.

Janine flipped through the other pages, she hadn't known you could buy things like this. 'It's not mine.'

'You're in charge of office supplies Janine. No one else goes in there.' George was frowning, but the side of his mouth twitched slightly.

She tried to stop her hand from shaking as she held the calendar out to him. 'I'm sorry. I don't know how it got there, but I promise it's not mine.'

He didn't take it, and she dropped it on top of his desk. The redheaded milkmaid on the front cover smiled at her.

'This kind of behaviour can't be tolerated in a workplace—' George stopped abruptly, unable to contain his laughter.

Her lips trembled as she tried to keep from crying.

'You should've seen your face!' he said, leaning back on his swivel chair roaring with laughter.

The skin on Janine's chest prickled hot with embarrassment, she could feel the blush running up her neck to her cheeks. 'I don't understand.'

'I got you a good one!' George said. 'Oh, come on, don't be like that. It was just a joke.' He stood up, walked around his desk and clapped a hand on her shoulder.

'You gotta lighten up if you wanna fit in around here, love.'

She bowed her head, trying to focus on the pattern on the carpet. She knew he would be looking at her breasts, her top button had come undone again.

'Yeah, good one,' she said.

'I bet you've never seen tits like that, have you?'

'No, I haven't.' Just hold it together until he gets bored, then you can leave.

The phone at her desk started ringing. 'I better get that.'

'Off you go.'

She looked up, he was grinning, and she could see the glistening of tears in the corner of his eyes. *I'm glad I'm so entertaining.*

By the time she'd shuffled back to her desk the answering machine had picked the phone call. She sat on her chair heavily, the wave of pain and nausea were almost unnoticed under the powerful shame.

The machine was set to play the message as it came through. It was George's nephew calling from a job to say he needed more supplies. She'd need to call him back right away, but she had to listen to the message twice to get the right number. Her brain didn't seem to be cooperating.

*   *   *

For the next two weeks Janine found pictures of nude women all over the office, in her desk drawers, stuck up on the kitchen cabinets or put in with the mail. George had taken great pleasure in telling everyone in the office about what he'd done, and all the boys were getting in on the joke. Janine smiled each time, and told them how funny it was, but each time she felt a little bit less like one of them.

When she came back from lunch one afternoon, she found a picture of a woman and three men, one for each of her orifices, on her typewriter. The images had become progressively more extreme, and this one made Janine exclaim in horror. She crumpled it up and threw it into the wastepaper bin next to the desk. Elena, who was in to do the books, looked up.

'You can't let them see they're getting to you, love. It just encourages them,' she said.

'I just wish they would stop, I thought it would have run its course by now.'

'It's a sign of affection, you know. You could always try beating them at their own game.'

'I wouldn't even know where to begin.'

Elena got up and came over to her desk. 'Never mind love. I know it's not in your nature to play tricks. You're doing a good job here, just let them have their fun until the next thing takes their interest.'

'How long will that be?' Janine heard the whine in her voice and wished she didn't sound so young and stupid.

'I don't know, hunny. Don't let it worry you, it's only a joke. I could talk to George but it would make it worse for you if I do. You gotta have a thick skin to work in a man's world.' Elena gave her a hug, squeezing Janine briefly into her fleshy, highly-scented bosom; it was sort of comforting.

Janine sat down at the typewriter and tried to get on with the invoicing. It was no use crying over the situation. She hadn't told John; he'd be jealous and probably think she'd done something to invite the teasing. She didn't need to give him any more ammunition at the moment. He'd taken the pregnancy badly and had been particularly mean to her since then.

7. Happy Birthday Janine

As Elena predicted, the boys at work lost interest in putting pornography in her desk drawers after several months. Perhaps they had run out of pictures, or wanted to use it for its original purpose, and not waste it on a girl at the office.

The pain in her abdomen settled down over time, although if John was too rough with sex, she sometimes got a painful reminder. She eventually went to the other doctor Elena recommended and got a prescription for the pill and a supply of oxycodone and Valium. She told herself she would only use it for emergencies.

In the six months after she had started taking the pill, she put on about three kilograms. She couldn't say anything to John, he wouldn't have allowed her to take it given he was sterile, but she wasn't ever going back to that dark, stinking room in Carlton. Gerry was the only person she'd told the whole story to, and while they were still friends, Gerry was busy with year twelve and didn't have time to see her.

On the twentieth of the month, she would be eighteen, she had been saving a few dollars from every pay she could put towards a birthday party of some sort. She didn't know what she wanted to do yet, but couldn't let her eighteenth birthday go unmarked. Perhaps she'd even call her mother.

'What are we doing for your birthday, lovey?' John asked in early November.

'I dunno. Nothing too big, but I thought we could go out for dinner or something?' Janine didn't look at him, she didn't want to give away how much she wanted this.

'Is that all? You only turn eighteen once.'

Janine looked at the floor. She could count on one hand the number of people she wanted to invite to her party. 'No, I just want something small.'

'You leave it to me. I'll organise a night you won't forget.'

*   *   *

Conveniently her birthday fell on a Friday, but she had no idea what to expect. John hadn't taken her out much; he usually left her at home since she was underage.

'I bought an outfit for you,' John said, holding out a black plastic bag.

'Really?'

He'd been complaining about how tight money was for weeks. Perhaps he was saving to put on a lavish night for her birthday. A warm rush flowed through Janine remember why she fell in love with him.

'Put it on, do yourself up nice, we're leaving in an hour.' He smiled at her and there was a mischievous twinkle in his eye. She hadn't seen him look that excited for a while.

In the bedroom, she tipped the bag out onto the bed. Black fishnet tights, a skimpy black skirt and a black corset top. It all looked tiny and she was surprised John would let her out of the house in it. He was usually so protective.

She put the top, then realised it was backwards. She shuffled it around and her breasts, bigger now she'd put on weight, spilled out a little. She tugged at it, trying get it to sit nicely, but no matter what she did, she looked lumpy and slutty.

The skirt was very tight, as she wriggled in she was afraid it wouldn't even zip up. She lay on the bed and sucked her tummy as hard as she could. She couldn't breathe or walk well, but she looked amazing.

'Fuck me.' John said as he looked her up and down. He'd come into the room as she was admiring herself in the mirror. 'You're just about falling out of that top, love.' John came over to her, adjusting her top so that it sat better, but exposed more of her breasts. He gave her a quick squeeze as he stepped back.

'Now you're ready to hit the town. Come on.'

Janine slipped her black high heels on, the same ones she wore to work.

*   *   *

The club was in King Street in Melbourne's CBD. The street was full of strip clubs and bikers, but with John by her side, Janine felt safe. He walked beside her, his hand resting on the back of her neck.

'Fuckin' fag!' A man yelled at them as they went by. He was balding, with a long scraggly beard and a black leather jacket. She didn't get time to look at the gang logo on the back before John pulled Janine into a doorway.

'Dickhead. If you weren't here, babe, I would have shown that guy what he gets for talking to me like that.'

She smiled up at her man, he was so tough. He'd made her put on a long jacket over her outfit so people wouldn't see her until they were in the club. She was glad she hadn't had to walk past those bikers with her boobs almost out of her top.

They climbed several flights of stairs stinking of cigarettes and piss before they came to a heavy metal door. John knocked and the door slid open. The stairwell had been dark, but inside the club was darker. There were a few black lights, she assumed they hung from the ceiling although Janine couldn't make out much in the gloom.

As her eyes adjusted, she realised there were hundreds of people inside. Most of them were dressed like she was; the women wore skimpy outfits, ripped stockings, studded belts; chains and safety pins were featured heavily. The men wore black, the details hard to make out in the gloom. Everyone had massive hair. Janine stuck out with her dirty blonde locks. She'd washed and blow dried her hair but compared to most people, including John, it was flat and lifeless.

The music was loud and droning, the bass line simple and repetitive, it rose up through her feet.

'I'll get us some beers. You stay here,' John yelled into her ear.

She leaned her elbow on a ledge which ran around a pillar near where she had been standing. With all the music John had played for her in the two years they'd lived together, she had still didn't understand what it was about the clanging, droning and screaming he liked. She never said anything of course, he knew much more about music than she did, but if she had her choice, she would she gone back to the Beatles albums and big band records her father had liked.

She hadn't thought about Dad for a long time. No time to be stuck in the past these days, but just that moment, she was struck by how lonely she had become. Her father was dead, and her mother might as well be. When she'd called her that morning, her mother had hung up as soon as she'd said hello. Even Gerry seemed to have forgotten it was her birthday.

Well, I have a loving boyfriend, I don't need friends or family.

She felt a tap on her shoulder and spun around. Now face to face with a tall thin man in his early forties, his face covered in white foundation and enormous black eye-makeup like a panda.

'You must be Janine,' he said. He took her hand, his own covered in rings and he had a huge leather cuff all the way up his forearm and kissed her knuckles.

'Uh,' she managed to say.

'I'm Spider, John said you'd be here tonight. Is it your first time?'

'Yes.'

Spider still had her hand, his thumb running back and forth over her skin. She wanted to pull away but didn't want to upset John's friend.

'You look beautiful.' He leaned his head close to hers and spoke into her ear. She flinched back a little.

'Thanks.' Janine looked around for John, she didn't want to be left alone with a man who called himself Spider. He made her skin crawl. John was at the bar having a conversation with a guy she didn't recognise. Like Spider, he wore all black and a lot of eye liner, enough that she could see it from across the room.

John saw her looking at him and raised his beer in her direction. He started pushing his way through the crowd to get back to her.

'How do you know John?' she asked Spider, who was still caressing her hand.

'From the scene. I saw his band a couple of times back in the day, but you're probably too young to know them.'

Janine was intrigued. John had briefly mentioned the band when they first met. 'I don't know anything about it. John doesn't talk about it.'

'Shame. They were great. Toured Australia a couple of times. They were pretty dark. Some promoters wouldn't touch them, but cult popular.'

Janine nodded. Spider was on a roll and she suspected once John reached them, he would stop the conversation.

'They had some pretty sweet on-stage antics. You know trying to be Iggy Pop. John wore these massive platform shoes on stage.'

'What did he play?'

'Rhythm guitar. They were a five piece, so they had a really full-on sound.' Spider looked in John's direction and leaned back to Janine's ear.

'I heard that they split up coz he was sleeping with the lead singer's girlfriend. I mean they were pretty free with the love, but there is a difference between fucking at an orgy and fucking behind someone's back. Y'know?'

Janine didn't know, but nodded anyway.

'Here you go.' John handed her a beer. The glass seemed small and he'd spilled a lot getting through the crowd.

'What have you been telling my girl, Spidey?'

'Nothing mate, talking about the good old days when we used to see you out a bit more.' Spider turned to her and winked. He had let go of her hand as John approached. Janine tried to gauge the dynamic between them, but it went beyond her understanding.

I hope I have friends who have known me that long when I'm their age. It was one thing for Gerry not to want to hang out so much, their lives were so different, but she thought she'd at least get a phone call on her birthday.

'Don't frown, baby. Gives you wrinkles,' Spider said.

'Sorry.'

'Did she tell you it's her birthday today. We've arranged something special. You don't turn eighteen every day.' John looked at Spider and they shared a look.

'No, you certainly don't.' Spider grinned at her and patted her thigh, just above the knee.

After her first beer, Spider insisted on buying her a cocktail. It was sickly sweet and very strong, she felt lightheaded afterward and she wondered if he'd put something extra into it.

The men wanted to be up the front near the musicians. Janine followed them and was buffeted around the mosh pit. She'd never been anywhere like it, she was exhilarated, but also scared. Her skirt rode up and her boobs tried to escape from the corset-top she wore. She couldn't help fidgeting with it as she tried to dance. One person groped her breast.

'Don't worry about it, love, it's just harmless fun, eh?' John said when she told him later as they were having a drink between bands.

'Copping a feel is mosh pit tradition. Nothing to worry about,' Spider agreed.

Maybe it was you doing it.

'That was the last band I wanted to see. The night is still young. Why don't we head back to mine?' Spider said.

'Very generous of you. You got anything fun at your place?'

'Plenty of fun stuff at my house.'

Sins of the Father

*　　　*　　　*

Spider's place was a warehouse in Collingwood. He had a bedroom in what used to be an office and several tatty couches, a mini-fridge, hot plate, kettle and toaster, outside in the main body of the warehouse. The November evening was mild, but inside the warehouse it was chilly.

'Have a seat, I'll grab some beers.' Spider indicated to the couches. He flicked on a radiant bar heater which did very little to take the edge off the chill.

Janine had sobered up considerably in the taxi on the way over. John and Spider clearly had something in mind and her stomach was doing flip flops inside her imagining what it could be, coming up with increasingly wild theories. She pulled her coat tighter around herself.

'You look a bit peaky, love,' John said, putting his arm around her shoulder. 'You want something to get you feeling a bit more chill?'

'What sort of something?' she asked.

'I've got most things,' Spider said, he was leaning against the sink, beer bottle dangling from his fingers, cigarette between his lips. 'Got some Valium, some nice oxys, got Charlie and horse if you're feeling more adventurous, but I recommend a 'lude.'

'I'll have a few bumps of Charlie, give Janine a lude or two,' John said.

Janine looked from her boyfriend to his mate, she wasn't sure what a lude was, and was sure if she asked them, they would laugh. She was eighteen now, and had to seem worldly. 'Okay.'

Spider gave her two small pink pills, which she swallowed with a swig of room temperature beer. Apparently, Spider's mini-fridge was mainly for show.

After about fifteen minutes, Janine felt a spreading warmth and sense of wellbeing. She had snuggled into John, who sat beside her on the couch, and Spider had taken a seat at the other end, near her feet.

'How about a foot massage, Janine. Does that sound good?' John asked.

She looked up and smiled, that did seem like a good idea, although she didn't say so aloud.

Spider picked up her foot, gently removed her shoe and started to rub her foot. At first his touch was ticklish, and she squirmed half-heartedly.

'Sorry, how's this?' Spider said, running his thumbs in circles across her instep.

'Mmmm,' she mumbled.

John reached his arm across her shoulder and started to rub her breasts. She was surprised he would do that in front of his friend.

John put his hands down inside her top, and Spider had moved from her feet up her calves.

'Are you having a nice time?' John asked, as he pushed her top down exposing her breasts.

'Yes, I like when you touch me, baby. Aren't we being very rude to Spider though?'

'We could invite him to join us, then it wouldn't be rude, would it?'

'You have lovely skin,' Spider said. He lifted her leg to his face and started kissing it.

Janine giggled. It was quite overwhelming to have two people caressing her like that.

'Why don't you give Spider a kiss?' John said. He pushed her into a sitting position and Spider moved towards her. He knelt between her legs as they kissed. It had been a long time since she'd kissed anyone other than John. It felt thrilling and naughty to be doing it in front of him.

John moved from behind her, gently turning her face to his, and kissed her. She could feel Spider's hardon pressed against her thigh. He stroked his hand up towards her groin, and she was surprised to find how excited she was when he slid her panties aside and dragged his finger across her pussy.

'She's a very good girl, you see how wet she is already,' John said, looking over Spider's shoulder.

'We should move to the bedroom, so much nicer than out here.' Spider removed his fingers and took Janine by the hand.

Spider's bed was a mattress on the floor, but the sheets smelled clean enough. Janine fell back onto the bed and giggled.

Spider had already unbuckled his belt and was pushing her knees apart. He looked at John, who nodded his head briefly, before he climbed on top of Janine and started to fuck her. Spider's cock was long and thin, it felt strange inside her. He thrust hard and fast and panted in her ear.

'Steady on,' John said, tapping him on the shoulder.

'Yeah, yeah, sorry.' Spider off the bed and John, who was now nude and erect stepped into his place. He slid into Janine's pussy, and she sighed at the comfortable feel of him. She tipped her head back and was surprised to find Spider's cock against her mouth.

She gagged as he tried to get the whole thing into her mouth, her eyes streaming. She pushed his hips back and tried to keep him at a comfortable distance. All the while John was fucking her more and more roughly, making it difficult to keep Spider's cock in the right place.

John slowed down a little and looked to Spider. 'You want her cunt or her arse?'

'I've always been a pussy man.'

'Fair enough.'

John pulled out. 'Stand up,' he said.

Janine stood up, her legs were unsteady beneath her and her arousal was starting to fade. 'I think I've had enough.'

'You've had enough when we're done. Now be a good girl and sit on Spider's cock.'

*   *   *

At least it was over quickly. Janine was still clothed, but not covered, her top and skirt both now more like a belt around her middle. She pulled the skirt down and her top up but couldn't find her panties or fishnets anywhere.

'Where's the toilet?' she asked.

'Up the back there, love.' Spider waved his arm towards a dark corner behind the bedroom.

Janine's legs were sticky with cum and she felt sick. *I shouldn't have let them get so excited.*

8. Work Christmas Party

Janine tried to forget what happened the night of her birthday. John didn't mention Spider after that night and Janine didn't bring it up.

Something had changed between them. John was colder, meaner, than usual, but his sexual needs hadn't changed.

At least I know I'm still desirable, Janine thought as she got ready to go to work.

The boys at work were behaving themselves and Janine was even starting to think that she might enjoy her job. She'd been there for a while and her skills had improved significantly over that time.

'Elena, do you think George would give me a raise?' she said quietly when the boss's wife was working on the accounts.

'I couldn't say, *koukla*. It probably depends on what day it is when you ask,' she replied.

'Right, of course.' Janine went back to typing out the invoices in front of her and tried not to be disappointed.

'I didn't mean to upset you.' Elena perched her ample Lycra-covered bottom against Janine's desk.

'I'm not upset,' Janine lied. 'I just, well, I've been here for a while and, the pay isn't very good. I'd like to be able to afford some nice things something, you know.

Nice clothes for work, like you.' She would never have worn what Elena wore, but it wouldn't hurt to be on her good side.

'Get away!' Elena flapped her hand dismissively. 'How about I tell you when George is in a good mood and you can go ask then?'

Janine was so relieved she almost burst out laughing. 'Thanks so much. I really appreciate it.'

'You're a good worker.'

*   *   *

It was almost a week later when Elena started jerking her head and wriggling her eyebrows at Janine.

'What?' she whispered.

'Go talk to George now, he's just made a big sale. And we had a good time last night, if you know what I mean.' Elena winked and waved her hand, causing her many bangles to clank together.

Janine swallowed and stood up. She'd never asked for anything before. She hadn't taken annual leave, other than over Christmas, because she didn't want them to have a reason to fire her. She smoothed her skirt down and caught sight of her scuffed shoes.

I'm going to use this raise so I can be a better employee to the company, and a better girlfriend for John.

George was a big man, overweight but still very active, and the odour of his sweat and cigarettes filled the room. When he had a lot of phone calls, he would close the door and the smell would be like a wall when you walked in. Clearly Elena didn't find it off-putting. Today it wasn't too bad.

His large dark-coloured fake wood laminate desk dominated the room, he sat behind it in a black leather swivel chair. In front of the desk were two black vinyl chairs.

Janine knocked on the door frame. 'Have you got a minute?'

'Janine, my love, I always have a minute for you. Sit down, sit down.' George beamed at her and waved her into a chair.

'How have you been then? Boys not giving you too much grief?' he asked.

'No, they had fun for a while there, but they've settled down now.' Janine looked at her hands clasped in her lap. The silence stretched out.

'You wanted to talk to me about something?'

'Yes, sorry. It's a bit awkward—'

'It's not about women's issues is it?' he interrupted.

'No, nothing like that.' She glanced at him briefly and he was visibly relieved. 'I'm wondering if we could discuss my salary—'

'I see what's happening,' he said.

Janine lifted her head again and George was smiling broadly.

'I've been wondering when this might come. You've been here and while and we've had you on the trainee wage.'

'Yes.'

'Well, how about we promote you to a full secretary, and we can increase your wage accordingly. Seems to me you don't need much in the way of training anymore. Elena says you're a hard worker and I don't believe my wife would mince words if you weren't. She'd have had you out on your ear if there were any problems.'

'Thank you, that would be great.' She was surprised how easily George had agreed.

'We'll get something made up for you to sign, and we'll make sure the next pay packet is on the new rate.' George stood up and came around the table towards her. Janine stood, and had to steel herself not to take a step back. She'd never been this close to George before and he was a towering hulk of a man.

He wrapped his arms around her, gave her a squeeze, and patted her back firmly. A little rough, but genuine. 'How does it feel to be a secretary?'

'It feels pretty good.'

George left one arm draped around her shoulder as they walked out into the general office space. 'Elena, she finally asked. You can put that through now.'

Elena grinned and clapped her hands together.

She wasn't sure whether to be flattered or suspicious that the boss and his wife had known she would ask for a raise before she did.

*   *   *

On her way home, Janine bought herself a bunch of bright, papery, native daisies. She couldn't wait to tell John. When she walked in the door the flat was empty,

John often had a drink with the boys after work. She put the flowers in a vase and sat them in the dining table then made spaghetti Bolognese, one of her favourites, although John preferred meat and three veg.

John arrived home a bit after seven. She was watching TV when he came in.

'Where's my dinner?' John was unsteady on his feet, he'd clearly had a few after work.

'It's in the oven baby, I waited till you got home so we could eat together.'

'Damn right you did. You don't eat without me.'

They sat at the dining table and John shovelled his food into his mouth. If there was one thing that suffered with his drinking it was his table manners. Janine ate delicately she had never been a big eater.

'Would you like to hear about my day?' she asked.

'Not really. But I'm sure you're going to tell me.'

She gave a nervous half-laugh. 'I asked my boss for a raise and he gave it to me.'

'Wow, when did you grow a spine?' John's face was set in a scowl. Janine's excitement started to ebb away. 'Any how much more money do you get now?'

'It's not much, twenty dollars a week more.'

'You'll have to put all of that into the household expenses. I don't think you realise how much I carry you in this relationship.'

Janine wished she hadn't said anything. She wouldn't be getting any nice new work clothes, or a haircut. If only she'd thought to lie, she could have kept the raise to herself. Although John would have been suspicious if she'd come home with new clothes.

She sighed; she was being selfish. 'I didn't know. I'm sorry I'm not contributing as much as you are. I'll try harder.'

'You are incredibly stupid, Janine.'

'I'm sorry.' Janine's eyes had started to sting. She told herself she would not cry. This is what being an adult was about. She had to pull her weight and if life was expensive, she would have to get better at making her money stretch.

*   *   *

When they went to bed that night, Janine still felt the pain of John's words sharply. She'd been so proud of herself and he had reminded her how childish she was. She couldn't expect to be praised for something that was a basic function of adult life.

John was already in bed; he had made a few lewd comments and she knew he would need satisfaction before she could sleep. In the bathroom she pulled the mirror towards her opening the cabinet behind it, and picked up the bottle of Valium she got from Elena's doctor friend. She wanted to go straight to sleep once John was done and her whirling mind would make that hard.

She filled her cupped hand with water and swallowed the pills. She only had six left and would need to get some more soon. She slid into the black satin sheets beside John. They felt vaguely sticky, and she made a mental note to wash them.

'Come here,' John grabbed her hips and slid her toward him.

He was quick this time, and when he rolled over to sleep afterwards, Janine was drowsy. It hadn't been long ago that she'd relished the attention he paid her, had felt rejected if they went more than a few days without making love.

Perhaps it's the pill, people say it makes you less horny, she thought as she let her heavy eyelids close.

Her pay rise was completely consumed by the household bills. It occurred to her that perhaps John wanted her to have no money for nice things, but she dismissed the thought. He loved her and it was only fair that she paid her share. She bought all the groceries but, as John kept reminding her, he paid for other things.

The next couple of weeks slid past then it was nearly Christmas. Last year they had gone up to see John's brother and his family, but it had not ended well. The office where Janine worked closed over Christmas, George and Elena took a couple of weeks off. Sometimes they stayed in a little fibro house they had in Rye. George's family, his brother and his family, Elena's sisters and their kids, mostly in their mid-teens and early twenties all stayed together. The stories from last year made Janine wonder if they liked spending so long in such close quarters, but teasing and bickering were how they showed affection.

Sins of the Father

There would be a party at George's house on the twenty-third of December, the day the office closed.

'Bring your boyfriend Janine, we'd love to meet him,' Elena had said when the invitations were passed out.

'I'll ask him.' Janine had wanted to bring John along, but she knew he wouldn't be likely to come. The night before the party, as John was sitting in front of the television with a beer, Janine decided to bring it up.

'Did I tell you my boss is having a Christmas party tomorrow?'

John turned his head toward her, perched on the arm of the couch. 'No. How long have you been sitting on that?'

'I thought I'd told you.'

'You're a shit liar.' He turned back to the screen. 'You're not going without me.'

'You'll come?' Janine couldn't keep the smile from her face.

'Seeing as you have so kindly invited me, how can I say no?' His sarcasm was cutting but Janine still was pleased.

'I'm so glad. Everyone's been dying to meet you.'

John grunted and she knew it was time to let him watch his show. He hardly ever wanted to do social things with her.

*   *   *

John arrived at the office to pick her up just before lunchtime. They would drive to George's so they could arrive together. Elena had taken the day off to make sure the food was ready. George had invited his important clients and suppliers as well as the staff and family, and when Janine and John arrived there were already a dozen people there.

George had a double-storey yellow brick house with a vast three car garage, which had two doors rolled open so guests could go through to the garden out the back. The front garden was almost entirely concreted, and a large, circular concrete fountain took pride of place in front of the door.

Janine took John's hand and led him through the garage to the patio. She recognised a few faces, but wasn't very good at remembering names. She was suddenly nervous John wouldn't like not knowing anyone. She looked back over her shoulder; he was scowling.

'Fucking wogs,' he muttered.

'Ssh,' she said.

'Don't worry, I won't embarrass you in front of the boss. But Jesus Christ, they don't do themselves any favours.'

The back patio had a roast lamb on a spit, and two trestle tables covered with food; one on either side of the sliding glass doors into the back of the house. Elena waved them over, she was standing next to several vast buckets of ice and drinks.

'Janine! This must be John.' She held out her arms to embrace them both. Janine accepted the hug, while John stepped back to avoid it. 'I'm Elena, this is my house,

George over there, is my husband and the owner of the company. We're so glad you could come.'

John mumbled something inaudible, Janine hoped it was pleasant.

'Thank you, we like it. Can I offer you a beer?' Elena said.

John's face brightened at the offer. 'That'd be great.'

Elena handed them each a VB from the bucket.

'What a spread,' Janine said.

'We can't let you go hungry; you might even get something to take home if you play your cards right.' Elena was beaming, the role of hostess suited her. She saw more guests arriving behind them and waved. 'You make yourself at home, there's no formalities, take what you want and make sure you try everything, alright, love?'

Janine nodded and Elena moved her attention to the new arrivals. John walked past the tables of food and sniffed disdainfully. 'Wog food,' he said, quiet enough no one else heard, but Janine's stomach still clenched in anxiety.

'Let's just try a few things, do you want to find a seat and I'll bring you a plate?'

John grunted in reply, and took her VB. He found a pair of white plastic chairs near a small table and sat down heavily, the scowl back on his face. She sighed and grabbed paper plates, and plastic knives and forks for each of them.

The spread was impressive, desserts at the far end of the table were covered in cling film, in front of her were several salads; potato salad with egg and bacon pieces, tabouleh, Greek salad with chunks of feta and olives, a rice salad with sultanas and carrot. She spooned out a little of each of them for herself and gave John the potato salad, he wouldn't like the others. There was flat bread and dips, she took a couple of pieces and a little of the hummus. There was a plate of something that looked like yogurt, which she didn't feel adventurous enough to try. And then there was the meat. Two trays of lamb from the spit, cold meats, a plate piled high with cold prawns, and an array of chicken drumsticks. She made sure John's plate had plenty of all of them and gave herself a small helping of the lamb.

John will probably say I've taken too much, but it's Christmas.

When she joined him, he raised an eyebrow at her plate. He'd finished his beer in the short time she'd been getting a plate fixed for him.

'You need another beer, baby?' she asked.

'Yeah. I'll mind your plate.'

As Janine walked back towards the ice buckets where Elena was still greeting arriving guests, something prickled in her belly. Maybe it wasn't a good idea to have brought John to the party. He could be the life of the party if he wanted to be, but when she looked over her shoulder at him, he was sullenly picking at his meat and potato salad.

'Your man seems lovely,' Elena said.

'Yeah.' Janine's cheeks heated. She'd been thinking such uncharitable thoughts about him, and here her boss's wife was saying how nice he is. *You're getting ungrateful and taking him for granted.*

'You need a refill?'

'Yes, please.'

Elena handed her another beer. 'You needn't worry. No one here will bite. I'll send one of my boys over shortly to make manly chit chat. Then he won't feel so like a fish out of water. It can be tough not knowing anyone.' She smiled and for a moment Janine wished Elena was her mother.

This would be her third Christmas without a family. Since her father had died it felt like she'd lost all her connections to the world. Her grandparents hadn't even tried to contact her in all the time she'd lived with John. It felt like they didn't care.

John had eaten all the meat she'd given him, along with half of the meat on her plate when she got back.

'It's not bad, the potatoes taste like feet though. I'm not eating that.' He tossed the paper plate carelessly on the ground near his feet.

'I'm sorry, hunny,' she said, handing him the beer.

'I'm waiting to see if the cakes are any good. If they're no good we're going home.'

'Okay.'

I hope he cheers up soon. I don't want anyone to see him in this mood. It had been so long since they were out together, not counting the club on her birthday, and John had been very pleased with himself that night.

The thought of her birthday put a lead weight in her belly. She hoped she'd never run into Spider again. She hadn't liked the way he touched her, and she really hadn't liked the way John behaved when he was with him.

She sat on the white plastic chair next to John as he drank his second beer. George came over to ask if they were doing alright, but was quickly distracted by other guests. Janine was quite happy to nibble away at the small portion of food she'd allowed herself, she had to be strict even at Christmas given how much weight she'd put on recently, and watch the goings on of the party. John's left leg jigged up and down on the spot and he tore the label off his beer in tiny fragments making a mess at his feet. She had smoked almost half a packet of cigarettes trying to calm her nerves.

'I think it might be safe to try the cake,' Janine said, turning back to John after seeing Elena unwrapping the tiramisu and other desserts. 'Should I get you something?'

'No, I'll get it. You'll get me rubbish.' John walked to the table; his feet seemed to clomp unnecessarily loudly.

'Are you having a nice time, John?' Elena stood next to him. Her voice carried across the back patio and Janine hardly had to strain to hear her.

'It's alright. Good spread,' John replied.

'You're a doll. You eat your fill. I don't want anyone to go home hungry.'

John grunted something that sounded like a thank you and clomped back to the chair. Janine didn't understand why he was in such a foul mood.

'Is the cake any good? Shall I get some?'

'You've had plenty,' he said.

'Sorry.' Janine clasped her hands together and squeezed them between her knees. She'd hoped the party would be an opportunity to get to know her colleagues better, to show off her partner, but she couldn't leave John alone. He didn't seem interested in conversation with anyone who came over either and Janine felt too awkward to carry on for long when he was barely engaging.

He had taken a couple of profiteroles, a big whack of tiramisu and some watermelon from the dessert table. He only ate the tiramisu.

'I'm going. Are you coming with me?' he said, dropping his second paper plate on top of the first between his legs.

'Okay. I'll just say goodbye to Elena.'

'Can't we just go?' John stood up and started walking back to the garage and towards the street. 'I'm not waiting.'

Janine couldn't leave the party without thanking her hosts, they had put out so much food and made such an effort to include her, but if John left without her, she couldn't be sure he'd let her in when she got home.

There had been one episode, not long after she moved in, when she hadn't done what John wanted and he told her she had to stay somewhere else.

'You clearly don't care for me at all. Humiliating me in front of my friends,' he'd said. Janine hadn't understood at the time how saying she was tired and didn't want to drink any more had humiliated him, but she knew better now. His pride was very important to him and being seen to follow his lead in social situations was how she showed him she loved him.

As she ran after John, she passed George. 'I'm sorry, we have to get home.'

'Oh,' was all George could get out before she was racing to the car.

'You're lucky I waited.' John revved the engine and pulled out from the curb with a squeal. 'That party was shit. It's alright to work with those people but don't hang out with those dago dickheads. You hear me?'

'I'm sorry. I'll tell them I can't come next time.'

9. Alone for Christmas

John was quiet when they got home. Janine waited for the criticism she was sure was coming, but when he was silent even at bedtime she started to really worry.

'Are you okay, baby?' she asked.

'Fine.'

'Alright then.' She climbed into bed; the sheets were cold to her skin though the day had been warm. She wanted a cigarette, but John hated her smoking in the bedroom. He said it would ruin the sheets. She lay, still and quiet beside him. He had turned his back on her, and she could tell by the rhythm of his breathing he wasn't asleep.

He'd never been silent before, not for this long. Usually when she'd done something wrong, he would tell her, often repeatedly to make sure she understood, but not today. She told herself not to fidget, her fingers wanted to tap but she held them rigidly against her belly so she wouldn't disturb him.

'If you're not going to sleep, fuck off to the lounge room,' he said, his low voice still seemed to boom in the quiet night.

'Sorry.' She got up and took a cigarette out into the lounge. The ashtray was full of butts from earlier in the evening; sitting in front of the terrible Christmas T.V. not speaking. It wasn't long until she heard his chainsaw-like snoring and was comforted he wasn't still lying there stewing. She smoked the rest of her pack before she dared trying to sleep.

The office was closed between Christmas and New Years' Day. She couldn't visit her mother, and her grandparents all seemed to have abandoned her. Gerry was finished school by now and Janine didn't know if she would be in Melbourne over the break to visit. She decided to call her in the morning. The glowing VCR clock showed nearly four in the morning, she snuck back into the bedroom.

When she woke up, John had already gone. She must have slept heavily to have not felt him get up. He usually crashed around the house; his footfalls echoing across the lino in the kitchen and thudding across the carpet.

There was a note on the kitchen table.

'Gone to stay with Mum. Don't do anything stupid. John.'

It was John's handwriting, but Janine didn't understand the message. He'd never spoken about his mother, Janine had assumed she'd died, and the idea of him leaving without saying goodbye left her feeling cold.

She didn't touch it, just left it sitting on the table. She made herself coffee and went to have a smoke before realising she was out. John didn't smoke much but she could usually bum one from him if she was out first thing in the morning.

She drank her instant coffee; two sugars and no milk, the same way John had his. She'd adopted a lot of his habits since she moved in, it seemed strange now. It was the first time since she'd moved in, she'd been in the house alone for any length of time. She walked around the empty house in an oversized T-shirt. Without John, the house seemed dirtier, older, more decrepit. She would clean it all up, make it nice for him when he came come. Maybe try to cut down on smoking to buy a nice bunch of flowers to welcome him home.

She sat on the couch with her second mug of coffee and flicked on the T.V.

The phone rang and startled her out of a daze.

'Hello?' she croaked. She coughed quietly to clear her throat and tried again. 'Hello?'

'Mum's sick.' It was John.

'What do you mean?'

'She called me yesterday, before the party. Cancer. They can't treat it. She doesn't think she'll last the week.'

'Oh my God.' Janine didn't know what to say. It certainly explained why he'd been so quiet yesterday. 'Do you need me?'

'No. I don't want you bothering my mum on her deathbed with your meddling and interfering.'

'I don't interfere,' she said, her voice turning nasal.

'Shut it, will you? I need to be here for a few days, so I'm leaving you alone. Don't fuck this up.'

'I won't. I want to help. Where are you?'

'I'm in Sale. Mum lives up here now. I'll be back in a week or so.'

'Alright. I miss you.' Her voice sounded small.

'Yeah. Bye.'

Janine hung up the phone carefully, her body moved in slow motion. She put her hands in her lap and started to cry. She was going to be alone at Christmas and her boyfriend wouldn't let her meet his mother even when she was dying.

There must be something really wrong with me. She sobbed into her hands. She cried until her head hurt and her eyes were swollen and sore. By the time she looked up it was getting dark outside.

Janine pushed the hair out of her eyes and went to the bathroom. She stripped off her T-shirt and showered, the warm water running across her skin felt gorgeous. When she had towelled herself dry, she opened the cabinet behind the mirror and took the last two Valium. She needed to sleep; everything would be better in the morning.

*   *   *

Christmas morning Janine woke up alone. She realised with John away there would be no presents from anyone. She wasn't sure what he'd bought her, he hadn't given her any hints. She'd bought him a fancy new silver cigarette lighter and had 'Love Always' engraved on it.

She was tempted to go through the cupboards and wardrobe looking for her gift, but it would make John angry. He had enough to deal with.

She scrubbed the floors, vacuumed the carpets, took the covers off the couch cushions and washed them. The day was bright and sunny and by the time she'd washed a load of sheets the cushion covers were already dry. She put on some of John's records, if he'd been home, he would have insisted he chose the music and handled the records.

She started to get hungry for lunch and looked in the fridge. There wasn't much.

Nothing's open, I'll have to make do with what's in there. She scrambled eggs and had it with the ends of the loaf of bread. She ate at the dining table listening to The Cure.

When she'd cleaned up after lunch, she despaired. The house was as clean as it was ever going to be and it still looked dark, dingy and falling down. There was only one more Valium and she didn't want to feel sad and alone anymore. John had a bottle of scotch but she had nothing to mix. She sat in front of the television and slowly drank the rest of the bottle, wincing a little less with each sip.

Janine woke up on Boxing Day on the couch. She'd passed out some time after midnight. Her neck and back twinged as she sat up and her head pounded, she had one of the tablets the doctors had given her which helped a little.

John hadn't called. She wanted to call him, but had no number to reach him on. He was so far away, and she couldn't even let him know she was thinking of him.

She picked up the phone and dialled Gerry's house. She hadn't heard from her for a while, but maybe they could hang out.

'Hello?' Gerry's mother answered.

'Hi.' Janine didn't know how to start. 'Merry Christmas.'

'Who's this please?'

'Sorry. It's Janine. I wondered if Gerry was there?'

'Hello dear.' Gerry's mother hesitated briefly. 'Let me get her for you.'

There was a long pause, Janine heard muted conversation but couldn't make out the words, then there was a scuffling sound and Gerry's voice came down the line.

'Hi Janine,' she said.

'Merry Christmas.'

'Yeah, you too.'

There was a long pause. 'I thought we could catch-up. I have a few days off work, John's gone to visit his mother. I haven't seen you for ages.'

'I have lots of family stuff on right now.'

'You don't even have time for a coffee?' Janine pushed harder than she would have usually.

'I'll check with Mum.' Gerry put her hand over the receiver and Janine couldn't make out what was being said.

'Mum says I can see you tomorrow. About eleven?'

'Great. I look forward to it.'

'Yep. See you at the coffee shop down the road from me, remember the one?'

'I remember.'

'I have to go.'

Gerry had hung up the phone before Janine had said goodbye. She clenched her teeth; her friend's mother had to force Gerry to spend time with her.

Maybe Gerry would tell her they couldn't be friends anymore. She had probably been hoping Janine would go away, and they wouldn't have to have an awkward conversation. Thanks for the memories and all that.

At least the shops are open today. Janine pushed away the sadness in her throat.

She looked down at herself, still wearing the dirty overalls she'd put on to clean the house yesterday. She sniffed; she needed a shower, a good meal and to stop feeling sorry for herself.

She had just turned the water on when she heard the phone ringing. *What if it's Gerry cancelling?* She briefly considered letting it ring out, then remembered it was probably John, and he would be livid if she didn't answer.

She flicked off the water and ran to pick up the handset in the bedroom before he hung up.

'Hello?' She sounded breathless.

'What were you doing?' he asked, his voice cold and clipped.

'Shower, sorry baby.'

'Right. I'll have to stay up here a bit longer. Looks like mum won't last the week and I have to sort out her shit when she dies.'

'Oh.' Janine folded her free hand across her belly, standing in the bedroom naked while her boyfriend's mother was dying. 'What can I do?'

'Nothing. I don't need you coming up here and getting underfoot. I'm staying in Mum's house while she's in hospital so I can start throwing shit away.'

'Don't you want to keep any of it? Won't your brothers want some of it?' Janine didn't have any idea what his brothers would want, they were so seldom mentioned she suspected John had had a fight with them. Both younger than John, his brothers lived in Sale, close to their mother.

'Why aren't they taking care of it?' she asked.

'They're both useless pricks. Sean's too busy being on smack and Greg is visiting his in-laws in Melbourne. They've got three little kids and apparently he can't bring them back from seeing their other grandparents to see his own mother's dying breath.'

'That's appalling. Are you sure I can't help? I don't want you to be alone.'

'Fuck, Janine, let me be. I was only calling to make sure you hadn't burned the house down.'

'What's your number there?' She needed a way to reach him, she didn't want to have to wait by the phone for days in case he was coming back.

'I don't want you calling me here.'

'Just for emergencies then.'

'What possible emergency could you have that would trump mum's death?'

Janine couldn't think of anything, she stammered down the phone line feeling more and more stupid as the pause drew out.

'I thought so. I'll call you in a few days.'

'I love you,' she said. He grunted and hung up the phone.

My poor baby, he's going through so much and he wants to push me away. There was nothing for her to do but wait. She went back to the shower and stood under the hot streaming water. It felt better to be clean, but her belly gnawed with a suspicion John wasn't telling her everything.

*   *   *

The next morning Janine felt almost hopeful about her meeting with Gerry. Would they be able to reconnect after all that time? Both out of school now, dealing with the world of jobs, and rent and other adult experiences.

Janine arrived at the café a little before eleven, she'd had a Valium before leaving the house to make sure she was in a good mood. She sat at a table facing the front window and waited. They used to go for hot chocolate or coffee every weekend when she was still at home, back before her dad died and everything changed. Her mother's house was five minutes' walk away, but Janine wouldn't go there. Having the phone hung up in your ear was one thing, but a door slamming in her face was more than she could bear.

'You want to order something?' The waitress came over to her, a tiny spiral bound pad in one hand, and a red, chewed-looking pencil in the other.

'I'm waiting for someone, we'll order together.'

'Righto.' The waitress walked back towards the kitchen. Janine was the only customer. It was quite warm in the sun streaming through the window, and Janine started to feel drowsy.

She snapped her eyes open when she heard the bell over the door tinkle, it wasn't Gerry but an older gent. The clock on the wall said ten past. Gerry had never been particularly good at being on time.

The door tinkled again, and Gerry's mother, Celia, walked in. She came to sit at the table with Janine, her face was drawn and serious.

'I thought Gerry was coming.'

'Hello dear. She was going to come. But...'

'But?'

Before Celia could answer, the waitress came back over. Janine ordered a cappuccino and Celia a pot of tea.

When the waitress was out of earshot again, Celia spoke. 'It's been very hard on Gerry the last few years. She felt you'd abandoned her.'

'I never did. I kept in touch.' Janine's voice was louder than she meant it to be.

'She doesn't want to see you, Janine. She has to focus on her studies and spending time with you is too painful for her.'

'Why is hanging out with me painful?'

Celia sighed. 'When you left school there was a lot of negativity—your mother said a lot of nasty things about you.'

'What things?' Janine's hands clutched one another under the table.

Celia's head whipped around, the waitress approached with their drinks. They were both silent until she was back in the kitchen, out of earshot.

'Vicky said you'd stolen from her. Said you were taking drugs and weren't to be trusted.' Celia held up her hand to silence Janine. 'I know she was exaggerating, but the school believed it. Gerry was teased for being friends with you. Vicky would drop in to visit us, wanted to be friends with me she said, she was so sad since you'd left, and you wouldn't speak to her.'

'She wouldn't speak to me.'

'Your mother has always been fond of wine. She would come to our place, drunk, throwing wild accusations about you. I had to tell her not to come in the end. I know you're not a bad girl, Janine, but Gerry can't separate what your mother said from reality.'

Janine sniffed loudly and realised she was crying.

'I'm sorry. I tried to tell her to give you a chance, maybe what Vicky said wasn't true, but with all the rumours flying around, Gerry doesn't want to risk being seen with you.' Celia put her hand on Janine's shoulder.

'But she was my best friend. My only friend.'

'I'm sorry.' Celia looked sad, but somehow it felt fake. She sipped her tea and said nothing.

'I may as well leave, then. I can't say it was nice to see you,' Janine pushed her untouched cappuccino away; it sloshed over the edges filling the saucer with dirty-looking beige liquid.

'You were never a mean-spirited girl, Janine. Don't start now.' Celia said as Janine was walking out the door. The tinkle of the bell as the door closed was maddening, she wanted to pull it off and smash it.

Janine hands were shaking so she shoved them into the pockets of her jeans. She stormed up the road, not thinking about where she was going. When she looked up, she was around the corner from her mother's house.

She'd walked off some of her anger but as she saw her mother's gold Mercedes parked in front of the house she grew up in, she wanted to scream. Without thinking about it, she marched up to the front door and slammed her fist against it four times.

'Vicky,' she yelled. 'Open the door right now and speak to your only child before I make a scene.'

Janine pounded against the door again before turning her back on the house. Her mother kept a row of pot-plants along the edge of the veranda in terra cotta pots. Vicky would spend hours making sure they had just the right soil moisture, that they were protected from pests, and too much sun. She took an unreasonable amount of joy from them.

'Vicky!' Janine screamed. Footsteps came towards her down the hall, the slightly unsteady click clack of heels, her mother had had a heavy night. Janine picked up the pot plant closest to her, a maiden hair fern, and threw it over the veranda railing onto the front path where the pot smashed, splattering dirt everywhere.

The front door opened behind her. 'What the hell do you think you're doing?' Vicky squinted her eyes against the bright summer morning.

'Hello, Mother.' Janine threw a second pot over the railing. It didn't explode as spectacularly as the first, deadened by falling onto the grass beside the path.

'How dare you show your face here.'

'How dare I? After the shit you've been telling people about me?'

'Keep your voice down.'

'Are you ashamed of me, Mother? Or of yourself? Let's have all the neighbours up and peering around the lace curtains. You can't pretend I'm dead, or overseas, or whatever you've told them.'

Vicky folded her arms across her skinny bosom and waited. 'Are you quite done?'

Janine was so angry she had nothing to say.

'You brought it on yourself. And yes, I am ashamed of you.'

'What did you tell my grandparents? They don't talk to me either.'

'I haven't told them anything except that you don't live here anymore. They don't know where you are. You've never tried to get in contact with them.'

'And no one thought it was weird I wasn't there for Christmas?'

'No. They didn't.'

Vicky seemed so calm Janine wanted to punch her just to get a reaction. It wouldn't make any difference. Her own mother had moved on with her life and didn't care about her anymore.

Janine kicked over another pot plant, one with large, flat, deep green leaves, and walked away from the house. She was wearing thin tennis shoes and as she walked her foot hurt where she'd kicked the plant.

What a waste of energy that was. Trying to reconnect with people who clearly didn't care about her. She was angry, disappointed and despairing. When she was far enough away from her mother's house, she wouldn't be seen by anyone she knew, she stopped and sat on a bench. She'd been crying and her face would be streaked with mascara. She opened her little mirror and tried to clean it up with spit on a tissue as best as she could.

She wanted oblivion and was out of pills. *Who do I know who has good stuff?* The first person to pop into her head was Spider, she shuddered. She had no money but maybe he'd be interested in an exchange. John didn't need to know.

Spider's phone number was in her address book, she'd copied it from John's once in case of emergencies. She walked to a phone box and called him.

The phone rang and rang, she counted eighteen rings before a sleepy sounding voice answered.

'What?' he said.

'It's Janine. I need—' she hesitated, why would she want to subject herself to Spider's sweaty hands if she didn't have to?

'Lovely Janine. You looking for a good time, eh?'

She shivered at how excited his voice had become. 'I need some party favours. I don't have a lot of cash.'

'Don't worry, love. We'll sort you out.'

'I'll be there in about an hour.'

'I can't wait.'

Janine hung up the phone and tried not to think about his breath panting in her ears.

10. Make You Own Fun

When Janine knocked on Spider's door she almost turned and ran away. This was the lowest she'd ever sunk. John would hate her if he knew she was doing, he could never find out.

Her taste for oxy and Valium had been increasing, it was a problem. She told herself she would stop before going back to work. She was in control, just needed a hand while John was away.

While she was telling herself all of this Spider opened the door. He was wearing saggy cut off black jeans and no shirt, his thin, pale, hairless torso on display.

'Come in, come in.' He grabbed her hand and pulled her into the dark warehouse. 'I'm so glad you called.'

He pulled her along behind him and sat her down on the decrepit couch. He sat beside her and his pupils were tiny, even in the gloomy room.

'You look good,' he said.

'Thanks. I can't stay long.' They both knew it was a lie. He smiled at her the way a wolf might smile at a rabbit.

'No worries, straight to business then.'

She shifted away from him, but she was right up against the arm of the couch, his leg was pressed against hers. She could smell his breath, sickly sweet and somehow oniony.

'What're you after then?'

'Do you have prescription stuff? Oxy or Valium?'

'I have some, sure, that's what you like?'

'Yeah.'

'How about I give you what I have in the pharmacy range, and throw in a few ludes, and a roofie or two.'

'Yeah, whatever,' she said.

'Now, about payment.' He put his hand on her thigh and started rubbing.

'No kissing.'

'Deal.'

She fought the urge to push his hand away. 'Can I have the gear then?'

'Payment first lovely.'

Janine closed her eyes. 'Of course.'

He stood up and held out his hand. She took it and they went into the back bedroom with the mattress on the floor. It was even dingier than she remembered.

*   *   *

At least it was over quickly. Spider didn't have much stamina. She pulled her jeans back on while he went to the cabinet beside the door. He pulled out a small baggy of white pills, some round and some ellipsoid. He pulled out a bigger bag of different pills, these were pale yellow, and dropped a few into the other bag. He spent a few minutes rummaging around and preparing a collection for her.

'These are my finest pharmaceuticals. You're a good lay. And don't mix the little red ones with any of the others, yeah?'

'Right.'

She reached for the baggy but he held it back. 'John doesn't need to know about this deal, yeah?'

'He'd kill me,' she said.

'Me too.' He handed her the baggy and she shoved it into her handbag. She turned and walked back towards the front door.

'I'll see you again soon, yeah?' he called after her.

'Yeah. Right.' She pulled the front door closed behind her, straightened her hair, and popped a couple of chewing gum pellets into her mouth. He hadn't kissed her, but she felt like she could still taste him, his smell was all over her skin.

A shower and some pills would fix everything.

*   *   *

The phone was ringing as she put the key in the front door. *That'll be John.* She fought with the lock, rushing to get to the phone before he hung up.

'Hello?' She panted down the line.

'Where were you?'

'Out for a coffee,' she lied.

'Mum's carked it. The doctor called me this morning. She's being cremated tomorrow and I'll be back the day after.'

'Oh honey, I'm so sorry to hear that. Are you okay?'

'I'm fine, you moron. I didn't even like Mum.'

'Sorry.' *He's only being cruel because he's hurting.*

'Who were you having coffee with?'

'No one.' Janine was a terrible liar. She could still smell Spider's rank breath on her skin.

'Really? Just having coffee on your own? Are you a loser or a liar, Janine?'

What answer does he want? Either way he'll use it against me. 'I guess I'm a loser.'

'Damn right. I've always told you that. You know I could do so much better. You're lucky to be with me.'

'I know. I love you, baby. I can't wait for you to get home.' Her ears were burning hot with shame.

'Stop grovelling. Are you gonna be there when I get home?'

'Yes, I'll make your favourite. What do you want?'

'Fuck, enough with the questions.' He hung up.

Her hands were shaking again as she put down the receiver. John wasn't usually so mean to her, perhaps he knew about what she'd done. But how could he? It was more likely the sudden loss of his mother, no matter how much he protested he didn't care about her. He was grieving in the only way he knew how; lashing out at the people he loved.

She stood watching the phone for at least five minutes before she picked up her handbag from where she'd dropped it next to the front door and drew out the bag of pills. She took one Valium and one oxy; she wanted to dull her feelings without going through her supply too quickly. She wouldn't be able to go back to Spider once

John was back if she needed more. She shouldn't have gone today.

*   *   *

Despite her resolution to go easy on the tablets she got through almost half the bag by the time John was back. He walked in at eight o'clock on the Friday night, a long neck beer in his hand. She'd prepared his favourite meal; lamb chops, mashed potato and veg, but she'd had it ready for six, and had it warming in the oven since then, to be sure it would be ready when John got home.

'Sit down, baby, I'll bring your tea over.'

John grunted and sat heavily at the dining table.

'Do you need another beer?'

'Yeah, and you can go out and clean out the car for me while I eat. I don't want to look at you.'

Despite the awful things he'd said to her over the years they'd known each other, it still hurt when he sent her away. He'd been gone for almost a week, the longest they'd ever been separated, and there was no welcome home, no romantic reunion.

The car was a in a sorry state; the back seat filled with empty bottles, beer and whiskey, a couple of soft drink cans, wrappers from fast food joints. He must have eaten out for every meal he'd had while he was gone and put all the rubbish in the car for the amount of trash she saw.

She pulled open the back door and a smell of unwashed, sweaty man and rank takeaway washed over her. It was so strong the spilled beer was barely discernible. She put the rubbish into the big bins before venturing back into the house to find some cleaning products to try to get the stench and spills out. The seats were vinyl, they would come up alright, but the carpets in the foot wells might be a more difficult task.

John was sitting in his armchair, the TV was on, and his eyes were closed.

'Was that supposed to be my homecoming meal?' he said, his eyes stayed closed.

'I thought it was your favourite.'

'When you don't ruin it, yeah. It was barely edible.'

She looked over to the dining table, he'd finished everything on the plate. 'I'm sorry, baby, I'll do better next time.'

'You finished with the car yet?'

'Not yet.'

'Leave the rest.' He opened his eyes and she saw what he wanted. 'Come on.'

He grabbed her upper arm and pushed her in front of him towards the bedroom. He pushed her down on the bed, face first, reached around her to unbutton her jeans, and pulled them, and her panties down.

She heard his belt buckle tinkling as he got himself ready. She tried not to tense up, but she wasn't ready for him.

'Slowly, baby,' she said.

'Fuck, you're so tight. You've been a good girl while I was gone.'

He fucked her hard for a few minutes before reaching climax. She was relieved it was over, after a week away she wasn't used to having her body used like that. She wiped her eyes, determined he wouldn't see the tears in them.

He smacked her bottom and laughed. 'I'm going to bed. You can go back to cleaning the car now.'

He pulled off his jeans, which had puddled around his ankles, and his faded black T-shirt. It wasn't long before he was snoring.

Janine spent another hour trying to get the car clean. It still smelled bad, but she covered it with cleaning sprays. She hoped it would be good enough. Guilt at what she'd done with Spider was gnawing at her belly, she wished she could take another Valium but she didn't dare while John was around. He would ask her where she'd got them. It was not an argument she wanted to have the day he got back.

*   *   *

The next night John took Janine to a New Year's Eve house party over in the western suburbs. Janine hadn't been over on that side of town and was completely disoriented when they arrived. The house had a white picket fence and white weatherboards. A few of the boards were flaking paint and there were cracks in the concrete of the driveway, making Janine stumble in her heels.

The party was out the back, they followed the driveway down to a wide expanse of lawn with a lone Hills Hoist in the centre. The garden had one spotlight attached to the back of the house, and no shrubs or flowers as far as she could see. It was quite busy already; enormous speakers had been dragged out onto the back veranda where a tall thin man seemed to have put himself in charge of the tunes.

John introduced her to the host, Amber, as they arrived. She was a was a petite, red-headed woman whose entire outfit, what there was of it, was white denim. She had teased and crimped her hair into a massive tangle on top of her head, Janine assumed it was so that she appeared slightly taller than she was. Even in five-inch white stiletto heels, she was shorter than Janine.

'I'm so glad you could come. I was sorry to hear about your mum,' she said, reaching out to hug John. Her head nestled into his chest and they embraced for longer than she thought was appropriate.

'I'm Janine,' she said, holding out her hand.

'Nice to meet you, I didn't know you were bringing anyone, darling.' Her last comment was directed at John and a look passed between them that made a sharp dagger of anger flash through Janine's belly.

'This is my girlfriend,' John said.

'Oh.' Amber frowned, then waved at some one behind then. 'Excuse me would you, darling?'

Janine watched her sway across to the new arrivals before turning to look at John. 'How did you meet her?' she asked.

'Friend of a friend,' John replied. She frowned again but decided not to pursue it.

John knew a lot of the people there and she spent the night following him around and trying to make meaningful additions to conversations she was barely following. So many names she didn't recognise, and many of the characters in the stories had several nicknames making it harder to follow.

They celebrated the countdown to midnight with sparklers and a raucous shout-sung version of Auld Lang Syne. Someone passed Janine a glass of champagne and she smiled up at John. He was distracted watching the red-head, Amber, who was busy snogging a thin man with equally enormous blond hair.

'Are you into her or something?' Janine said, her anger suddenly bubbling out her mouth.

'What?'

'Amber. You seem pretty keen on her. I thought you were mine.'

'You don't own me, Janine.'

'So, we can see who we like? I didn't realise that was part of the deal.'

'You can't.'

'What does that mean?'

'What do you think it means? I do what I want, you stay at home and keep things nice for me. That's all you're good for.'

The anger Janine had been holding down since John returned boiled inside her. Leaving her alone at Christmas, the dismissive comments, the casual cruelty, it was all too much now she knew he wasn't even being faithful.

Without thinking, she dropped her cigarette and slapped him hard across the cheek. 'How many sluts have you slept with while I've been making sure you had hot dinners? Cleaning up after you? Giving you all my wages? How many?' She drew her hand back to slap him again and he caught her by the wrist.

'You don't get to do that again.' He was holding her so tightly she thought he might break her arm.

'Let go.'

'We're going.' He dropped her wrist and moved his hand to the back of her neck. 'Get in the car,' he said into her ear, digging his stumpy fingers into her flesh and pushing her in front of him.

In the car he was silent, Janine started to become frightened of what he might do.

'I'm sorry, baby, I didn't mean it. I was jealous.'

'Don't speak.' He took his eyes off the road to glare at her and the car swerved over the double lines into oncoming traffic. He pulled the wheel back and corrected with a few honks from the other drivers.

'Do you think you should be driving?' she asked.

Without taking his eyes off the road John flung the back of his hand at her. It caught her squarely in the nose. Pain flared through her face and her eyes started to water immediately. She put her hands up over her face and felt wetness coming from her nose. She looked down at her bloodied hands.

She snuck a sideways glance at him before reaching into the glove box, pushing a wad of serviettes into the base of her bleeding nose. Neither of them said anything for the rest of the drive home.

When they got there, John stormed into the house. She followed, the serviettes still jammed into her face, but her eyes had mostly stopped watering by now.

John was in the bedroom, pulling her clothes out of the wardrobe and throwing them on the floor.

'Get the black garbage bags from the kitchen,' he said over his shoulder.

'What? Why?'

'You don't live here anymore.'

'You can't—I don't have anywhere to go,' she stammered. Her mind felt full of cotton wool.

'I don't care. Yes. Amber and I have been sleeping together for a while. Once she's moved in here, she'll have no reason to snog idiot wannabes like Finchy.'

Janine looked around; her heart was pounding so hard she thought she might faint. 'It's the middle of the night. You can't throw me out.'

'I can do anything I want.'

She stood, dumbfounded in the doorway to the bedroom. John turned to her, his face red and blotchy with fury, and pushed past her to the kitchen. He came back with the bin bags and started to shove Janine's clothes into them.

'This isn't happening,' she said.

'It's happening. I should have thrown you out months ago, but I didn't because I felt sorry for you. You're so pathetic, I'm sick of it.'

He had filled one bag and was about to start a second when Janine realised he was serious. *I need to get my baggy,* her mind ticking over excruciatingly slowly.

She walked to the bathroom, her feet dragging across the carpet as though she were half asleep. She shoved her toiletries into her handbag, luckily it was voluminous and usually not very full. She slipped the baggy out from behind the bathroom drawers without John seeing it and dropped them into her bag too.

John had one bulging garbage bag in each hand and was dragging them towards the front door, still ajar form where they had charged through earlier.

He tossed the bags onto the front lawn and turned back to her.

'Out.'

'You're the only thing I have, baby. Please, I'll be better, I'll do whatever you want.' She was crying now, her words were muddy with tears and stuffiness from her swollen nose.

'Too late. I'm sick of the sight of you.'

'No, baby please,' she said.

John walked towards her, his face dark with rage. She cringed away from him but couldn't seem to make her feet move. He grabbed her by the hair and dragged her to the front door. She squealed in fright and pain before he pushed her forward, she stumbled down the front steps and landed hard on her shoulder.

John closed the door and turned off the front light. It was three in the morning on New Year's Eve. Janine had no money, no friends and nowhere to go.

11. A Place to Sleep

Janine sat down on the curb at the end of John's driveway and cried. She had no idea what she was going to do now that she'd been thrown out, again. John hadn't been himself recently, but she had never even considered he might have been cheating on her, or that she was on the out.

It was a mild summer's night but she shivered. She was exhausted and didn't want to sit on the cold, hard concrete anymore. She rummaged through her bag and popped a couple of tablets she hoped were Valium.

She stood up, slung her handbag over her shoulder, picked up the two bulging black plastic bags containing everything she owned, and started walking towards the payphone. It was out the front of the convenience store around the corner. As she approached, she was surprised to find it open.

She didn't have much money on her, but needed cigarettes. The old man behind the counter looked up when the bell chimed as she opened the door. His curious look turned into a scowl when he caught sight of her two bin bags and swollen face.

Don't you judge me mate, you've got no idea. 'Hi.' Janine's voice sounded adenoidal. Her nose was swollen and painful.

'What'll you have?'

'A pack of Winnie blues, um, and this.' She held up a Violet Crumble bar. She wasn't hungry but the sugar and chocolate were too tempting to resist.

The old man accepted her money and said nothing more. After stuffing the chocolate bar into her handbag and lighting a ciggie, she pulled the bin bags into the phone booth with her. Who could she call? She stared out the window until she'd finished her smoke and for some time afterwards.

The first person she thought of was Gerry. Even though it was clear Gerry didn't want to see her, maybe the fact that she was literally facing a night on the street would change hers or Celia's mind.

'Hello.' Gerry answered sounding mostly asleep.

'It's Janine.'

'I thought Mum told you not to call here.'

'Don't hang up, please.' Janine fought to keep control of her voice, the tears that had stopped were close to breaking through again.

'You've got two minutes.'

'John's thrown me out.'

'And?'

'I—' Janine had expected Gerry to soften at the news, but her voice was hard. 'Can I stay with you for a little bit till I get myself sorted out?'

'No. I don't want to see you.'

She heard the phone crackle as Gerry hung up on her. *When did she get so mean?*

Her hands were shaking as she looked for another coin. She had no other friends. Perhaps one of her grandparents, but she didn't really think turning up on their doorstep, bloodied and despairing, would endear her in their eyes.

The only other people she knew were George and Elena. They were kind-hearted, genuine people, but they were her employers.

Can I really continue to work for them after they see me like this? Will I lose my job as well as my home? Her mind raced through versions of the phone call with Elena. For some reason she was always the one who answered the phone.

'What time do you call this?' George said.

'Sorry. It's Janine.'

'Why are you calling me at this time of night? You sick?'

'No, I'm not sick—can I talk to Elena?'

George grunted and called his wife's name. Janine flinched away from the phone as he shouted at the other end.

'Janine? Love, what's happening? It's very early for you to be calling.'

'Is it? I'm sorry. I lost track of time.' She had a watch but God knows where it was, or if she even still had it.

'It's okay, *koukla*.'

'Sorry, umm. I have a bit of a situation.'

'Do you need to take some time off? We don't come back to work for another couple of days. Sweetie, you know you can talk to me about anything.'

The Valium had started to kick in and the world seemed to be far away. 'John's thrown me out. I—' she stifled a sob pretending it was a hiccough. 'I don't have anywhere to sleep.'

'Oh, darling. You will stay with us. I'll look after you, you don't worry about a thing. Where are you? I'll send George to get you.'

'George is not going out to get anyone,' he said in the background.

'Shut-up, *malaka*, you do as you're told.' Elena's voice had taken on a hard edge that brooked no argument.

'What's happened?' he said, his footsteps coming towards the phone.

There was a muffled sound and Janine listened to them talking for several minutes. She couldn't quite make out what was being said, although Elena was clearly winning.

'Janine, where are you? George will come now.'
She told her.

'You stay there. Don't worry. It will all be fine.'

'Thank you.' Janine's throat had become dry and her voice came out as a squeak.

*   *   *

George showed up about fifteen minutes later in his hotted-up car. She could hear it several streets away. By then she'd finished the Violet Crumble bar and done what she could to tidy her face with spit on a tissue she found in her handbag.

'You look terrible,' he said.

'So do you.' He was wearing a purple satin shirt and track suit pants. He had a lot of gel in what was left of his hair, and he seemed to have glitter down one side of his face.

'I was about to go to bed when you rang.'

It was New Year's Day. The party last night seemed so far away. It was like it was someone else's life.

'Well, get in. Is this everything?' He raised his eyebrows surveying her overflowing bags.

'I left in a bit of a hurry.' She wiped her finger under her nose, it had started to bleed again. She threw her bags into the boot and climbed into the low-slung passenger seat of the orange sports coupe George drove.

'Boyfriend give you that nose?' George said, after driving in silence for a few minutes.

'He's not my boyfriend anymore.'

'Probably for the best. Can't go 'round punching young ladies in the face.' He glanced at her; her cheeks heated with shame.

As they drove, he stole glances at her but didn't say anything. For a man who could talk the back leg off a donkey, as he would say, he was strangely quiet.

'Can I ask something?' he said, as they pulled into the driveway.

'I guess.'

'If he said he was sorry, would you go back?'

'He'd have to be really bloody sorry. He won't though. Upgrading to the new model.'

George grunted. He probably meant it to be comforting. They got out of the car and Elena greeted them at the door in a satiny leopard print dressing gown.

'Oh Janine. Your face.'

'I know.'

'This man is no good for you. I knew it when I met him last week.' She drew Janine into her chest, holding her tightly.

Janine sank into the embrace for a moment, but it was claustrophobic being smothered in Elena's ample flesh, and her perfume, usually too strong from across the room, was overpowering. Her nose started to throb.

'Okay, Mum, let her go,' George said, giving Elena a pat on the shoulder as he walked into the house.

Janine had not ventured inside the house when she was there a little over a week ago, before everything had fallen to shit. The interior was in a mid-seventies style; cream carpet and dark woodwork dominated. The entrance way led to three steps up to the formal dining and living area. The walls were covered in stuff; decorative plates, prints of famous artwork, photos of smiling similar faces she assumed were family. Even a terrarium coffee table sat in the centre of two vast cream leather couches.

She knew her boss was doing well but she hadn't realised how well. She resented the small pay rise she'd wrangled out of him, but then felt a sharp pang of guilt. *They've invited you into their home, be grateful.* The voice in her mind sounded like Vicky.

'I'm going to bed, finally,' George said. 'Elena will see you're sorted out, but I think sleep is what we all need before thinking about anything else.'

'Yes, yes, shoo.' She smiled at him as he trudged away. 'Do you need to eat first? You look very pale. Are you sure you don't need to see the doctor about that nose? I know one place that will be open.'

Janine could barely follow the rapid succession of questions. 'George is right, I need to sleep I think.'

'Alright then, love, follow me. You leave all that there, we'll sort it out later.'

Janine had bent to pick up her bags but was so relieved not to have to drag them behind her she thought she might cry. Again.

The room Elena showed her to was obviously the guest room. Even with her stuffed-up nose she could smell potpourri and faint dustiness. The bed looked small, a double probably, almost lost under at least eight large pillows with lacey cases. Elena threw several pillows on the floor, pulled down the corner of the doona and stood, hands on hips, surveying the room.

'You let me know if you need anything—actually, just take what you need. I'll be dead to the world for some time. It's been a busy night.'

'Thank you.'

Elena left the room, closing the door behind her with an uncharacteristic softness. Alone in the oddly impersonal room Janine wondered if she'd made the right decision. These were her employers. Allowing them into her life to this extent gave them so much more power over her. *What other choice did I have?*

She slipped into the filly nightgown Elena had laid out. Her clothes dumped in a pile at the foot of the bed. The mattress was soft, and the linen smelled clean. She could take another tablet, to make sure she had a good rest, but she decided to keep them for emergencies. In a big, soft bed, in a quiet neighbourhood, after a night of no sleep she didn't expect it would take her long to fall asleep.

She lay with her eyes closed, thoughts running around and around in her mind. When she woke up some hours later, she realised she'd fallen asleep quite quickly.

*　　　*　　　*

Living with Elena and George seemed to be the only solution for the short term however it didn't take Janine long to realise that she could not stay there.

Each morning the three of them would climb into George's car and drive to work. Elena was like a mother to her, looking out for her in her own way, but George seemed to resent her. She couldn't get away from them; all day at work and then all evening at home. She was expected to eat dinner with the family, sometimes their sons would be there, other times just the three of them. If she tried to go into her room to read or be alone, Elena would be upset. She never said anything directly, but complained loudly to George how ungrateful and antisocial their guest was. Janine knew it was probably a guilt trip, honed by years of manipulating her sons, but it was too much to bear. Every night after their meal she would watch television. Elena and George would take one enormous cream leather couch, while she sat on the matching couch on her own.

In the middle of February George first asked her for rent. She had known it was coming, but she hadn't realised just how much he wanted to charge her. She didn't know much about the rental market but it was more than half her wage. Given George was paying her, it seemed particularly unfair he wanted her to pay that much back in rent.

She'd managed to save most of her money since coming to stay with them. Elena had refused to take her contribution for the food she ate, nor for bills coming in.

'I'm going to start looking for somewhere else,' Janine said over dinner. They were having roast lamb with salad. Elena was very fond of lamb, though Janine thought it tasted fatty.

'You know you're welcome to stay with us as long as you like, now that you're paying rent, you're just the same as any lodger,' George said around a mouthful.

'I know, but I think I should really learn to stand on my own two feet. You've been so kind to me, more like a family than my real family...' Her own mother didn't even know where she lived now.

While she'd been staying with Elena and George, she hadn't used many of her pills. She still had a few in her supply for when things got really bad, but there was something about their perpetual presence that made her hesitate. She didn't want them to know she was taking them. They knew everything she did, so if she ran out and had to get more, Elena would know.

The next few nights she started looking for places to rent in the local paper. They were expensive but it seemed she could afford something quite nice for the amount she was paying George.

'Will you give me a rental reference?' she asked Elena the next day at work.

'Of course, darling. You know you don't have to go.'

Something in the way she put the two thoughts together made Janine wonder if she would give her a good reference. She clearly liked having Janine around, her own sons were off with their wives.

'I know. It's something I want to do.'

'Independent woman. I like that.' Elena slammed the stamp in her hand down on the paper to drove home her point.

*   *   *

The first house she looked at was a one-bedroom unit out the back of a larger house in Brunswick, a granny flat. The ad in the paper had read:

> 1BR detached. Own kitchen and
> bathroom. No couples.

When she had called the number to arrange a viewing the woman who answered spoke very broken English. After a brief conversation where Janine felt she should raise her voice in case it helped with understanding, they arranged a Saturday afternoon appointment.

The house was painted white brick, with a long driveway along one side, and a large concrete bird bath in the front yard. Janine knocked on the frame of the wire screen door and waited. She could hear someone shuffling around inside and thought about knocking again.

'Hello? Mrs Bianchi? It's Janine.'

'Yes, yes, I come.' The voice came from inside, shuffling continued for some minutes before the door finally opened.

Mrs Bianchi was extremely short, Janine was not tall but was at least half a head taller, and almost as wide as she was tall, had a ruddy complexion, and wore all black and a dusty looking floral apron. Janine guessed she was about seventy. She wiped her hands on the corner of the apron, Janine wondered if she had been cooking or from habit.

'You come,' she said, waving her hand beckoning Janine behind her. Despite the length of time it took her to answer the door the old woman moved quickly down the long driveway and through the vegetable garden in the back yard to a tiny, weatherboard cubby.

'This is for you. You rent this.' She unlocked the door with a key she produced from somewhere in her enormous skirt and pushed it open.

The door had dropped in its hinges and dragged along the floor, Janine squeezed herself through the small gap she'd managed to create. The old lady stayed outside, apparently having no interest in showing her around.

Inside was dark and hot. All the blinds were drawn, and the air smelled musty and old. She wondered how long it had been closed-up for. She felt around for the light switch and the single bare bulb shed a sullen yellow light on the room. It was even smaller inside than it had looked from the outside. A single bed along one wall, a bar fridge with a microwave on top, small sink, about thirty centimetres of bench space and some cupboards along the other wall. Next to the kitchenette was the door to the bathroom. As cramped and small as the rest of the bungalow, it was tiled in dull orange-brown with a toilet in the same colour.

The place looked clean, apart from the air of disuse. *At least that's something.* She lingered in the unit, not wanting to appear too quick before returning to the relative cool of the outside air. The sun was almost blinding after several minutes in the dark granny flat.

'You like, yes? You take, yes?' Mrs Bianchi asked.

'It's not for me. I'm sorry.'

The old lady harrumphed loudly and pulled the door shut with a grunt. She stood with her hands on her hips and pointed back down the driveway. 'You go.'

Janine shrugged and turned back toward the road. Perhaps the old lady was personally affronted that she didn't want to live in a tiny, hot room. It was much smaller than the place she and John had shared, more of a bedsit, no wonder the ad specified no couples.

*   *   *

About two weeks later Janine waited outside another house ready to inspect. She had tried calling four other places, but none sounded right for her. This property, in Fitzroy, seemed like the perfect option. The area was rough; several large blocks of housing commission flats marred the view of the city skyline. She stepped over a broken beer bottle lying smashed across the footpath as she entered.

The house itself was a slightly run-down terrace house, the door and window trims had been painted a deep brick red and the exposed brickwork was highlighted by the white moulding running along the veranda roof line. In places the white wrought iron had started to rust, leaving brown tears dripping towards the ground. There was a small patch of garden, it looked as though it hadn't been tended recently; mostly hard packed mud and in the corner near the front fence, a gnarled rose battled on, a few leaves clinging to its spindly upper branches, but no blooms.

Janine knocked on the door of the house, her hand came away slightly sticky from something covering the large, deep red door knocker. The woman who answered the door was frazzled-looking but about her own age.

Her hair was bleached blonde and stood up around her in the remains of an elaborate, teased up-do. Her eyes were ringed what was left of her black eyeliner and eyeshadow that may have once been a vibrant shade of blue.

'Oh shit, I thought you were coming tomorrow,' the blonde said, pulling at a stray lock of hair.

Janine hesitated. 'Should I come back?' She didn't want to come back, she'd come all the way here from Elena and George's place. The bus trip had been sweltering and taken more than an hour.

'Nah, fuck it. You're here now. Plus at least this way you'll know what you're in for.'

Janine laughed nervously and followed her into the darkness of the interior of the house.

'It's small and needs a bit of fixing up. On the plus side, the landlord doesn't give a shit what we do in here, but on the downside, he doesn't do much in the way of repairs. Rent is cheap though, so I guess that's what you're after right?'

They had come through the lounge room at the front of the house, followed by two tiny bedrooms, then the kitchen and bathroom at the back. It reminded Janine of a train carriage the way the rooms were all in a row.

'I'm Phoebe, by the way.' The blonde stuck out her hand as though she had only just remembered.

'It was you I spoke to on the phone.'

'Yeah, right.'

Someone in the first bedroom closed the door. 'Is it just you then?'

'Yep, my boyfriend stays over sometimes, but I stay there sometimes too. Kinda evens out. This one will be yours.'

The room was only large enough for a double bed, a small table and chair. Janine turned around to see a large dark wood wardrobe.

'That comes with the room, the bed and everything else is Jason's, he's moving out.'

Janine nodded, and sniffed the air; a fragrance of unwashed socks, something she thought might be tomato sauce, and faint undertone of mould. For a bachelor room it seemed tidy. The bed was unmade, but the sheets looked clean enough.

'When did you say it was available?' Janine asked. It seemed simple, well located, despite the slightly rough area. She didn't have anything worth stealing anyway.

'Jason's already sleeping at his new place – moved in with his girlfriend – so he's paid until the end of the month but if we find someone sooner he'll clean out his shit and you can pay him the difference.'

'Cool.' Janine was unsure for a moment what happened now. 'Do you have any questions for me?'

'Nah, you seem cool. I asked you most of them when you rang. You think you want it? I get a good vibe off you,' Phoebe said.

'Yeah, I think I would like it.' Janine smiled. She had been dreading this meeting in case it was as bad as the last one. She had also been dreading going back to Elena and George's place a failure again.

'Sweet. I'll have the estate agent give you a ring and we'll go from there.'

'Great.' *That was easier than I thought.* 'Actually, do you think Jason will need the bed and stuff? I don't have anything, so if he wants to sell it, let me know. Save him the hassle of moving it out.'

'Cool, I'll ask him.'

Janine excused herself and Phoebe walked her out. As Janine sat in the bus home, this time a pleasant temperature but stinking like unwashed feet and stale urine, she was pleased with herself. She was a proper adult for what felt like the first time in her life.

Maybe this time things will work out for me.

12. Family Reunion

Janine moved into the house in Fitzroy three weeks later. She had a bit of money saved up and was able to buy the bed from the old housemate as well as pay the bond. Phoebe had moved on to a new boyfriend and he was constantly popping over so they could have noisy sex.

It seemed as though things might be looking up for her, and Janine started to wonder if there was something around the corner that would blindside her, but it didn't come.

Elena and George had not taken her moving out very well but, as time went by they reduced the number of times they referred to her abandoning them. Janine couldn't understand why it was so important to them—she'd put them out by living in their spare room. It wasn't as if they needed more family to look after, with their own children and extended family always visiting.

She felt a bit guilty but had felt worse living there. Now she was able to go out at night to a bar or see a movie without Elena getting upset.

The cooking was a loss though; Janine had never been a good cook and living with Elena emphasised how much she had to learn. Oddly, she had shown no desire to teach Janine how to cook. Perhaps they were jealously guarded family recipes, but Elena probably preferred to be the only one in the kitchen.

'You wanna come out with me and Bob tonight?' Phoebe asked, putting her head around Janine's door as she got home from work. Phoebe worked in a clothing store around the corner in Brunswick Street, and finished later than Janine.

Janine looked down; boring work clothes, a pale pink blouse and black pencil skirt. 'Where are you going?' she asked.

'Probably Perseverance, down the road. Nothing fancy, but I wouldn't wear that,' she waved her long-fingered hand at Janine's outfit, 'you'll never pick up looking like a workaday stiff.'

Janine laughed nervously. 'Right, of course.'

'We're going in about half an hour, okay?' Phoebe said over her shoulder as she walked away.

Despite going out more often and getting some of her confidence back, Janine was worried about going out with Phoebe and Bob. They were so trendy; Phoebe with her bright-coloured fashionable clothes and Bob, in expensive suits and shiny shoes. Phoebe said he was a futures trader, whatever that meant. He clearly had a lot of money and probably had his teeth whitened; they were unnaturally bright.

She decided to wear a short black dress with layers of ruffles dripping from her waist to the hem, she wore black stockings and her trusty black pumps along with a short blue cardigan. The autumn evenings were chilly but it would be stuffy inside.

The three of them walked the short distance to the pub, Phoebe and Bob arm-in-arm, Phoebe giggling and chattering while he was quieter. It was early enough to still be largely empty, so they found a booth in the back of the main room and Bob got them all a beer.

'I don't usually drink beer but here, if you're not drinking beer, you go somewhere else,' Phoebe said, handing Janine her pint.

'Thanks.' The beer was cold and bitter, she hoped it would improve as she drank.

Janine slowly made her way through her beer and half a packet of cigarettes before they were joined by two men.

'These are my work colleagues, Craig and Frank, this is my gorgeous girlfriend, Phoebe, and her housemate, Janine,' said Bob, introducing them. They all shook hands; Craig's hands were warm and smaller than seemed proportional to his lanky frame. He had short dark blond hair which he'd slicked straight back with product; Frank and Bob both had identical haircuts. Frank was stockier, almost fat compared to the other two men, and kept dabbing his forehead sweat in the stuffy, smoky pub.

Craig slid into the booth next to Janine and Frank pulled up a chair from a nearby table. The conversation was immediately dominated by work talk among the men. Janine smiled and nodded but didn't understand the lingo. Frank was the butt many of their jokes, though, and she joined in on the teasing without really knowing why.

Next to her, Craig's thigh was pressed against hers and he would punctuate his sentences by patting her on the knee. Craig had fine high cheekbones, soulful hazel eyes and well-shaped, thin lips. There was something about the way he looked at Janine that made her feel she was the only woman in the room.

He was clearly as wealthy as Bob and attractive enough to have any woman he wanted. *Nothing wrong with a bit of flirting, even if he is out of my league.*

'What do you do for work, Janine?' Craig turned to look at her and she struggled to remember what her job was.

She giggled and looked away, trying to compose herself. 'I'm a secretary in a family plumbing business.'

'Sounds great. I love a good family business, although sometimes you get a bit of family drama seeping into work, I bet, eh?'

She turned her gaze back to Craig and giggled again. 'Sometimes.'

'I reckon you're great at your job, Janine, you look very conscientious.'

'Thanks.' Her cheeks were very hot now, and it wasn't just the beer. Craig's hand had been resting on her thigh for several minutes by this time and she would have let him do whatever he wanted to her.

'I need to go to the toilet,' Phoebe announced across the babble at the table. She stood up and lingered by the booth.

'Janine, are you coming?' she asked, her eyebrows wriggling in a pointed way.

'Yes, sorry.'

Phoebe wanted company to go to the bathroom for some reason. Craig slipped out and his hand brushed against her bottom was she went past. When she looked back at him, he winked at her. *Clearly not an accident then.*

Phoebe grabbed her hand and dragged her through the now busy, noisy pub towards the ladies' bathrooms.

'You absolute slut,' she said, beaming.

'What do you mean?'

'You've got Craig eating out of your hand. I've only met him a couple of times and he's never taken a shine to anyone as quickly as he did with you. Bob says he can be a bit standoffish around women, but looks like you've charmed him.'

'I didn't do anything, honestly.' Janine's heart had started to beat a little too fast, she didn't want to upset Phoebe.

'I'm teasing, you duffer.' She turned and went into a nearby stall. 'Are you keen?' she called over the door.

'I think so. He's very suave, but I don't know what they're talking about.'

'I never do. Been seeing Bob for weeks and I still have no idea what he actually does at work. I guess it's nice to have a bit of mystery about a person.'

'That's true—'

'What were you going to say before you stopped then?' Phoebe pushed past her to the sinks and scrubbed her hands vigorously.

'Should I play hard to get? Or be keen?'

'Whatever you think is best, looks like you're interested though, so I think he'd see through you.'

Janine smiled and felt the heat rise in her cheeks again. 'I'm not a very good actress.'

Back at the booth, Craig had bought them a round of vodka and orange juice. 'It's so much classier than beer, don't you think, Janine?' His voice was deep and rumbling, not quite loud enough for everyone to hear, he was just speaking to her.

'I'm not much of a beer drinker,' she said.

'What's your usual drink then?'

'Um,' she hesitated. She wanted him to think she was sophisticated like he was. 'I quite like white wine.'

'An excellent choice for a discerning young lady.'

Craig turned his attention back to the men's conversation, draping his arm around her shoulders. It felt good to be close to his side, he smelled of menthol cigarettes, and a musky, woody cologne she couldn't remember the name of. With any luck she would smell like him when she went home. She hoped he wanted to come home with her, it had been a while since she'd had sex, and even longer since she'd had really good sex. Her libido had taken a knock when John had introduced her to Spider, but since she'd moved in with Phoebe it had returned a strong as ever.

*　　　*　　　*

A little before three in the morning Craig walked Janine home. They stood on the veranda and he kissed her. His clean-shaven cheeks were soft and cool against hers. He kissed her gently at first, then more urgently, grabbing her around the waist and pulling her towards him. She could feel his hard-on through his clothing, and her body responded.

It felt like they kissed for a long time; hours, days, years, before he pulled away.

'I'd better get going,' he said.

Janine was breathless and a little confused. 'You aren't coming in?'

'We've only just met. Let's not rush things.' He smiled and his face lit up, even in the darkness she could see the twinkling energy in his eyes.

'I guess I'll see you around?'

'Here's my card, it has my number on it. Call me and we'll set up a proper date.' He winked and gave her a brief peck on the lips before turning to walk away down the narrow street. 'See you soon, Janine.'

Her legs felt unsteady beneath her. She hadn't been kissed like that possibly ever, and she'd never met a man who didn't want to sleep with her as soon as she let him.

He obviously wanted to, his body had given him away, but had restrained himself.

Slipping her key into the lock she let herself in. She flopped onto the bed and kicked off her shoes, her mind was spinning, and her body was still tingling and alive with Craig's touch. She inhaled deeply and was caught with a waft of his cologne.

Janine lit a cigarette and stared at the ceiling thinking about what it would be like to sleep with Craig. She didn't bother to undress and when her cigarette had burned itself down to the butt, she dropped it into the ugly glass ashtray on the floor next to the bed, rolled over and fell asleep.

The next morning, she wandered out of her room feeling a little hung over and sticky from sleeping in her clothes. Phoebe's door was closed, and the sound of Bob's rhythmic snoring told her they had made it home too. She made herself a cup of strong, black instant coffee and sat in the loungeroom. Despite having only just woken up, it was nearly midday, and a beam of sunlight made a bright stripe on the wall near her head. She closed her eyes so she could enjoy its warmth without being blinded.

I can't call him tonight, that's way too soon, maybe tomorrow. She smiled to herself.

*   *   *

Craig was a romantic. When she had eventually called him on Tuesday evening, she had left a message on his answering machine. He had taken her out every other night since then; dinner, movies, cocktails on the weekends. He insisted on paying for her and liked to flash his money around. It was a novelty to be treated like a princess and Janine was falling for him hard.

Despite the initial kiss on the veranda, Craig didn't have a high sex drive. He loved kissing and touching her, but the sex itself was over as soon as it had begun. Janine was disappointed; she became extremely aroused and nowhere near satisfied when he was done, but it was preferable to being used as a sex toy the way John had used her.

When they had been dating for just over three weeks, Craig asked about her family.

'I don't really have any family,' she said.

'Don't be silly, everyone has family, I want to know where you came from.' He stared into her eyes to intently she had to look away.

'My father died when I was in high school, and I don't have any brothers or sisters.'

'I'm sorry baby, that must have been really hard for you.'

'It was.' She shook her head. 'My mother made it even harder.'

'What happened?'

Janine wasn't ready to tell him about how she'd behaved. She was ashamed of how snotty she'd been as a teenager. Vicky might have been an alcoholic control freak, but she was still her mother. It hurt that their relationship was so damaged she wouldn't even acknowledge her own daughter.

'It doesn't matter,' Janine said, looking at the dull grey carpet in her bedroom.

Craig took her hand and stroked it with his thumb. 'It matters to me. You don't talk about your family; it makes me sad to think you don't have anyone.'

Tears prickled Janine's eyes. It was too hard to talk about it, she had lost so much when her dad died, and the years since then had been such a struggle, she saw that now. She could only blame herself, if she hadn't been such a terrible daughter, and friend, they wouldn't all have abandoned her. Even John threw her away in the end.

'I've got you, and Phoebe and a couple of other people. I'm okay.' She closed her eyes and hoped he would drop it.

'You'll always have me.' He kissed her forehead and they sat in silence for a long time. She was glad of these moments; they were so close they didn't need to talk all the time. She dared to think maybe this was a man she could grow old with.

'I'd really like to meet your mother,' he said.

'I'd like that too, but she won't see me.' A tear that she'd managed to hold back slipped out of the corner of her eye, she brushed it away. *I won't cry about this anymore.*

'That doesn't sound very nice. Maybe I can work on her for you. I can be very convincing you know.'

'I don't think that's a good idea.'

'Don't worry, princess, I won't make her angry. Parents love me. I'd like to help you repair that rift. A girl needs her mother.'

And she did. There was a hole in her heart she didn't want to admit was there, but the fact her mother, and her grandparents, had been removed from her life hurt deeply.

'I guess it can't hurt to try. She can't not speak to me any more than she does now.'

'That's the spirit, pumpkin.'

*   *   *

After trying to call her mother and having her hang up in her ear, she gave Craig Vicky's phone number, hoping he could work his magic on her. They didn't talk about it for a couple of weeks and Janine thought he must have given up or been knocked back.

'We're having dinner at your mum's on Sunday,' he said on Thursday morning.

'What?' Her heart had started pounding in her chest and she felt a little dizzy.

'Are you alright? You look a bit peaky?'

'I'm okay, I thought she refused to speak to you since I didn't hear anything about it, and now we're going to have dinner with her? It's a lot to take in.'

'She said you'd be like this.'

'Like what? She threw me out of the house at sixteen and hasn't spoken to me since and now you just casually announce we're going for Sunday dinner?'

'Vicky said she'd tried to find you.'

'That's a lie.'

'Now babe, don't let's make this a bigger deal than it needs to be.'

'You have no idea what I went through with her.'

Craig put his hands up in surrender. 'You're right, I don't. I'm sorry. I thought it would be a nice surprise to see your mother. I can tell her you're sick if you want to postpone.' He stroked her face and smiled the smile that always made her melt, and she couldn't stay angry anymore.

'It's okay. Don't believe her over me, though. She's been really awful to me.'

'She makes it sound so reasonable, but I know you were out on your own at a young age. I promise nothing will change how much I love you.'

A shiver ran through her, as though he found exactly the thing she was worried about and spoken it aloud. 'As long as you still love me, and believe me after we've met her…'

'Of course, silly, your mother can't tell me anything that will make me think you're less than perfect.'

He brought his arms around her and held her tight, she breathed in his scent and was instantly calmer. *I'm hardly perfect, but I'm glad he thinks I am.*

*   *   *

Janine spent Sunday feeling increasingly sick with anxiety. Her hands were sweating and she couldn't eat. Craig spent the day with at her place playing *Super*

Mario Bros on the *Nintendo* he had bought her for the house. He said it was for everyone but whenever someone else wanted to play he became sullen. In the end Phoebe and Bob stopped asking. Janine usually watched him play or flipped through a magazine but today she couldn't seem to sit still.

'What's going on? You're so jumpy. It's ruining my game.' Craig's character had just fallen down a pipe and died.

'I'm sorry, I'll go into the bedroom if you like,' Janine said, getting up from the couch.

Craig sighed. 'You don't have to do that. I know you're worried about seeing your mum.' He stood up and started to rub her shoulders before drawing her into an embrace.

'She's probably really sorry you haven't spoken for so long. It must have been hard on her too. Try not to think of the worst.'

Janine rested her head against Craig's hard, muscular chest and sighed. He hadn't showered yet and he smelled of old cologne, cigarettes and coffee, it was comforting to be close to him, breathing him in. He was a great listener, sometimes he'd rather cuddle than have sex and that was nice for a change, but with his scent filling her nostrils she wished he would just carry her into the bedroom and have his way with her.

'Why don't you have one of my Valium? Might take the edge off.'

She looked up at him, her eyebrows drawn together in a frown. 'I didn't know you had Valium.'

'I don't like to advertise it, it's only for emergencies and it seemed like you could use some.'

'You think of everything,' she said. Since they had been spending time together, Janine had avoided using her diminishing stash of prescription drugs, she wanted to impress Craig. Now she wouldn't need to be quite so strict.

Since they were his pills, Janine took two; within half an hour she was much more relaxed about the whole situation.

Craig drove to the house in Camberwell where she'd grown up. It was odd to see the path, the veranda, the front door with its stained glass inset panels on either side. She wondered if perhaps the door had had a coat of paint.

Thoughts wafted through her mind without causing her much concern. Craig took her hand and they walked up to the door together. He rang the doorbell, that was new, and the sound of synthesised chimes came to her through the closed front door.

Her mother swung open the door shortly afterwards and there was a moment of intense silence between them. She looked Janine up and down, then turned to Craig to give him the same treatment.

'You must be Vicky, it's so lovely to meet you.' Craig held out his hand for her. It took several long moments before she responded, taking his hand, wrist limp, palm down, to shake it.

'You'd better come in,' she said, dropping Craig's hand and walking away down the hall.

Janine couldn't bring herself to say anything yet. Her mother had barely acknowledged her and even through the fuzz of the Valium rejection hurt.

As they went past her old bedroom, she was not surprised to see her mother had filled it with sewing, knitting and other bits and bobs. She would never have thought her mother would enjoy handicrafts, but perhaps she needed something to keep her hands busy.

The kitchen smelled as though she'd recently mopped it with bleach. Janine couldn't figure out what they would be eating as there was no evidence of cooking.

'I hope you like terrine Craig, I have one chilling in the fridge with a salad.'

'Sounds delightful,' he said, looking around the room and taking it all in. 'You certainly keep a tidy house, Mrs Barrett.'

'I don't have anyone else here to make a mess. I like to keep on top of things.'

A glass of red wine sat on the kitchen bench. *Of course she'd already started.*

'Can I offer you some wine?' Vicky met Janine's eyes for the first time since she'd arrived, Janine told herself she wouldn't be the first to look away.

'Thanks, Mum. That would be great.' She didn't break eye contact until her mother turned away to pour.

'Red alright?'

'Yes, fine.'

Craig looked from one woman to the other, then made a face at Janine she interpreted to mean 'be nice'. Janine rolled her eyes but tried to keep her cool.

*   *   *

Conversation over dinner was mainly between Craig and Vicky. To keep her promise to herself to be nice, Janine said very little. It seemed to suit her mother, who didn't ask anything about her life but showed great interest in Craig; listening intently as he explained what he did on a daily basis. Janine had heard it before and it made no more sense this time than the other times he'd told her; moving money from one place to another but somehow you end up with more than you started with.

Vicky loved to talk about money, before long Craig had convinced her to show him her share portfolio so her could get a better return out of it.

Janine yawned pointedly, stretching her hands up towards the ceiling.

'Would you like coffee, Craig, or perhaps some chocolate mousse?' Vicky said.

'If it's not too much trouble, thank you.'

The food had been uncharacteristically good and she doubted Vicky would have improved that much since she'd left.

Despite the fact Vicky hadn't yet said anything directly to upset Janine, her nerves were on edge, the

Valium had worn off and she hadn't had enough wine to take its place.

'Can we go soon?' she asked, keeping her voice low.

'It's not late, it would be rude to leave before dessert.'

'This isn't fun for me, you know.'

'I think you're being a bit hard on her. I promise we'll go as soon as we've had dessert.' He put his hand in hers, giving it a reassuring squeeze.

The chocolate mousse was passable, if Janine had been feeling generous, she might have enjoyed it. Craig made nice with her mother as she ground her teeth trying not to scream. They left her mother's house a little before eleven o'clock.

'You didn't tell me your mum was so interesting,' Craig said as he drove them back to Janine's place. She yawned and her jaw crackled.

'You said we could leave straight after dessert.'

'Don't be a sook, babe. You haven't seen your mum in ages, of course she wants to catchup.'

'She only talked to you, doesn't give a shit about me.'

Craig put his hand on her knee. 'You're tired, I'm sure it's been a stressful evening for you. Next time it won't be as hard. You've broken the ice now.'

She looked over to him, catching his eye briefly before he returned to watching the road. He was smiling so broadly she thought he might hurt himself. *What's he so pleased about?*

She was not looking forward to a next time. Her mother would use any suggestion of vulnerability to crush her daughter and Janine didn't need that in her life. Craig was a good guy, stable, had a good job, didn't demand too much from her, she didn't need her mother coming in and sowing doubt or picking fights.

Craig stayed the night and was up before seven to go to work. He kissed her goodbye as he tiptoed out of the house. Janine stayed in bed, watching the grey light around the edges of the curtains, waiting for her alarm to go off.

Maybe I am expecting the worst of Mum, she must have had a really hard time with Dad's death and I behaved badly. Craig might be right; she didn't know how to patch things up without looking like the bad guy. She thought herself in circles until the alarm bleeped.

13.   The Deal

Over the next couple of months Craig insisted that they visit Vicky every other Sunday. He had no relatives in Melbourne, and said he missed having a family around him. Elena didn't take too kindly to the news that Janine has let her mother back into her life.

'Your mother should be ashamed. No matter what my kids did, they would always be welcome.' She made an exaggerated spitting gesture to emphasise her point.

'I dunno, she was doing her best.'

'You ended up on the street, sweetheart, remember when you came to stay with us? It was only because I knew your mother wouldn't, we took you in. If she had been less of a—well, I would have marched you over there and told her to look after you properly.'

The vehemence Elena displayed reminded Janine why she sometimes wished she were her mother. Then again, with the high expectations she put on her children, Janine thought maybe it was for the best she wasn't.

After working with the family for a nearly three years, Janine had started to get bored with the constant drama between Elena and her sons.

I could start looking for another job, things are going well with Craig, and living with Phoebe is okay, so maybe it's time to try for something more challenging.

George usually skim read the newspaper at lunch time, but once he was done with it, he lobbed it into the pile next to the bins. Janine took lunch after her boss so she could take the job pages home to look at later. She had tried looking through them while she ate, but other employees wandered through the lunchroom and it seemed suspicious to hide the pages every time someone went past.

'Good for you getting into something more lucrative, babe. You could branch out into shares or futures with me if you get any savings.' Craig leaned down and kissed her hair as she pored over the ads one night after work. They'd been out to a fancy new restaurant in Hawthorn, a Japanese fusion place. Janine had come home hungry as she couldn't bring herself to eat half the food on display.

'It'll be a while before I have much to invest.' They had discussed her financial situation several times since they'd started dating seriously. She knew he was trying to help but she became defensive when he asked about money.

Her mother had given him ten thousand to start investing in bonds and he had already given her nearly a thousand back in dividends. An unbelievable return, according to Craig. Janine wished she had the money to make those sorts of investments, but with John and the move, and her living expenses, she had very little saved.

'Look at this one,' Craig said, leaning over her to point.

Skilled Secretary cum Girl Friday
required for busy family business.
Croydon Location. Salary plus
benefits.

'It's too far away, I'd never be able to get there on the train.'

'If you bought a car, it wouldn't be too far away.'

She turned to look at him sharply. 'Where am I going to get the money to buy a car from?'

'I could loan you a little bit if you needed it. You'd pay it back in no time on that wage.'

'You don't have to do that.'

'I know, hunny, but I want to. You work so hard and you'll never get ahead in life without taking a leap.'

Janine chewed her lip and didn't answer. It seemed too good to be true, she wanted to give him time to change his mind.

'You could always go to the bank, but they'll give you a higher interest rate than me–I wouldn't charge you any.' He winked.

She smiled; he could be so generous sometimes. 'Okay, I'll apply for this one and *if* I get the job, I'll let you loan me the money for a car. Nothing fancy mind you; a reliable run-around.'

'Of course, baby. Something that suits you.' He grinned at her and pulled her closer to him on the couch.

Despite their minimal sex life, Craig was the best boyfriend she'd ever had. He must have been ambitious to be a stockbroker, otherwise he couldn't afford the lifestyle he had, but she was glad he wasn't jealous of her goals.

*   *   *

Janine called the office of *Goodman & Sons Carpentry and Building Services* the next day from the phone box down the street from her office. She didn't want anyone to overhear and was offered an interview the day after.

I'll have to call in sick. She placed the received gently back on its cradle and turned to fight her way out of the booth. No matter where she was the door for the phone box always jammed.

As she was shaking the door trying to jiggle it loose, she decided to call Craig at work to give him the good news instead.

'I got an interview!' she said as soon as he answered.

'That's fantastic. I knew you'd blow them away. Do you need to borrow my car tomorrow?' he said, before lowering his voice to continue. 'Maybe I could take the day off and come with you?'

'You don't need to do that.'

'You keep saying that. What time is it?'

'Eleven.'

'We could have lunch afterwards. My treat. Please say you'll come.'

Janine chewed the inside of her lip for a moment. 'Okay, that sounds like fun.'

Back at her desk it was all she could do not to grin from ear to ear. Things were starting to look up for her. Her mother was being less of a bitch, mostly due to Craig's influence, and she getting ahead in her career, despite all the worries she had about never having finished school.

'You look like the cat who got the cream,' Nick said. He was the elder of Elena's children and the one who teased her the most.

'Buzz off, Nick.'

'Were you on the phone to your boyfriend at lunch time then? I saw you twirling the phone cord like a schoolgirl.'

'I was not.' Janine's voice was a squeak of outrage.

'You're such an easy target, Janine. I thought you would have learned to be tougher after working here for so long.' Nick laughed at his own joke and wandered off back to his van.

I won't miss that. No matter how many times she told herself it was affectionate, the teasing and practical jokes played on her were always hurtful.

She tucked the note with the interview time and address into her purse, slipped it back into her handbag and dropped it under her desk.

*   *   *

Craig stayed the night so he could be there in the morning to help her prepare for her interview. Janine had thought it would make more sense to stay at his place in the city, but he had insisted. She'd never been to his apartment.

'It's so empty and flashy. I'm much happier with you here,' he had said when she asked about it. For someone who liked to show off his car and suits it seemed odd he didn't want to show her his apartment.

Craig drove down to Croydon, an eastern suburb of Melbourne Janine hadn't had much call to visit. Flat and industrial, with the hills surrounding them. According to the directions from the receptionist, the place they were looking for was on the corner of two main roads.

'That was it back there,' Janine said, craning her neck to watch the building retreat into the distance. Craig always drove fast so they went right past it.

'Ah, balls.' Craig slowed the car and they pulled onto the shoulder so he could make a U-turn and head back.

The place was a flat looking rectangular building, on one side was a caryard with huge flags clapping against flagpoles in the breeze. Janine expected the crossroad to be a lot bigger; there weren't even traffic lights.

'If she said it was next to the caryard, I would have seen it earlier,' Janine muttered.

'What?' Craig asked.

'Never mind.'

He turned into the caryard and turned off the engine. 'I'll have a look around here while your inside. There's no rush. I'll be here when you're done. Are you ready to wow them?'

Janine grimaced. 'Ready as I'll ever be.'

She checked herself one last time in the side mirror of the car before Craig kissed her on the forehead.

She stepped out of the car, straightened her skirt and flicked her long blonde hair off her shoulders. She'd chosen a slim-fitting black skirt, her trusty black pumps, a red, frilly, button-down blouse and a black jacket to finish it off. Craig had insisted on the shirt. 'You need a bit of colour, shows you have some personality, but not too much.'

The caryard was quite large and, despite being next door, the walk to the office felt interminable. The click-clacking of her heels on the uneven footpath echoed loudly in the flat open area.

Once inside the offices of *Goodman & Sons Carpentry and Building Services*, she looked around for a receptionist; an enormous, dark brown desk, holding a phone, a typewriter, and a few stacks of papers sat in the corner, but no one was behind it. The rest of the room was decorated in shades of brown; the carpet was a dirty beige, two corduroy couches in chocolate, even the water cooler stand was brown, although the bottle was the usual blue.

I'm glad I wore some colour.

There was a small chrome bell on the desk, which she dinged a couple of times. It wasn't very loud. The wall behind the large desk was taken up with a mirrored window. Perhaps the other staff were able to see her standing there even if they hadn't heard the bell.

Janine waited for someone for the full ten minutes until it was exactly eleven o'clock when a small, rotund, balding man came bustling out from behind the mirrored glass.

'You must be Janine.' He held out his pudgy hand towards her.

'Yes, that's me.' She took his hand and his grip was surprisingly firm.

'I'm Barry Goodman, the owner. Sorry, there was no one to greet you, that's the job you've applied for you see and there isn't anyone in it.' He laughed heartily; Janine smiled but didn't understand why it was funny.

'Come through. Can I get you a coffee?'

'That would be great, thanks.'

He led her back through the door in the mirrored wall into what was clearly the main office and warehouse.

'We moved into this building about six months ago, haven't quite got the hang of it yet,' he said, as they entered a small kitchenette area. The whole back of the building was one vast room. The end nearest the reception area had four desks, grouped to face into each other, each covered in a concerning array of papers and tools. Towards the back were two large roller doors, one raised, the other closed, and two white vans.

'How many staff?' Janine asked. It seemed bigger than George's business, but it could have been the layout.

'It's me, my two sons, two apprentices, and a couple of contractors who come and go depending on the job.

My wife used to do reception and the books but she's—well she doesn't anymore. You want milk and sugar?'

'Sugar, no milk, thanks,' she replied. The look on his face when he'd mentioned his wife made Janine think she'd left him not the company. She filed that away to think about later.

*   *   *

An hour later Janine walked briskly back to the car yard where Craig waited for her.

'How did it go?' he asked as she approached. He was lounging against the bonnet, the bright red paintwork glinting in the sunlight; he looked like a model.

'Oh babe, I think he really liked me. We got on so well, and everything in the job is just like what I do for George but they're a bit bigger, so I have room to grow and learn more stuff. Maybe even some bookkeeping.' She couldn't help grinning to herself.

'What did I tell you? Knocked 'em dead.'

He took her in his arms and planted a kiss on her lips, she thought for a moment he might dip her. She generally didn't like public displays of affection, but it was a special occasion.

'He hasn't offered me the job yet, but I'm confident.'

'Of course, you are. I'm going to take you to the revolving restaurant up in the mountains.'

Janine clapped her hands together in excitement. 'I've never been there.'

He's really spoiling me; I was so worried he didn't really care about me but maybe he's the one. She stepped into the lowslung sports car.

'I'm so proud of you for going after a better job. I know George and Elena have done a lot for you, and you're part of the family, but you have to admit when you've got everything you can out of someone.' Craig patted her knee and started the car.

'What do you mean?'

'Just you shouldn't feel guilty about leaving. You don't have to stick around with them.'

It hadn't occurred to her that she was betraying George and Elena's generosity. She'd been with them through some hairy situations, it felt ungrateful to be looking for another job.

Janine spent lunch and the drive back to Fitzroy worrying about how she was betraying her new family. She knew how much it hurt to be thrown out of a family and now she was about to walk away from one that had welcomed her in.

'You okay? You seem quiet,' Craig said in the car when they parked in front of her place.

'I'm okay. Don't worry about it.'

'You were so excited, maybe it's starting to sink in that a new job will have lots of new challenges and all the rest but I know you're capable.' He kissed her on the forehead while reaching across to pop open her door.

'I know I said I'd spend the day with you but since we're back a little early, I thought I'd just go see a couple of clients, set a few things up. Is that okay?'

'Of course, babe. You drove me all the way down there, you can have the afternoon.' She wanted him to stay and stroke her hair as they watched a video, but his work was important.

'See ya then,' he said.

She swung the door shut and he sped off down the narrow street. Phoebe wouldn't be home for a couple of hours yet, and she had the house to herself.

*   *   *

By the time Phoebe arrived home after six o'clock, Janine had vacuumed and mopped the floors, done a load of washing now drying on a rack in the lounge room, and prepared a lasagne. She wasn't usually a cook, but thought it would be nice to eat a home-cooked meal for a change. Craig loved eating at the most exclusive restaurants, but she sometimes just wanted homemade. Even visiting her mother, they ate store bought foods.

Janine's limited repertoire was a few staples; steak and chips, sausage and mash, lasagne, and apricot chicken she'd learned from the label on a can of apricot nectar, but she tried hard.

'Something smells good,' Phoebe called from the hallway.

'I made dinner, if you want some.'

'When would I ever say no to that.' Phoebe looked immaculate as always. She wore a dress in dark red plaid, tight at the waist it fell in enormous ruffles to the hemline at her knee. She wore a wide elasticised black belt on top, a matching plaid bolero jacket and black stilettoes.

'I don't know how you can work in those shoes,' Janine said.

'You'd be surprised what the human body can get used to,' she said with a wink. 'So, why the cooking?'

'I'm not sure. I thought I would be celebrating.'

'But you're not?'

'No, I mean, I don't know.'

'Why don't you start from the beginning.' Phoebe sat down at the kitchen table and watched as Janine served large slabs of lasagne with the garden salad she'd cobbled together from stuff they had in the fridge.

'I had a job interview today,' she started. She told Phoebe about the interview, and the lunch date.

'Why are you not sure? Sounds like you had a fantastic day.'

'I don't know whether I should be leaving. They've really helped me through a hard patch. Craig says I shouldn't feel bad about it, but I do.'

'Are you gonna work there forever?'

'No, but it was only little while ago I was living with them.'

'That's true. You don't want them to think you're ungrateful.'

Janine took a bite, chewed it carefully and swallowed. 'It won't kill me to stick around a bit longer, I'm sure Craig will understand.'

'Gotta do what you gotta do, love. This was great by the way. You should shame-cook more often.' Phoebe laughed and took her plate to the sink.

*   *   *

Janine went back to work the next day feeling guilty. She had told them she had a doctor's appointment and wasn't sure how long it would take, so she needed the whole day. She was convinced Elena knew it was a fake reason but she hadn't been challenged.

Just before lunch Nick came into the office. He smelled like shit; he must have been doing some sewerage works. Usually, they tried to pass off those jobs to local contractors or the apprentices, but it looked like he'd had to do it himself.

'Hi Nick.' She felt sorry for him.

'You have no idea what I've been through today. Literally, you wouldn't believe it if you saw it.'

'Geez, can I do anything?'

He thought for a moment and shook his head. 'Nah. Is Dad around?'

'Still in his office I think.'

'Get him to come out the back, don't wanna stink up the office.'

'Will do.'

'Can I bum a couple smokes off you too?'

She had half a pack, and had hoped to stretch it till Monday when her pay came through. Nick was hovering by the doorway out to the car park, trying not to touch anything.

'Of course, take the rest of mine.' She stood up and took it to him. The stench as she got closer was overwhelming. She wanted to ask what had happened for him to smell and look like that, but it wasn't the right time.

Nick disappeared back outside, and she went into George's office.

'Nick needs to see you out the back,' she said, sticking her head around his door.

'Got his dick stuck in his zipper again?'

Janine was shocked, George was crude but not usually he had a bit of a lead up to a comment like that.

'C'mon Janine! I'm only teasing. You know we only do it coz we love you.'

'Yeah, of course.'

George walked past her and out to the carpark before she was able to get her mind together. Somehow having him say the words out aloud made it all seem so real. She couldn't take the job in Croydon now. Even if they offered double her current salary, she wouldn't be able to forgive herself. Maybe in a year, after the memory of arriving on their doorstep with all her worldly possessions in black bin bags had faded.

Craig will be disappointed. He was so keen on me getting a better job.

Sins of the Father

*   *   *

Craig worked most of the weekend, so the next time she saw him was when he picked her up to go to her mother's for dinner.

He honked from the car pulled up outside her flat. There were often no parking spaces and he didn't like leaving the expensive car in the street if he didn't have to.

Janine shoved her feet into her shoes, the scuffed black pumps she wore everywhere, and sighed. She needed new shoes, better clothes, and a car. It was all very well resolving to stay with George out of loyalty, but she still looked like a poor person, so Craig told her.

'You hear back about that job?' he asked as she closed the passenger side door.

'Not yet. I think I'll tell them I'm not interested.'

He shot off down the street, accelerating hard then having to brake hard at Brunswick Street. 'What do you mean? I thought you said it went well.'

'It did, but I think I should stay with George a while longer.'

'Your loyalty means nothing to them. It's a cutthroat world out there, you have to be more assertive.'

'It's not the right time.'

Craig sighed heavily and swung the car around a corner aggressively. 'I know you'll make the right decision for you, but it's not what I'd do. You won't get ahead in life by being sentimental.'

It was oddly mercenary to hear him talk like that. After everything he'd said about how she needed to maintain her connections, to rekindle her relationship with her mother and now this.

'I haven't said anything about it to Mum, so can we just keep it under our hats?'

'Sure, whatever you think is best.' He patted her knee and stared straight ahead.

Dinner with Vicky this week started with vegetable soup, blended so one couldn't guess the ingredients, although it tasted like mainly cabbage. The main was grilled fish with green beans, carrot and cauliflower, all blanched and cooled, far too crunchy for Janine's tastes, and desert was chocolate mousse, again.

Craig had kept the conversation light, he generally carried most of it on these visits. Even after so many months Janine found conversation with her mother difficult; anything she said was twisted and thrown back at her as a criticism.

'Janine turned down a new job this week,' Craig said, taking a sip of his red wine. His third glass for the evening.

Janine's eyes widened and she looked at him pleading to let the topic drop.

'Did she really? I didn't know she was even going for a job, but to have an offer and turn it down. What on earth made you do something so stupid?'

Janine watched the dancing light of glee in her mother's eyes. 'I haven't been offered it yet.'

'Yes, but you said you weren't taking it. It's the same,' Craig said.

'And pray, what was the reason for this decision?' Vicky aimed the question at Craig.

'She says she owes the other business. I've tried to tell her it doesn't make good business sense but she's overly emotional sometimes.'

She clenched her fists below the table. 'You talk about me like I'm not here. I can make my own decisions, thank you very much.'

'Of course you can dear.' There one thing worse than her mother's acerbic disapproval was patronising indifference.

'Forget I brought it up. I needed to talk to you about a business proposal, Vicky, I think you'll be very interested in.'

Vicky's gaze lingered on Janine for a moment before she turned back. 'Yes?'

'It might be better if we step into the study. I have an investment opportunity which might be better to discuss in private.'

'Yes, very good dear. Janine doesn't need to listen to our boring money talk. Clear this up, will you?' Vicky waved her hand over the dinner plates.

As her mother and her boyfriend walked away, heads drawn close in quiet conversation Janine wanted to scream.

What were that talking about? Why wasn't she invited? It wasn't as though her mother's finances were a secret, although in the years they hadn't been speaking she supposed that could have changed. Her mother didn't trust her, and what stung more, was Craig encouraged it.

Janine stacked the plates in the dishwasher, clanging them loudly in frustration. She cleared the table, wiped everything down, finished off the remnants of mousse and they were still not done.

At close to eleven o'clock she finally had had enough. She stormed down the hallway to the study, her father's study which her mother had clearly commandeered since his death and flung open the door.

'It's time to go.' Janine stood, hands on hips.

Craig and her mother were sitting side by side on the brown leather couch going through some paperwork. From where she stood it look like a contract.

'You just need to sign the last page, and I'll get it all set up,' Craig said, before turning his attention to Janine. 'I'm sorry it's so late. I didn't mean to leave you on your own so long, honey. We'll be done in just a minute.'

She was furious. He'd apologised to her as though he was really sorry, and now she felt ridiculous and still angry. 'I'll meet you in the car,' she said.

Craig was true to his word and followed her out in a couple of minutes.

'That was a bit rude,' he said, climbing into the driver's seat. He smelled of whisky and had a cigarette hanging out the side of his mouth.

She let out a sort of grunt of annoyance. 'I'm tired and I want to go home.'

'I know. I'm sorry it got so late.'

You said that already. 'What was Mum signing anyway?'

'She's investing in a new firm I've just got on the books. She doesn't have a very good investment strategy so she's sold her shares and signed over part of the value of the house onto a mortgage so I can invest it. It'll give her a much better return than what she had before.'

It sounded like an awful lot of money. 'Isn't that a bit risky?'

'Hardly! This is the surest thing I've come across in years. No need to worry.'

She didn't know anything about investments, and Craig did it for a living, so she sat back and tried not to be annoyed at being left out of the conversation. It would have been boring anyway.

14. Working Too Hard

'Why haven't you offered me the deal you offered Mum?' Janine asked when pulled up in front of her place.

'You've never liked it when I talk to you about money.'

'Well, I don't especially, but it seems weird you talking to her about that stuff.'

Craig pulled her hand into his lap and looked into her eyes. 'You're really upset aren't you, babe?'

'No,' she lied.

'I can see it. Listen, this firm only takes investments over a hundred grand, I knew you didn't have it so I didn't want to make you feel bad by bringing it up.'

'Oh.'

'If you like, I can keep an eye out for an investment that might suit you. How much savings have you got?'

Janine swallowed and didn't answer.

Craig squeezed her hand. 'When you have a thousand, let me know and we'll see what we can set up. Okay?'

'I worry you're ashamed of me. You have so much more money and—'

'It doesn't bother me how much money you have. Honestly. You're a hard worker I respect that much more than rich arseholes who don't have to work.'

'Like Mum?' she said, a smile creeping across her face.

'I never said that. I think I better go before I get myself in any more trouble.' He leant over to kiss her, it lasted barely a moment and she was reminded how long it had been since they'd had sex.

'See you soon then.'

She click-clacked her way up the brick path to the door, turned her key and was inside the house without looking back. She didn't know why she was so angry with Craig. Angry and horny.

It should have been a relief he got on so well with her mother, and was trying to help with her money. Her mother had never really worked, and since her father had died, she didn't have the income she used to. She'd told them she lived off the interest on her investments and given she didn't have a mortgage on the house her expenses were pretty low. But the greed in her eyes when Craig had talked about the work he did, and the returns he was getting for his other clients made Janine shudder.

Concern for how she presented herself in public, constantly buying the most expensive clothes, and perfumes, and wines was one thing, but naked money-hungry desire was something new. Janine threw off her dress and shoes and climbed into bed, she was too annoyed to bother cleaning her teeth or wiping the makeup off her face.

She flicked the radio on quietly so that she could listen while she fell asleep. It was one of the only things to help quiet her mind when she got worked up. John couldn't stand any kind of noise while he slept and she'd spent long nights lying awake next to him. Craig didn't mind it so much, although she tried to avoid it when he slept over.

Her hand reached down to her underwear and slipped under the band. She had liked getting herself off, it seemed dirty, but there was no way she'd ever sleep while she felt so pent up. Her hand was never as good as a man, but it scratched the itch long enough for her not to nag.

*   *   *

Craig called her at work on Tuesday to say he would be snowed under at work and not to worry if she didn't hear from him. The call only lasted a couple of minutes before he had to get back to it. Then on Thursday Barry Goodman left a message on the answering machine to tell her she hadn't got the job.

On Friday night, when she arrived home from work, the house was empty. She'd planned to go out for dinner with Craig and a few of his mates, arranged weeks ago, but she hadn't heard anything from him. She walked into the kitchen and saw the huge bunch of red roses the table, wrapped in deep red cellophane and interspersed with white baby's-breath.

She picked up the flowers and inhaled deeply, they didn't have much perfume. The card was addressed to her.

I'm going to have to cancel our plans
tonight. Investor meeting in the city
is likely to go late. See you soon, all
my love, Craig.

Janine closed her eyes and sighed. She would be
having pizza and watching TV alone on Friday night,
again. Craig really did work much too hard sometimes.

After the roses came Janine didn't hear from Craig
until the next Thursday. She started to worry and left a
message on his answering machine every day. The first
message was to thank him for the roses, then to say she
was looking forward to seeing him. On Thursday she was
getting desperate.

'I don't know what's happened to you. My mind is
racing, I hope you're not hurt. Please call me back.' She
gripped the phone in both hands to stop it shaking as she
replaced it on the cradle.

Only an hour later the phone rang again and she
jumped from the couch to answer it; she wanted to make
sure that she got there before Phoebe.

'Janine?'

It was her mother. 'Yes.'

'Do you have Craig's phone number? I have left him
several messages and he doesn't call back so I thought I
might have the wrong number.'

'Why have you been calling him?' Janine's belly
filled with rumbling anxious waves.

'He said I needed to sign something else last time he was here. I want to make sure the deal is going through. I've put just about everything I have into this scheme, Janine, and if your boyfriend isn't trustworthy, you've ruined me.'

'I've ruined you? I had nothing to do with it. You were the one talking without me and making rash decisions about your finances.'

'I will not be lectured by you about money.' Vicky's voice had taken on a clipped and disappointed tone that Janine had thought they'd left in the past. She sighed.

'What's his number?'

'He's not returning my calls either. The last I heard he had some important investor meeting. I have to go. Craig might be trying to call me.'

She hung up the phone and it rang immediately. 'Hello?'

'Hi hunny.' Craig's smooth voice was like wine down the phone line.

She felt the receiver slipping from her grasp as relief washed over her. 'Where have you been? I've been calling you.'

'I know, I saw the little red dot on the answering machine but I thought I'd call you rather than listen to the messages. What did I miss?'

He hadn't answered her question. Her relief became tainted with suspicion. 'Where were you?'

'I told you, I had an investor meeting, and then they wanted to go to Tassie to the casino down there, and when you have a big investor wanting to relieve himself of a bunch of money you don't just say no—'

'I thought they had phones in Tasmania,' she interrupted.

'They do.'

'Seems like the only reasonable reason for you not to speak to me for over a week and make me think you're dead in a ditch somewhere.' She sounded like her mother, she took a deep breath and started again. 'I'm sorry. Are you back now?'

'Yeah, I thought I'd come visit you, if you like, but if you're going to be mad then I won't bother.'

'I'm not mad,' she lied. 'Come around.'

'Alright, be there soon.'

Craig wasn't usually a big drinker, so surely he wasn't too drunk to call the whole week, and he had always let her know when he had to travel for work before. Something wasn't right but she couldn't put her finger on it. Best to put it out of her mind until he was in a better mood.

An hour later she opened the front door to let Craig in and was surprised at the state of his clothes.

'When did you get back?' she asked.

'About midday.'

The hairs on the back of her arms stood on end, he didn't meet her eye as he walked past her into her bedroom. He lay back on her bed and kicked his shoes off.

'Should we watch something? It's not too late,' she said.

'I'm pretty tired.'

'Do you need a shower?'

'I probably should.'

She went to the linen cupboard and pulled out a fresh towel. When she returned to the bedroom Craig had stripped down to his boxers, his clothes in a pile on the floor. He looked much thinner than when she last saw him and couldn't seem to keep still.

'Thanks,' he said. He dropped his boxers and wrapped the towel around his waist. While he showered, Janine picked up his clothes, folded them neatly and stacked them on the chair. It wasn't like Craig to toss his suit around. When she picked up the shirt it had smelled wrong; ammonia, or even a hint of urine.

Whatever he's been doing in the casino it wasn't bathing or changing his clothes.

She had few items of Craig's clothing he'd left behind at her place over the time they'd been dating. Janine always took pride in carefully washing, ironing and putting them away so they would be clean if he ever needed them. It was quite a collection now. She selected a white t-shirt and a clean pair of boxers for him to sleep in; he didn't believe in sleeping nude, he'd said 'it feels too exposed.'

As he slept Craig ground his teeth so loudly it kept her awake and when her alarm went off at seven, she was staring at the ceiling and trying not to be angry.

She turned to him, and gently shook his shoulder. 'Time to get up,' she said. Craig slept on, his teeth scraping over one another. Sighing, Janine slipped out of bed and started making breakfast; toast, coffee and a cigarette.

She took a mug of coffee into the bedroom for Craig, but again she couldn't wake him. Never before had he slept through an alarm, being shaken and the smell of coffee. Maybe he was sick. She put the coffee down, sat next to him and spoke loudly. 'You have to get up.'

No response. She slid open one of his eyelids and finally he roused. 'Get off. I'll be there in a minute.'

Janine showered, blow-dried her hair and swept it into a French roll. It was a skill she'd recently acquired from Elena, who in turn had been taught by her extremely camp, and very talented hair-dresser Jacques.

Craig was still sleeping as she applied her makeup in the bedroom. She opened the blind, switched on the light and bumped around the room hoping to disturb him, but he showed no signs of getting up; his coffee was untouched.

At five minutes to eight she gave up. 'Babe.' She shook his shoulder, he mumbled something unintelligible. 'I'm going to work. You need to get up, you'll be late.'

He batted her hand away.

'Fine, stay there.'

She picked up her handbag, shoved her feet into her trusty black pumps and stomped out of the house.

*   *   *

The phone on her desk rang at two o'clock that afternoon and something inside her tummy fluttered. *That will be Craig.*

'Hello, Janine speaking,' she said, making sure she used her professional voice.

'Baby. I'm so sorry about this morning.'

She sighed. 'I'm at work.'

'I know, I'm across the street in the phone box. Can you come talk to me, please?'

Janine looked around the office, George was in the middle of an animated phone conversation, Elena was busy typing something, and the rest of the team were out.

'Hang on,' she said, pulling the handset away from her ear and covering the mouthpiece. 'Elena, do you mind if I pop out for five minutes? Craig wants to talk to me.'

'No, darling, you do what you need to do. I'm here.' Elena's heavily-plucked eyebrows had climbed halfway up her forehead, but she said nothing else.

'You there, Craig? I'm coming down now. You can have five minutes.'

'Fantastic.'

She stepped outside the dingy grey building where she worked. Since she'd started the colours on the sign had faded, and the wall had become a dirtier shade of grey. It had looked so spick and span back then, but now it had lost all of its gloss. She walked towards the phone box on the corner. The street was mostly empty, Craig leaned against the phone box, his hands in the pockets of his pants. He was wearing the same suit he'd worn yesterday, but he might have put on a clean shirt.

She frowned as she came to a stop a few feet away from him. She fished out a cigarette from her handbag and lit it.

'Thanks for coming out,' he said.

She harrumphed.

'Can I have one of those?'

She held out the pack to him. He took one before going on.

'I know you were worried about me this morning.'

'You could say that.' She wasn't going to make this easy for him.

'I had a few too many uppers while I was at the casino. The investors really wanted to party hard, and I couldn't say no.'

She took a long inhale from her ciggie, blowing it out and watching it drift across him.

'I don't usually do that much. You know me, I'm so moderate most of the time.'

'Yeah, you are. You trying to impress the investors by going harder than they did, were you?'

'No, nothing like that.'

She raised her eyebrow.

'Okay, maybe I was. They're so rich, baby, I had nothing on them. I needed them to think I was in their league.'

'And you came home to me on the comedown, stinking to high heaven, passing out and sweating all over my bed sheets.'

'I thought you wanted to see me.'

'I do, but not like this. You look terrible.'

He sighed and looked at the ground. 'I know.'

'You wouldn't see my mother in that state, why would I want to see you so off your tits? I missed you, I was worried about you, but coming to see me in a state doesn't make me worry any less.'

'You'll be happy to know I got them to sign the agreements this morning, so I won't need to schmooze them again.'

Janine flicked ash onto the ground. 'Not calling me for a week. What was I supposed to think? You could have been anywhere, doing anything. You could have been dead.'

'I know, I'm sorry, baby. I won't do it again.'

Suddenly Janine was afraid she'd pushed him too hard. What if he decided she wasn't worth all the hassle and next time just didn't come back? 'I love you, Craig. Mum loves you.'

'I let you down. I'm sorry. I'll make it up to you.'

'It's okay. I have to go back to work. I can't just leave whenever you need to talk to me either, so next time wait till I'm home?'

'Of course, you're right. I forget other people's jobs aren't as flexible and self-directed as mine.' He leaned forward to kiss her temple. 'I'll do better next time. You're such a trooper.'

'Thanks.'

'I'm heading home now, and I'll be around on Sunday afternoon for dinner with your mum. Love you.'

'Love you too.'

He kissed her, but Janine pulled away quickly. She didn't want any of George's sons seeing her. She'd long ago learned to keep her private life well away from them for her own safety.

'What did Mister Fancy pants want?' Elena asked as she sat down at her desk.

'To apologise.'

'What for?' Elena's eyes lit up and she tottered over to Janine's desk for the full story.

'Don't tell anyone this okay?' Janine started every conversation with Elena this way. Sometimes it got back to George or her sons, but it seemed less likely when she added this at the beginning.

'Cross my heart, darling.'

'He was at the casino in Hobart for a week without telling me, and then we he got home he was shitfaced.'

'Oh my God. What was he doing down there?'

'Work.'

Elena crossed her arms up under her ample bosom. 'I hope you told him he was a *malaka*.'

'In my own way.'

'Good girl.' Elena patted her on the shoulder and went back to her desk satisfied she knew the whole story and could concentrate on her work again. If only it was as easy for Janine to slip back into her tasks. Her mind kept going over and over what he could have got up to on a week away without her.

She shook her head. He was barely interested in sex; it wouldn't be like him at all to have cheated on her. Except he barely drank and didn't take drugs either.

*   *   *

She spent Saturday pottering about at home and had dinner with Phoebe. She told herself she wouldn't chase Craig, if he wanted to make it up to her, he'd need to do the work. He arrived on Sunday afternoon just after four o'clock.

'I got you something,' he said. He was standing in her kitchen as she made herself an instant coffee and a green tea for Craig.

'Oh?' she said, watching her spoon swirling the black, sweet coffee.

'Here.' He handed her a small box about the size of a coffee cup in pale blue-green cardboard.

'What is it?'

'Open it.' He was grinning at her. She placed his cup on the counter in front of him and opened the box. The box was very silky and smooth and as she slid the white ribbon away, she saw the label, 'Tiffany & Co.'

'It's too much,' she exclaimed.

'You haven't even looked yet.'

She carefully pulled off the lid of the box to reveal a gorgeous wristwatch. The face was white with a pale gold surround, gold roman numerals and black hands. The label sat in the centre of the face, and displayed the date on the right, next to the little knob used to change the time. The black leather strap was smooth and glossy.

'It's really too much,' she said. It must have been worth a grand or two at least.

'I wanted to show you how much you mean to me. I went to Tassie to get those investors, but I came home for you. I need you to know how important you are to me.'

'I don't know what to say.'

'Say thank you and try it on.'

'Thank you.' She tried to put the watch on her wrist, her hands were shaking.

'Let me,' Craig said, taking the watch in his hand and securing it on her arm. 'I wonder if your mother will say anything.' He winked.

'She's going to die. She's always wanted a beautiful watch, maybe a Rolex, but this is even prettier.'

'Rolex's are flashy. I didn't think that would suit you.'

Janine felt her cheeks flush with embarrassment and delight. 'Thank you,' she said again.

Craig came around the table and slipped his arms around her waist. He lowered his lips to hers and kissed her deeply; he hadn't kissed her like that for a long time.

Immediately her pulse quickened and her groin tingled. She didn't want to get too excited, often he would kiss her until she was bursting then tell her he wasn't in the mood, but it was no good, she had never wanted him more than she did right now.

'Shall we go to the bedroom?' he purred in her ear.

He really was spoiling her. Not only did she get a beautiful watch to show off to all her friends and to her mother, she might even have a night with him that left her satiated.

Craig usually liked to make foreplay last as long as possible; he would explore her body with kisses, running his hands all over her, driving her crazy. This time when she shut the bedroom door he unbuckled her pants, pushing them down around her knees.

'Turn around,' he said, pushing her against the door firmly.

A shiver of anticipation flowed down her spine. She heard him lick his fingers, then felt him slip them between her legs. He pushed his groin against the back of her thigh, she could feel his hard-on through his pants. 'Do you like that?'

'Mmm,' she said. She heard him unbuckle his own pants and slip them down. He rubbed the head of his cock across her pussy, it was slick and ready for him. She tilted her pelvis and pushed back against him.

The next moment he was inside her, it felt like he was bigger than usual, perhaps he was more into it than he had been in the past. He slid in gently, and she gasped. She put her hands up against the back of the door. He grabbed her hips and started to thrust; slowly at first, then faster and deeper.

Oh God, it's never been like this before. Her body was tingling and sizzling all over. She could hear him panting next to her ear, and she let out a low groan, perhaps more like a purr.

'You're going to make me come,' he said.

She pushed back against him as he started to thrust frantically. With a grunt and a sigh, he climaxed. They stood, leaning against the door for a moment, before he moved away. He pulled his pants back on and flopped onto the bed. Janine followed him and nestled into his shoulder as they lay together.

'Thank you,' she said.

'My pleasure.'

*   *   *

All through dinner with Vicky, Janine kept smiling to herself thinking of the afternoon. She hoped it was a sign that Craig had a renewed interest in her, and perhaps it would be the start of a new phase in their relationship. She'd have to go back onto the pill if he was going to be more spontaneous about sex though. It made her feel bloated and a bit cranky but she really didn't need a baby in her life messing it up.

'So how is my investment doing?' Vicky asked, her fifth glass of red wine in her hand.

'It's doing well by all accounts. Much too early for any kind of returns of course. They pay out quarterly.'

'I see.' She sipped her wine, her eyebrows drawn together in a deep frown. 'I explained to you, I'm sure, that I live off the income from my investments, and given I've put quite a lot of my money into your scheme I will need it to pay out regularly.'

'Don't worry,' Craig said, 'I'll have something for you in a few weeks.'

Vicky sniffed. She must have put too much into the investment with Craig and was feeling the pinch, Janine thought to herself. Her mother wouldn't like having to curb her expensive habits so she could stay solvent. It made Janine smile. All her life her mother had lived off someone else, first her father and then her father's money and life insurance. She'd didn't work and spent most of her time having coffee with her cronies and going out to expensive luncheons.

'I promise I'll have some returns for your soon,' Craig said, putting his hand on Vicky's forearm. She seemed to soften; her shoulders released from where they had hovered around her ears.

Craig was oddly quiet on the drive home. 'Are you staying with me tonight?' she asked.

'I've got an early meeting. I think I'll crash at mine.'

'Are you okay, you seem . . . was it what we did earlier? I thought you had fun.'

'I did, baby. I was just thinking about work.' He stared straight ahead at the shiny, wet tarmac.

'Of course.'

15. A White Picket Fence

Now Craig had secured the big investors, he was around much more. He spent the night frequently, but the sex seemed to have been a fluke. Janine found herself hornier than usual now she knew it could be like that. Even in her early days with John she hadn't had such a good time, a new world had opened up to her.

One Wednesday morning as she and Craig were getting ready to head off to work it occurred to her she should have had a period. She wasn't very good at keeping track, but she went back over the last few weeks; it had to have been at least six weeks since she'd last had one.

'Oh God,' she said, flicking through the pages of her diary hoping she'd counted wrong.

'What?' Craig stood behind her and rubbed her upper back. It felt so good when he touched her like she immediately had a surge of blood to her groin.

She shook herself. 'I'm late.'

'It's not even eight yet.'

'That's not what I mean. Do you remember when's the last time I had a period?'

'Sorry? I—' The hand on her back had stopped moving. She turned to look at his face and he was staring blankly ahead. 'You mean—'

'I think I should do a test.'

'Yeah. Let's not get too carried away before we know for sure.' His face was a ghastly shade of grey.

'Don't worry. I'll get rid of it.' *I've done it before.*

'Hang on. I never suggested that. I'm just, you know, surprised. I thought you were on the pill.'

'I stopped taking it. We weren't, well, you know, we don't have that much sex and you usually wear a condom anyway, so I stopped.'

'Right… and the time before visiting your mum, we didn't.'

'I thought it would be okay.' Janine felt tears stinging her eyes. She should have made sure this didn't happen again. After the ordeal the last time she knew better but here she was, again.

'I've got to get to work. You get the test and we can decide what to do after we know for sure, okay?' Craig bent down to kiss the top of her head before walking out the front door. His eyes still had a faraway look as though he was in shock.

Janine had wanted to be someone's mum for as long as she could remember; when she was little, she would put dolls up her shirt, give birth to them, nurse them, push them around in their tiny prams. As an only child she swore to have at least two children so they wouldn't be lonely. And now she was considering killing another baby. All of her emotions happened at once. She sat at her kitchen bench and wept.

After a very long time, Janine wiped her eyes and looked at the clock—ten minutes to nine. She picked up the phone and left a message for Elena and George to say she'd be late in. She wasn't going to spend the day wallowing, that would be the worst thing she could do.

When she arrived at just after ten o'clock, Elena looked worried.

'Are you okay, hunny?' she said. 'You should have taken the day off.'

'No, I'm okay. I just had a bit of a rough morning and knew I wouldn't get here on time.'

'You're like our daughter remember. We care about you. You can tell me, *koukla*.'

'I know. Maybe in a little while.'

Elena stepped forwards and engulfed her in squishy flesh. Janine made no attempt to pull away. It took all her concentration to stop herself bursting into tears again.

'It's okay, really,' Janine said, once she'd been released.

'If you say so.'

Janine sighed. She'd have to tell her. On the way into work she'd stopped by the chemist to buy a home pregnancy test. She would have to wait until she got home so no matter what the result, she would be able to cry in peace.

The day dragged by, they had finished a couple of big jobs recently, but all the paperwork had been done, filing put away and the phones weren't ringing. In a week they would have end of financial year to deal with, but she couldn't start yet. She sat at her desk, tapping her cigarette packet against the tabletop.

'Are you going to do that all day?' Elena said, perching her bottom on the edge of Janine's desk. She plopped a cup of instant coffee in front of her. 'You probably don't need any more coffee, but eh, it's instant. May as well be mud.'

Janine smiled, or tried to. She felt too.

'You tell mamma what's happened and I will take it to my grave.' Elena's enormous, over-made-up eyes held hers.

'You promise no one will hear about it?'

'Cross my heart.'

After the shit she'd put her bosses through with John, she didn't think much would change how they saw her.

'I think I'm pregnant.'

'You think?'

'I'm late. I haven't done a test yet.'

'Hmm.' Elena took a sip of her coffee, it would be black with three teaspoons of sugar. Janine took hers with black with two. She knew all of their coffee and tea habits. She'd been there long enough.

'And this baby, it is Mister Fancy pants', yes?'

'Yeah.'

'Did you tell him?'

'This morning. He looked like he would be sick.'

'Hmm,' she said again.

It wasn't like Elena to be so quiet. Janine was disconcerted by the pause and was very tempted to start blurting things out, but she sipped her coffee instead.

'Best to make sure first. Then, when you know for sure, you tell this boy of yours that he must marry you.'

Janine nearly choked on her coffee. 'I don't think that's how it works.'

'It was for me. You know George and I were pregnant before we got married.'

'I didn't.'

'You never were good at maths were you.' Elena shook her head and clucked in a matronly way.

Now Janine thought of it, George and Elena's wedding anniversary, their twenty-fifth, had been two years ago, but their eldest son was twenty-eight in September. She laughed. Elena must have been heavily pregnant at the ceremony.

'It was different back then,' she said.

'Bullshit. Nothing is different. Men want to be told what to do. They want you to be their mother and their wife. You just tell this boy that he must do the right thing. Once he knows what's expected of him, he will come through.'

'And what if he doesn't?'

'Then he is no good and you are better off without him. But really, darling,' she put her hand out and cupped Janine's jaw, 'he will stay. You are a beautiful girl, and he is a nice boy. It will be alright.'

Janine looked away. Despite everything she was still her boss and crying in the middle of the office where George or one of the other blokes could walk in at any second was horrifying.

'You can do a test tonight and tell me tomorrow what happened. If you have a baby, I will spoil it rotten. You know my boys are so slow to give me grandbabies.'

Janine smiled and continued to look at her desk. Elena patted her on the shoulder before tottering back to her desk. Could she have a family with Craig? He had everything sorted out, he had never expressed an interest in children, but maybe she could convince him. She couldn't kill another baby, she wouldn't.

*   *   *

At home she peed onto the tester stick and sat on the edge of the bath waiting ten minutes for it to change colour. *A watched pot never boils*, but she couldn't tear her eyes away.

'How much longer are you gonna be? I gotta piss!' Phoebe's voice cut into her thoughts and through the solid pine door between them.

'Sorry. I'll be out in a second.' She opened the door and let Phoebe in. As soon as the bathroom door closed, she knew she should have put the tester somewhere out of sight.

She listened to the flush of the toilet, and the trickle of water as Phoebe washed her hands. She was always much more thorough than Janine with hand washing, though it didn't translate to being tidy around the rest of the house.

'Your test then?'

'Yep. Is it done yet?'

'Not yet. Does Craig know?'

'We talked about it this morning, when I realised I was late.'

'Ah, that's what the storm out was. I vaguely heard him stomping down the hallway but when I got up you were out so I forgot about it.'

Janine jiggled on the balls of her feet, itching to check whether the test was ready, but knowing in her heart it wasn't.

'You keeping it?'

'I want to.' She was shocked to hear herself say it out loud.

'Is that why Craig was pissed?'

'I don't know. He just went pale and left. I'll call him tonight when I know if it's real.' Janine's eyes travelled across Phoebe's shoulders to where the test sat on the side of the sink.

'Just look, will you?'

She felt slightly sick, the palms of her hands were slick with sweat and she nearly dropped it.

'Positive,' she said.

Phoebe came into the bathroom to look for herself. 'Well, fuck.'

'Yeah.' Janine placed the stick back on the edge of the sink. Phoebe gave her a quick hug before retreating to her room. She wasn't much for dramas where she couldn't poke fun at the people involved.

The phone in the house was on a fairly long cord, but it didn't reach all the way into Janine's bedroom. She had been meaning to buy a longer cord so she could chat to Craig without being overheard but had never gotten around to it.

'Hi, you've reached Craig—'

Answering machine. 'It's me. Call me back.'

She hung up, waited a few seconds before dialling the number for his beeper. He carried it everywhere with him but when he was in Tasmania, he hadn't returned any of her pages. Perhaps she had the wrong number, but she tried anyway. Hopefully he would call her back soon. If he was still talking to her.

She flicked on the TV and surfed the channels. She found herself shouting answers at the contestants on *Sale of the Century*. She hardly ever got them right, but it didn't stop her playing along. It was almost distracting enough to forget the gnawing worry lodged deep in her belly.

When the phone rang half an hour later, she jumped to answer it.

'Craig?' she said.

'Yes. I got your message. Did you do a test?'

'Yeah.'

'And?'

'We're pregnant.'

'That's amazing news!' He sounded jubilant.

'But you were so worried this morning?'

'I know, it was a shock. I needed to process it. I didn't plan on having kids but now you're pregnant.'

'You want to keep it?' She tried not to get her hopes up.

'Of course. I want to have a little family with you, in a little house, maybe get a cat.'

Janine started to cry. 'Oh my God. I was so scared.'

'Don't cry, it's okay. We're gonna be a family.' He was speaking really fast.

'I—'

'What?'

'I thought you would dump me.'

'Why would I do that, silly. I love you.'

If she hadn't been sitting on the couch at that moment, she might have fainted. Her ears started to make a low buzzing sound and Craig's voice became faraway.

'I'm coming over, okay, we'll celebrate. Champagne. Wait, you can't have champagne. I'll bring chocolate. See you soon.' He hung up the phone and she listened to the beeping tone for a while before she put the handset down.

*   *   *

Craig arrived fifteen minutes later, and Janine was still reeling from his turnaround. For once in her life things were going her way but she still felt an uneasy restlessness in the pit of her stomach.

'I'm so happy to see you, baby.' Craig was smiling broadly and sweating. 'I came over as soon as I heard from you. I got you these.' He held out a bunch of red roses, that looked a little crushed.

'Thank you.'

They were standing in the loungeroom, Janine held the flowers to her chest, they were vaguely warm.

'I had to run to get a taxi,' Craig said, as though he had read her mind.

'Do you need a drink or something?' *What happened to the car?*

'Have you got any white wine?'

'I don't know. I thought you were bringing chocolate and champagne?'

'I forgot. Sorry babe, I was just so excited.'

She nodded. 'I'll see what we have.' She left him there; she could hear the slight jangling of the figurines on the bookshelf as he bounced his leg up and down. He seemed strung out. After the week in Tassie he had sworn it was a fluke, but it seemed he'd had a little something before coming to see her. She put the crushed roses into a vase, filled it with water and set it on the kitchen bench. Craig was flicking through TV channels, she heard snatches of conversation, or music, before he switched to another station.

She took a breath, filled the kettle and put it on to boil. Opened the fridge, she saw Phoebe had an open bottle of white wine in the door; they'd apologise later and buy her more.

When the kettle had boiled, she made herself an instant coffee, and poured Craig a wine. The combination seemed so incongruous she almost laughed.

'You sure you're okay?' she said, putting his glass down in front of him on the smoky glass coffee table.

'Just excited. I was worried this morning, I know you saw my face, and it was a shock, I thought I'd have longer to set myself up before bringing a family into my plan but I spent the day going over some things, and I think it's going to be great.'

'You want to be a family?'

'Did you think I was going to let you raise this baby without me?'

Janine was silent. Craig's smile gradually faded.

'You thought I wouldn't want to keep it? I can't believe you thought that.'

'My ex, John—well, let's not go into the details.'

He pulled her to his chest and held her head there. 'I would never make you do that. It's against everything I believe in. Children are a blessing and we have to cherish them.'

Janine smelled that same acrid sweaty odour she'd smelled weeks ago, not as bad, but it was still there. She pushed herself away. 'I always wanted to be a mother. I thought it would be further down the track, but I guess your little guys are too strong.'

'They take after me.' He grabbed the wine and slurped half a glass in one gulp. 'Sorry, look at me behaving like a slob.' He put his glass down, smoothed his suit jacket and stood up. He reached into his pocket and pulled out a small navy-blue box.

'Oh my God,' she squealed.

Craig knelt in front of her, awkwardly positioned between the couch and the coffee table, with the TV burbling in the background and a wild look in his eyes. 'Janine Barrett, will you do me the honour of becoming my wife?'

'Oh my God,' she said again. He took her left hand and slid the ring onto her fourth finger. It was a gold band with a string of sapphires on each side of an enormous diamond.

'Does that mean yes?'

'Yes, yes. Of course.' She reached out to hug him, shaking a little. For the rest of the evening, she sat beside him on the couch and stared at the ring. Once he'd asked her the question, he seemed to calm down a lot, *he must have been so nervous*. By ten o'clock he was snoring with his head back at an uncomfortable angle while Janine tried to get her mind around everything that had happened.

When she'd woken up, she was just plain old Janine, and when she went to sleep, she would be a mother and a fiancée. Two of the things she'd yearned for, for so long had been dropped into her lap, and yet she couldn't seem to shake the worry something wasn't right.

She left Craig there on the couch when she went to bed. When she woke up, he had crawled in beside her and was snoring lightly. She snuck out to go to the toilet, on her way back from the bathroom Phoebe was in the kitchen.

'What happened last night? I heard a bunch of excited talking and then you just watched TV.'

'Well…' Janine held out her left hand and wriggled her fingers.

'You're fucking with me.' Phoebe grabbed her hand and inspected the ring. 'He proposed?'

'Yep.'

'And you said yes?'

'Who would say no? He's handsome, rich, in love with me, and wants the baby.'

'You can say that again.'

'I mean, he's way out of my league, but I'm not thinking about that.'

Phoebe let go of her hand and stood, arms crossed against her chest, leaning against the fridge. 'You always put yourself down, Janine. It's a bad habit.'

'I know.' She looked down at her hand and watched the glinting light from the diamond as she moved her fingers. 'It's all so fast.'

'It's not fast. Don't try to find something wrong with this. Just be happy, yeah?'

Janine sighed and looked up at her friend. 'You're right. It's about time I had something go my way.'

16. A Wedding and a Baby

When Janine went in to work on the next day Elena saw the ring immediately.

'He proposed?' she said.

Janine felt the blood rush to her face. 'Yeah.'

'You are having a baby and wedding? My God, it's so exciting.' She was speaking at top volume.

'Keep it down, I'm not ready to tell the whole world yet.'

'Okay, but it won't stay a secret for long with a rock that size on your finger.'

She was right, as soon as George saw her, he knew, he told his sons, and they told the rest of the staff. All day she had a string of men sitting on the edge of her desk talking about her fiancé. She got no work done and Elena was rushed off her feet answering the phone calls Janine kept missing.

'I'm sorry about today,' she said as she picked up her bag to go home that night.

'You have nothing to be sorry about. These men are such gossips they needed to hear every detail from you, now they have what they need it will be back to normal tomorrow. Come here.' Elena wrapped her in her arms and rocked her back and forth. 'I'm so happy for you. Didn't I say it would all work out?'

'Yes, you said.' Janine couldn't stop smiling. Then she remembered she was unlikely to get such a warm reception from her own mother, despite all the comments Craig was too good for her. She pushed the thought from her mind. Soon she would need to think about practicalities, where they would live, what they needed to buy for the baby, what colour to make the nursery in their new house, and what she would wear to the wedding. There was so much planning to do and she couldn't wait start buying bridal and baby magazines.

Craig hadn't mentioned anything about a date, but Janine had decided the wedding would need to be before the baby was born, otherwise what would be the point of having one? By her reckoning, she was eight weeks pregnant which meant she had at least another eight weeks before she started to show. It would probably be alright for her to show a little but definitely not after the six-month mark.

Phoebe looked through magazines with her and came home with new recommendations for wedding venues and other services after work each day.

'I ask my customers, if they look old enough to be married, where they went and who did their catering and stuff. It's great, everyone gets really on board when I tell them my best friend is getting married. Most people love to talk about themselves.'

'Am I really your best friend?' Janine asked.

'Of course. Don't tell Fay though, she's been my best friend for longer, but you're both equal in my eyes.'

Phoebe winked. She had broken up with Bob at some point in the last few weeks, but Janine hadn't seen much evidence that she was heartbroken. Leading up to the complete disappearance of Bob from conversation and from the house, they had seen less and less of each other. Phoebe's time was freed up to hang around the house and talk about Janine's future.

'Are you moving into Craig's place? I mean it makes sense, he's got a much better apartment in the city,' Phoebe said, they were sitting together in front of the T.V. one evening. Janine had a coffee and Phoebe had red wine. Janine wished she had red wine.

'Yeah, I guess.'

'What do you mean?'

'He hasn't really talked about how it's going to work, and besides…'

'Besides what?' Phoebe prompted after a lengthy pause.

'I've never actually been to his place.'

Phoebe gasped. 'Seriously? I assumed you had. But you don't ever stay out overnight, he always stays here.' She stared off into middle distance, her hand poised mid-page-turn. Janine stared at the bride in her spectacular white satin cupcake-like dress.

'I don't want to make a big deal out of it.'

'I hardly think it's making a big deal for you to ask where you'll live once you're married. Or actually, to ask when you're getting married. You're working to a clock here.' Phoebe patted her belly. Janine curled herself away from Phoebe's hand. In the two weeks since she'd found out about the baby, she had developed a sense of connection and a protectiveness of the person growing in her belly. She'd read through the baby magazines she bought the foetus was now the size of a raspberry. It seemed absurd to feel so connected to the tiny berry in her abdomen. She didn't want to think of names yet, but she'd started referring to it to herself as Cherry.

It was hard talk to Craig about stuff like where they'd live. He was such a big thinker, working on the next big project and the mundanity of it made Janine feel shy to bring it up. At the same time, she needed to figure it out. She didn't want to end up having moving in a rush, or leave Phoebe in the lurch with rent, especially when she'd been so supportive lately.

'I'll talk to him,' Janine said.

'It's not just about his life you know, it's your life together now.' Phoebe finished her glass of wine. She went to the kitchen and came back with her glass refilled with the slightly vinegar smelling cask wine.

'Don't make that face, you love this stuff.'

'I know but everything smells different, mostly worse, than before.'

'Cheers to pregnancy hormones.' Phoebe raised her glass.

When she went to bed that night, Janine lay looking at the dark ceiling unable to fall asleep. When Craig was there with her, everything seemed to be going well, he made her feel safe and cared for, like he had everything under control, but when he wasn't there, she kept coming up with problems and questions she had no answers to. She turned over onto her stomach, felt nauseated and rolled onto her back again. *I'm going to get some answers from him.*

*   *   *

Craig came over on Friday night after nine o'clock, he had been schmoozing clients, but he smelled like bourbon and cigarettes.

'I'm not drunk,' he said as soon as she opened the door.

'Thanks for clarifying,' she said. He pushed past her into the kitchen.

'I'm having a coffee. Do you want one?' she asked.

'Have you got any wine?'

'No, I'm pregnant, remember? I don't drink alcohol anymore.' She'd managed to give up drinking completely, but her coffee and cigarette consumption went up to compensate for it.

'Right,' he mumbled, opening the fridge to peer into it.

Janine didn't think he was as drunk as he seemed. 'We need to talk.'

'Sounds ominous.'

'It's not really.'

He swung the fridge door shut, having found no miscellaneous beers or unfinished wine bottles. 'What about coffee then?'

Janine boiled the kettle and made them each a cup before they moved into the lounge room. Phoebe had gone out for the evening in search of a new boy toy.

'I've been looking through these magazines,' she said, pushing a pile towards him across the smooth glass surface of the coffee table.

'They look good.' He didn't look at them.

'The thing is, I need to have a date or at least an approximate date to work towards if I'm going to make any enquiries. Phoebe and Elena are happy to help me with organising, I know you're run off your feet with work.'

Craig mumbled something into his coffee cup as he took a sip.

'We also need to work out when I'm moving into your place. And what I need to bring with me or sell. I'm sure your stuff is much better quality than mine.' She gave an embarrassed half-laugh. She hated talking about money, but it was worth the discomfort now to get a few things settled so she could get on with planning.

'Right. About the apartment. It's much too small for you and a little one, we'll have to get another one. I'm sorry I didn't say so earlier but I haven't had time to scratch myself let alone think about stuff that's so far off.'

'It's closer than you think,' she said under her breath.

'Huh?'

'If we want to get married before I'm the size of a house and move in as soon as possible after that there isn't really that much time. A couple of months at most.'

'Shit.'

'Yeah. It's all pretty soon, but,' she patted her belly, 'this little Cherry is setting the timeframe from now on.'

'In that case, I trust you to make the appropriate decisions. I'll make sure I'm there for the wedding and if you find a nice apartment you want me to look at, send me the details and I'll be there. You're more than capable of managing this.' He smiled at her and kissed her forehead.

'I'm so glad we got that settled then. I'll make arrangements for the wedding to be as soon as possible and I'll get onto looking for apartments tomorrow. What can you afford to pay in rent?'

Craig made a noncommittal noise and looked away. 'We're probably looking at two bedroom, somewhere in the inner suburbs where it's still cheap. Whatever you think you can pay half of will be fine.'

It occurred to her she wouldn't be able to work for a while after the baby was born. Her mother had never worked, but Janine was determined not to rot at home hiding her misery and resentment in wine. What she could afford to pay half of now would have to be paid for entirely by Craig's salary for the next couple of years at least, but it wasn't the right time to talk about that. She'd got the information she needed from him and she would be able to get on with bookings and planning.

*   *   *

Her mother was not particularly interested in the news that Janine was pregnant. She and Craig visited her for Sunday dinner, but had been there twice before Craig had felt it was the right time to mention it.

'You'll have to take the engagement ring off, so she doesn't ask about it,' he'd said. Janine had been unhappy but she knew Vicky's mood was an important factor in how the news would be received. Now a few more weeks had passed, Craig was able to give her a cheque for her first dividends from the new deal he had, so he thought it was a good time to let her know.

'What's that on your hand, Janine?' Vicky asked, as soon as they were in the door.

'We have something to tell you,' Craig said.

'I should hope so, given the size of that ring.'

'We're engaged, Mum.' Janine smiled at her, hopeful this would meet with her approval.

'Are you pregnant?' she asked.

Craig and Janine looked at each other briefly.

'I was joking, but I see by your guilty faces that you are. Well done getting up the duff. Always such a lady.' Vicky curled her upper lip in disgust.

'Now Vicky, she might be pregnant but that merely sped up the timeline on something that was bound to happen anyway.' Craig was using his smooth-talking sales voice. 'She put no pressure on me, and I made the call to propose marriage and to accept my responsibilities as the father of her child.'

219

'You're sure it's yours then?'

'I don't appreciate you speaking to my fiancée in that tone,' Craig said, putting his hand out to shush Janine.

Vicky crossed her arms across her chest. 'My tone? You're here with my slut of a daughter to tell me she's gotten herself pregnant and you're permanently attached to her while draining me dry without anything to live on.'

'Now you bring it up, I have something for you.' He took the cheque out of the breast pocket of his navy pinstriped suit. 'These is your quarterly earnings. You'll see that your investment is tracking at twenty-five percent increase over the year.'

Vicky snatched the cheque from his hand and eyed it greedily. Janine had seen the cheque was for nearly fifteen thousand dollars, a sizable quarterly income for someone without a job. 'If you are as good a husband and father as you are in the stock market, all my objections are moot. Except who you're marrying but you've made your bed.'

Janine's heart was pounding in her chest and she was so angry she might draw blood digging her fingernails into her palms.

'It's supposed to be a happy announcement. You're going to be a grandmother!' Craig said.

'I had hoped I would be a lot older before that happened,' Vicky mumbled, before turning to lead them into the kitchen for a pre-dinner glass of wine.

*　　　*　　　*

Elena was as excited as Phoebe to help Janine plan for her wedding and her baby. She had no daughters of her own and the self-appointed role of mother of the bride was one she relished. The business's accounts had taken a back seat as she planned Janine's perfect wedding and birth.

'You need to get a venue to hold at least two hundred people,' Elena said.

'I don't know two hundred people,' Janine replied.

'Don't be silly, of course you do. You only need to fill half, Craig will have the other half, that's only fair.'

'I don't even think I could bring a hundred.' Janine shook her head. 'We're not like your family. My dad's funeral was only fifty, and that included all his army mates.'

Elena screwed up her face. 'I have never understood why you don't have more friends. You're such a nice girl.'

What about Gerry? The last time they spoke Gerry had denounced their friendship and said she didn't want to see her anymore, but that had been a while ago, and things had changed since then. Janine had certainly grown up a lot, mostly under the influence of Craig, and was in a much better position.

'What's eating you?' George asked as he came into the office. He was returning with lunch although it was only a quarter to twelve. He said it was because of his early starts, but Janine thought it more likely he liked to have lunch twice. He was stout but hadn't changed size in the years she'd been working there.

'Secret wedding business.'

George threw his hands up in an exaggerated exasperated gesture but smiled as he went into his office with what smelled like fish and chips. He was also keen on the idea of a big wedding, but whenever his opinion was asked about either the ceremony or the baby he agreed with Elena. Janine had thought this might be because he didn't have an opinion about such frivolous, girly things, but after a couple of weeks, she started to understand he was avoiding taking any point of view opposing his wife.

That evening as she walked home from the tram stop, Janine's thoughts drifted back to Gerry. She used to have her phone number in a little purple address book she'd been given by her grandmother at some point in her early teens. Most of the phone numbers she called regularly she knew by heart; Craig's pager, Craig's home and offices numbers, Vicky's number. She had looked for the little book when she and Craig first got together, to add his details but hadn't been able to find it. It had not come with her after being thrown out of John's house. She bought a new one, plain black and much more grown up.

The household copy of the white pages was being used to prop up one side of the couch in the lounge room. It had lost a leg somewhere in transit from the footpath up the road to their lounge, so she called directory assistance.

'Directory Assistance; what name please?' a friendly woman's voice answered

'Anderson in Camberwell please.'

'Do you have a street? There are a couple.'

'Oh, yes. Radnor Street.'

'Thank you.' There was a click and an automated voice read her the phone number. There was a time, before she lived with George and Elena when she had known the number without having to look it up, but not now.

Janine's hand hovered over the keypad. On the one hand, if Celia answered, she wouldn't stay on the line long enough for her to explain. On the other hand, if Gerry answered the phone, what could Janine say to make sure she stayed on the line?

She pressed the numbers. One, two, three rings, she couldn't help counting them. It seemed to take an inordinately long time before there was a slight knocking sound as someone picked up the receiver on the other end and spoke.

'Hello?' Gerry said, no gatekeeper this time.

'Don't hang up,' she said, and pressed on before Gerry could tell her to get off the line. 'I'm getting married, and I want you to come.'

There was a long silence. Janine told herself to hold her tongue and wait for a response. She didn't want to scare Gerry or annoy her by talking over her.

'I'm really pleased to hear it, but I don't want to revisit that part of my life.'

It felt like a blow to the stomach, but at least she hadn't hung up the phone. 'Despite our recent differences you were by best friend growing up. I don't want you to miss out just because I've been an idiot.'

There was a long sigh on the other end, but Gerry said nothing.

'I've met a really nice guy, a stockbroker, and he wants to marry me.'

'That's great. I can't really talk now.'

'I know you haven't forgiven me for John. At least I think that was the problem, we didn't really get to talk about why you didn't want to see me.'

'I'm not going to get into this with you. I'm hanging up now.'

'We're having a baby too,' Janine blurted.

Gerry laughed, a completely humourless sound. 'There's the Janine I know. Got yourself up the duff and roped some poor man into marrying you.'

Janine was shocked, why would her best friend be so angry with her? 'I thought you'd be happy for me.'

'I'm happy without you in my life, Janine. You're a bad egg. I knew all that shit you said about your dad couldn't be true and then you went off and lived with John and now you've tricked some guy into a wedding with a baby. You're the worst person I can think of.'

'What do you mean, all the stuff about Dad?'

'You told me a bunch of bullshit about what you did together, and how he loved you. It was disgusting lies and I can't understand why you thought I would believe it.'

Janine didn't know what to say. She'd never been explicit with Gerry about her and her dad. And now she was being written off like a dumb, manipulative slut.

'I never lied to you.' She sighed. 'I guess you don't want an invitation to the wedding then?'

'No. And don't call me again. I want nothing to do with you.' Gerry hung up the phone and it clanged loudly. Janine took a few deep breaths and lowered the receiver. How could someone she'd known for so long, who had been her best friend for years not want to be included in her special day?

It hurt more than Janine would have liked to admit. She found it hard to maintain friendships and the one she had counted as her most important was irrevocably gone.

Fat, hot tears spilled from her eyes and ran down her cheeks. She cried silently, nothing like the howling despair she'd felt when John threw her out nor the hollow, numb feeling after her father died. She missed having a best friend. Phoebe tried, but they hadn't grown up together, weathered the schoolyard teasing and scandals, and conspired against their parents together.

Janine sat with her face in her hands for a long time, until her tears dried up and she was drained and empty. Phoebe came home after dinner out with her new boyfriend. Janine was glad she only heard one set of footsteps approaching.

'Hey love, how was your day?' Phoebe called down the hallway.

'Oh hunny, what's happened?' Phoebe noticed Janine's post-cry face immediately.

'Gerry won't come to the wedding.'

'Is that your high school bestie?'

'Yeah.'

'That's tough.' Phoebe sat on the couch next to Janine. She smelled like cigarettes and incense. 'We knew she wasn't keen, so it's not really a surprise, is it?'

Janine sniffed. 'I guess not.'

'It's still hard to hear, I know.' Phoebe pulled Janine's head toward her lap and stroked her hair. She was too tired to cry anymore. The quiet comfort helped.

They sat in silence for a while, until Phoebe began to fidget under Janine's head.

'Has your leg gone to sleep?' Janine asked.

'How did you know?'

Janine sat up and scrubbed her palms into her eyes. 'Enough of that.'

Phoebe got up and got ready for bed. Janine took out a notepad and started to write down everyone she needed to invite to the wedding. It wouldn't be a very long list; her mother, her three remaining grandparents, her father's sister and her family, and a few people she had been friendly with at high school, people from work. She had thirty or so people for her side, and knowing Craig, he wouldn't have any family, a few friends and perhaps a client or two. Despite Elena's insistence, they couldn't fill a two-hundred-seat venue. Craig would have spent whatever she wanted on a big, fancy wedding, but it wasn't her style. Better to have something simple, elegant, she would go all out on a big poufy dress, but otherwise low key.

At nearly midnight it was too late to call Craig and past her bedtime. She rubbed her hand across her lower belly. She wasn't showing yet, but she had become attached to her little Cherry.

17. A Small Delay

Three weeks later Janine had found the perfect wedding reception venue; a small restaurant in Fitzroy North serving Greek food would let them rent out the entire space for the evening. She had decided they would get married in the registry office in the city in the afternoon with a few people to witness it and invite the larger crowd to the reception dinner.

Craig had been noncommittal about the suggestions she'd made, and with Elena and Phoebe's prompting, Janine had started making decisions without him.

'I've booked the reception venue for the tenth of September,' she said as they were walking home from having dinner at a little Vietnamese place around the corner from her place. Craig had been staying with her almost every night.

'What? We didn't agree on anything. Shit, the tenth is only a couple of weeks away.'

'We need to get married before I start to show too much. You haven't shown any interest, so I did it myself. We can't wait much longer.'

Craig slipped his hand out from hers and folded his arms across his chest.

'What?' she asked.

'I wish you would have discussed it with me.'

'I did. I've talked to you about this every night since you proposed, but you haven't been listening.'

He stopped walking and she turned to look at him, hunched against the chilly August evening. 'We need to talk about this wedding, Janine.'

'Yes, we do. But not in the street.' She turned away and walked back to the house. Despite the cold night she was flushed with anger by the time she arrived home.

Once inside she went straight to her bedroom and threw her coat off onto the chair. She sat down, her arms and legs crossed and waited for Craig to follow her.

'Don't be mad, baby,' he said. He sat on the bed facing her and put his hand on her knee.

'Why would I be mad?'

'I have to tell you something.'

Janine jiggled her foot up and down and said nothing.

'I'm going to have to put off the wedding.'

She had known it was coming. He didn't really want to marry her, he had proposed out of obligation and wanted to back out. 'It's too late to terminate the baby,' she said. It wasn't strictly true, but she didn't want to lose her little Cherry.

'I want to marry you and I want the baby, but we have to postpone it. I put all my cash into the deal your mother bought into. I can't actually pay for wedding right now. I but I want this to be a proper big day for my princess.'

'I haven't even told you how much it will cost yet.'

'I know baby, I've been looking over my finances, you know, since we found out. I wanted to make sure we could have a good life and get started on the right foot, and even five grand for the wedding will make it hard to pay rent on the new place and buy all the baby stuff.'

'Right.' Janine couldn't look at him. Her eyes were welling with tears and when she looked down at the carpet they escaped down her cheeks. 'You've always had so much money, bought whatever you wanted and now you're skint?'

'Exactly. I've thrown all my money away. I have some savings but that's the money I live off. I'm not as rich as I seem to be.'

She looked up at her fiancé and saw the shame in his eyes. 'It's okay.'

'Really? You haven't paid a deposit or anything have you?'

'No, it's fine.'

'I promise I will always look after you and the baby. You have my word. I will be more responsible with my money and make sure I work hard to have security for you.' He knelt in front of her and put his hands onto her belly. 'This is my future, our future. A marriage is just a piece of paper. You and me and the little one, we're what's important. This is my family now.'

Looking down at Craig, seeing the tears swimming in his eyes and the crack of emotion in his voice. He wanted to give her the wedding of her dreams. It must have been torture to admit he couldn't pay for it.

'We'll be okay.'

'You promise?'

'Yes,' she said, with a sigh. 'Let's not mention it to Mum. She's bound to give me shit about it enough without admitting we can't pay.'

He laughed huskily. 'You're probably right. We'll tell her the venue we want is not available till next year and I simply won't have another one.'

She smiled and kissed him. There was the man she knew, the confident smooth talker, not this trembling mess kneeling in front of her.

*   *   *

Her mother didn't ask about the wedding plans, so Janine didn't tell her for nearly six weeks.

'You're going to have to have this wedding soon or you'll be too big to pretend you're not pregnant.' She had finished her tiny serving of fat-free, sugar-free, and in Janine's opinion, flavour-free, chocolate mousse.

'Didn't we tell you? We've had to delay the wedding. Craig found an ideal venue, but they're not available until June next year. I'll have had the baby by then and won't need to worry about it.'

Vicky jolted in her seat, causing the small glass bowl that had contained the mousse to fall onto its side. 'You can't serious; having the baby before you get married? I thought you had moved beyond your slutty behaviour.'

Janine clenched her hands into fists under the table.

'It's my fault really, I have my heart set on this quirky little place in Brunswick Street, I know the owners, they're good friends, but they're very popular for wedding receptions.'

'I see.' Vicky schooled her face back to a calm veneer, but the pity for Craig and disdain for her daughter weren't completely hidden. 'I'm tired tonight. I'm afraid you won't be able to stay and chat.'

Craig stood up when she did and started to gather up the remaining dishes. Janine thought if she moved, she might explode and the white-hot rage in her belly would flow out of her mouth in words she couldn't take back. Craig would be devastated if she undermined all his hard work by letting her mother get under her skin.

'I'm sorry to hear you're tired. Maybe you had a bit too much to drink,' Janine said. 'We'll get out of your hair.'

She took Craig's elbow and led him to the front door. 'See you next time, Vicky,' he said over his shoulder.

'You can let go now,' he said, when they stepped onto the little path back to the car.

Janine looked over to him, she'd almost forgotten he was there in her singlemindedness to get out of the house. 'Sorry babe, was I hurting you?'

'No, it's okay,' he said rubbing his upper arm. 'She really got to you, didn't she?' Craig got into the driver's side.

She made a noncommittal noise. They drove along in silence, *Ring My Bell* played softly over the radio.

'I'd like you to talk to me. I know it's been hard with your mother over the years, but I can't help you unless you let me in,' he said.

'I don't want to talk about it.'

'I think it would make you feel better to tell me what's wrong.' He put his left hand on her thigh, darting a quick look at her then turning his eyes back to the road.

'She called me a slut.'

'Did she?'

Janine clenched her jaw. 'Yes. She says it all the time. It was never true and always made me angry.'

'Right.'

'I mean, that's why she threw me out of the house, in the end. She was jealous of the relationship I had with my dad, and after he died, I was a bit wild and she didn't want to deal with it.'

'Why was she jealous?'

'God knows.' Janine sniffed. 'He liked spending time with me more than he did with her.'

'Oh.'

'He was in the army, so he wasn't home much. We were very close, he said I was his special girl. Me and Mum got on okay when he wasn't there, she largely ignored me but that was fine. When he was home, she seemed to have it in for me. Of course, my dad was always taking my side in arguments.'

'I had no idea.'

Janine looked out the window at the thin drizzle which had started to fall. Despite spring having arrived over a month ago, the cold, damp weather lingered. 'Now you know. Whenever she makes some comment about me being a slut, I remember how she chucked me out.'

'There's never an excuse to treat anyone like that, no matter what they've done. I promise, as long as I'm around, you'll never be out in the cold again.'

Janine leant over and rested her head on Craig's shoulder. She was glad he was in her life, so what if it they had to wait a few months to get married. It was only a piece of paper; what they had between them was much more.

*   *   *

Elena had been disappointed to hear the wedding was pushed back, but she redirected her energy to getting ready for the baby.

'We won't tell the boys that it's been delayed, they wouldn't know when it was supposed to be in any case,' she'd said.

When Janine went in to work the day after the scene with her mother, Elena wasn't there yet. Often Janine was the last person to arrive, the others would get there well before nine o'clock. She sat at her desk and set herself up for the day; checked the answering machine and opened the mail.

It was nearly ten-thirty in the morning when Elena arrived looking haggard and unwell.

'Are you alright?' Janine asked, going over to see her as soon as she walked in.

'Don't worry about it.' Elena was pale and had large dark circles under her eyes.

'I am worried about you.'

But I'll leave it for now. She made them both a coffee, and sat on Elena's desk, the way she had so many times before.

'Here. Now, tell me what's going on? You're never this late.'

'It's nothing.'

'I don't believe you.'

Elena sighed and sipped her coffee. 'George and I are fighting.'

'Why?'

'He says he wants to hire a new person when you go off to have the baby and I want to keep you.'

'Oh.' Janine hadn't thought about what would happen with her job when the baby came. It seemed naïve now.

'I want to get someone for six months while you're getting used to the baby and then have you back, but George said if we're teaching someone how to do everything, we have to keep them.' Elena sniffed. She wasn't wearing makeup.

'What happened then?'

'I slept on the couch, not that I got much sleep. George didn't wake me when he went to work, which is a feat in itself, usually he stomps around so loud he'd wake the dead. And now I'm here and he is not. We never fight.'

Janine put her hand on Elena's shoulder, and tried to ignore the guilt in her stomach. They had been like parents to her, better than her own, and now George was going to throw her away just like her mother and John and Gerry. She gripped the handle of the coffee cup too hard and it dug into her fingers.

George wanted to get a new receptionist, fine, but she was angry she hadn't seen it coming. They were a small family business and couldn't afford to train someone new only to have her come back, with divided loyalties, six months or a year later. It seemed natural she would have to resign, have the baby and then see how things went.

And she was angry Craig hadn't said he would support her to do the stay-at-home-mum thing, at least for a while. She knew being home with the baby was important, especially in the early stages, and he made good money. Maybe she didn't need to work anymore, except to stop herself going stir crazy.

'It's okay, Elena, I'll resign when it's time for the baby to come. You don't have to fight with George about it. I haven't even decided if I want to come back to work, Craig is such a great earner.'

'Sweet girl. Thank you.' She stood to give her one of her strangling hugs. 'You will bring the baby to visit us, though, won't you? I love babies, all the boys say they don't care, but they coo and fuss as much as me.'

'Of course.' Janine didn't know if she'd have time to visit her old job with a new baby, but it was a nice idea.

*   *   *

When she got home, Craig was sitting on the couch with a beer in one hand and the TV remote in the other.

'You're home early.'

'I had a few meetings and there wasn't much point going into the office afterwards.'

Janine perched on the arm of the couch and looked down at him. He seemed to have lost something, his spark, in the last few weeks. 'I think I want to take a few years off work to be with the baby,' she said.

He turned to her, alarm fleeting briefly across his face before he calmed it. 'Of course. You gotta do what's best for the little one.'

'My mother didn't work at all after I was born, but once the kid is at school, I'll definitely be ready to work again. I don't want to end up like her, a shell of a person filled with red wine and competitive friendships.'

Craig smiled up at her then turned back to the TV. She was reassured they were on the same page and went to the kitchen to put together something for dinner.

*   *   *

The next couple of months slipped past in a blur of routine. Janine's belly swelled and Craig stayed with her every night. Probably to keep an eye on her and the baby.

Janine became more uncomfortable sleeping and moving around, and the worst was still to come. Despite the fact George wanted to get rid of her when the baby came, he was as caring and jovial as always.

The lead up to Christmas was stressful for Janine. The years she didn't have contact with her family meant she became quite anxious about having a fight with her mother. Vicky had invited her paternal grandmother, Claire, to the Christmas lunch she was hosting.

'And when will there be another dividend payout from this investment, Craig?' her mother asked on the Sunday before Christmas.

'I'm sure it will be in mid-February some time. They seem to be paying out in six-month increments.'

Janine was shocked to think her mother had spent the whole of the fifteen thousand from the last pay out. Surely Vicky didn't have many expenses, although she had mortgaged part of the value of the house into the investment, something Janine thought was a bad idea, both Vicky and Craig disagreed.

'The first payment was for a quarter and it's been much longer than that now. If I'd known how unreliable the income would be, I might have rethought the amount I invested.'

'I understand the frustration, but as I mentioned, when you're talking about investments with this high return you sometimes have to accept that they're not run like clockwork. If you need emergency funds, I'll be happy to help out.'

Vicky scoffed. Janine tried to suppress a smirk; she would never accept a handout or even a loan from her daughter's boyfriend. It would be much too humiliating.

'Do you want me to bring anything to Christmas lunch?' Janine asked.

'I don't think so.' Vicky's face showed her disdain for the idea. In the time since they had rekindled their relationship Janine hadn't once got her to agree to eat at their place in Fitzroy. Perhaps her mother didn't trust her cooking or didn't want to risk the car on the streets. Janine had stopped asking.

18. Family Christmas

On Christmas morning Janine woke at just after eight o'clock. They were due at Vicky's for lunch at twelve. She rolled over to face Craig.

'Merry Christmas, babe,' she said.

'Mmm, Merry Christmas,' he mumbled, his eyes stayed closed.

Janine left him to sleep, he would be cranky if she made him get up. She walked through the loungeroom to the small kitchen and saw that there was a gift-wrapped in gawdy red and green paper under the spindly plastic tree that wasn't there last night. She picked it up, the note read: 'To Janine, From Santa'.

She slipped her fingers under the tape and got the paper off almost intact. She always felt particularly accomplished if she managed to get the paper off without any tears. Inside was a black box, about fifteen centimetres square. She pulled up the lid to reveal a yellow cassette Walkman with matching yellow headphones. A broad grin spread across her face. She'd mentioned a while ago she wanted one and Craig hadn't said anything about it since then. She thought he'd forgotten about it, but he had been keeping it under wraps to surprise her.

Janine put the gift down on the coffee table and bounded back into the bedroom.

'Oh baby, it's the best thing. Thank you so much.' She kissed him all over his face until he was forced to flutter open his eyes.

'What's that now?'

'The Walkman. I thought you hadn't heard me.'

'I don't know what you're talking about.' He smiled. 'It's from Santa, isn't it?'

'Yes, but I know it's from you. Santa's not real.'

'He most certainly is. You must have been a very good girl this year.'

Janine's cheeks grew hot as she flushed.

'Now, now, you have been a good girl. I told Santa so myself.' Craig laughed and kissed her. It might have been to keep her quiet, but Janine didn't care. Any time Craig showed any kind of interest in her physically she took full advantage.

They had sex; there was quite a long period of foreplay and giggling but the act itself was quite short. Janine wondered how Craig would respond if she pleasured herself, but then realised she had to pee instead. The growing baby inside her placed increasing pressure on her bladder. She sighed, pulled on a light dressing gown and went back out to the bathroom.

When she had finished, Craig was making her a coffee; black with two. In the beginning of their relationship, he had teased her for enjoying Nescafe, but he made it for the both of them most mornings now.

'Coffee?' he said.

'You read my mind.'

The morning was cool for summer and the warm mug was comforting.

'What shall we have for breakfast?' he asked.

'Mum will have quite a spread I'm sure, so maybe some toast and vegemite?'

'It's Christmas, you don't want to be a bit more adventurous?'

She smiled and looked around at the orange laminate benches and pale pine cupboards. 'Alright, peanut butter and honey.'

'That's more like it.' He winked and placed a couple of slices down in the toaster.

*   *   *

Janine made sure they were at her mother's place in plenty of time. At five to twelve they parked out the front and turned off the engine.

'Are we going in?' Craig asked when she had been sitting there for about a minute without moving to leave the car.

'Mum won't be happy if we turn up early. Best to wait here until it ticks over midday.'

'It's only four minutes… three now. Surely, she won't mind. She never has for Sunday dinner.'

'Sunday dinner has nothing on Christmas. Mum will be making final adjustments and whenever anyone turned up before the appointed time for a do, she made them regret it.'

Craig shook his head. He probably didn't believe her, but he hadn't been through the ordeal. In primary school, Vicky had been very active with the other parents at the school and had invited a large number of people to an end-of-year party. It had taken her the entire summer to stop talking about the one family who arrived ten minutes early. Added to which they were a single mother and a little boy from the year below Janine. They weren't invited back.

As soon as the clock struck the hour Janine got out of the car and walked up to the house. Her mother opened the door to greet them and gave her air kisses on both cheeks.

'Lovely to see you,' Vicky said. 'Didn't bring any wine then?'

Janine clenched her teeth. 'You told us not to.'

'Hmm.' Vicky raised an eyebrow.

Inside it was overly warm and stuffy, filled with the smell of roasting meat. The table was set for six, her mother, herself and Craig, Claire and two more. Perhaps her mother had invited her own parents. It would explain why she was cooking instead of buying and reheating. A glass of white wine sat sweating on the bench, from which her mother took a large slug.

'Who else is coming?'

'Claire and your Nanna and Pop.'

'Really?'

'There's no need to take that tone.' Vicky put her wine glass down with a heavy clank.

'What tone?' Janine pretended innocence.

'You haven't been to the last few Christmases—'

Not that it was my idea.

'And your grandparents and I have seen a bit more of each other.'

Janine said nothing, she had never understood the distance between her mother and her grandparents. She didn't know much about them except they lived out in the Yarra Valley, in wine country.

'You look nice, Craig dear,' Vicky said. Craig wore a middle grey suit, a white shirt with no tie, and tan coloured loafers. He had recently bought the suit, said it was an excellent deal, although too hot for the jacket in the house. He shrugged it off and draped it across the back of the chair at the head of the table.

'Thanks Vicky, I made an effort to look nice. Just for you.'

'You're too smooth.' Vicky flapped her hand at him, Janine thought she was being too flirtatious, even for her.

The doorbell rang. 'I'll get it,' Janine said. When she opened the door, her grandparents stood in front of her. They seemed very old and very small, yet sprightly.

'Hello dear, we're here to see Vicky. Have we got the right house?' Carol, her grandmother said.

'It's me, Janine.'

'Oh, my dear. Haven't you grown? Goodness, your mother didn't tell us you were expecting.' She put her hands out to caress Janine's belly. It was odd to be touched by a near-stranger, but Janine was used to it.

'Good to see you, love.' Her grandfather's voice was rough and raspy, as though he needed to clear his throat. He held an unlit pipe between his teeth. He had been told often enough wasn't allowed to smoke in the house but seemed to liked the feel of it anyway.

Once she had hugged them both and her grandmother, Carol, had stopped trying to feel her baby bump, she led them down the hallway to the kitchen.

'You didn't say Janine would be here, and with one on the way,' Carol said, her voice a little sharp.

'Didn't I?' Vicky said.

'No, you certainly didn't tell us about her news,' her grandfather, Ted said, looking at Craig leaning on the kitchen counter in his shirt sleeves.

'Pop, this is my fiancé, Craig,' Janine said.

'Craig, is it? And what do you do with yourself?' Ted went over to Craig and pumped his hand vigorously.

'I'm a stock trader, mostly.'

'Stocks? Hmm, I don't go in for that sort of thing.' Ted stepped back and was looking pointedly at the jacket over the chair in what appeared to be his seat. Janine hoped there would be no macho displays of pride before they'd even eaten.

'Sorry, let me move that for you.' Craig placed his jacket on the next chair. 'Some people think stocks are too risky, but I have a good track record of great deals and excellent returns. I do alright.'

'I can see that.' Ted looked him up and down, apparently taking in the quiet, but expensive, taste of

Craig's clothing. 'I'm sure Vicky thinks you're just the bees' knees, does she?'

'I can't speak for her, but she seems to like me.' Craig smiled, his white teeth shining. It was his selling smile. Ted nodded, he squinted at Craig a moment longer before turning back to Janine.

'And he's responsible for this—exciting state of affairs?'

Janine giggled; her heart was pounding under the scrutiny of this man she barely knew. 'Yes. We'll be married early next year.' She waved the ring in his direction.

'In my day, we got married first.' He sniffed and sat down at the head of the table.

'Now Dad, we don't want to spoil Janine's good news with our old-fashioned ways.' Carol put her arm around Janine's shoulders and squeezed. 'How long now, dear?'

'I'm due in March.' Janine smiled. She never tired of talking about the baby or the wedding plans, such as they were.

'You're young and healthy, I'm sure it will be a breeze and you'll be able to come visit us with the little one.'

'Of course.' It seemed odd she was expected to feel a connection to these two people. She hadn't seen them since she was eight-years-old. After a fight, something about her father, they had refused to visit. Janine thought it would have been her grandfather's doing, he was a prickly sort, and her father was never one to back down when he thought he was right. Her father probably won. Perhaps it was only since his death they had come back into their daughter's life.

'Did you use the recipe I sent you, dear?' Carol asked. Vicky rolled her eyes, a gesture that made her look more like a sulky teen than an upper middle-class woman in her forties.

'Yes, Mother. It's roast beef exactly as you used to make. Complete with your duck fat potatoes and Yorkshire puddings.'

Janine's mouth started watering at the sound, since becoming pregnant her appetite had been unpredictable. Some days she would be too nauseous to eat much at all, sometimes bananas, cigarettes and coffee were all she had, other days she was so hungry she could barely keep her mind on the job. She would have to go down to the corner shop for emergency chocolate and sausage rolls, sometimes together. Despite the toast she'd had earlier she was suddenly ravenous.

'When do you think we'll eat?' she asked, her belly rumbling noisily.

'It'll be ready when it's ready,' her mother said.

'I'm sure you could spare some bread and butter for the poor girl; she is eating for two you know.' Carol went to the breadbin and started looking around for a snack.

'I'm okay, really, I can wait,' Janine said. Her belly growled again, even more loudly than before.

'Can't deny yourself when you're hungry. Think of the little one,' Ted said.

Janine was surprised to hear her grandfather getting in the middle of the unfolding drama.

'I haven't got any bread. She'll have to have something else.' Vicky opened the cupboard, moved a few items, before turning back to them. 'Here, have a couple of these. That ought to keep you from wasting away in the next ten minutes.'

Janine said nothing and took the dry water crackers her mother had shoved in her direction. Her mother had found the least appetising thing in her cupboard as a punishment.

It was just as well she had something to keep her going, the roast turned out to be bigger than Vicky had anticipated and they didn't sit down to eat until well after one o'clock. Janine had eaten the entire pack of crackers by then. She had a large serving and another half serving of the roast, with potatoes, vegetables, gravy, and five Yorkshire puddings. Her mother's face became more pinched with every mouthful, but her grandparents and Craig, all encouraged her to eat while she was hungry.

Claire had arrived at half past twelve, carrying two bottles of red wine. Ted visibly tensed when she arrived. She sat between Janine and Ted, opposite Craig. Vicky and Carol were at the other end of the table.

Whatever Ted's problem had been with her father, it included Claire. Janine suspected Vicky had always wished Claire was her mother, rather than Carol. They were much more alike, concerned with looking their best at all times, and spending money on clothes and accessories to make sure other people knew their status. Claire was unlike her mother though as never denied herself, particularly when it came to food. Claire served herself a large portion of Christmas dinner with all the trimmings but didn't have seconds; 'Saving room for the pudding,' she said.

After pudding they all moved to the back veranda to enjoy the mild sun of the late afternoon. Christmas in Melbourne was always either swelteringly hot, the kind of heat where you wanted to hide inside the house and wait for the sun to go down or freezing and pouring with rain and no in-between. This year the top temperature had been thirty-five degrees Celsius, not too bad, but the roast beef had made the house stifling, even with the air conditioning on high.

Outside a small breeze blew and her mother had brought out chilled white wine to sip while they digested the enormous meal. Janine looked at the cool, pale yellow liquid in Craig's glass with envy. Vicky wouldn't buy any soft drinks, too much sugar, so she had had only chilled water for the entire afternoon.

'I'd like a glass of that please, Mum,' she said.

'It's bad for the baby,' Vicky replied.

'One drink won't do her any harm,' said Claire.

Her mother's lips pressed into a thin line, but she said nothing. Claire poured out a small glass of white wine and handed it to Janine. The first sip reminded her how much she missed it. She wanted to do the best for the baby, so she had been very strict about alcohol consumption. She savoured the flavour, swirling it around her glass and around her mouth before she swallowed. She wondered if she'd ever really appreciated it before.

'I couldn't stomach any alcohol with your mother,' Carol said. 'The very idea of wine made me feel I might be sick.' She smiled.

'I certainly won't need a second one. I'm absolutely giddy,' Janine said.

'The body goes through so many changes. Did you have any morning sickness?'

Janine told her grandparents about the trials and joys of her pregnancy so far, both grandmothers seemed fascinated. Ted gazed off into space, Craig was content to listen while Vicky's foot jigged up and down and her fingers drummed on the glass tabletop.

'That's quite enough, thank you, dear,' Carol said, laying her hand over Vicky's fingers. Vicky pulled her hand away sharply and glared at her mother.

'You're ridiculous! You were never interested in my pregnancy! If I'd turned up to Christmas dinner unmarried and six months gone you would have disowned me.'

'They were different times, and you weren't unmarried, were you?' Carol said.

'Don't speak to your mother like that.' Ted said at the same time. Janine had thought he hadn't been listening. Vicky picked up her glass and stomped back into the hot, stuffy house.

'We'd about given up ever having a grandchild when you came along. Bill had thought he couldn't have children. But then along you came. We couldn't have been more pleased to have you.'

Claire made a face at this comment. Her mother's parents hadn't been around much, no doubt Claire thought they were negligent.

What if her father had been infertile and she was someone else's baby? Janine's parents had been married for some time before she had come along. She had always been a Daddy's girl, but she looked more like her mother, a fact she constantly lamented; her pale hair was never quite blonde, her tendency to pudge around the middle and her short stature. Bill had been lean, tall, and dark.

Janine had never suspected her mother of cheating before that moment. With her father off with the army for long periods, what would have stopped her? Chronically unhappy, and obsessed with being the best in the neighbourhood, her friends had always been women. Perhaps Bill made a deal where he would take the child in as his own as long as Vicky stayed?

It would explain why they had stayed together. She had always assumed it was stubbornness; unable to admit they'd made a poor choice they battled on miserably to maintain the façade.

The sun wouldn't set until almost nine o'clock tonight. Janine looked through the windows towards her mother tottering around the kitchen in her high heels, angry and cleaning.

'That wine's gone straight to my head, I need to go home and have a lie down,' Janine said.

'Of course. It's been a big day.' Craig leapt up taking her mostly empty glass and trotting inside with it.

'It was lovely to see you all. I'm sorry I have to leave.'

'You've done well, love. You look after that baby, we're very keen to meet our great-grandchild.' Carol took her hand and helped her out of the stiff plastic chair.

She hugged each of her grandparents and promised to keep in touch before heading back into the kitchen. Vicky stood leaning on the bench; her skinny arms folded across her chest.

'I'm sorry we're going early, Mum. The meal was lovely.'

'I told you wine was a bad idea.'

Janine sighed. 'Yes, you did. I'll see you for Sunday dinner then.'

Vicky harrumphed.

*　　　*　　　*

The car ride home was silent, Craig taking his cue from Janine's mood. They sat together on the couch and watched stupid Christmas shows without saying much to each other. Janine felt a bit nauseated, perhaps from the wine, or from overeating, or from her mother's comments.

When they went to bed, she lay on her side, facing away from Craig, and her mind kept going over and over the conversations.

'That was weird,' she said.

'I wasn't going to say it, but there was something there.'

'My parents were married for five years before I was born.'

'Oh?' Craig said.

Janine let the silence sit between them for a while before she answered. 'I don't look much like my dad.'

'Oh.' Craig's voice dropped.

'If I wasn't my dad's baby, I don't think my nan, Claire, knows. She's been there for me the whole time, why would she be, if she knew we weren't related?'

'Maybe she knows and doesn't care? Or you're a miracle baby. It's not very nice to think your mum cheated.'

'You're right, I shouldn't assume things.'

Craig kissed the back of her neck and put his arm around her belly. 'Goodnight, Mamma.'

'Night,' she said. But Janine couldn't sleep. It might not have been very generous to think of her mother like that, but it explained so much. Why she resented Janine, the misery and tension between her parents. Since her father's death her mother hadn't dated anyone. And she was no happier now, than she had been before.

19. Home Sweet Home

Janine spent the days between Christmas and New Year's Day hanging out with Craig. He was distracted and restless.

'We need to sort out the new place. Once the baby comes, we can't stay here.'

Craig seemed to have moved in, though neither of them mentioned it, and she couldn't expect Phoebe to live with a baby as well.

'I'm sorry I haven't been able to help out with the house hunting. Work has been hectic. I'll have some money coming through soon, mid-February at the latest, and then we'll be able to move. It's just too hard to move while I'm waiting for the next big payout.'

'I don't understand why you don't get a proper salary.'

'I get paid when my investors do, I take a percentage. Sometimes it's only three months, sometimes it's longer. You know I've been generous when I've had the money to be. Don't make me feel bad about it being a slow time.' Craig looked at his bare feet where they sat on her scuffed red-brown carpet.

'I never wanted you to feel bad, I just want my baby to have the best.'

Sins of the Father

Janine felt her cheeks become hot. She didn't like to talk about it, but there were things her mother had done she swore she wouldn't do. Her parents provided a roof over her head and food on the table, they were never poor, but Janine had never believed her mother wanted her, and her father, who loved her so much in his way, was only around a few months of the year. A child needed a mother and father who loved them.

'You're going to be great you know.' Craig smoothed her hair away from her eyes and kissed her forehead. 'I'm going to get you a cold towel, you feel really hot.'

'Thank you.' She was very hot, the weather didn't agree with her condition and she was constantly covered in a sheen of sweat. Craig returned with a small hand towel that he'd soaked in cold water. She lay the towel around her neck and let it drip down her shoulders and back. It was blissfully cold for a few minutes before her body heat warmed it and she felt sticky again.

Craig watched cricket on the television, sitting forward on the couch, his eyes following the play intently. When they'd first met, he'd spent so much money on her; flashy meals, and cars and jewellery, but that Craig had been replaced with this mooching, bogan Craig who couldn't pay his way. The flashy cars were gone, he didn't have one at the moment, and he spent more and more time at home during the day. December and January were quiet, with people away and businesses slow, but it bothered her. She was carrying his baby, and once it arrived, her salary would be gone. She pushed the thought from her mind and reached for Craig's hand. He squeezed her back, but didn't turn away from the TV.

*   *   *

Janine's last day of work was February 14, three weeks before she was due. The doctor had explained it wasn't good for her to continue to work too close to the birth, and to make sure they were ready and to give herself a chance to rest in the last difficult weeks. She was so relieved the pregnancy was almost over she cried several times on her last day. She found it hard to sit behind the desk, working around the bulk of her belly, she couldn't walk quickly and became very hot and winded if she tried to do anything strenuous. The baby had also taken to kicking her during the night and her sleep had been very disturbed.

Craig had bought a cot and a pram and a few other things, he'd had a small pay-off but he still didn't have bond for a new place to live. Just before home time on her last day, Elena called everyone together for an afternoon tea. She'd been busily creating sweet desserts for days; leaving them in the fridge and insisting that no one eat any until the farewell. Janine had come very close to eating one of the profiteroles, thinking it wouldn't be noticed, until Elena caught her in the act.

Elena dinged a teaspoon on the side of her cup to call everyone's attention. 'I know you've all come here to say goodbye to our lovely Janine.'

'And to eat,' said her youngest son.

'A bit of shush now,' George said.

256

'Janine has been with us for a long time, she first came to us as a young girl and has grown into a beautiful woman and soon-to-be mother.' She beamed at Janine. 'It's been a pleasure to sit across the room from her for these last years, to watch the ups and downs of her life, and I think this time she's onto a winner. So, from everyone here, our family to yours, we'd like to give you this gift.'

Elena handed Janine an enormous box. Janine unwrapped it, and inside it was a huge array of baby things; rattles, jumpsuits, cloth nappies, blankets, hats and booties. It was everything she could ever need and Janine started to cry.

'Don't you cry, *koukla,*' Elena said, wrapping Janine's upper body in a tight hug. 'This is no time for crying.'

'Thank you,' she said, her voice muffled by Elena's embrace. 'I don't know how I'm going to get it all home.'

'Craig can't come pick you up?' George asked.

'He's got no car at the moment, dear,' Elena said, saving Janine having to say it herself.

'What kind of bullshit man doesn't have a car,' he grumbled. 'I'll give you a ride then.'

'Thank you.' Janine found it hard to talk around the lump in her throat and tears streaming down her face.

When George dropped her home later that day, Janine was still tearful.

'George, this is Craig,' Janine said, as she came into the lounge room. George had his hands full carrying the box, many of the gifts inside didn't all fit back in after she'd pulled them all out.

Craig was on the couch wearing beige shorts and a red polo top. He had brought several of his suits with him when he had unofficially moved in, but he seemed to have fewer clothes now than when they met.

'Hunny, this is my boss.'

'A pleasure to meet you.' Craig stood, wiped his hand on his shorts and held it out to George. With his hands full, George couldn't shake Craig's hand and there was an awkward silence between them.

'Take the box and put it somewhere will you.'

'Of course.' Craig took the box from George and put it on the floor next to the coffee table. Janine bit down the urge to tell him that was an unhelpful place to leave it.

'Can't stay, I'm afraid,' George said.

'Thank you for bringing me home.'

'Walk me out, will you?'

Janine followed George back into the street, the late afternoon was still scorching and the old terrace was cooler than the air outside. Janine squinted in the sun and held a hand up to shade her eyes.

'You deserve the best, Janine. If you ever need me to come sort out your fiancé, you just give the word.' George's face was dark and serious.

Janine giggled. 'You're sweet, I'll be sure to keep in touch.' She leaned over to give him a kiss on the cheek.

George waved from the driver's seat of his ute as he pulled away from the curb. He must have been doing his gruff father routine with her to hide his emotions, she thought to herself. How could he not like Craig?

Inside, Craig was watching TV again and had not moved the box of baby things.

'Baby, can you find somewhere for all that stuff to go? I need to have a rest, it's been a big day.'

'Sure, I'll get to it in a minute.'

Janine sighed. 'Are you too busy watching *Family Feud* to help your heavily pregnant fiancée? You were in exactly the same position as you were when I left. What happened to the go-getter I knew when we first met?'

'You think I've done nothing all day? You think I like saying no to you? To not having enough money to get us a new place? I don't need to stick around an hear any more.' He stood up and stormed out of the house.

I shouldn't have made him feel small. I'll make sure he knows how much I love him, no matter what, when he comes back.

*   *   *

For three days Janine waited. She tried paging Craig, but he'd left his pager in the house. He had never left her for so long since the trip Tasmania with his investors.

'I think I should call the police,' she said. It was not the first time she'd said it.

'I know you're worried, but he's a grown man. He'll show up eventually,' Phoebe said. Each time Janine brought up the police, she had said something similar. Janine was sick with worry and the baby wouldn't settle; she kept wriggling and kicking. Sitting was uncomfortable, lying was uncomfortable, the only thing that really made her feel less like the world was spinning out of control was pacing up and down the loungeroom with the television on in an effort to distract herself.

She heard a key turning in the lock and she rushed to the doorway to see who it was.

'You're back,' she squealed as Craig closed the door behind him. He glanced up at her, looking tired.

'I brought you something.' He walked towards her, one hand tucked behind his back. Janine threw her arms around him and kissed his face, cheeks, eyelids and lips. He stood stiffly and received her affection.

'What is it?'

He held out his hand, and in it was a key. 'I got us a new place.'

'Oh, Craig. You didn't have to; I could have waited. I've been so worried about you. Where have you been?'

'Doesn't matter now.' He sighed heavily and sat down on the couch. 'I was so angry with you the other day. I didn't want to admit I'd been letting you down. I haven't been putting in as much effort into the business as I should have and I certainly hadn't made any progress on finding us a place to live. The baby will be here any day now and we're still living in a share house.'

He looked so sad and tired. She wanted to know what he'd done for the last three days, but she didn't want to pepper her poor fiancé with questions.

'I'll make you a cup of tea.'

'Have we got any beer? It's been so hot.'

'I'm sure we do.' Janine went into the kitchen and looked through the fridge, the only beer they had was in the cupboard. 'There's no cold ones.'

'I don't care,' Craig called from the other room.

She returned to the lounge, handed him the beer and sat down next to him on the couch. She ran her hand over her belly. 'She's finally calmed down. She's been tossing and turning since you were away.'

Craig popped open the can of lukewarm beer and took a sip. 'I'm sorry I worried you and the little one.'

'It's okay.'

'What are we going to call her anyway?'

The last scans had shown that the baby would be a girl. Janine had been through a long list of names but Craig had not shown any interest.

'I thought Chloe was nice,' she said.

'My grandmother's name was Chloe. It was pretty unusual at the time, but I've always liked it.'

'That's settled then,' she said, snuggling down beside him. Craig put his arm around her and rested his hand on her belly.

'You're the best thing that's ever happened to me,' he said.

*   *   *

The house Craig had found them, was a small brown brick house in Brunswick. Two large bedrooms, lounge, kitchen, and a study or smaller bedroom. The bathroom was tiled in orange and brown and the floors in the kitchen were a matching dark brown tile. It was a little lacking in the looks department, but it was solid, well maintained and clean and fully furnished. The neighbours on either side grew vegetables in their front and back gardens, and the area seemed quiet and safe.

'It's beautiful!' Janine said when they had finished looking around. 'How did you find it?'

'I know the owner, he's out of town for the next couple of years doing a deal with an investment bank in Singapore. I didn't want to bother him originally by asking if we could use it, but when we had that fight, I knew it was time to pull up my socks and provide for my family.'

'We'd better get our stuff over here then. We don't need to pay two sets of rent, and once the baby comes, I won't want to move anything.'

'I've already thought of that. We only have to move our clothes and some of the kitchen stuff. It should only take a couple of carloads. I've organised a car for the next couple of weeks from a mate of mine. I'll do all the lifting and you can tell me where things have to go.'

'I love you so much,' she said. The surge of warmth she felt towards him was overwhelming. She had always wanted someone to look after her, and take pride in being a good partner and father.

Sins of the Father

*   *   *

Craig had underestimated the amount of stuff they had, but they had moved into the new house by the end of the week. With both of them not working it was easy to get everything sorted. The tail end of summer was still blisteringly hot, and Janine was unable to do much packing or lifting.

Craig wasn't any good at cooking, so she made sure he had a good supply of cold beer and food at the end of the day.

The baby wasn't due for another two weeks, but Janine felt she would burst at any moment. Her bump had dropped and her pelvis had shifted making her waddle. She was exhausted from the move and the heat and spent a lot of time on the brown velour couches resting.

The Monday after they moved in Craig got up and went to work. 'Now you're settled here I can get back to work. I'll see you later, baby.'

The first day alone in a new house Janine wondered if she'd made a mistake. The house was strange, and she didn't know anyone nearby. Phoebe promised to visit but she worked during the day. She had no energy to clean or cook elaborate meals, and she was bored, alone in the house.

In the late afternoon, when she wanted to cry, she decided to go for a short walk. There was a convenience store on the corner and the main road not too far away. She would think of something she needed to buy as an excuse and chat to whoever was working there. Perhaps try to get some information on the local maternal health nurse or community house.

She pushed her swollen feet into a pair of pale pink thongs, splashed water over her face and went out. It was not at hot as it had been, but still over thirty degrees Celsius according to the temperature gauge on the veranda. She waddled slowly down the road, making sure not to tire herself out too much on the way. They needed more milk and bread and she had a craving for peanut butter.

The shop was dimly lit and blessedly cool compared to the heat of the afternoon outside. The air conditioner placed over the door created a sheet of cold air, causing her to shiver as she walked through the hanging plastic strips into the shop. As her eyes adjusted to the low lighting, she saw several sets of shelves, closely packed and jammed with products. Everything she could want, and a few things she couldn't ever imagine needing. The fridges were at the back of the store, and she shuffled down to pick up milk. The bread was at the front, she ran her eyes over the various products on her way. When she was up close, the bread seemed a bit stale and she considered not getting any, but the idea of peanut butter toast was firmly planted in her mind.

'Where's the peanut butter?' she asked, putting her bread and milk on the counter.

'Let me show you.' The woman behind the counter looked to be southern European; Greek or Italian, and a little shorter than Janine. When she stepped out from the till she eyed Janine's belly.

'I still have two weeks would you believe it?' Janine said.

'You look about ready to me!' The woman smiled.

The peanut butter was more expensive than it ought to be, but Janine didn't mind. Now Craig was back hard at work she could spend a bit of money.

'I've just moved in up the street. Do you know where the maternal health clinic is? Or a mums' and babies' group?' she said, after they'd gone through the payment.

'Yes, dear.' The woman gave her complicated directions to a neighbourhood house which seemed to be quite close.

'Can you write down the address? My baby brain won't remember all that.'

'Silly me. Yes, yes.' She wrote the address and then drew a tiny map on a piece she ripped off from a roll of butcher's paper behind her.

'Thank you, you've been such a help, and it's so nice and cool in here.'

'Any time you want to come have a chat, you feel free. I know it can be lonely if you're in the house alone with the baby. I'm Francesca.'

'Janine. I'll be back, you can count on it.'

20. An Exciting Arrival

Janine settled into the house and Craig went out to work every day at eight a.m. He didn't come home until after six. Since the place was furnished, it didn't take long to unpack the few boxes they had.

A few blocks away on Sydney Road there were plenty of shops, though only one sold baby things. It had been hot every day since they moved, and Janine had to make sure she walked slowly and had plenty of water on her daily outing. Of course, it meant she needed to pee more often; she had introduced herself to a number of shopkeepers in attempts to relieve herself on her trips.

The baby was due on the sixth of March, she had made arrangements with the local hospital. Everything was ready to go. Being home on her own all day, after working for so many years, and school before that was tough. Daytime television was woeful, although she found herself drawn into the dramas unfolding on the midday talk shows.

When she had the first contraction on Sunday, two days before she was due, she thought it must have been a false alarm, the doctor had told her the name of them but she didn't remember. She had another one about ten minutes later. Then her waters broke, soaking through her shorts and all over the kitchen floor.

She called Craig's work number, but no one answered, she paged him to call her urgently, but she didn't want to wait around until she heard back from him.

She called her mother. 'My waters have broken.'

'What do you want me to do about it?' Vicky said. She sounded drunk; it was only one o'clock.

'I don't know what I'm doing. Am I supposed to go to the hospital?' Janine tried to steady her breathing.

'Didn't you write this all down when the midwife told you? Wait for the contractions to be five minutes apart for two hours. Then you go to hospital. Isn't Craig supposed to be taking care of you?'

'He's at work, and he's got the car.'

'Stop panicking. You have a while to go yet. Wait for him to come home or call you back and if your contractions are two minutes apart and he's still not home, call a taxi and go to the hospital.'

Janine choked back a sob. 'Can't you come and get me?'

'I don't think so.'

'Are you drunk?'

'I had a couple of wines with lunch. I'm not drunk, but I wouldn't like to drive in case the police decide to make an example of me.'

Janine grunted as another contraction started. She slammed down the phone and did her breathing exercises.

She waited for Craig to call her back and kept track of the contractions. They were steady at ten minutes apart, but they were getting stronger. She paced up and down in front of the TV and smoked the rest of her packet of cigarettes in an effort to calm down. Each hour she called Craig at work, and each time it rang out. She didn't even know if it was the right number.

By six o'clock, when Craig walked through the door, her contractions were five minutes apart and had been for an hour.

'We have to go.'

'What? Where? I just got home.'

'I've been calling you since lunchtime. It's time to go—fu' Janine stopped talking abruptly as a particularly strong contraction set in. Craig's face drained of colour and his eyes widened.

'Oh, shit. You mean? Oh, shit.'

'Get the bag,' she pointed to the hospital bag she'd packed during the afternoon. 'I'll wait in the car.' She held out her hand for the keys.

Craig continued to splutter uselessly. Janine took the keys from his hand, picked up the bag and marched out the door. She slung the bag into the back seat and eased herself into the front passenger seat. It was still warm outside but had cooled over the course of the afternoon. It took Craig long enough to come out to the car for her next contraction to have started.

He managed to drive her to the hospital without getting lost although he babbled on about his day the entire way. Janine was in no mood for prattle and so distracted by her labour pains she couldn't follow what he was saying. At least he didn't need her to respond.

Janine's daughter, Chloe, was born at ten thirty the next morning after keeping her up through the night. She was exhausted and gasping for a cigarette, but they'd hooked her up to the gas in the end and she wasn't in too much pain.

The baby had barely any hair and weighed just over three kilograms. She had muddy blue eyes and after an initial bout of crying, settled down to sleep in the cot next to her mother. She was wrinkled and red, but she was the most beautiful thing Janine had ever seen.

*   *   *

Craig was very unsure of the baby, he made light of it, but he avoided holding her. Whenever her did he seemed to be very stiff and awkward. Janine laughed the first time the nurse handed him the tiny baby.

'You need to hold her head,' she said.

'Oh, right.' Craig held perfectly still, holding the baby in his hands outstretched. He couldn't seem to get her into a comfortable position, and was unwilling to put her against his chest.

'You won't bond with her like that.' The nurse reached out and rearranged Chloe into the cradle of his arms, and then went to attend to the other patients.

'Look, she likes you,' Janine said, watching her daughter blinking uncertainly up at her father. She didn't really think Chloe had much idea what was going on, but wanted to encourage Craig. He needed to get used to holding her and or he would be no help at all once they got home.

Her mother turned up to see them that evening, Craig had gone back to work to sort out a few things.

'This is my granddaughter?' She wrinkled her nose in the baby's direction.

'Yes, don't you just love her?'

'Doesn't look like much.' Vicky peered down her nose to where Chloe was nestled next to the bed.

'She's only just been born, give her a break.' Janine laughed nervously.

Her mother made a noise that could have been agreement. She stayed about twenty minutes, trying to make small talk before she made an excuse and left. Janine had always thought her mother had about as much maternal instinct as a block of wood, but it was strange to see it in action.

Janine stayed in the hospital for three days, to make sure she didn't have any complications from what the doctors told her was a relatively simple birth. As painful as it had been, she hoped the worst was over. Craig came to take her home in the afternoon. He'd remembered to fit the baby carrier into the back.

'It wasn't easy, given it's a two door. I don't think we'll be able to leave it in there permanently. I might need the car to drive clients,' he said.

'If you're going to be at work with the car, I guess that's fine. We'll have to put it in for the weekends though,' she replied.

At home he'd built the cot in the spare bedroom, moved some of the furniture out into the garage so all the baby stuff had a place. It looked quite strange to have new white baby furniture in a room with pale orange wallpaper and carpet the green-brown colour of the baby's poo.

Craig worked every day and Janine was left at home with the baby. Chloe was a good girl, she slept a lot and breastfeeding seemed to come naturally, but Janine was lonely. The local playgroup didn't take infants as young as Chloe, but she enjoyed hanging out at the neighbourhood house talking to the other mothers. They cooed over the baby and she felt less alone.

Despite her mother having no job, she was too busy to come visit often. Janine hadn't expected much, but she had turned up with a couple of casseroles and a few groceries.

'I can't stay, but you needed a few things to get you through the first couple of weeks.' She said when Janine opened the door. Vicky put the food in the fridge and left the other groceries of the dining room table and went to leave. Janine thought she was almost as uncomfortable with the baby as Craig, although she had a lot more experience.

'Tell Craig I need to speak to him, will you?' Vicky said.

'What about?' Janine held the tiny baby to her chest, absentmindedly rubbing her back in small circles.

'I still haven't had any more money from his investments. I didn't want to say anything to you, you know, but he really needs to pay me soon.'

'I'll tell him.'

Vicky left the house and Janine went back to sitting in front of the TV. Craig still hadn't paid her mother? At Christmas he'd said mid-February, and she had been so caught up with moving house and preparing for the baby she hadn't thought to check with her mother whether the payment had gone through. Neither Vicky nor Craig had mentioned it for months, she had assumed it was paid.

Craig's working hours were getting longer now the baby was here. Janine was exhausted with caring for her all the time. He arrived home at seven o'clock that night.

'Hey, baby,' he said, strolling in to give her a kiss on the forehead.

'Hi. Can you take her for a second?' Janine said, pushing Chloe into his hands.

'Uh, sure.' He held her stiffly and stood in the middle of the dining room as Janine went back to getting through some of the piles of laundry that seemed to have sprung up since the birth.

'Mum came 'round today. She brought a couple of casseroles. There's some in the fridge if you're hungry.'

'How's your mother?'

'She's okay. She said you hadn't paid her the dividends she's owed.'

'Really? I'll have to chase that up.'

'You didn't check?' Janine stared hard at her baby's father. *Could he really have forgotten about that?*

'I was pretty busy, getting ready for the baby and making sure we had enough business to cover the new expenses, especially now you're not working.'

Janine felt heat rising up her throat. 'Excuse me?'

'I didn't mean it like that, I know you're working hard looking after Chloe. But I have to put a lot more effort into the business now I'm the sole breadwinner.'

'Whatever you say.' She was exhausted and emotional. 'I'm going for a walk, make yourself dinner. I'll be back in time for the eight o'clock feed.'

'Wait. I can't—'

'Can't what? Look after your own child for an hour or so? I haven't even been out of the house today. You have no idea what it's like being stuck at home with only her for company.'

Craig's mouth hung open. Before he could respond she had picked up her handbag and stormed out of the house.

In late March, the temperatures during the day were still in the high twenties, but at night would drop quickly after the sun set. Janine wished she had thought to bring a coat but she would warm up if she walked briskly. She was exhausted but out in the cool evening air she felt a weight lift from her shoulders to be away from the baby, even for a short time.

Craig really needs to step up with her. He wouldn't do any of the night changes and couldn't do any of the night feeds. He needed to go to work and to sleep, but Janine resented him. His life had barely changed since she got pregnant, he still got up and went to work every day, he played sports with his work buddies or clients on the weekends. Her life was totally turned on its head— no job, she'd moved to a new house, lost contact with Phoebe and the Fitzroy crowd. She was alone and completely beholden to Craig for everything.

It wasn't fair. She wanted to go back to work, having someone at home to debrief with after work. Sometimes, even though she looked forward to the moment Craig got home, she wished he would take the baby and let her have a proper rest.

The streetlights glowed yellow and the air smelled like rain. She brushed away the couple of errant tears sliding down her cheeks.

How did it come to this? How did I end up with a boyfriend who is too afraid of the baby do his share of caring for her? If she'd known how hard it would be, and how useless Craig was, she wouldn't have had the baby. She loved Chloe more than she'd loved anything in her whole life, she would die for her, but she still wished she was alone several times each day.

21. A Long Wait

'I have been living off credit cards for months, Craig. This is unacceptable. Why can't I be paid on a schedule like every other investment?' Vicky stood next to the dining table with her hands folded across her chest.

In the two months since the baby came along Janine and Craig had only been able to visit her mother for Sunday dinner a couple of times. Craig was always off doing something for work. Vicky had shown up one Thursday evening after leaving messages with Janine and trying his office number for two weeks without success.

'I know it's hard, I'm sorry it's taking so long. I might be able to transfer you some of my own money to get you by. You need to have faith, I'll come through for you, just like I did the first time.'

'That was almost a year ago.'

'How did you go through all that money since then, Mum? What have you been doing with it?' Janine said. She was bouncing Chloe gently on her shoulder waiting for her to burp. She had become used to the little girl's rhythms and while she had no idea what she was doing most of the time, they had some fun together.

'Most people make more than double that. And I have a mortgage to pay off. I have given your boyfriend all my investment capital, and taken money out of the house, so

I can live in the manner to which I'm accustomed and he's now refusing to pay me.'

'Now Vicky, I never said I wouldn't pay you.' Craig seemed unflappable in the face of her mother's distress.

'It's too late. I want to withdraw the investment. You're obviously mismanaging it and I want it back.'

'It's not as simple as that. You need to find a buyer for the stocks and futures you've bought, and then there will be taxes to pay on the increased capital.'

Vicky slammed her hand on the dining table and the baby started to wail.

'Ssh! You've upset Chloe,' Janine said.

'I don't have enough money to live, he's being a total prick about it and you're taking his side. I knew it was a mistake to let you back into my life. Look what you've done.'

'Calm down, everyone. I'll get you some money. I can't do it right now, but I'll bring something around to you tomorrow okay?' Craig put his hand on Vicky's shoulder, she shrugged him off.

'I'd better see a good sum tomorrow or I'm going to the police.'

'I understand you're upset, but this isn't a police matter. What would you say even if you did go?' Craig was almost laughing at her now.

'Come on, Craig said he'll sort it out, it's time to go.' Janine had managed to stop Chloe screaming but she was still unsettled. No good would come from her mother sticking around. She held Chloe to her shoulder with one hand, walked between Craig and Vicky and tried to shuffle her in the direction of the front door.

'If this isn't sorted out tomorrow, I am going to the police,' Vicky said as she left. The weather outside was cold and dark, May in Melbourne was always surprisingly cold, Janine thought. She closed the front door and leaned her back against it, took a deep breath and went back to face her fiancé.

'Your mother really needs to calm down. There's nothing I can do about her spending habits; she should have made that money stretch further.'

'Don't you blame her,' Janine said quietly, she was still livid and didn't want to further upset the baby by raising her voice. 'You said it would be stable and reliable, she thought it would only need to last three months, not nine. A sure thing, I believe were your words. You better make it right; or she will go to the cops.'

Craig went to the fridge and pulled out a bottle of beer. He went to the deep brown velvet recliner and sat down in it before he answered. 'Let's say I do give her some of my money to tide her over, as you seem to suggest. Then we, the baby, won't have any money coming in for another few months. You're not in a position to do anything except spend my money so unless you can get your mother off my back, we're all going down the toilet.'

He was so calm, it shocked her. He had no intention of sorting out the money and just hoped Vicky would go away. Janine didn't believe Craig had no money in his savings. When they met, he had so much ostentatious wealth he couldn't possibly have run out of all of it.

'If you don't make this right with Mum, I'll go to the police with her.' She turned away from him and went into the nursery. She lay Chloe down in her cot and sang her a silly little song she'd made up that put her to sleep every time.

She wondered if she would sleep in here tonight. This wasn't a spat that would sort itself out if they all had time to calm down. There was a real problem and if he couldn't figure something out, how could they possibly continue to function as a family?

*　　　*　　　*

Janine fell asleep in the old rocking chair she used for breastfeeding, and stayed here all night. Chloe barely woke up, as though she too was exhausted from the fight. First light crept through the window when the baby started to cry and stir, Janine picked her up. This was her favourite time of the day, when Chloe was still sleepy and the day was just beginning. In the afternoons she became restless and lonely, but first thing in the morning, the sight of her tiny daughter, all wrapped up, made her smile.

I'm so lucky to have you in my life. 'It's been rough along the way, but now we have each other everything will be okay. We're a team, you and me.' She stroked the baby's hair as she nodded her head against Janine's chest. 'Let's see what Daddy's doing, hey?'

The floor was cold under her feet as she walked through the house. He wasn't in the lounge or kitchen, he wasn't in their bedroom, and obviously wasn't in the baby's room. There was one other bedroom, but it was crammed with junk and bits of excess furniture. She went out the back in case he was having a cigarette on the steps, but he wasn't there either.

She looked out the front window and his car was gone. *It's too early for him to be at work.* She hadn't heard him leave during the night. She went back to the bedroom and opened the wardrobe; his clothes were gone. As were his toothbrush and all his expensive creams and colognes.

'Fuck,' she said aloud.

She got her cigarettes and lit one, pacing up and down the hallway trying to figure out what she should do. Craig had bailed. She wasn't sure who deserved her anger most; Craig, her mother, or herself for thinking he'd be different. She finished her cigarette and lit another one from the butt. She picked up the phone and called her mother.

'You haven't seen Craig, have you?' she said when Vicky answered.

'It's eight in the morning—where has he gone?'

'I don't know. I slept in the baby's room after you left and when I got up, he was gone. Packed all his shit and left.'

'Get dressed. I'm coming to get you and we're going to the police.'

'What for?'

'To report my money stolen.'

'He hasn't stolen your money, I'm sure there's a reasonable explanation.'

'Really? Leaving his new baby in the dead of the night is a reasonable thing to do, is it? Be serious, Janine. He's gone.'

Janine heard a clatter as her mother threw the phone handset. She stood there, stunned until her cigarette had burned down nearly to her fingers, she stubbed it out quickly.

She put the baby down, crying in protest, and went to her bedroom. She stood in front of the wardrobe, staring at the spaces where his clothes used to be. She ignored the plaintive wailing coming from the other room and tried to think.

Janine didn't know who the landlord was for the house they lived in, how much rent they paid or when it was due. More than she could afford now she wasn't getting a wage, certainly. She would be eligible for a government pension but how long it would take to come through, and what she needed to do to get it were beyond her understanding at that moment.

Obviously, her mother was no help, she had burned through everything she had waiting for another payout from Craig's magical investment. Either it never existed or had tanked and he'd been too ashamed to admit it. Janine guessed the second, he'd spent so much time talking up how safe it was, how good the returns would be, now he'd lost all the money and didn't want to tell them.

Which left her grandparents.

Vicky's parents had seemed accepting of the situation at Christmas but when it came down to providing for her, would they turn their back? They hadn't come to visit the baby, even after Carol has promised they would. And Claire, the only grandparent she'd ever really known and trusted. A woman who had shown her love and care since she was a baby but who, now she thought about it, she didn't know much about.

All the daydreaming was interrupted by a loud rap on the front door. Her baby was crying in the next room and her mother was waiting at the front door.

'Hold on,' she shouted. She threw off yesterday's clothes and found some others that smelled clean. She hurriedly grabbed her handbag, the baby's bag, and picked up her daughter.

'I'm sorry, I'm so sorry,' she whispered. Chloe was cold to the touch and shivering; she'd been unwrapped while Janine was trying to figure out what had happened to her life. She opened the front door to find her mother looking as though she would boil people alive with her glare if she could.

'You shouldn't let her get so upset.' Vicky looked at the baby.

'I know.'

'Get in the car.'

Vicky insisted on going to the Camberwell Police Station. It was one of the longest half hours of Janine's life. She held Chloe against her chest and shushed and hummed to her all the way. She glanced over at her mother's hand; her knuckles were white and her jaw rippled as she clenched and unclenched it.

The building was dark red brick with square, white trimmed windows and the word, Police, written in large white metal letters across the front. It was quintessentially art deco and Janine wondered if it had been built for the cops or if they'd moved in later. Chloe was asleep again, wrapped tightly in her blankets and snuggled against her chest. She lent down to sniff her hair, it no longer held that new baby smell, but was still intoxicating.

Her mother stormed up to the desk officer and banged her hand on the bell unnecessarily hard. The constable behind the desk raised an eyebrow at her and moved the bell out of reach. He looked about twenty-five, with wispy sandy-blond hair and didn't seem very authoritative.

'Can I help you?'

'We are here to report a theft,' Vicky said.

'I see, let's get some details from you first.' The young constable took out a pen and paper, ready to take notes. Vicky gave him her name, address, date of birth in a terse tone.

'And what's been taken?'

'About two hundred thousand dollars.'

Janine saw the edges of her mother's mouth twitch in satisfaction as the officer's face went slack for a few moments before he schooled it back to impassiveness.

'I see. I'll just need to speak to someone for you. If you'd like to have a seat.'

'Thank you.'

'You never told me he had so much of your money,' Janine said, she wanted to yell, but the baby was still sleeping against her.

'It wasn't any of your business. It's still not, except you brought that lying scum into my life.'

'Why did you give him so much? Was it everything you had?'

'I don't have to justify myself to you.'

'No, but if you'd told me outright you were giving him all your assets and re-mortgaging the house to get in on this deal, I might have told you not to put everything on one basket.'

Her mother crossed her arms.

'Didn't it seem a bit risky?' Janine asked.

'Craig had an answer to all of my questions. He was so sure the investment was solid.'

'He always sounded sure. It didn't mean you should believe him.'

Vicky scoffed. 'I'm sure there were so many times you didn't trust his judgement. When exactly did you realise that he was full of shit? Before this morning I mean.'

Janine opened her mouth, then closed it. She hadn't ever thought he was full of shit, had trusted him with everything. The only reason she hadn't given him her own savings, meagre as they were, was because he said she couldn't invest with so little. Was he trying to protect her from his scam? Did he know he would leave her with the baby one day and felt guilty about taking her savings? It didn't seem likely he would have scruples about her and not about her mother, unless it was all some sort of terrible mistake.

'I never did. I believed everything,' she said.

'I thought so.' Vicky was pacing up and down the waiting area, her black high-heeled shoes tapping across the tiled floor. Janine smelled burnt coffee and her belly rumbled reminding her she hadn't had breakfast. Suddenly she needed to sit down.

The constable had come back to the desk at some point during their conversation, Janine turned to him. 'How long do you think this will take? Do we have time to get coffee or something to eat?'

'One of the detectives will be with you shortly.' His eyes dropped to the sleeping bundle on Janine's shoulder. 'I could probably get you some coffee and biscuits. How old is the little one?'

Vicky rolled her eyes and continued to pace.

'She's just about two months. Such a sweetheart really, but we didn't have time for breakfast before we raced over here. Her father left us some time last night, you see, and I was a bit distracted.'

The constable's face crinkled momentarily in a frown.

'He's the one who took the money, I think he knew we were onto him. Or at least that Mum was.'

'I see.' He tapped his pen on the notepad in front of him a couple of times. 'I'll be back in one tic.'

He returned after a couple of minutes with a tray holding two paper cups of coffee, and several Monte Carlo biscuits.

'You're a lifesaver,' Janine said.

The coffee was weak and milky, almost grey, but at least it was hot. The biscuits were delicious, and despite her mother's glare she ate all but one, which Vicky took with disdain.

They waited almost half an hour for a detective to come down to see them. He walked out into the waiting room wearing a grey suit, a pale blue shirt and no tie. He seemed harried and self-important.

'Vicky Barrett?' he said.

'Yes.'

'Follow me please.'

Janine stood up to follow them and he put up his hand. 'Just Mrs Barrett.'

'Oh.' Janine sat back down heavily.

'They want to talk to everyone separately, you see' the desk officer said. 'It might be a while, if you want to take the baby out for a walk?'

'Yes. Good idea.' Janine didn't want to go for a walk but the idea of sitting in the waiting room for her mother was an even less attractive prospect. 'I'll be back in about half an hour. Mum and I came together so please don't let her leave without me.'

'Sure thing.' The constable nodded and she pushed open the swinging doors into the chilly late-autumn morning.

Janine wandered down towards a cluster of shops not far away. She bought a bacon and egg sandwich and managed to eat it before Chloe woke up and wanted to feed. She had a piece of cloth she draped over herself and the baby while she fed.

'We don't allow that here.' A snooty-looking man in his middle years came over to her. He seemed to be in charge.

'I won't be long. She's getting fussy and she's just started.'

'I'm sorry but you'll have to leave.'

'You can't see anything. What's the problem?'

'As I said, we don't allow that here.'

Janine sighed. She fished out some money from her purse and flung it on the table. She tried to grab her handbag and the baby's bag with one hand, while not detaching her from her breast. Trying to balance all her bags in one hand was worth it to avoid the screaming of a partially fed baby.

She struggled back to the police station, by which time Chloe had finished on one side and wanted the other breast. She was starting to grizzle and wriggle as Janine pulled open the door and flung herself inside.

Her mother wasn't there; no surprise she hadn't been gone very long. She sat down in the first chair and swapped the baby to the other side, trying not to flash the constable or the old wino who had joined the waiting list while she was out.

This was why she didn't like to go out much with the baby. It wasn't the first time someone had disapproved of her feeding in public. It made no sense to Janine; it was totally natural and surely better for the baby than a bottle but the looks she got from people made her wish she could disappear.

Once Chloe had had her fill, and was burped, she was sleepy again. She didn't do much more than eat, sleep and shit at the moment, but at least she wasn't crying. Janine wished she had the pram; she was getting tired of holding the baby.

Vicky came out with the detective in the grey suit after about twenty minutes.

'If I could speak to you now, Ms Barrett?' he said.

'Can you take her?' Janine looked at her mother expecting her to say no.

'Fine.'

Janine handed over the baby and followed the detective back into the police station. The walls were brick, rendered and painted white. The paintwork was grubby in places, and Janine didn't want to think about why.

The detective took her into a room with a tape recorder, a white laminate table and four chairs.

'Have a seat.'

Janine sat down.

'Your mother has given me the rundown, but I need to hear it all again from you. So, if you could start at the beginning.'

It was surreal to describe how she met Craig to a police detective. How their relationship had developed, how he had got her back in touch with her mother. Then won Vicky over, and then the details dried up, she had been excluded from the financial conversations.

'You weren't privy to the actual deal?' the detective asked.

'No.'

'You didn't see any paperwork signed, or money handed over?'

'No,' she said again.

'Hmm, makes it a bit tricky.'

'What do you mean?'

'It's much harder for us to say he stole the money if there's no witness to the transaction.'

Janine didn't understand. 'But I heard them talking about it, it was an investment. It definitely wasn't a loan or a gift.'

'That helps, but even so.' The detective ran his hand across his chin. The tiny stubble made a rasping sound against his palm. There were no sounds in the room other than his noisy breathing and the tick of the tape recorder.

'What happens now?' she asked.

'I have all I need. We'll be in touch with your mother if we have any luck tracking Mister Wilson down. I wouldn't hold your breath.'

The rest of the conversation and the walk back to the waiting room were a blur. The sound of Chloe's crying brought her out of her dream-state. Vicky thrust the infant into her hands as soon as she stepped back through the waiting room door.

'Thank you for coming in, Mrs Barrett, Ms Barrett. We'll be in touch.' The detective made it sound disturbingly final. Janine was exhausted and pushed her emotions down to deal with later.

'Let's go.' Vicky marched out to the car, leaving Janine to collect up the baby's bag and follow her.

22. Caring for Mother

A week went by and Janine hadn't heard anything from her mother or from Craig. She went down to the corner shop occasionally for some company, it was terribly lonely without anyone to talk to all day and all night. She was afraid to call her mother but in the end she became worried.

'Mum?' she said.

'What d'you want?' her mother's words were very slurred. Despite apparently being out of money she had managed to keep herself stocked with wine.

'I'm worried. I haven't heard from you.'

'I never call you. Why did you think it would be different now?'

'You didn't hear from the police then?' Janine bit the inside of her cheek, no good getting angry at her mother.

'No. They're useless.'

Janine heard fingernails tapping on a hard surface. Her mother wasn't usually this curt. 'Okay well. Um, I'll see you on Sunday then?'

'Do what you like. You always do,' Vicky said and hung up the phone.

She put down the phone receiver and went to look for the phone number of the detective at Camberwell. If her mother wasn't interested in following up, she certainly was. The possibility of Craig being innocent diminished with every passing day.

As soon as she got back to the phone Chloe started crying, it was feeding time again. Janine let the little card sit on the timber laminated table under the phone and went to tend to her. She had wondered if Chloe knew her father had left; she seemed more grizzly in the last week. Of course, it might have been because Janine had had no rest from her.

She flicked on the TV as she put the baby to her breast. It was children's stuff, furry blobs and crafts made from egg cartons and toilet rolls. She sat listening to the gurgling and gulping of her baby under the squeals and clangs from the television and closed her eyes.

The baby woke her, she had fallen asleep sitting on the brown velvet armchair. When her milk had run out the baby started to cry. She switched sides and told herself she wouldn't fall asleep this time. All the books said it was best to sleep when the baby slept, but every time Janine went into the bedroom, she smelled Craig. His scent was on the sheets, the bathroom smelled of his cologne, and whenever she tried to sleep, she would cry instead. The best sleep she had was on the couch or in the rocking chair next to Chloe's cot. At least there she wasn't reminded she'd been abandoned with a baby, no job, no boyfriend, no idea what she was doing and a mother who barely spoke to her.

Once Chloe had finished feeding, she was sleepy and calm. Janine wrapped her in her blankets and went back to the couch. She fell asleep almost instantly, with the sound of the kids shows in the background.

It must have been a few hours after she lay down, she woke up again. Chloe was awake in her cot but apparently happy enough lying there looking around. Janine picked up her daughter and bounced her on her shoulder a little.

Then she remembered the detective. She called the number he'd written on the card; a main reception line, and his extension written in pencil. His number rang out, so she called the front desk.

'Camberwell Police Station, Constable Pierce speaking,' said a warm male voice.

'Yes, uh, I'm looking for one of the detectives,' she said.

'They've all gone home for the day. Do you want to leave a message?'

'Uh, yes.' Janine looked at the clock in the hallway, it was almost seven, she'd slept longer than she thought. 'Please let Detective Cochrane know Janine Barrett called to see if there was any news.'

'Ms Barrett, you came in last week with the little one and your mother was it?'

'You remember us?'

'I don't often get such well-behaved babies, so she was memorable.'

Janine laughed, put the phone between her ear and shoulder and adjusted her hair. It wasn't twirling but it was close.

'You're very sweet to say so. If you could pass on the message.' Janine didn't think it was a very good idea to flirt with the officer when it was her ex-fiancé, or perhaps current fiancé depending how things worked out, who'd been the subject of her complaint.

'Sure thing. I'll let him know.' There was a pause and Janine wondered if he was going to say more.

'Thanks for your help then, Officer.'

'Before you go,' he blurted.

'Yes?'

'I don't think you'll hear anything from them. This sort of thing doesn't usually come to much. People like your man, fraudsters, they're pretty good at covering their tracks. He'd have a stash of cash somewhere, maybe even a bolthole, and you'll never see him again. Best to get on with your life as though he's not coming back. I mean, if you want my opinion.'

If he was flirting with her, he was doing a terrible job. 'Thanks for your help,' she said again. She hung up and kissed Chloe's sparse blonde hair. 'Seems like it's just you and me, kiddo.'

Despite the sleep deprivation and baby brain and the stress of everything that was going on, Janine couldn't rest. Her mind kept going over and over everything she had to do and what could go wrong. Everything had fallen apart, the life she'd dreamed off with a house and a baby and a husband had disappeared with Craig.

*   *   *

It took Janine three weeks to get her single mothers' pension sorted out. Some forms to fill in and bureaucratic hoops to jump through but all in all easier than she thought it would be. The pension wasn't a lot of money, but it would stop her and Chloe from starving and might even pay the rent. Craig hadn't left anything about arrangements with the landlord, despite looking through every scrap of the paperwork left in the house. Janine would have to wait until they contacted her about unpaid rent. She wasn't happy about it, but didn't have much choice.

Vicky had her and the baby over for Sunday night dinner every fortnight, though getting there was much more difficult now she had no car. Craig had taken it when he went, at least he'd left the baby carrier if she ever got another car later. Every so often she would call the office number in the hopes he might pick up. Last week she dialled the number only to hear a recorded message; it had been disconnected.

The journey to Vicky's place involved walking to the tram stop, a tram to the city, a train to Camberwell, then walking to Vicky's house. She refused to pick her and Chloe up from the station. Probably because she was drinking so heavily these days, she didn't trust herself to drive.

To get back to Brunswick in the evening, Janine had to leave at twenty minutes past eight. She would arrive at her mother's about six o'clock, the journey each way could take an hour and a half on Sunday timetables. Part of her thought it wasn't worth trekking all the way across Melbourne every other week, but as one of the few regular social outings she held onto it.

Despite allowing her to visit for dinner, her mother made sure Janine understood she was in the doghouse. They didn't talk about money, nor about Craig or the lack of progress the police were making. If Janine made the mistake of bringing any of these topics up, her mother would get up from the table and leave the room. Sometimes she would not return before it was time to leave. Janine said goodbye through the closed bedroom door and trudged back home.

One Sunday in late July, her mother looked worse than usual. She had become more gaunt since Craig disappeared; having replaced almost all her food intake with wine. She watched her mother sway down the hallway towards the kitchen, her clothes and shoes as immaculate as ever, but there was not much left to fill out the dress she wore.

Janine sat at the dining table, Chloe nestled quietly against her shoulder. Her mother wasn't wearing any jewellery. It had always been a point of pride for her mother to show exactly how wealthy she was by wearing large, often gaudy but very expensive gold jewellery. Rings, bracelets, necklaces, she even had one particularly awful gold and pearl brooch. Today she had none of these on. She wasn't even wearing the wedding band.

'Mum, what's happened to all your rings and stuff?' Janine asked, sure that her mother would simply leave the room, but too curious to leave it alone.

'I got rid of them.' Vicky waved her hand dismissively.

'All of them?' Some pieces Janine had hoped to inherit one day, there were a few heirlooms in among the chunky gold items.

'Yes. It's all gone.'

'Why?'

'I had to. The police are doing nothing about this hole you've left me in, and I needed the money.'

'They would have been worth thousands.'

'They were. I'll have to sell your father's records and stereo soon. My jewellery only just covered the debts I'd accumulated since… well.'

Janine was appalled; her mother would sell everything before trying to get a job. She had to admit she hadn't thought about what it would be like for her mother with all the money gone and a mortgage to pay back. Of course, Vicky would be much too proud to do that to get some sort of unemployment benefit from the government.

'And what about when you don't have anything left of Dad's worth selling? Will it be the silver next? Or the car?'

'Don't be ridiculous.'

'I'm not the one selling everything to feed my wine habit.' As soon as it had left her mouth, she knew it was a mistake. 'Why don't you ask Nan and Pop? They could help, couldn't they?'

'You think I didn't ask? They said I had made my choice marrying Bill and my daughter had done exactly the same thing. They were quite clear that this was my bed and I would have to lie in it.'

Ted had won the argument again. He was not a violent man but from what Janine had seen of him, he had a temper.

Janine desperately wanted to say she was sorry, she'd been blinded by love, the appearance of wealth and prosperity, and have her mother forgive her. But it wouldn't make any difference.

Vicky picked up her glass, still half filled with red wine, and took it to the kitchen bench. She refilled it without saying another word and walked out. Janine heard the bedroom door close behind her. Since having the baby Janine's appetite had been much bigger than before. It must be producing milk to feed Chloe. She put the baby into her pram, tucking her in firmly, and went to the fridge. She found the dessert, chocolate mousse as always, but there was almost nothing else in there. She looked in the freezer and saw a bag of frozen peas and a bottle of vodka.

Mum never liked spirits before. Her mother had fallen into a deep depression, but Janine had no idea what she could do to help. She was on a pension, trying to spend as little as possible, waiting for the day she would have to pay back rent. She lit a cigarette, and took the mousse back to the table. She waited for her mother to yell something through the door about smoking in the house, but it didn't come.

Janine ate her mousse in silence, it didn't taste like much, she wasn't sure whether that was because it was a terrible no sugar no fat version or because she was worried about her mother. No noise came from the bedroom, and Janine started to get the creeps.

She knocked on the door. 'Mum?'

No answer. She counted to ten in her head and knocked again. Still nothing. The creeping feeling wouldn't go away, so she turned the handle.

'I'm coming in.' Janine swung open the door to see her mother lying, fully clothed, on top of the bed. She'd finished off the wine and there was a bottle of pills on the bedside table. A cold hand gripped Janine's belly.

She went to the side of the bed and touched her mother's hand. It was cold and clammy. She shook Vicky's shoulders. 'Mum. Are you alright?'

Vicky's eyes jerked open. 'Get out. You have no right to be in here.'

'Sorry.' Janine leapt back from the bed, surprised at the quiet, cold anger in her mother's voice. 'I wanted to make sure you were alright.'

'Bit late for that now, don't you think?

Janine didn't know what to say.

'Just fuck off. You've done quite enough damage already.'

'Alright. Bye, Mum.' Janine backed slowly out of the room. She took Chloe and the pram and left. She'd never seen her in such a state before, even when she'd thrown Janine out of the house. The hatred in her eyes burned as brightly in spite of all the alcohol and Valium she'd ingested.

As she walked to the train station, one hand holding her jacket tightly around her throat against the bitter wind, Janine wondered if she'd gone too far. Give Vicky some space to let her anger subside. As a teenager she'd asked forgiveness before her mother had been able to stew over the incident. It suited her mother to be the martyr in some ways, suffering but still able to have everything she wanted: the house, the status, the friends. Perhaps she'd alienated her friends with her drinking or maybe she had tried to cut down her spending and her friends didn't want her in the group anymore. Vicky had never been good at sharing, but as Janine thought back over the last few months, there had been fewer stories about Harriet's grandchildren or Stacey's horses or any of the other names.

Maybe a call to her grandparents would help; surely she could convince her grandmother to do something? Her mind went over and over the possibilities on the long journey home to her empty house. If she wasn't careful, Janine would slip into the same patterns as her mother. She needed to find herself some company, and Chloe would need a father figure as she grew up.

23. A New Man #2

Having resolved to get back out into the dating world, since Craig wouldn't be back, Janine started looking for ways to meet people, maybe even a man. The neighbourhood house was no good, full of women mostly, the corner shop was not better, although Francesca was nice for a chat. She couldn't take Chloe into pubs, even if she did it wouldn't do much for her chances. The weather was cold and wet, so she couldn't hang out at the beach or in the parks. The best she could come up with was hanging around in the cafés on Sydney Road.

Most of the other patrons were older Greek and Italian men, she suspected they had been told to get out of the house by their wives and were passing the time before dinner when they would be welcome back. She and Chloe were quite popular with the old gents who would coo and fuss over the baby, taking turns to hold and play with her. A few younger men came by for lunch, the tradies would be in for their sandwiches at eleven, they must start very early for lunch to be at eleven o'clock.

One fellow, a tall, thin streak of a man with wild blonde hair that looked as though he never brushed it, took a shine to her. Whenever they were in the café at the same time he would hang out with her. Sometimes he bummed a cigarette, but today he offered her one.

'Thanks,' she said as she held it to her lips. He leant over and lit it for her. 'Such a gentleman.'

He blushed bright red as he stood up. 'I owe you a couple.' He held the container of lasagne loosely in his left hand and shifted his weight back and forth, rocking on his feet. His boots were filthy, covered in mud, his work pants were the standard workman's blue, his shirt and jacket were the same colour. Janine smiled at the idea of him dressing in the morning, going through a wardrobe filled with blue and carefully selecting just the right shade of faded for the day ahead.

'Do you mind if I sit with you?' he asked.

'Sure.' Janine looked around at the half empty café, none of his workmates were around, she wondered if he'd been put up to it. 'What are you working on?'

'We're digging holes,' he said with a smile. He peeled open the container and dug into his lunch with a plastic knife and fork which looked cartoonishly small in his long-fingered hands.

'Digging holes? Fascinating.' She regretted her sarcastic tone as soon as she'd said it. 'We're just on our daily outing, aren't we, Chloe?' She faced the baby so she wouldn't have to see his reaction.

'She yours? She's gorgeous.'

'Yeah, it's just me and her now her Dad's—' Why was she telling him that? She hadn't even got his name. 'I'm Janine by the way.'

'Bernard,' he said, dropping his knife, wiping his hand and holding it out to her. She shook it, warm and calloused, as she'd imagined. 'Some dudes shouldn't be allowed to father kids. A girl as cute as you has to bring her up on your own.'

Janine was surprised by how angry he sounded. She wasn't quite sure what to say, so she took a sip of her cappuccino and waited.

'Me mum ended up in the same position, when my little sister was three our dad just fucked off. Never heard from him again. I can't fathom it, y'know?'

'I'm sorry to hear that.'

'Mum did her best but money was always tight. I'd never do that to my kids.'

Janine smiled at him. He was sweet in a slightly overbearing way. He made his way through his lunch at record speed, when the container was empty, he took a deep breath and pushed it across the table.

'I know this might be coming on a bit strong, but umm, I'd like to give you a ring sometime.'

She had been waiting for the question, but the flush of blood to his cheeks when he asked her made her want to giggle. 'That sounds nice. I don't get out much, there's not much you can do at night with a baby.'

'That's alright, I'll think of something she can come along to.'

She took out a pen from the baby's bag and wrote her phone number on a napkin. Bernard took it and grinned broadly.

'Thanks, luv.' He turned to Chloe, as she lay gurgling in her pram. 'See you soon, cutie.' He pinched her cheek and the baby frowned, as though considering whether to cry, but didn't.

Janine watched his long, thin frame as he ducked out the front door, through the dangling plastic strips and strode off down Sydney Road. 'You don't like strangers much, little one, I know, but he won't be a stranger too long,' she said to Chloe. She patted the baby's tummy gently, finished her coffee and started for home. The old fella behind the counter nodded at her with a smile as she left; he knew what was going on.

*   *   *

When she arrived home in time to make her own lunch, the same as always, a ham sandwich with lettuce, tomato, salt and pepper, she couldn't stop beaming. He wouldn't call for at least a few days, such were the rules of dating. She didn't have an answering machine, so she would have to be around when he rang, although she had nowhere else to be.

She sat down in front of the TV with her sandwich and a glass of Coke and watched the midday movie. She would feed Chloe after she ate; breastfeeding on an empty stomach tended to make her feel sick.

As Chloe was settling in to the second side for this feed, the phone rang. *It can't be him already.*

'Hello?' she said.

'Yes, is this Janine Barrett?' a rough male voice said.

'Yes, speaking.'

'This is Detective Cochrane, with the Camberwell Police. Have you got a moment?'

Janine shifted in her seat; it had been months with no word from the cops. 'What can I do for you?'

'We've been trying to get onto your mother. I wondered if you'd heard from her?'

A cold, icy feeling gripped her belly. She sat up straighter, and Chloe lost her hold on her nipple and started to cry. 'Sorry, hunny,' she said. 'One second,' she said to Cochrane. She used the moment's delay in repositioning the baby to calm her thoughts.

'I haven't spoken to Mum since, it must have been Sunday, not the one just gone, the one before. She cracked the shits with me, so I thought she was just sulking.'

'Does she often ignore the phone?'

'I wouldn't have thought so.'

'I see. We've tried to phone her, to discuss her case, and I dropped around there a couple of times, but she didn't answer the door.'

'Right.' Janine wanted him to say something reassuring but the detective let the silence stretch out between them. 'Do you want me to try her?'

'If you could. We have some matters we need to discuss, and to be frank, I'm concerned for her welfare. She seemed out of sorts the last time I spoke with her.'

You can say that again. 'I understand, Officer.'

'Detective,' he corrected her.

'Yes, Detective. I can go around there—' she glanced at the time, almost two o'clock. 'I could go today, but I don't have a key. If she decides she isn't talking to me there isn't much I can do.'

'I appreciate it. Tell her to give me a ring as soon as possible, will you?'

'Okay.'

Cochrane gave her his number and they hung up. Janine didn't understand why she should spend her afternoon chasing down her mother when the cops were perfectly capable of going over there themselves. If Vicky didn't want to talk to them, she wasn't likely to let Janine in, and she'd have dragged the baby all across the city for no reason. But she'd promised to go.

She burped Chloe, changed her nappy, and put her back into the pram. Janine checked herself in the mirror, grabbed her things, and went back out into the street.

Normally Janine would nap in front of the afternoon shows, she still didn't sleep well in the bedroom, and she could feel herself nodding off on the tram into the city. She bought another coffee when she changed to the train at Flinders Street.

When she arrived at East Camberwell train station, she was desperate for a pee, but there was no public toilet. The walk to her mother's house was about ten minutes and she hoped she'd last that long. Since the baby came, her bladder was more unreliable than it used to be. If her mother didn't let her in, she'd squat in the garden.

Thankfully Chloe was happy in her pram, awake but keeping herself entertained flailing her hands in front of her face in an uncoordinated fashion. Janine smiled down at her little bundle, even with everything Craig had done, her baby was the best thing in her life.

She dragged the pram up the steps in front of the house and knocked on her mother's door. The plants in the garden around the veranda were looking dry and brown. Perhaps she'd paid someone to take care of it, and it was one of the many expenses she'd had to cut.

She hopped from one foot the other holding her knees together. 'Mum. You need to let me in or I'll wet myself on your front step,' She yelled.

She stopped to listen, pressing her ear to the door, heard nothing, and decided to pee in the garden at the side of the house. Once she'd relieved herself, she went back to the pram at the front door. Chloe had fallen asleep, her chubby forearm lying across her face.

'Mum? Are you in there?' She used the knocker again, then started banging her palm against the door. 'I'm coming around the back.'

She struggled with the pram back down the veranda steps and followed the gravel path around the side of the house, past the spot where she'd peed, and onto the patio at the back. She pressed her face against the windows as she went past, but she couldn't see anything; the curtains were all drawn.

The French doors leading out to the patio were closed, and locked. Usually, Vicky only locked the doors when she wasn't home, but Janine couldn't imagine where she would be at four o'clock on a Thursday. Through a gap in the blinds, she saw at least five wine glasses left around the kitchen. The dirty dishes made Janine anxious.

She's been drinking more, but I thought she was okay. She tried to think of a way of getting into the house. There was a door in through the garage, it wasn't usually locked.

Chloe would be alright on the back patio while she tried the garage. She walked to the front of the house and turned the big metal handle of the garage. The heavy door swung out and up with a groan, at least she was in. There was no car, and she wondered if maybe her mother was out. Still, she'd come all this way, and had to check. The door into the house wasn't locked, and she walked into the laundry. There was a smell in the house like bad breath, but stronger, sour and slightly rotten. She walked back through the house to the kitchen, opened the French doors and pulled the pram inside. It was as cold indoors as it was outdoors. With Chloe safely in the stinking kitchen, Janine went to the other rooms in the house. She opened the junk room that used to be her bedroom, it was almost empty, only a couple of cardboard boxes stacked in the corner. She went past the formal living room; her father's stereo was gone.

She found someone to buy it. Her mother's bedroom was at the front of the house, opposite the formal living room. The smell got worse as she moved through the rooms. Her mother's bedroom door was closed, Janine took a breath and knocked on the door.

'Mum, it's me. Are you okay in there?' She didn't wait for an answer and pushed her way in. The smell was pungent, vomit with undertones of alcohol, and body odour. The room was so dark she could only make out vague shapes. Covering her nose and mouth with her sleeve, Janine flicked on the light.

Vicky was lying on the bed, face down. There was a pile of dried vomit on the floor near her head, red wine from the stain.

'Mum?' She shook her shoulder gently. It was still warm, but so thin she was skin and bones.

'What?' came the muffled reply. Her mother hadn't moved and Janine thought for a moment she'd imagined her response.

'What's happened? Why didn't you answer the door?'

'I didn't want to.' Vicky wiped the back of her hand across her mouth and rolled onto her side. 'You've checked on me, you can go now.'

'How long have you been lying here?'

'Does it matter? Fuck off, will you.'

Janine recoiled, her mother didn't swear. 'I can't. You're lying in a pool of your own sick.'

'That's my business.'

'It's my business too! Cochrane, the detective, sent me over here to check on you because you wouldn't answer the door.'

'I don't want to speak to him either. Incompetent, the lot of them. No leads in months, and they leave me slide into poverty.'

'I think you should come home with me. Until you're feeling better.' Janine regretted saying it immediately, but she didn't have a choice. She couldn't leave her here in the filth and emptiness. They could sell the house and start again. A sharp sadness rippled through Janine, this was the house she'd grown up in, it held so many memories, she didn't want to see it go.

'Why would I go with you?'

'You don't look well. You can't keep living as you are.'

'Going to save me from myself, are you? With no job, and a new baby?'

Janine bit the inside of her cheek to stop herself screaming. 'Fine. Stay here in a pile of vomit, selling things off until you live in an empty house.'

Janine watched Vicky's eyes glaze over as she lay back on the bed. Back in the kitchen, Chloe was grizzling and fidgeting, perhaps the smell was getting to her too.

'Let's go bubba. Leave your stinky Nan to wallow on her own.'

*   *   *

She spent the ride home trying to calm Chloe, who refused to settle. Usually, she was so good on public transport. She got looks from various people judging her for her crying baby taking up all that space with the pram in the peak hour rush. It wasn't her fault she was upset; it was all Vicky. *Why didn't she come with me? Being on her own in that house must be so depressing.*

When she arrived back home at nearly six o'clock Janine was exhausted and starving. She had to call her grandparents. It wasn't her place to rescue her mother, but she couldn't stand by and let her fall apart either. She didn't have Ted and Carol's number; she'd never needed it before.

Chloe was wailing now. The trip home had made her increasingly upset, nothing Janine did soothed her, so she sat in the rocking chair to feed her. For a while Chloe was too distressed to latch on, but eventually she found the nipple. Janine was so relieved at the silence she started to cry. Not only for Chloe, for herself and her mother as well. Since Craig had left, she had been so busy trying to keep herself and the baby alive she hadn't had any time to think about it.

Everything was out of control. It had seemed okay but now she saw things had been deteriorating for a while. The night he'd come home from Tasmania stinking and edgy, the massive payout he'd given Vicky all those months ago should have been an indication it was too good to be true, but she'd trusted him. A handsome smooth talker. He had treated her better than anyone she'd ever been with, but it had all been a lie.

She swapped Chloe to the other side lay her head against the rocking chair. For what seemed like the hundredth time, she asked herself how it had come to this. How had she not known that the deal was fake? that Craig didn't really care for her?

She didn't deserve a nice house, a family, a husband. Maybe her mother was right; everything she'd ever done led her here: alone, living off welfare. She hadn't had any other choice, but what if she'd done things differently? Would she have found her mother in a puddle of sick?

But then she wouldn't have Chloe. She was about the only thing she still loved after everything that had happened. She pushed her finger into the tiny hand and smiled as it curled around hers.

'I'm going to make sure you have it better than I did. I promise,' she whispered into the wispy blonde hair.

She was about to drift off to sleep when the phone rang. The sound must have startled the baby, she turned her head and her ear filled with milk.

'Dammit,' Janine said aloud. She grabbed a cloth to blot the milk away and hurried to the lounge to answer the phone.

'Yes?' she said.

'Sorry, is this a bad time?' the man's voice said.

Janine took a breath; she couldn't place him yet. 'Who is this?'

'Bernard. You said I could call.'

'Goodness, from this morning.' It seemed so long ago.

'Yeah, I didn't want to miss my chance. I don't buy into that waiting thing. It took me long enough to say hello.'

Janine laughed. It seemed so silly that this man thought she was intimidating enough to worry about saying hello to. 'Hello then.'

'Sorry, I guess it's a bit out of the blue. I'll call you another time.'

'It's fine, really. I've had a weird day.'

'Okay, if you're sure.'

'I'm sure.' She sighed; it was nice to have a conversation that wasn't going to blow up in her face. 'What have you been doing today? In the seven hours since I saw you?'

'It's been almost nine, I'll have you know.'

'Right, nine.' She smiled.

'Got home about four, and I've been trying to think of reasons not to call you since then. But I've done everything I can think of, bar rearrange my sock drawer, so I gave in.'

Janine didn't want to talk about her day, it was too soon, and she barely knew this man. She asked him about his work and after a little bit of prompting he turned into a chatterbox. It was easy to talk to him, or at least to listen to him talking.

Her belly grumbled and she remembered she hadn't eaten since her sandwich at lunch time. 'I'll have to go; I have to get dinner on.'

'Of course, sorry. I eat so early I forget that it's dinner time for everyone else.'

'It's fine. I'll talk to you soon, okay?'

'Okay, wait,' he said.

'I'm still here.'

'I meant to ask if you wanted to have dinner on Saturday. I'll come pick you up, we can go somewhere with a highchair and a kids' menu.'

'That sounds nice. I'll confirm with you later okay?'

'Right, yep, okay. Bye then.'

'Bye Bernard.' She hung up the phone and shifted Chloe to her other shoulder. Bernard clearly had no idea about babies; Chloe was still too young to eat solids, but it was sweet of him to think of it none the less. She put Chloe on the rug in the lounge and went to see what was in the fridge. She only realised, staring into the fluorescent and mostly empty depths of the fridge, she hadn't got his number.

24. Who's the Mum Here?

For dinner Janine ate toast with peanut butter and promised herself she would go to the shops in the morning. It was harder trying to shop when she had to take the baby with her. And with only one person to cook for no incentive to make anything new or interesting. Although she put the groceries under the pram and didn't have to carry them home, she wished she had a car. With the pension she wasn't going to starve, and she hoped to be able to afford the rent but she couldn't justify the expense of taking a taxi home. She often ate convenient foods; toast, eggs, and baked beans, plus cigarettes had gone up again.

Bernard called her the next day and told her he would pick her up. She remembered to ask for his number so she could call him back if anything went wrong, not wanting to stand him up if something happened with Chloe and she couldn't come out.

'I understand you have to look after her first, but it will be fine. You just gotta make up your mind and everything will go your way,' he'd said before hanging up the phone.

I'm sure everything in your life had gone the way you wanted it to through the power of positive thinking. It wasn't fair to gripe about his attitude, but a lot of things had gone wrong for her, and of all the things she expected to land her in trouble, settling down and having a baby with a gorgeous, wealthy, handsome man hadn't been high on her list. She didn't deserve someone handsome or wealthy and believing she did landed her in trouble. Bernard was tall, blonde and angular, his face was a little bit alien, and a touch feminine. He wouldn't have been called handsome, but he wasn't ugly either. He seemed easy to read, and she wanted someone who couldn't lie to her the way Craig had.

*　　　*　　　*

Janine wasn't going to drag her and the baby all the way over to her mother's place again if she could help it, but leaving her mother without checking in for over a week until Sunday dinner seemed too long. Vicky still wasn't answering the phone.

She remembered her promise to call her grandparents. She'd been through her address book, and as expected, didn't have their number. Clearly Vicky was no help, so Janine had to go back to the phone book.

Her maternal grandparents lived on a tiny farm in the Yarra Valley. There were ten Goddards in the White Pages, she could eliminate half of them immediately as being in the wrong area, which left five numbers to call.

The first two weren't the right Goddards, the third didn't answer, but on the fourth call her grandmother answered.

'Hello, Carol speaking,' she said.

'Hi Nan, it's Janine.'

'Oh.' There was a pause.

'Are you still there?'

'Yes, dear. I'm sorry, I wasn't expecting to hear from you. It's been quite some time since Christmas.'

Janine felt the words like a punch. She had promised to invite them to meet the baby, she had meant to be a good granddaughter and cultivate a proper relationship with them, but she had been so caught up in her own repetitive, empty life she'd forgotten she had family who were waiting to see her.

'I'm sorry. It's been really busy with the baby and everything since Craig left.'

'What?' Carol sounded shocked.

'Oh.' She hadn't told them. Maybe they didn't know about the money either. 'A few things have happened since Christmas. I thought Mum might have told you.'

'We don't speak to Vicky much.'

'Right.' Janine didn't know what to say. There was so much to tell her, but it was so hard to start. Chloe gurgled in the background.

'What's the baby's name, dear?' Carol prompted.

'Chloe.'

'Very pretty.'

Janine's blood pumped in her ears. 'Here's the thing. I'm worried about Mum. Long story short she lost a lot of money and I don't think she's very well. I don't have a car and I'm a single parent now and I can't go to check on her very often. I called to ask if you would go.' The words tumbled out in a rush.

'Goodness. You're going to have to go back to the beginning, dear, and explain it all more slowly.'

Janine took a deep breath and tried to lay out everything that had happened since she last saw her grandmother. When she said it aloud it sounded awful. She was quite tearful by the time she finished on the puddle of vomit and the empty house.

'That's where I wanted your help.'

'I'll have to talk it over with Pop. I don't know if we can be running up to the city willy nilly because your mother refuses to live with the consequences of her decisions.'

'It's not her fault that Craig was a crook.'

'No, but she put all her eggs in one basket with him, and of course she's not got a job, like a normal person might in her situation. She was always one for being kept.'

Janine was shocked by how angry her grandmother sounded. She'd thought it was because of Ted's stubbornness that they hadn't seen each other for so long, but now she wondered if Carol was just as bad.

'If she was really in such a pickle, she could call us and ask for help herself, but she won't do that either. There's nothing I can do for her.'

'What if she's really sick? Shouldn't we do something?' Janine asked.

'You said yourself you're too busy to check on her. I might be her mother, but she has made it abundantly clear our meddling in her affairs is unwelcome. She'll

317

come to her senses eventually, she always did as a child. She needs to learn her lesson. Speaking of lessons—' Carol took a breath and continued. 'Your child is a bastard, and while I was willing to accept you were going to get married and make a real family, I see I was being naïve. Any child born out of wedlock is doomed to bring down all those around it. Ted and I want nothing to do with you or your illegitimate child. I don't know how you got this phone number, but you'd do well to forget it.'

There was a heavy clunk as she hung up the phone. Her grandmother had been distant all through her childhood, now she knew why. She was bitter and inflexible; Vicky had inherited the trait.

Chloe started to cry; it was time for her feed again. If nothing else the kid was a good eater and growing at an unbelievable rate. In the TV dead zone of the early afternoon she sat in Chloe's bedroom in the rocking chair. She should be more concerned about her mother, go over there to check on her, but it seemed such a hassle. To take the two-hour ride on public transport each way to be thrown out of the house like she was last time. She didn't have a key, what if next time she couldn't even get in?

Something would have to give eventually. It might be sooner rather than later, but she didn't have the energy to care anymore. Janine had her daughter to think about now and couldn't spend all her time worrying about a mother didn't want her there.

Bloody Craig. If he hadn't pushed her to get back in touch with Vicky, she wouldn't feel so guilty and defeated right now. Of course, he was responsible for more that she didn't want to think about. She looked down at the fair, downy hair on Chloe's head and was glad she'd met him, even after everything.

*   *   *

On Saturday night Bernard arrived for their date five minutes early. Janine was trying to coax her hair into something resembling a fashionable style. When she heard the knock at the door, she nearly dropped the hairbrush in surprise.

'I'm coming!' she yelled. She trotted down the hall to pull open the door. 'You're early,' she said.

'Sorry—' Bernard looked her up and down and smiled. 'You look great!'

'I'm not ready yet.' She pointed the hairbrush towards her unruly blond hair. 'Have a seat, you can talk to Chloe.'

'Righto.'

She rushed back to the bathroom, she took one look at the wild state of her hair, partly teased up and a long way from being ready. She sighed and started to brush it out. She pulled it tight and put it up in two small buns. It wasn't what she'd hoped for, but at least this way she didn't look as though she'd electrocuted herself. She had one final look in the mirror in her bedroom; she'd chosen a long, loose-fitting denim skirt, and a knitted jumper she'd found in an op shop on one of her trips up Sydney

Road. Not great, but she didn't have any baby vomit or food stains on her clothes, and her squishy baby tummy wasn't obvious. It would have to do.

When she came into the loungeroom Bernard was tickling Chloe's belly as she lay on her blanket on the floor. She smiled at the tableau before he looked up to see her.

'Why'd you change your hair? I liked it.'

'Sorry, I gave up and did something simpler. I'll do something big next time. It's hard to have time to doll yourself up with this one wanting your attention all the time.'

'But she's so cute.'

Janine smiled. 'Yeah, she's alright.' She scooped Chloe up off the blanket and went to settle her into the pram. 'Where are we going then?'

'I asked the boys at work where there was a good spot where we could take the little one. They reminded me about a pub in Reservoir. It has a playground and stuff, although she's too little for that.'

'Yeah, she can sit up and roll over but that's about it.' Janine laughed. 'Let's go then, I'm starving.'

Bernard stuck out his right elbow. 'Follow me.'

Janine slipped one hand under his arm but struggled to push the pram at the same time.

'I'll take her if you like,' he said and took over driving the pram.

They went out to the street. He had driven his work car, a white ute in need of a good wash.

'We can put this in the back, and you'll have to hold her.'

'Okay then.' Janine didn't think it was very safe, but what could she do. The pram was much too big to put into the cabin with them. 'How far is it?'

'About ten minutes I reckon.'

'Should be okay then.' She took Chloe out of the pram, making sure she was wrapped up securely in her blankets, and Bernard put the pram into the tray of the ute. He tied it to the front railing to stop it rolling around as they drove. She stood and watched him; the cab of the ute was too high for her to climb into holding the baby.

'Jump in,' he said.

'Can you take her, and then hand her up?'

He looked from her to the passenger seat a couple of times, then put his hands out to take the baby. Janine clambered up and he handed back the bundle. She was glad Chloe had just had a feed and was quiet. She hoped it would stay that way for the rest of the evening. It would be a nightmare trying to get back if Chloe decided to start bawling.

It took longer than ten minutes to get to the pub, but Bernard managed to fill in the time telling her about the boys he worked with. It sounded like a nice crew, the sort of blokes she used to work with at George and Elena's business. A short sharp stab of sadness went through her belly when she remembered they didn't want her back. Now Craig was gone, she'd have to find somewhere close to home and a crèche for Chloe. She didn't want to stay on the single mother's pension forever, sitting at home on her own watching daytime T.V. only talking to the baby.

The pub was called The Rose and something, she couldn't read the sign's cursive script; a flat building with a carpark in the front and the back. Inside the huge dining room had with square wooden tables, round backed wooden chairs and dark green patterned carpet. It was hazy with smoke and she realised she hadn't brought any ciggies. *I'll have to go without, I guess.* She followed Bernard pushing the pram into the main dining room.

The waitress sat them in the smoking area and brought a highchair. 'Can I put the pram over in the corner for you?' she asked.

'Sure,' Janine said. If she needed to change Chloe or get any of her things, she'd have to run over to the corner, but it made more sense to put it out of the way.

'Have you been here before?' she asked when they were seated.

'Yeah, a couple of times with the boys. We generally go out after work on a Friday. We're working over near you these days, but the job before was in Preston and we came here a couple of times.'

'What's good? I don't go out much.'

'I usually get the chicken parma. I'm a man with simple tastes.' He winked at her, and she felt colour rise up in her cheeks.

'Sounds pretty good.'

'Right, I'll go up to the bar, they don't come 'round to take your order. You want a beer or something?'

'Oh...' She hadn't had much to drink since she found out she was pregnant. It might be a good way to let go of some of her worry. 'I'll have a house white, but only one, I'm not used to it since having Chloe.'

'Righto.' Bernard stood up and went to the bar to order.

Chloe was too small for the highchair they had brought. She could sit up on her own, but Janine was concerned that she might slip down or pull herself out. She put her hand on the baby's leg and rubbed her thumb up and down her chubby calf. It was reassuring to have her close. She wouldn't have been able to come if she'd left Chloe with someone. Apart from having no-one to call on to baby sit, they hadn't been separated since she was born. The idea of getting back to work was tempting, she missed adult conversations and being useful, but going a whole day without Chloe made her feel as though she might die.

Bernard came back to the table with a pint of dark coloured beer and a glass of white wine big enough to make Janine feel dizzy just looking at it.

'You said one, so I asked them for a big one. They're very generous with their servings.'

'Wow. I might have to take half my dinner home with me.' She was only half-joking. She had never been a big eater, and although she was eating more now, she was breastfeeding, she still wouldn't be able to eat as much as he could.

'Maybe they'll give us a doggy bag.' He winked and sat down heavily. 'Tell me about you.'

'There isn't much to tell; my life is centred around this one.'

Bernard nodded and took a sip of his enormous beer. 'And her dad? Not around anymore.'

Her belly clenched involuntarily. 'No, he's out of the picture.'

'Fucked off, did he?'

'That's the short version.'

'Only version I need. Some blokes—you don't abandon your baby, it's just not on.'

'I'm glad to hear there are some gentlemen left in the world.'

'Plus, she's so cute. I could eat her up!' He leaned over and gummed at her fingers. Chloe squealed in delight and kicked her little legs.

'I think she likes you.' Janine smiled. A child needed a father figure, but she had to make sure he was loving and kind; although after the lies Craig told she wasn't sure she could trust appearances. She certainly couldn't trust handsome men.

'I've always got on well with kids. Never had any of me own but—' He stopped abruptly.

'I'm sorry to hear that. You'll make a great dad one day.'

Sins of the Father

Bernard sat in brooding silence for a little longer than Janine was comfortable with. She didn't want to break it with questions. He'd tell her when he was ready.

'My ex and I tried for a while, but never conceived. Turned out she was on the pill the whole time. Lying whore ran off with a mate of mine.'

'My God. I had no idea.' Janine's hand went still on Chloe's leg who hadn't picked up on the mood and continued to wave her little hands around happily.

'Anyway, enough of that.' Bernard shook his head and looked out the window. For the rest of the evening he talked about work, then football, then back to work; carefully sticking to topics that wouldn't bring up difficult memories for him perhaps. She felt for his pain, having been on the receiving end of plenty of lies. Hopefully it meant that he valued the truth as she did. Their meals were gigantic; her chicken parma was almost the size of her head, and totally covered up the chips underneath and part of the salad was warm where it had been trapped under the chicken.

She'd been so hungry when they left the house, but after a little wine, she couldn't even finish half her meal.

'Are you going to finish?' Bernard asked. He'd got through all of his and was eying off her plate.

'No, do you want it?' She had been looking forward to having the leftovers for dinner the next day, but she wouldn't get possessive of a meal he'd bought her.

'Great, thanks.' He pushed his plate to the side, picked up hers and put in front of him. He managed to get through most of it. He sat back and rested his hands on his belly. On his skinny frame he looked only a little rounder. He must be very active at work to stay so thin and eat so much.

Bernard drove her home, helped her get the pram out of the back of the truck and walked her and Chloe to the door.

'I had a nice time. Thank you,' she said. He looked at her lips as though trying to decide whether to kiss her.

'I did too,' he said. He moved his gaze to the ground before coming back to her face. He took a breath and leaned in to kiss her, gently pressing his closed lips against hers. She held the kiss, but her mind kept drifting to Chloe, squirming in her pram in the cold night air.

She pulled away. 'I'll see you soon.'

'Okay then.'

'Thank you for dinner, we'll have to do it again sometime. Maybe I could cook? Then we wouldn't have to worry about taking the pram in the ute.' She hadn't intended to invite him over for their second date, but taking Chloe out again seemed too hard. It had been pleasant, but next time she would get a babysitter, or leave Chloe with Vicky for a night. The thought reminded her of the state she'd found her mother in last time they saw each other.

'I love home cooking,' he said. He took her hand and gave it a squeeze. 'I eat a fair amount though, so um, maybe cook for three.'

'Deal.' She craned her neck up to kiss him on the cheek. 'I'll call you,' she said and let herself into the house.

'You better.' He was grinning, clearly not concerned she hadn't invited him in.

*　　　*　　　*

In the morning, she woke up freezing after kicking off one of the blankets in the night. She didn't remember her dreams but felt unsettled. It was Sunday, her day to go to Vicky's for dinner. She reached for the phone beside the bed and dialled her mother.

It rang and rang, but no one picked up. Her mother usually had an answering machine but maybe she'd sold it or turned it off. Camberwell was a long way but Janine wouldn't have forgiven herself if she hadn't at least tried to go on as normal. It was the sort of thing her mother would do; pretend everything was fine to keep up appearances.

Janine had thought a lot about what she would do if her mother was in a drunken stupor on a day she was expecting company. She got up and puttered around the house, played with Chloe, tried to read a book but fell asleep and it was still not time to leave.

When it was finally time to go, she called her mother's number again, on the off chance she would pick up. She didn't. There was nothing to do except head all the way over there and hope for the best.

On the tram there was a man rocking back and forth muttering to himself. It didn't sound coherent although she occasionally caught a word or two; she gathered his neighbours were watching him. Thankfully, he got off a few stops later and she didn't have to push her way past him in the city. The train to Camberwell was almost empty, unusual for that time of a Sunday afternoon, but perhaps there was a big football match on, she thought.

The road to her mother's house was eerily quiet. She was sure it was just her imagination. Janine dragged the pram up the steps to the front door and was caught in the face by a leaf blown up by a sudden gust of wind.

Goosebumps broke out along her arms despite the warm coat and scarf she'd wrapped herself in. If it was an omen, she didn't understand it.

It all looked much the same as the last time. She took a deep breath and rang the doorbell, listened for the sounds of footsteps approaching down the hallway, but heard nothing. On a normal day, her mother would wear towering stilettos or clunky square-heeled pumps. She would clump or clip clop down the hallway, depending on the outfit and sometimes on her mood, but now it was silent.

'Fuck.' Janine didn't want to leave the pram on the veranda, so she carefully manoeuvred it down to the path and swung open the garage door. The car was there, perhaps it hadn't moved. She hoped her mother hadn't lain in a puddle of her own sick for days.

The door into the house from the garage was unlocked, and she pushed the pram inside. The smell of vomit and misery was lessened, but she could still catch wafts of it from time to time.

'Mum! I'm here. Where are you?' she called.

She pushed Chloe into the kitchen, put on the brakes and went to look for Vicky. This time she headed straight to the bedroom. There were puffs of bleach and potpourri as she walked up the hallway.

'I was coming. Impatient,' Vicky muttered, emerging from the front bedroom. She looked skeletal. Janine wondered how she hadn't noticed before; sunken cheeks and eyes, her hair brittle and wiry, knees sticking out like lumps from between her twig-like calves and thighs. She had always been obsessed with her diet, but it was a shock to see how she had wasted away. It must have started before the baby was born.

She thought back to Christmas, surrounded by food and couldn't remember her mother eating much, only drinking. All the times she would make meals and barely touch them, claiming she'd had a big lunch with the ladies in one of her clubs; book club, wine club, whinge club.

'Jesus, Mum. You look terrible.'

'I've had the flu.'

'That is not why you were lying in a pool of your own vomit.'

Vicky brushed past her, the bones and ligaments in her feet sticking out as she tottered down the hallway. 'Why did you come the other day? I could have called the police for breaking and entering—'

'I didn't break anything,' Janine said. Her mother didn't acknowledge the baby and she felt a small stab of hurt in her guts. 'I was worried. The police called me to see whether you were okay.'

'Why would they do that?'

'Because they want to give you an update or something, and they couldn't get you to answer the phone or come to the door.'

'Update my arse.' Vicky stood by the kitchen bench, leaning her bony behind against the stainless-steel sink and poured herself a glass of rosé. 'On what exactly?'

'They wouldn't tell me; it's your case remember?' Janine crossed her arms over her chest. It still stung the police didn't share whatever news they might have had with her. She might not have had any savings to steal, but Craig had screwed her over at as much as her mother.

'Mmm.'

'Is that all you have to say for yourself?'

'I might have missed a few calls, I got rid of the answering machine.'

She didn't say she'd sold it.

'Don't you get a pension from the army, as a widow?'

'You only get that if your husband dies at war.' She twisted her face into a sneer and Janine fought the urge to leave right then.

'You can't keep living like this.' She reached out to the pram and jiggled it back and forth, to calm Chloe but she needed something to do with her hands so she wouldn't smack Vicky across the face.

'What choice do I have?'

'You could get a job, for one.'

'They just fall off trees, do they? I have no experience in the last twenty years, I don't know anyone in the business world, and everyone I know is a housewife— they wouldn't be able to help me even if I wanted to.'

Janine sighed loudly. 'You want to be miserable. You've always wanted to be miserable. Even before Dad died you were so set on being a martyr.'

Her mother's lips compressed into a thin line. Despite her skinny arms, she would still be able to slap her hard enough for her ears to ring.

'I'm sorry,' Janine said, too tired to have this argument. 'Maybe we should go.'

'I won't have you wasting the food I've made.' It was a close to a peace offering as Vicky was likely to get.

'What's on the menu?'

'Chicken Kiev. A fellow on the television said it was the latest thing.'

Janine tried not to let her surprise show; had her mother cooked? She sat down at the table dragging the pram after her so she could keep rocking it.

The chicken was dry, covered in breadcrumbs and fried. It seemed so absurd her mother was fading away from malnourishment and this is what she chose to serve. Accompanied by a flavourless salad of iceberg lettuce, shredded carrot, cherry tomatoes and cucumber. Janine knew better than to ask for dressing.

'You can still come live with me in Brunswick. I have a spare room,' she said, although the room wasn't exactly spare, it was filled with the old furniture she couldn't throw away but didn't want to use. 'You could rent out the house and at least pay the mortgage.'

'You want renters living in this house?'

Janine should have known it wouldn't be any use. The house itself was nothing if not the location. Brunswick was far too working class, far to ethnic, to ever be Vicky's home.

'It was just an idea,' Janine said, pushing her half-eaten chicken to the side. Despite being hungry she couldn't make herself eat.

They spent the rest of the evening barely talking, the silences between them seemed to be thick with unspoken words, but neither of them would say anything further. Janine had offered her help twice and her mother was in no mood to offer anything in return. Perhaps all the wine and lack of food had scrambled her brain, or she was the same stuck-up bitch she'd always been. Too fancy for her parents, and her husband, aspirations of grandeur. Everything she'd worked towards, the house, the marriage, her child, had all turned out wrong for Vicky. Feeling pity for her mother was worse than being angry. At least when she'd been angry it was okay to leave her.

'I called Nan and Pop.' She didn't know why she'd brought it up, standing in the hallway about to go home.

'Oh?'

'Nan told me to stick it. She didn't even want to meet Chloe.'

'You told her about Craig leaving then?'

'I told her the whole story.' Janine looked down, afraid to meet her mother's gaze.

'Saves me doing it. It couldn't have lasted. They can't stand me. It was a surprise they wanted to come to Christmas to be honest. I thought Mum might have been dying but she's still hanging on.'

Janine didn't know what to say. Her mother needed help but refused to see sense. It should have been obvious she wasn't thinking clearly to see the way she'd starved herself, but Janine had held out hope her mother would accept.

'Well. You can come stay with me anytime, if you want company or something.'

'If I ever get that desperate, I'll give you a call.'

Janine clenched her teeth and flicked the brakes off the pram with more force than necessary and her toes smarted as she walked towards the train station.

She wondered whether she could call the police, say her mother was a danger to herself, but she wasn't convinced they would take her seriously. Was she bad enough to have her committed? Janine wanted to get her treatment, but it seemed excessive to have her thrown into an institution.

*   *   *

When she got home at nearly ten o'clock, Janine was exhausted. She held Chloe in her arms on the couch for a while, taking comfort from the little girl smiling up at her. She never held a grudge, she cried when she was sad or hungry or tired or cold and smiled when she was happy. Moments like this she was envious of her daughter's simplicity.

Janine wanted to talk to someone, she fought the urge to call Bernard; it was late and he would have work in the morning. Plus, she didn't really know him. She couldn't burden him with her mother's breakdown, or whatever it was.

For the next three days, Janine expected the phone to ring at any moment. Her mother might see sense and ask to stay, even if only for a couple of days, or else a call to say she'd died. It seemed melodramatic, but Janine couldn't stop the images of her mother, motionless, face-down on the bed popping into her mind.

She had an appointment with the mother and baby nurse on Wednesday after lunch. Apart from the regulars at the coffee shop, it was the first person she'd spoken to all week.

'Are you doing alright, love? You seem tired, I mean, more so than usual,' she said after they had measured and weighed Chloe.

'I'm fine,' Janine said.

'Are you sure?'

Janine's bottom lip quivered; she pressed her lips together to stop it. 'I'm going a bit stir crazy. Her dad isn't with us anymore, and my mum's not well.'

'I'm sorry to hear that.' The nurse glanced down at her notes. 'You didn't mention the father had left last visit.'

'I didn't think you'd need to know. I'm still here.'

The nurse smiled a tired smile as though she knew more than she was letting on. 'If you're sure then I'll see you in two weeks.'

Despite her protestations that she was fine, Janine was disappointed how quickly the nurse moved on. It was three o'clock, all the school kids were out clogging up the streets with their loud chatter. She saw two blonde children, five and seven, walking on either side of their dad, holding his hands. He had the same sandy blond hair and wide-set eyes. He didn't say much, instead encouraging them to talk.

She was only about fifty metres from her house but it seemed so much further. Her legs started to fold under her, the next thing she knew she was sitting in a heap on the concrete footpath, bawling and gathering a gaggle of concerned parents and confused looking children.

'Are you alright, love?' The sandy blond man asked.

'I don't know,' she sobbed.

'It's alright,' he said. He knelt next to her on the footpath and rubbed her back. Soothing circles, the way she liked. Her dad had done it when she was small, Craig had done it when she was upset. She sniffed back a big wad of snot and wiped her sleeves across her face.

'I know it's hard. Especially when they're little and you're not sleeping much.' His voice was so soothing. His kids were hovering behind him.

'Is the lady sick, Dad?'

'I don't think so mate. Just having a bad day, right?' He turned to her.

'Yes. I'm just having a bad day.' Janine struggled to her feet. Chloe had started to grizzle and scrunch up her face. 'I'm alright, bubba.'

'Are you going far?' the man asked.

'I'm just up here. If you want to just come with me till I get in the door, that would be really helpful.'

'Wanna come with this lady to her house? Make sure she gets home okay?' He addressed the children. They looked at one another then back to him before nodding warily.

'I'm not crazy, I promise. I'm just a bit sad,' she said. 'Like your dad says, I've had a bad day.'

'I have bad days sometimes,' the younger one said. He seemed to have decided she was alright really.

'Adrian stepped on your sandwich one time, you cried about that when you got home.' The older boy seemed to be following his brother's lead.

'Yeah, Adrian is a poo-head.' He looked at his dad to see if he would get in trouble. The man frowned but said nothing.

They walked along, it wasn't far, and by the time the five of them arrived at Janine's drab brown brick house she felt better. The younger boy had explained, in great detail, why his favourite dinosaur was pterodactyl.

She had calmed down significantly, something about his inane prattle, not demanding anything from her had given her some perspective.

'I think I'll be alright now,' she said. 'Thank you.'

'I hope you feel better tomorrow,' said the younger boy.

'I'm sure she'll be okay,' his dad said. 'We might see you around later, when this one is a bit bigger, maybe.' He smiled at her and she felt a little flutter in her belly. Apart from his eyes being slightly too far apart he could have been a model. His jaw and cheekbones were chiselled as though from marble, and his eyes were a cool steely blue that make it hard to look at him for too long.

'Say bye-bye, boys.'

They both waved and said goodbye. She turned up the driveway into her house and sighed. Her little family needed a father figure. She would call Bernard to keep him interested. He seemed to be happy to have Chloe around and he was a straight shooter; she didn't expect any great deception from him.

25. It's Only Temporary

Janine sat down to dinner a couple of hours later and there was a knock at her front door. She sighed, looked longingly at the chops and mashed potato she hadn't even started, and stood up.

Her mother was standing on the front step, wrapped up heavily against the mild evening, and holding a small overnight bag.

'I've been thinking about what you said.' Vicky stepped into the house. It was only the second or third time she'd ever been there, and not since before Craig left.

'Come in,' Janine said pointlessly, watching her mother glide into the house. She seemed to have found some reserve of energy and poise deep down inside her.

'I'm just having my tea, there is a bit left if you want to join me.' It wasn't really enough for two, but Vicky didn't eat much, so it would stretch.

'That would be lovely.'

Janine had expected her to say no but put together a plate with the remains of the mash, one lamb chop, and some frozen vegetables. They ate quietly, Chloe sat on the highchair smacking a small pile of mash with her palms and smearing it around her face. She wasn't quite ready for solids, but Janine thought it was cute to watch her pretend to eat.

'I spoke to a real estate agent this morning. He's going to list the house for rent, partially furnished.'

Janine said nothing, it was too surreal.

'I know you mentioned renting the other night, and I thought it was ridiculous, but then I called Holly and she mentioned that her niece and her family were looking to come down from Sydney, and I thought if I got renters with good references, who would take the house as is, it would be alright. I'm not going to settle for the first to apply though, obviously. I'll be very careful screening.'

'Of course,' Janine said. She chewed and swallowed her last mouthful. 'You'll stay here while the place is on the market?'

'Yes, the agent thought it would be best if he could get in to make arrangements without me getting underfoot.'

'Right.'

She had managed to make the whole thing seem like her idea. It would have been galling if it weren't so tragic; her mother had never accepted help from anyone not counting the income of her husband, but here she was, bags packed, asking to stay with her daughter. *Maybe now she's here she'll eat more and drink less.*

Janine took the plates into the kitchen and stacked them next to the sink. She didn't have a dishwasher and Vicky wouldn't get her hands dirty in the sink. 'Your room isn't made up, you'll have to give me a hand with it.'

'Alright.'

At the dining table her mother's small frame seemed even smaller with the weight of her financial problems. Having stepped out of the grand house in Camberwell had stripped her of some of her power. She looked old, and crooked in the dark-stained pine chairs.

Chloe needed a bath, having rubbed potato all over herself, squashed it into her clothes and hair. 'Let's clean you up then,' Janine said, picking her up. 'Make yourself at home, Mum.'

Janine went about her usual routine, largely ignoring her mother; a grown woman who could entertain herself.

Once Chloe was bathed and dressed, she put her down to sleep. She would probably wake at two or three in the morning for a feed, but she usually only woke once these days. When she came back into the lounge, her mother was still sitting at the table, staring into space.

'Want to help me get your room set up?' Janine said, putting her hand on her mother's shoulder, as though to a child. Vicky didn't seem to have the strength to react. She picked up the overnight bag and went back down the hallway to the spare room.

There were three sets of drawers in one corner, a white laminated desk, sized for a child, and a king single bed. The bed frame was dark oak, bulky and not to Janine's taste, but the mattress was firm and clean.

'It's bit of a junk deposit, but we should be able to make it nice for you.'

Her mother stood in the room, eyes glassy. Janine put the overnight bag on the desk and went to get sheets from the linen cupboard. She didn't own any single bed sheets, but there were a few sets that had come with the house. She still hadn't quite figured out the nature of the deal with this house. Craig had left nothing and no-one had turned up asking for rent yet, so she hoped she could stay on indefinitely. No doubt a fantasy, she put away a portion of her pension cheques to make sure she could pay when the time came.

*　　*　　*

Vicky showed no interest in getting her house ready for renters. In the days after she arrived unannounced, Janine watched her lose all the energy she had found to get to Brunswick, she sank into the bed in the spare room and didn't come out much. Janine told herself she wouldn't give her any money.

Her mother must have gone out to get wine at some point, when Janine arrived home from her daily outing to the coffee shop she found the first of many empty bottles in the bin. Although she asked her mother to join her at the dinner table each night, their conversation was minimal on the rare occasions she came out of her room.

Bernard came around for dinner the weekend after her arrival and Janine had tried to warn him but he was such a prolific talker he barely heard what she said.

'Hey, gorgeous!' he said when she answered the door. She had Chloe in her arms and her mother was hiding in the bedroom.

'Hi.' She stood on tiptoes to give him a quick kiss on the cheek. 'Come in. You remember I said my mum was staying with me?'

He was already sitting on the couch, making himself comfortable. 'What? You never said that.'

'I did, but that doesn't matter. She probably won't be joining us, she's not well at the moment.'

'I hope she doesn't give me whatever it is.'

'It's not contagious. She might pop her head in, I didn't want you to be surprised.'

'Right.' He sniffed and seemed to be thinking it over. After a moment he nodded his head and held out his arms. 'Give her to me, I'll keep her outta trouble while you finish dinner.'

Janine handed him the baby. He was very good with her, and she smiled to herself that she'd found a man who not only liked her but seemed to like her daughter too.

'What are we having?' he asked, his eyes fixed on Chloe's smiling face.

'Chicken and mushroom pasta. I saw it on a cooking show and thought I'd give it a whirl.' As she said it, it occurred to her it might not have been a great idea to try out a recipe the day she had company. It was too late now. Next time she'd make something form the old standards.

In the end she needn't have worried, the meal was delicious, the chicken and mushrooms tender and creamy and the pasta al dente. Bernard told her all about his week at work, all the dramas between the men in the team, their partners and children, a couple of them even complained about their parents. It was fascinating to hear how much he knew about his co-workers. She had never known nearly that much about Elena and George, and she'd lived with them. He was good at getting people to confide in him, but with her, he mostly talked. At least she didn't worry about running out of things to say. He polished off a huge plate of pasta and accepted a little more when she offered. She'd made enough for six and they'd eaten more than half.

After dinner an awkward silence came over them as she sat back at the dining table. She had cleared away all the dishes and put Chloe into her cot. She was sure he wanted to kiss her, but they were on opposite sides of the table.

'Should we watch some TV?' she asked.

'Yeah, sounds good,' he said.

They went to the dark brown velvet couch, one of the only items she liked that had come with the house and sat at each end of the sofa. Janine switched it on to some Saturday night movie. An American cop going after some bad guy or other, few words and a lot of violence. She was about to change the channel when Bernard shuffled closer to her.

He turned to her and she felt his breath on her neck. She wanted to kiss him, but she thought he liked to be in charge. She waited, feeling his nervous energy coming closer to her.

In the end she turned to him, his face only centimetres hers and kissed him. A chaste kiss, lips on lips, and for a while he was stiff. She thought he might pull away, but he melted towards her, parting her lips with his tongue, and gently probing her mouth and lips. She was excited, she hadn't been kissed in a while and, since Chloe had been born, her sex drive had been higher than while she was pregnant. She felt heat spreading from her groin and her nipples became erect. There was wetness in her bra and she hoped that she hadn't started lactating. As much as Bernard might like Chloe and accept her single mother status, she didn't think he'd be into milk.

He put his hands out around her waist and drew her towards him, her knees were pushed into his groin and she could feel the hot, hardness there. They had left all the lights on in the kitchen and loungeroom, and it was much too bright. Especially with her mother in the spare room, she kept listening for the sound of the door handle turning.

'What's wrong? Should I stop?' he asked. She had stiffened at the thought of her mother walking in.

'No—let's go into the bedroom. I don't want to get busted.' She laughed awkwardly.

'Right, that would be shit.' He stood up, adjusting his crotch, and held out his hand. 'After you.'

Bernard closed the bedroom door with his foot and pushed her back onto the bed playfully. She giggled and he climbed up next to her.

They spent a long time kissing and exploring each other's bodies with their hands. He was tall, and skinny, under his shirt he had fine hair running in a line up from his groin and a tuft in the middle of his chest. His body was different from anyone else she'd been with, Spider had been skinny, but small and wiry with cold, clammy skin. Bernard seemed to be on fire; every part of him she touched burned under her fingers.

He was a gentle lover. By the time they got to intercourse Janine thought she might swallow him whole and his tender thrusts were disappointing, however he was consistent and lasted much longer than any of her other lovers. When they finished, she hadn't had an orgasm, but she was quite satisfied none the less.

He fell asleep almost immediately, leaving Janine to listen to his breathing and the sounds of the house.

She heard her mother get up and pad down the hall to the kitchen. It felt like she had gone back in time, when she'd lived at home, she was sure her mother had heard what went on with her father. Sometimes she thought it must be why she was so snarky when he was home from the army. Vicky had never been particularly maternal, but when Bill was away, they had a routine, a grudging ceasefire, but when he was back and Janine got more attention than Vicky, the delicate balance was lost.

Having her mother living with her now had seemed like the only option, but she hadn't quite thought through the practicalities. Vicky was in her house, not the other way around. When she was sulking in the bedroom, there was no conflict but what happened when she decided to come out was yet to be tested. She rolled over and tried to get to sleep against Bernard's smooth, hot skin.

*   *   *

She didn't sleep well; Bernard was like a hot water bottle. She'd spent a most of the night with her leg out of the blankets. He hadn't stirred when she got up to feed Chloe in the night, and he was still sleeping soundly when she crawled back in afterwards.

She woke early in the morning, despite the lack of sleep. She left him there and took a long shower, washing her hair and luxuriating in the hot water on her skin. She went to the kitchen in her dressing gown, the fluffy towelling one she liked in winter. Her mother had taken a portion of the pasta, she was eating even if it was when no one was watching her.

Janine made coffee, she took a mug down to Bernard and wafted the scent towards him. He stirred a little but didn't wake. She left the cup on the bedside table and went to sit in the rocking chair in Chloe's room. She watched her baby sleep, tiny hands opening and closing and her face scrunching itself into different expressions. She'd read somewhere it was a way to develop the muscles and try out the expressions as they slept. She sipped her coffee and pulled her feet up under the hem of the dressing gown.

Bernard was stable, someone who could be a masculine role model for Chloe. If her mother managed to get herself together to rent the house, she would have money coming in and maybe wouldn't stay with Janine. She couldn't believe it was what Vicky wanted, to be living in a tragically suburban brick house in Brunswick with her daughter. She wouldn't have told her Camberwell friends about the change in her circumstances.

After an hour Janine was hungry, and Chloe had woken for a feed as well. She made toast with peanut butter and sat with the baby in front of the television. The early morning cartoons were mind-numbing but they kept her mind off the man sleeping in her bed. It was only just after eight o'clock, too early to wake him on a weekend.

She fell asleep with Chloe in her arms and woke to a kiss on her forehead.

'You looked so cute, I didn't mean to wake you,' he said.

'Hi.' She smiled up at him, his hair was sticking out at amusing angles and his face had the slightly squashed look of a long sleep. 'I got hungry, but I can get you something if you like.'

'I saw the coffee on the bedside table, but it's cold. I'll make you another one, you're busy.' He pointed to the small shape in her arms.

'Thank you.' She directed him to where the coffee stuff was, the bread and peanut butter were still on the bench. The quiet domestic scene made her hope one day she might have a little house for her and the baby, and a man to make it a home.

After he'd eaten, Bernard came to sit with her on the couch. He still smelled like sex, and it reminded her of what they'd done the night before. It had been a while since she'd felt so erotically charged. He rested his head on her shoulder and mumbled something.

'What was that?' she asked.

'I said, I wish I didn't have to go.'

'Have you got something on?'

'Yeah, gotta go do some garden stuff for mum. She seems to think it's a good idea to give me jobs to do so she gets to see me. I can't complain too much, gives me something to do with my hands while she tells me all the gossip.'

Janine smiled; he had inherited his mother's gift for talking. 'It's good you take care of her.'

She heard the tell-tale squeal of the door of the spare room swing open, and tensed. Bernard lifted his head from her shoulder and rearranged himself. It was sweet he wanted to look nice for her mother.

Vicky came into the kitchen, she picked up the kettle. 'You didn't make one for me?' she asked, her voice raspy from sleep or wine, Janine couldn't tell.

'That's my fault,' Bernard said. He sat forward on the couch as though about to leap to her aid.

'And you are?'

Janine clenched her teeth, apart from it being none of her business who Janine had to stay in her own house, she had told Vicky she was having a friend to visit, and his name. 'This is Bernard, remember? I told you he would be coming for dinner last night.'

'Yes, you mentioned having company for dinner.' She sneered the last word and Janine had to bite her tongue to keep from snapping back.

'I'd better get going,' Bernard said after an extended pause.

'Do you want a shower?'

'Nah, it's okay.' He was uncomfortable, Janine refused to let her mother ruining this relationship. He had pulled his clothes back on and only had his boots to slip back onto his feet. Janine stood up to see him to the car.

'I'm sorry about Mum,' she said, as he pulled open the door of his ute.

'It's okay. I do have to get going.'

'It's my house, she's staying with me. If she doesn't like who I have to visit she can find somewhere else to live.'

'Don't be too hard on her, I'm sure she's just being protective.' He smiled, a broad toothy grin and he seemed so young. 'I'll see you soon.' He kissed her hard on the lips, reminding her once more of his gentle and competent lovemaking.

'I can't wait.' She winked and turned back to the house. She waved and he beeped his horn as he pulled away.

26. My House, My Rules #2

'Do you have gentlemen callers often?' her mother asked. She sat at the dining table, her hands steepled together over the cup of coffee. Dishevelled and gaunt but doing her best to appear haughty.

'I'll only remind you of this once; this is my house, you are staying here as a favour. If you don't like the choices I make, you can either leave, or keep quiet. I am not going to justify myself to you.' She spoke as calmly as she dared. The warm, tender feelings from the night before had vanished and a hard, hot rage had formed in her belly.

'Is that how it's going to be? You convince me to leave my home after thirty years and now you tell me I have to live by your rules?'

Janine unclenched her hands, which had formed fists beside her. 'I never forced you to leave. It was either rent or sell the house and live somewhere else. I'm trying to do the best by you, but if you're going to behave like this, you can go back to your empty house until you choke on your own vomit or they default on your loan whichever comes first.'

Vicky sat perfectly still for a long moment. Janine expected her to throw the cup of coffee but she didn't. She stood up silently and went to her room. Janine let out her breath and turned to look down at Chloe. She put the baby down for a while on the lamb's wool rug on the floor, she liked to stare at the ceiling and kick her legs. Janine tidied the kitchen and made another coffee.

She was just about finished drying the dishes and putting them away when she heard her mother's bedroom door open again.

Vicky tottered into the kitchen, she'd made herself up, put on a black cocktail dress which was both ill-fitting and inappropriate for ten in the morning, black heels and an over-sized black fur coat. Janine hadn't even realised she still had that coat.

'I'm going out,' Vicky said, picking up her handbag and car keys.

'Are you sure you're up it?'

'I may be forced to live here, but you will not tell me what I can and cannot do.' Vicky swayed a little and Janine realised she must have been drinking from her stash in the bedroom while she changed.

'You look a bit peaky is all.'

'Keep your pseudo-concern to yourself.'

Janine sighed and turned back to the dishes, any attempt to keep her in the house probably only encouraged her to leave. She heard the front door close and her mother's car start in the driveway. She squealed out onto the road and roared off down the street.

If she kills someone with that car because of her drinking I'll never forgive her. Such a hard thought she felt guilty immediately.

She had no concept of how long her mother might be gone and decided she would stick to her usual routine.

It was mid-afternoon, after she'd returned from a walk down to Sydney Road for a pastry that she started to worry something was wrong. There was nothing to do except wait. To call the police or the hospitals this early would be paranoid, but she felt an almost irresistible urge to do it anyway.

Night fell and still her mother didn't return. Janine distracted herself by walking to the fish 'n' chip shop and bought a hamburger with the lot for dinner. She paced around the lounge; even the television wasn't enough.

She gave Chloe her nighttime feed and put her to bed. It was no good waiting up for her mother to come home. For all she knew she'd gone back to Camberwell and drunk herself into a stupor. Janine went to bed shortly afterwards, with one of the sleeping tablets she'd stashed from the last time she went to see the doctor. She made a mental note to get some more.

*   *   *

Janine woke feeling groggy and strange. Chloe was screaming in the other room and she wondered how long she'd been in that state.

She pulled herself out of bed and staggered down to the nursery, each step made her vision jar nauseatingly. The last time she'd taken one of the sleeping pills had been before Chloe was born and it hadn't occurred to her she wouldn't hear her crying.

'I'm so sorry, baby, I'm so sorry.' She scooped up her daughter, placing her against her shoulder and bouncing. Usually this would calm her quite quickly, but Chloe wouldn't be soothed.

'Ssh, shush now.'

Outside the sky was slate grey, dawn was coming. Janine had missed the feed she usually did in the middle of the night. 'Poor little thing, you must be starving.'

She tried to feed her in the rocking-chair but Chloe was too distressed. Janine was tempted to put her back into the crib and crawl back into bed. The fog of the sleeping pill clouded her mind and her eyes slipped closed as she rocked back and forth.

Eventually Chloe had calmed down enough to feed. Janine fell asleep several times and jerked awake when her head lolled to one side or the other. When she'd eaten her fill, the sun was fully risen although the day was still cloudy and grey. The baby went straight back to sleep once she'd finished but Janine thought she'd better stay up.

In the spare room where her mother had been sleeping, it smelled musty and there were two empty wine bottles on the floor next to the bed, but no sign of Vicky. The tight, sick feeling in her stomach was back, even stronger than yesterday.

*   *   *

Janine dozed on the couch with Chloe on her lambswool on the floor when she heard a knock at the front door. It took her a while to register the noise, the sleeping tablet had really knocked her around, or maybe exhaustion, she couldn't tell.

Her hair was a fly-away mess of tangled blonde which she smoothed down as best she could on the way to open the door. She looked down at the grey tracksuit pants and oversized windcheater she was wearing. She wouldn't normally be seen in the outfit but it had seemed unnecessary to dress properly. She hadn't even made it to the café this morning.

She turned the deadbolt and pulled back the door, squinting a little at the pale, cold winter sunshine. On the doorstep were two uniformed police officers. One tall man, broad-shouldered, no neck to speak of, and big flat hairy hands, the other was a tall slim woman, her black hair pulled severely back from her face so she looked surprised.

'Can I help you?' Janine asked.

'We're looking for a Ms Janine Barrett,' said the woman.

'That's me.'

'I wonder if we could come inside,' the male officer said, his eyes travelling up and down her messy appearance. She crossed her arms across her chest, hugging herself.

'Sure, I guess.' She turned around and led them back through the house to the lounge. 'Sorry about the mess, the baby, you know.'

Chloe lay on the floor kicking her legs and burbling. At least someone was having a good time. She waved towards the sofa but the police both remained standing. 'Can I get you some tea, or something?'

'No. Why don't you take a seat, Ms Barrett.'

'Janine is fine,' she said.

'Janine,' the man started. 'I'm Sergeant Robert Frank and this is my colleague Constable Eliza Torres. We're her from the Brunswick West station. You really should sit.'

Janine sat on the couch, her heart had started to flutter in her chest and she was painfully aware of how tall and imposing they both seemed as she looked up their noses.

'I'm afraid we have some bad news,' Frank went on.

Janine felt she was supposed to say something but had no idea what was expected.

'It's your mother. We understand you're the next of kin.'

'What's she done? She was staying here you know. She was going to get the money, if that's why you're here. We just need some more time.'

'What? No, we've found her,' Torres said.

'As I was saying, we've found her, and her car, near the corner of Melville Road and Hope Street after a single car collision with a light pole.'

The fluttering in Janine's chest stopped, she couldn't breathe. 'Oh my God, is she alright?'

'I'm sorry. She was taken to the Royal Melbourne Hospital and was pronounced dead on arrival,' Frank said.

'What? When?'

'She died in the early hours of this morning, it took us a while to locate you.'

'I guess this place is in Craig's name.'

'Who's Craig?' Torres asked.

'My boyfriend—ex-boyfriend.' Janine corrected herself. 'How did you find me?'

'The Camberwell boys had this address.'

'Oh.' Janine sat back on the couch, part of her wished that it would swallow her, and she wouldn't have to think about any of this anymore.

'Ms Barrett? Are you alright?' Frank asked. She wasn't alright, she had to concentrate all of her energy on keeping her breaths coming in and out. The room was spinning and she might be sick.

'You don't look very well. Torres, get her a glass of water, will you?'

Janine stared up at the off-white paint of the ceiling. She felt someone press something cold and hard into her hand. She looked down to see the glass of water and was almost surprised the police officers were still there.

'What now?' she said.

'We need you to make a formal identification of the deceased and then you'll need to make funeral arrangements.'

It sounded like hard work. A shiver ran down her spin and she sloshed some of the water from the glass over the back of her hand. 'What happened exactly? You said single car?'

'Yes. From what we can tell, there were no skid marks, it doesn't look like she tried to stop herself. She may have fallen asleep at the wheel, her blood alcohol was extremely high,' Torres trailed off.

'Or she might have done it on purpose. It's difficult in these situations to know what happened,' Frank said.

'But no one else was hurt?'

'No. Only Mrs. Barrett.'

'I guess that's a blessing. She's—' Janine sighed. 'She's been quite unwell recently. I'm not altogether shocked.' She reached up to wipe the tears away from her cheeks, unsure if they were tears of grief, or shame, or relief.

'We'd like you to come with us now to make the ID,' Frank said. 'You can come with us in the police car or follow along if that's more convenient.'

'I don't have a car.' Janine glanced down at the baby. 'Can she come with us?'

The officers looked at each other. 'There isn't a baby seat fitted. Can you leave her with someone? A neighbour maybe?'

'I don't know anyone. I would have left her with Mum, but…' The silence hung in the air between them. Static crackled through the radio and a loud car rumbled past outside.

'We'll have someone come and pick you up,' said Torres.

'Okay.'

'We'll see ourselves out.' Torres pulled out a business card and left it on the dining room table before ushering Frank back out the front door.

Once the cops were gone Janine remembered how to breathe again but felt as though a massive weight sat on her chest. Her eyes were blurry with tears and she wanted it all to go away. Maybe if she wished hard enough, she would wake up and it would all be a dream; Craig would be here, his investments would be legit, her mother would still be alive, everything would be okay.

She squeezed her eyes shut but it didn't help. She lay back on the couch gasping, trying to make sense of what her life had become.

*   *   *

Janine had told herself that she would do a better job than Vicky, she would be a better mother and have a more successful life. When she'd asked Vicky to come and live with her it was to protect her from herself, and from the storm Craig had created. Now her mother lay in a morgue cold, alone and it was her was more than Janine could cope with. She had no more sleeping pills, but her mother had vodka.

She stood in the bedroom for a long moment before she could bring herself to take the dead woman's drink. Chloe was in the lounge, maybe crying but Janine was beyond caring. She needed to numb the hurt and anger inside her and the baby would wait.

When she got through half the bottle, she had sufficiently blurred the edges of reality and could leave the house and do what she needed to do.

*   *   *

The cost of the taxi to and from the morgue were more than she had spent on herself in months. The whole ordeal took nearly three hours and by the time she was home again Chloe was wailing to be fed and Janine needed a lot more alcohol to take the edge off everything she was feeling. She took the rest of the bottle of vodka from the spare room, her mother hadn't stayed long enough for it to be her room, sat in front of the TV and attached Chloe to her breast. She sloshed through the remainder by the time Chloe had finished feeding, lay her head back against the couch and closed her eyes.

She woke to the sound of the phone ringing.

'Hello?' Janine said.

'Oh, it's Carol dear. Are you alright?'

'Nan.' She breathed the word. If anyone would understand the complicated way she felt, it would be Carol.

'We heard about what happened. The police gave me your number dear; I didn't write it down last time we spoke.'

You never wanted to talk to me again last time.

'I just thought you might need a hand with the baby, now that you're having to do all that funeral business and what-not,' Carol continued.

'I thought you would be doing the funeral?'

'No dear, we're much too old to be doing that.'

'I don't know what to do.' The world had shifted on its axis and she regretted drinking so much, her mind felt fuzzy and unresponsive.

'You'll be fine. The funeral director will do most of the work. It's expensive though, dear, you'll have to work out some sort of payment plan, or try to get someone who is willing to wait for probate to go through, I know you don't have much.'

'You won't even cover the costs? I understand you don't want to do the work.' Despite her fuzziness the thread of her grandmother's conversation was finally coming through; she'd called to say she wouldn't help.

'No dear, it should come from the children.'

Janine's mouth worked up and down trying to find the words to describe the bile and anger now bubbling in her belly.

'We'll come to see you in the next few days, to make sure you're getting on alright.'

'No, don't. I'm doing fine.' Janine didn't want Carol in her house looking for reasons to criticise her.

'Nonsense, we'll bring you some casseroles and have a cup of tea. Alright, we'll see you soon.'

Janine hung up the phone with a sense of apprehension. Her grandmother, the same woman who had wanted nothing to do with her and her bastard child, had invited herself around to check up on her.

Despite the rollercoaster of emotions she'd felt in the last day or two, the thing she felt now was dread.

27. The Empty House

At some point in the next few days Bernard called her; her sense of time passing had stopped with the visit to the morgue and the alcohol didn't help. She must have invited him to visit as she woke to insistent knocking at the front door.

'Oh, hi,' she said.

'Geez, I thought you'd be happy to see me.'

'I am.'

'But?'

'You know how I said I'd had a bit of a shock?'

'Yeah. Should we go inside to have this conversation?'

'Right. Sorry.' She stepped back to let him into the house. It was messy and probably smelled of dirty nappies and alcohol. If she'd remembered he was coming she might have tidied up. A slow burn of shame started in her belly.

'Fuck, what happened here?' He looked around the disaster of a lounge room.

'I was about to tell you—'

'I think I need a cuppa tea for this. If there are any cups, or tea for that matter.'

'There's always tea.' She tried to smile as he followed her to the kitchen to watch the kettle boil.

'So, what's happened?'

She sighed. 'Mum died.'

'Fuck me. I figured it was something bad, given the state of the house but I did not expect that. I'm so sorry.' He reached forward and drew her into a crushing hug. She could smell his body, slightly stale from working all day, and was comforted. 'She seemed okay. What happened?'

'She crashed her car into a light pole,' she said, her voice muffled by the fabric of his shirt and the tears that had started to stream down her face.

'Jesus.' He stroked her hair awkwardly. 'Are you coping? I mean, you know you smell like a homeless person, right?'

'Hey!' She tried to push him away, but he held her firmly.

'I'm teasing. Want me to watch the rug rat while you have a shower or something? I can make my own tea.'

'Good idea. I haven't been doing much except drinking and sleeping.'

She poured hot water over the teabag and handed the mug to Bernard. He was doing his best to show he cared for her, but his words had fed her shame. Not only was she responsible for driving her mother away, but she was allowing her death to destroy her house, dignity, and care for the baby. If this was the sort of mother she was, she had no right to criticise Vicky. At least she'd always been there to make sure she was clean, had food to eat and a roof over her head.

Janine went to the bathroom, turned on the shower and stripped off her days' old clothes. She had no idea whether there was anything clean to put on afterwards. *Pull yourself together*. She had responsibilities, to her mother and her daughter, and couldn't fall apart.

Janine shuddered to think what Carol would say if she saw the state of her. Her grandmother made Vicky look reasonable. The shower helped her feel almost human again, and despite being a little bit drunk from earlier, she was thinking more clearly than she had in days. Dressing in a pair of jeans, a clean T-shirt and jumper she went back to the lounge to Bernard.

He was sitting on the floor, with Chloe lain along his legs. He was talking to her in a singsong voice and she seemed to be making noises in response.

'Having a good chat?' she asked.

'She's been telling me all about her day, haven't you? Yes, you have.'

She smiled and went to sit next to him. 'You need me to take her back?'

'Nah, I'm alight. I was gonna tidy up, but she's too darn cute.'

Janine rested her had on Bernard's shoulder. 'You're a good man.'

'I try,' he said.

Janine wanted to stay there, leaning on him. While Bernard entertained Chloe, Janine cleaned up. Put on the washing machine, emptied the bins, and washed the dishes. Each thing she ticked off her mental list made her feel lighter; the act of cleaning was washing away emotions she couldn't deal with. She swept the kitchen but didn't vacuum; Chloe hated the noise and she was being so good with Bernard it would be a shame to ruin it.

'My grandmother says she's coming to drop off some casseroles.' She was standing in the kitchen, waiting for the kettle to boil again.

'That's nice of her.'

'I'm not sure. She told me she wanted nothing to do with me and Chloe a couple of weeks ago when I asked for help with Mum. A bit convenient now I'm on my own she wants to walk back into my life.'

'Don't be too hard on her. She's trying to comfort you. Remember she just lost her daughter—it's your mum's mum, right?'

'I guess.'

Carol was hardly the sentimental type. If she was trying to reconnect, she should at least give her the benefit of the doubt.

Janine looked at the time, after six o'clock. 'I don't have any food in the house.'

'Let's order pizza, my treat. Then maybe tomorrow I'll take you to the shops.'

'You're not working tomorrow?'

'It's Saturday. This thing really must have knocked you if you've forgotten what day it is.'

'Yeah.' It wasn't just grief that made it hard to keep track of days, the monotony of caring for the baby and having no visitors made everything blur together.

*   *   *

Janine slept better with Bernard there with her and the house looked much better than it had, but she was still filled with dread when her grandmother showed up on her doorstep at nine o'clock the next morning.

'Hello dear, you look dreadful. I hope you've been looking after yourself properly,' Carol said.

'Come in, please.' Janine was still in her pyjamas and robe, but at least the baby was fed and gurgling happily.

'And how's my little girl?' Carol bent to pick her up. She was cradling her grandchild when Bernard surfaced from the bedroom, wearing only a pair of track-suit pants.

'Who might you be?' Carol asked, her voice sounded cheerful and her mouth curved up in a smile, but there was a chilliness in her eyes that set Janine on edge.

'Bernard, lovely to meet you.' He stuck his hand out confidently. Perhaps he was used to finding random members of her family in the house when he got up.

'You live here, do you?'

'No, got me own place up the road. Keeping Janine company in this difficult time. She's a single mum, you know, that's hard enough…'

He was skirting around the topic, everyone in the room, except the baby, knew what he meant.

'That's very sweet of you.' Carol's tone did nothing to reflect the sentiment of her words. She frowned deeply and jiggled Chloe on her hip.

'Coffee, Nan?' Janine said.

'That'd be lovely.'

Bernard retreated to the bedroom, Janine hoped it was to get dressed, while she made the coffee.

'I've come to talk to you about the funeral arrangements,' Carol said.

'I thought you weren't getting involved?'

'I'm not. But there's a certain decorum expected and I wanted to make sure you wouldn't bring us down with any ill-advised guests or tacky ceremonies.'

'Thanks.' For the first time Janine realised there were worse mothers than Vicky.

'I don't want this Bernard invited to my daughter's funeral. I'm sure he has his—uses, but he isn't family.'

'Sure.' Janine sighed. She'd hoped to have a friendly face there to help get through the funeral. Carol had a point, he barely knew her, but the thought of attending alone with all her mother's friends, and her stone-faced grandparents made her want to call the whole thing off.

'I think that's stirred now, dear.' Carol pushed her hand away and took her cup. Janine stood, her mouth agape at the rudeness for a long moment before she could calm herself enough to go back to the dining table.

'Sit down, dear.' Carol had taken the chair at the head of the table. 'As far as I know, you're set to inherit all your mother's assets, such as they are. You know she refinanced the house to go into a deal with Craig and the debt will now need to be cleared. You'll have to sell the house; you'll never earn enough to pay the mortgage since you didn't finish school.'

'Couldn't I rent it out?'

'Don't be stupid, dear. You won't get anyone to pay enough to get rid of the mortgage. Your mother was quite idiotic to think the investment scam would be enough to live off and pay back the bankers.'

'Oh.' Janine took a sip of her coffee and stared down at the light-coloured pine table. Her childhood home, the one she'd driven her mother out of with Craig's web of lies. Over the last few months her mind had often come back to how she could be so naïve to trust him? He was too good to be true and she'd been so desperate for love she'd glossed over anything that seemed questionable or strange.

Bernard come into the kitchen, dipped his head to Carol and set about making himself a cuppa.

'Sort out the sale of the house as quickly as you can. The longer it sits accruing debt, the more stuck you'll be. Sell off her things as well, nothing in the house is worth keeping.' Carol lowered her voice to a hissed whisper, she obviously didn't want Bernard to hear her.

'I'll get onto it first thing on tomorrow.' Janine said. She wished she could think of a polite way of telling her grandmother to buzz off, but nothing came to mind.

'I'm sure you can manage it dear, but I do worry about you. Alone with a new baby.'

Janine felt the hackles on the back of her neck rise. 'I'm doing okay, really.'

'You know we could take the baby so you can sort out the mess your mother has left behind.'

'I couldn't do that, but I'd be glad of a hand with the funeral and the estate stuff.'

Chloe wouldn't be in any physical danger with Carol and Ted, but all her instincts screamed against it. Janine had ignored her instincts plenty of times, and it had always turned out badly. This time she was determined to protect Chloe if it was the last thing she did.

'As I say, dear, we're happy to take the baby for a while, but the death arrangements fall to you. I'm sure your mother appointed you the executor, that's not a responsibility to shirk lightly.'

'You're right.' Janine clasped her hands together and watched Chloe wriggling in her grandmother's grasp. 'Looks like she needs feeding, I'd better get on. Thank you for dropping by. I'll be in touch if I need a hand with Chloe.'

Carol glanced at her half-finished coffee. Janine sat up straighter and prepared for the criticism she was sure was coming.

'You know what's best, I'm sure,' Carol said. 'Do keep in touch.'

'I will.' Janine stood and took the baby back.

She followed Carol to the door to see her off. She stood on the front step, waving Chloe's little hand at

Carol's car as she drove away. 'Nosey bitch,' she muttered.

'Is it safe to come out?' Bernard asked from the hallway behind her.

'She's gone.'

'What a piece of work.'

'You think so?' Janine turned back to Bernard, still shirtless and wearing a lopsided grin.

'Come to meddle and criticise. You'd never know it was her daughter who'd died.'

Janine made a noncommittal grunt.

'Why don't you feed the munchkin and I'll make you some eggs for breakfast.' He reached out to stroke her cheek with the back of his hand. Such a tender gesture she felt she might break down and cry.

'I don't think we have any eggs.'

'I'll grab some. Take it easy—you're grieving remember?'

She nodded. He didn't need to remind her what she'd lost. She had hated her mother; the arguments, the interfering and criticism, but she was now starting to see she'd learned from the best. Carol was not only critical and manipulative but covered it up with false friendliness. At least with Vicky if she didn't like you, you knew about it, if she didn't like something you'd done, she'd tell you. Carol's agenda was totally hidden with motives Janine could only guess at.

*   *   *

For the next week Janine did her best to juggle the baby, the estate, and finalising details with the police. It was difficult, but she felt useful again.

The police had contacts in the funeral and estate business, and she managed to find help for both. She walked through the house in Camberwell, the estate team had emptied it to sell everything worth selling, and taken the rest to the op shop. The empty house echoed as she walked over the bare floorboards.

She stood at the door of what had been her bedroom. A tear slipped down her cheek to realise it was over. This would be the last times she ever stood in this house. She'd put it on the market and the real estate agents would put display furniture in it shortly. She'd considered coming to the open house and auction but it would be too hard. Everything she'd loved, and hated, about her life growing up in this house was gone; a shell for some other family to put their lives into.

In her mother's bedroom all that remained of her life were the depressions in the carpet where the furniture had stood; queen-sized bed, dresser with the big ugly mirror, the bench at the foot of the bed where her mother had put on her shoes every day for twenty-five years, all gone.

Even the smell of the house was different, everything steam cleaned and deodorised, lemons and bleach.

'You ready to go, hun?' Bernard said, startling her.

'Yeah.'

He'd come with her on his day off to make sure she had company. He'd been such a rock for her, staying with her every night, even getting up to soothe Chloe when she cried sometimes. Janine didn't want to admit it, but she was getting used to having him around.

It wasn't love, not like with John, or Craig, but she was much better off with a nice, stable guy who was kind to her. She'd learned it was time to settle for good enough, and Chloe needed a father. No child of hers would grow up without a paternal figure and Bernard was very patient with her.

'Want me to drop you home? I got a couple of things to get done and I'll be back tonight,' he said. He'd bought a baby seat for the ute. It looked ridiculous in the middle of the bench seat but she'd cried when he showed her.

'That's fine.' She leaned over to give him a peck on the lips before buckling herself in and checking Chloe was secure in her capsule.

*　　　*　　　*

Janine opened the front door of the house and immediately something seemed off. A smell in the air; a little bit woody but also like incense.

Craig's cologne. She shook her head; she must be tired if she was hallucinating smells.

She put Chloe down in the play pen. Not quite at the stage where she could sit up or crawl around the baby could roll over and entertain herself gurgling and mumbling. Sometimes Janine would sit watching her; the most perfect thing in the world. On paper she had everything she wanted; a nice boyfriend, a nice house, a gorgeous baby, but something was missing. Was it the element of danger John and Craig had both had? Maybe she'd get used to it, but maybe she would always be a little bit empty.

This is the life I choose. This is what I want.

Janine went into the bedroom and changed into comfortable clothes. Whenever she left the house these days, she made an effort to dress up—no good all those work clothes going to waste sitting in the wardrobe, but she'd put on some weight after the baby and they were all too tight.

Down to her bra and knickers she realised there was someone else in the house.

'Who's there?' she called.

'I let myself in.' Craig was standing behind her in the hallway.

'What the fuck? Where have you been?'

'You've let yourself go, Janine.' His eyes travelled up and down her nearly naked figure.

'Get out of my house.'

'It's not your house, Janine. I know you haven't been paying rent since I left.'

'You have no right to come waltzing back in here like you own the place. And where's Mum's money? Hmm?'

'It's gone. You won't see that again, and the case against me with the police? That'll die with her, you know. I had hoped to be in an out before you got back.

Wanted to grab a few things now I'm not a wanted criminal anymore.'

Janine's ears were ringing she was so angry. She couldn't string words together and felt rooted to the spot. The man who'd ruined her life, the man responsible for her mother's death, was standing in her house as though nothing could touch him.

'I've done whatever I wanted with whoever I want for a long time. You and your cunt of a mother won't change that.' His voice was icy. It was as though he was another person entirely. 'I'm just grabbing a few essentials; pieces of couture I couldn't let you keep. You don't mind, do you?'

'I told you to get out.'

'You're not in a position to demand things, Janine. I'll go when I'm done.'

'I'll call the police.'

'Go ahead. The house isn't in your name, so I'm not trespassing. The things I'm taking don't belong to you, I'm not stealing.' He stepped towards her and she recoiled. She grabbed her dress from the bed and held it in front of her.

'Do whatever you're gonna do and get out.' Her heart was beating so fast she could barely hear anything over the thudding in her ears.

'I'm almost done. Just wanted to say hi before I left.'

He was in the house the whole time and waited until I was half-naked to show himself? She shuddered. She had known since he left, he was a bad man but this calculating, cold, arsehole was not the man she'd been in love with. How well he'd kept the mask in place while they were together.

He opened and closed wardrobes in the next room. She wanted him out, but as he said, there wasn't much she could do about it. And then she remembered Chloe.

She dropped the dress, pulled on a windcheater and jeans and hurried out to the lounge where the baby was lying on her back kicking her legs. She scooped up her baby. *He better not touch you or I'll kill him myself.*

Janine took the baby with her into the bedroom, slid down onto the floor, and rested her back against the closed door. She hoped it would be enough to keep Craig out.

'I have what I came for. See you around Janine.' Craig said, his voice back to the chipper tones she was used to.

She waited for him to close the front door behind him, then counted to one hundred before she got up. He hadn't taken much, some of the clothes and bags hanging in the wardrobe in the spare room. She went into the baby's room and put Chloe down for a nap. She probably wouldn't sleep but at least Janine would feel better knowing she was safe in her cot. The rocking chair was bare; Craig had taken the knitted blanket he had bought for her to use when she was up at night feeding. A small sob left her mouth before she put her hand over it.

She sunk to her knees, silently shaking. It felt as though she'd been waiting for this day ever since he left and now it was really over.

He would never be brought to account for the things he did; he was much too clever for that. It was her own fault she'd been drawn into it in the first place.

Bernard walked in about an hour later. She was still sitting on the floor in the baby's room.

'You alright, baby?'

She nodded.

'What's happened? Have you been crying?' he asked.

'It's fine, really.'

'I understand if you're upset about the house.'

'It's not that.'

He came to sit next to her. She'd leaned against the wall staring at the baby. 'What is it? You can tell me.'

She sighed. 'I'm going to have to change the locks.'

'Why?' Bernard's voice went up in alarm.

'Craig came by for his things. I didn't realise he still had a key.'

'Piece of shit, you should have called the police.'

'And told them what? The guy whose name is on the lease is here, come take him away?' She was so tired. She wanted to feel safe, like things were going her way and for once.

'You never told me this place is in his name.'

Janine studied his face; she couldn't work out if he was angry or not. 'I don't know how to change it. I don't know who the agent is. Honestly, I thought they would have sent me a letter demanding rent by now.'

'You haven't been paying rent? For how long?'

'Who do I pay it to?' She frowned, he was making a much bigger deal of this than was necessary.

'I'm sure you could have found out if you tried hard enough. Did you try the bond authority? Or the tenancy union? Or calling the real estate agents in the area?'

She looked down at her feet, her socks were getting threadbare on the toes, they'd need mending shortly. She looked back to Bernard. 'I guess I never got around to it.'

'Sometimes I wonder how you manage to function. Honestly.'

If she hadn't been so exhausted, she might have been offended. Craig had never been mean. Then again Craig had stolen two hundred grand of her mother's money and left her holding the baby, literally. Maybe it was good Bernard said what he felt. At least she knew what he was thinking.

'I'll do it on Monday.'

'If they haven't asked for it yet it can't be very important.' He leaned over to kiss her forehead. 'Did he say hi to his daughter?'

'Didn't even look in here. It was like he was a completely different person. I knew he was a piece of shit, but he was always charming. Today he was scary.' She grabbed Bernard's hand and squeezed it.

'I know a locksmith. I'll give him a ring now and see if he'll come over. I don't want him wandering around with a key.'

'Thank you.' She had thought about saying he didn't have to, that it would be fine, but she wanted to feel safe. It would make Bernard feel important to sort this out for her.

He got up and went to the lounge to call his friend and arrange to come around.

'He'll be here first thing tomorrow,' he said from the other room. Then he popped his head around the door of the nursery. 'Need a cuppa?'

'Yes, please.'

He dipped his head in a nod. She got up, splashed her face with cold water, and took Chloe out to the kitchen to be with him. She watched him pottering about making coffee for the two of them. When he was done, they sat on the couch and watched TV.

*   *   *

Bernard's mate came around to change the locks in the morning and charged mate's rates, for which she was grateful. The sale of the house and estate hadn't yet gone through and she was using money she'd set aside for back rent to cover her expenses.

The next few weeks slipped by in a haze of boredom and routine. Bernard stayed with her almost every night. He was good with Chloe and would occasionally make dinner as well.

When the time came to auction off her family home Janine couldn't quite believe it was happening. She stood in the kitchen inside listening to the bids. They'd set a reserve to the amount of the mortgage and her mother's debts, plus a healthy amount she could put away for a deposit on her own house one day down the track. They'd had no luck finding who was renting out the place in Brunswick. Even Bernard was stumped.

The real estate agent walked back into the house with a grin plastered across his face.

'We've got a bid for $356,000. I think you should take it. It's well above the reserve and a good price for the area.'

'Jesus,' she said quietly. 'Of course, take it.'

The agent went back outside and confirmed the sale. There was a small round of applause and then he brought the new owners into the kitchen where she and Bernard and Chloe waited to fill in the paperwork.

She looked at the buyers, a young couple, the sort of people her mother would have approved of living here. As she signed and initialled the contracts of sale, the hollow feeling grew in her belly.

More than half her life had been spent in this house. A lot had happened since she left home six years ago. She's become a mother, been homeless, and made two disastrous choices in men. She looked at Bernard, staring out the window at the back garden.

28. Best Interests of the Child

Bernard drove the three of them back to Brunswick. A shiver run down Janine's spine.

'Someone walk over your grave?' Bernard asked, taking the baby's capsule out of the cab.

'It's nothing.' She hoped it was nothing.

They went inside and Janine flicked the kettle on. 'Cuppa?'

'Yeah, ta.' Bernard put the baby in her playpen and went to the couch. It was a Saturday afternoon and he would want to watch the footy. She didn't care for it, but he seemed to be very invested in who was winning.

'Who's playing?' she asked.

'Collingwood and Hawthorn.'

'You don't go for either of them.' His team was Footscray, she was sure.

'Nah, but I need to watch for the tipping.'

She stirred two teaspoons of sugar into his tea and nodded. He needed to enough knowledge to keep up with bantering to the other blokes at work.

She sat down next to him, placing his tea down careful not to block his view. 'Thanks, love,' he said without looking at her.

There was barely time to take a sip of her tea before there was a knock at the door.

'I'll get it,' she said.

Her grandparents were both standing on her veranda, she was so surprised she couldn't find any words.

'Hello, dear. Are you going to invite us in?' her grandmother asked.

'Yes, okay.' She stepped back to let Carol and Ted in.

'It's a bit of a dump, isn't it, love?' Ted said.

Janine clenched her teeth together it didn't seem the time to start a fight. 'I was just having a cuppa, do you want one?'

'No thank you, we won't stay long,' Carol said.

Bernard turned the volume all the way down on the T.V. and stood beside her.

'We've come to tell you that we want to take the baby,' Carol went on.

'Of course, you can take her for a visit. She'd love to see her grandparents.'

'We meant permanently.'

Janine tried to make sense of what had just happened. She had expected criticism but never this.

'Why would we let you do that?' Bernard said after a lengthy pause. His voice was very quiet and Jannie turned to him. His face seemed calm, but his hands were fists beside him.

'I don't know who you are. This is family business,' Ted said.

'I'm Janine's boyfriend, and I'm pretty sure you can't walk into someone's house and demand their baby.'

'Boyfriend? Gee, she certainly moved on quickly. You could be anyone, I won't have criminal types hanging around my granddaughter.'

'Criminal types? The fuck you mean by that?'

'No good getting all worked up in front of the child. I know a bad sort when I see one.' Ted sniffed and looked over to the playpen. As he started to turn back everything seemed to go into slow motion. Bernard took a step forward and swung his fist at Ted's head. Janine tried to stop him, but she wasn't fast enough. It took a very long time for Ted to fall to the floor, he knocked his head on the dining table on the way down. Carol had started to screech.

'I'll show you worked up, old man.' Bernard bent down as though to hit Ted again.

'Stop it,' Janine shouted. Ted was a crumpled heap on the floor, suddenly looking much more like the old man he was, and a cut on his head had started to bleed profusely.

'Call an ambulance, stupid girl,' Carol said.

Bernard stalked away, slamming the front door after him. Janine looked down at the cut on her grandfather's head; he was badly hurt.

She called the ambulance; they'd be there within five minutes. She sat on the floor pressing a tea towel against the cut as the woman on the phone had told her to.

Carol paced up and down muttering to herself. 'Goes to show who you're consorting with,' she said.

'What did you think would happen? Barging in and announcing you want to take Chloe?'

'If you weren't unfit before, your boyfriend has seriously assaulted an old man. We'll easily take your child and make sure she doesn't turn out like you did.'

'Over my dead body.' Janine got up to open the front door.

'What's happened here?'

'Her psychotic boyfriend struck my husband, for absolutely no reason at all, and he cut his head when he fell.' Carol rushed up to the paramedics. 'He's run off now, thank heavens, but he could be back at any minute. We need to take the baby too, she can't be left in this environment.'

'Is the baby injured?' the taller of the two ambulance officers asked.

'No, she's fine. You can't have her,' Janine said, shouting over her grandmother to be heard.

'Unless the child is in immediate danger or has sustained an injury, we can't intercede.'

'Fat lot of good you are.' Carol spoke under her breath, but Janine heard every word.

'We need to get this gentleman to the hospital, his wife can come with us, but you'll need to come on your own.'

Carol glanced at Janine, still standing in the middle of the dining room floor covered in blood from the head wound and clutching the soaked tea towel.

'Don't follow us. We'll be reporting this to the police, and I will do everything in my power to have the baby taken away from you.' Carol snatched up her small navy-blue leather handbag and rushed out the door toward the ambulance. Janine had no idea where Bernard had gone but was relieved he hadn't come back yet.

Chloe was wailing; standing, holding the bars of her playpen to keep herself upright, her small face was covered in snot and tears. Janine looked at her bloody clothes and hands.

I can't pick her up till I've cleaned this off. She ran to the bathroom and threw her clothes into the bathtub before hurriedly rinsing the blood from her skin.

She put on her dressing gown and came back to the baby. Janine paced around the lounge and dining room, singing softly to Chloe. It took fifteen minutes to get her to calm down. Not long after she fell asleep.

Instead of putting the baby down, Janine held her for hours, until Bernard showed up well after dark. He had to come back at some point—his ute was in the driveway and he had work on Monday.

He had a key, and she heard him fumbling with the lock on the front door. She stayed on the couch, unsure what sort of mood or state he'd be in.

'I'm in here.'

He grunted something indistinguishable and slammed the front door shut.

'Are you alright?' she asked.

'Been better.' He looked dishevelled, his hair was sticking up around his head, his shoes and the bottom of his pants were muddy and he smelled of cigarettes and wet dog.

'Where did you go?'

'Been walking around. I was angry.'

Janine said nothing.

'Is he alright?' He couldn't look at her. At least he knew it wasn't okay to go around smashing old men in the face.

'They went off in the ambulance. Carol wants to take the baby. She said they'd go to the police.'

He sighed. 'I need a shower.'

'Okay.' She watched him trudge down the hallway into the bathroom. Her bloody clothes were still in the tub. She hoped he wasn't squeamish. The water came on, then the sound of his boots hitting the floor as he took them off. She'd never known what to do when men were angry—her father had never been lost hist temper, John had his moments, but she learned to avoid it. Craig never showed his anger except in the last visit. He must have spent a lot of time biting his tongue. Bernard was easy to read, if not so easy to control. She'd wanted to punch her grandfather too.

Bernard stayed under the water for a long time, when he came out, he went straight into the bedroom. Chloe was happy to go back into her playpen, so Janine went to check on him.

'Feel any better?'

'I guess.'

He had crawled into bed, nude and still a little damp from the shower. She took off her robe and slipped in beside him. 'It'll be okay.'

'Wait and see, right?'

She kissed the back of his neck as she played big spoon and waited until he fell asleep. She couldn't expect him to be strong all the time.

*   *   *

'I'm sorry about your grandfather,' Bernard said in the morning when she opened her eyes.

'How long have you been awake?'

'A while. I didn't want to wake you.'

'That's sweet.' She reached forward to kiss him, and just as he started to kiss her back, she heard Chloe crying in the next room. 'Every time.'

He smiled up at her as she put on her dressing gown and went out. *She must be hungry, my boobs feel like they're going to burst*. Bernard brought her a coffee while she was nursing. He seemed haggard; it must have been awful knowing he'd put an old man in hospital.

When she'd finished feeding Chloe and her coffee was gone, she looked the lounge. There was stuff everywhere—no wonder Carol thought she was unfit.

Janine tidied all the plates into the sink, she was elbow deep in the hot soapy water when there was a knock on the door.

'I'll get it,' Bernard said, levering himself off the couch.

He walked to the door and opened it, there was some muffle speaking she couldn't catch.

'You can't do that!' he said loudly.

She didn't hear the response, but she dropped the plate she was washing and rushed to the door. A woman in a beige suit stood there, with two young police officers behind her.

'Are you Janine Barrett?' the woman asked.

'Yes,' she croaked, she knew what was coming but she didn't want it to be true.

'I'm from Child Protection. We have an interim order to take the child, Chloe, from the home pending a formal investigation.'

Janine's ears were ringing. She could see the woman's lips still moving but didn't understand what she was saying.

'Do you understand?' the woman said, her voice loud and slow as though Janine was an idiot.

'Surely you can't do that,' she said at last.

'This is a court order, I don't want this to get ugly, for the child's sake, but I am perfectly entitled to take her.' She seemed calm, but Janine thought she saw a spiteful glint in her eye. 'It would be best if you cooperated.'

'Where are you taking her?' Janine was rubbing her damp hands up and down the sides of her thighs.

'She'll be given to a care home for a few nights. If we can resolve the issue by then, you'll have her back, if not she'll be set up with a foster carer.'

'I've never been apart from her. She means everything to me. I'm not a bad mother.' Janine started to cry. All her anger and fear had disappeared and all that remained was emptiness.

'I'm sure you're a good mother. I'm just doing my job. If you would step aside.'

Bernard's jaw rippled and she had a vision of him punching the social worker woman in the face as he had with Ted. Instead, he took her hand and led her back into the lounge. He sat on the couch, his face slack and glazed.

Janine ran into the nursery, grabbing Chloe's favourite things. If she had to be separated from her baby at least she could be comforted by little rabbit, or the blanket she liked.

'You have to take these, they're her favourite.'

'We have everything she needs at the home,' the woman in the beige suit looked down her nose at the rabbit. Chloe liked to suck on the ears, and it looked dishevelled.

'Please. I don't want her to be sad.' Janine held out the blanket.

The woman harrumphed but took it. The two police officers were silent. One stood near the door of the lounge keeping an eye on Bernard, the other followed the social worker back to where Chloe was. Janine picked her up.

'Chloe, you have to go with the nice lady, okay?' She was sobbing and Chloe was confused. 'It's okay baby, I promise it's only for a little while. I'll get you back.'

'I'll take her now.'

Janine handed her over and Chloe looked at her mother, her little face puckered in confusion and ready to cry.

Janine trailed behind them as they walked out of the house. Chloe was buckled into the back of the police car, the social worker got in beside her. Janine could barely see through the tears streaming down her face. She felt as though she couldn't breathe.

They drove off without another word, Janine was holding the paper the social worker had given her. She wanted to throw it away, but she wouldn't get Chloe back like that. She shivered in the cold morning air.

'Come back inside. Close the door.' Bernard was hovering behind her in the hallway.

She turned around; the house was so empty. Without Chloe it was all just stuff. Shit she'd accumulated.

'You did everything you could,' Bernard said.

'Get out of my house,' she said, her voice barely more than a whisper.

'What?'

'I said, get out of my house.' She couldn't look at him.

'What did I do?'

'Don't you get it? This is all your fault.' All the anger she thought she'd lost came surging back, her hands were trembling with adrenalin and rage.

'I'm not the one with crazy relatives who want to take my kid.'

'No, you're the one who punched her grandfather. I don't want to look at you right now.' She turned away and left him standing there, the cold breeze followed her back through the house until she shut the bedroom door on it.

There was no coming back from this. It was what she deserved. Chloe would be better off with Carol and Ted. She lay face down on the bed, numb, and closed her eyes. Nothing mattered anymore.

29. Epilogue

1995, four years later

Janine tried to sit up straight in the hard wooden pews, but it was so hot and stuffy she just wanted to sleep. Her dress was tight, and her shoes were pinching her toes. The little girl next to her ran her fingers over the Bible in the back of the pew in front of them.

Her grandmother, Carol, lay in the closed casket at the front of the church, the minister was going on about the valley of death or something, and Janine's mind was on her daughter.

Child protection had given custody of Chloe to Carol after the incident with Bernard, but when her grandfather had died a few months back and her health started to fail, they decided Chloe could go back to her mother.

It was all a bit of a whirlwind, in the years since Janine had been up and down, sometimes she held a job, and sometimes she would slip into old habits taking too many Valium. Since her baby had come back, she'd been better about that, had made sure the house was clean and tidy when Child Protection visited, and her that boyfriend was out. He had come around to the idea of having a kid in the house, though mostly seemed to get Chloe to run to the fridge for beer when he ran out.

Squeezing her eyes closed, Janine willed herself to cry, but no tears came. Carol had been a bitch till the end, didn't even let her have visits with Chloe.

Surprisingly, the little girl had turned out okay, apparently not fussed about living with a woman who claimed to be her mother, but that she didn't know. Janine put her hand on her daughter head. *We'll be alright, you and me.* Chloe smiled back at her.

Keep reading for a sneak peak of:

The Mother's Fault

By Fleur Blüm

Out now

Chapter 1

2015

Chloe Barrett looked at the incoming call from her mother on the screen of her mobile phone and sighed. She declined the call and turned back to her friend, Mel. They were out on the town, Mel's boyfriend was the drummer in a band, The Inflatable Cocks, and they were playing at Red Plum Bar. It wasn't Chloe's usual scene, slightly too grungy in her opinion, but she wanted to support her friend, who wanted to support her boyfriend. Plus, Mel had promised to be her wing-woman for the night.

The bar was down one of Melbourne's many alleys, still hanging onto its pre-gentrification vibe. On the door frame as they entered, along with a sign stating: 'No shoes, no shirt, no service' the management had taped an additional rule: 'NO DICKHEADS'.

The rule was somewhat redundant given Chloe couldn't tell the difference between patrons and staff; they all looked pretty rough.

She tugged the hem of her short, flared, neon orange skirt.

'No one wears colours at Plum,' Mel said earlier in the evening as they were dressing.

'Pretending I'm more of a rock chick than I am isn't going to get me anywhere,' Chloe had replied.

'Alright, you can keep the skirt but you'll have to wear a band t-shirt on top.' Mel scrunched up her face and held out a tight black tee with a band logo on the front. Mel dated exclusively from a never-ending pool of grungy musicians who were destined to be 'the next big thing' in the Melbourne band scene, so had quite a collection of T-shirts. Lead guitarists and front men held the most social capital, then bass players, placing drummers lowest in the hierarchy. Keyboard players didn't rate a mention, if the band had keys, they weren't hard-core enough for Mel.

Despite any reservations about getting in with Chloe's outfit, the bouncer barely glanced at their ID before waving them through. The venue was cave-like;_ dark, narrow and long, painted black with huge paste-ups of famous rock musicians plastered on the walls. The bar took up several metres directly in front of the door with more photos of musicians hanging in dinged-up frames above it. Back lights shone through opaque white and tan plastic masquerading as marble, below the countertop.

The stage at the far end of the room covered in scuffed black paint_ was backed by a deep red crushed velvet curtain. It stood empty for the moment, but music loud enough to make conversation difficult pumped through the sound system. A few people milled about, not many, but it was still early.

'The band room is this way,' Mel said, pulling Chloe behind her in the other direction, away from the stage, past the bathrooms which smelled relatively fresh, to a nondescript door. Mel knocked a couple of times before barging into the room.

The room was larger than Chloe expected but still cramped with the four members of The Inflatable Cocks, their gear, their respective girlfriends and guests.

'You made it, babe!' Mel's boyfriend, who went by Robbo, said from her left. He was a towering, bulky man, which made sense for a hard rock drummer. His long dirty-blond hair and biker-beard were not to Chloe's taste.

'You remember my friend, Chloe,' Mel said to no one in particular, before standing on tip toes to kiss Robbo with rather more enthusiasm than was necessary. Chloe looked away. She'd met the guys in the band a couple of times before but was still not comfortable enough to hang out without Mel as a buffer.

Though quieter in the band room than in the main bar, the music was still loud enough to make silence seem like _her best response. When Mel and Robbo separated, Mel dragged Chloe over to a decrepit-looking black vinyl couch, pulling her down to sit beside her, with her boyfriend on the other side.

'Are there other bands on tonight?' she asked.

'Yeah, we're headlining, so we're on last, but we gotta be here early coz the other bands use our drums and amps,' the lead singer, whose name might have been Steve, said. Chloe nodded. The group went back to discussing their set and other band-related stuff, Chloe sat quietly; she had no experience with the band scene.

Chloe's hands felt unnaturally empty without a drink in them, and the buzz from the couple of wines she had before coming out were starting to wear off. 'I'm going to the bar, does anyone want anything?'

'Get me a JD and coke, babe,' Mel said.

'Sure.' The band members were drinking beers from the fridge, no doubt part of the rider, and didn't need anything else, why buy drinks when you can get these free?

Chloe was bombarded with music which was much louder than she remembered. The bar was more crowded but nowhere near the sweaty crush she expected when the band played. She ordered two JD and cokes; they weren't her drink of choice, but it was easier than screaming two different orders across the bar.

As she waited for the barman to return with the drinks, Chloe noticed the man standing next to her. Slim and wiry_ and over six feet tall_, he stood half a head taller than Chloe, even in her high heels.

'Hi,' he said leaning towards her so she could hear him over the music. When he turned to her it felt like he could see straight into her mind, and all her secrets.

'Hi.' She was surprised how good he smelled; orange, leather, and musk perhaps. He wore tight black jeans and a black T-shirt which hugged his slight frame under a battered leather jacket.

'I'm Eddie.' He held out his hand toward her.

Her cheeks warmed in a blush as she took his hand._ A slightly crooked, aquiline nose sat in a strong face, which made him look intriguing, rather than detracting from his appearance. The eyes which seemed to see deep into her were pale, perhaps hazel or very light brown, hard to tell in the dim light of the bar.

Chloe giggled; he was so hot, and his hand still held hers.

'What's your name sweetheart?' he prompted.

'I'm Chloe.' As she looked down, finally able to break his gaze, her drinks appeared on the bar. 'It's lovely to meet you.'

'What?' he said, yelling over the music.

'I said it's lovely to meet you,' she said, leaning in closer and catching his scent again. It was rare for her to go to pieces over a man, but something about him threw off her equilibrium.

'Both for you?' Eddie's eyes fell on the two drinks she held, one eyebrow cocked.

'No, my friend is in the band room.'

'Why don't you take her drink to her, then meet me in the alley? We can talk out there. I need a smoke.'

'Okay.' Chloe could feel the stupid grin plastered on her face, but couldn't seem to pull herself together to act cool. She rushed back to the band room.

'I'm going outside for a smoke,' she said, handing Mel her drink.

'You don't smoke,' Mel replied, a knowing grin spreading across her face. 'Have fun. The boys are on at eleven.'

Chloe nodded.

The Mother's Fault

Out in the alley a group of about fifteen people clustered around a couple of tin boxes on the ground which served as ashtrays. She had tried smoking a few times in her teens, but given her mother had been a heavy smoker it had never seemed attractive. More like a waste of money and terrible for your health. Smoking inside venues had been banned for eight years now, since before she was legally allowed into bars and nightclubs. She much preferred bars without the smoke haze.

Eddie leaned one shoulder against the graffiti-covered wall of the narrow laneway. His collared leather jacket reminded Chloe of James Dean, the cigarette dangling from his lips adding to the impression.

'Chloe, you found us.' He grinned and beckoned her to stand by him. She hadn't brought a jacket with her, usually she spent enough time inside dancing, surrounded by other people. She crossed her arms across her chest, hugging herself for warmth, her cold drink dangling from her fingertips.

'You want one?' Eddie offered her a smoke.

'No, I'm okay.'

He shrugged and turned back to the conversation, which seemed to be focused on the latest football results. Chloe didn't care for sport much, but she knew enough to follow the talk.

'You cold, hun?' Eddie turned to her as he stubbed out his cigarette.

'A bit.' She wanted to appear tough, but after ten minutes in the chilly laneway she was thinking of going back inside.

'Here,' Eddie opened his jacket and wrapped it around her, pressing his body against hers. She was sure it wasn't just the alcohol or the jacket that warmed her cheeks. As she pressed up against his trim, lean torso, the attraction deepened. 'You smell nice,' he murmured, his warm breath brushing her cheeks.

'Thanks.' She had no idea what an appropriate response was. Clearly, he was interested, using his jacket as an excuse to get close. He was hotter than the guys she was usually attracted to, and seemed kind and thoughtful. Maybe she'd struck it lucky early in the night.

Eddie finished his beer and stubbed out another cigarette. 'The music will be starting soon, you coming in with me?'

'I should check on my friend.'

'You know the guys in the band?'

'The drummer's girlfriend.'

'Wow, you'll have to introduce me. I hang around the scene a lot, but I don't know many of the guys personally.' Eddie squeezed her shoulders inside his jacket. 'Come on, it's freezing out here. Find me on the dance floor when you're done.'

Chloe smiled and nodded. She started to pull away, out of the coat, but Eddie held her close to him until they were back in the venue. With a wink, he slipped his jacket off and went toward the stage where the first band of the night was setting up.

'How did you go?' Mel asked, grinning. She and the others were hanging out near the bar now to watch the other bands. Perhaps the riders had run out too.

'Alright. Hung out with the smokers for a bit.' Chloe couldn't help grinning.

'You must have scored, you look smug. What are you doing in here then? Get back to the boy and close the deal.' Mel winked.

This was exactly what Chloe hoped would happen, but she still felt guilty leaving her friend. She stepped back into the main room and worked her way to the front where the first band had started to play. Eddie had a beer in hand and she wished she'd bought another drink. It would have to wait now; it was rude to go to the bar while the bands were playing.

The music was hard, fast, loud, and heavily distorted, Mel had described it as a punk and metal night. The vocalist screamed incoherently into the microphone, but the band members were in time and probably in tune. Chloe caught herself bobbing her head along with the rhythm of the guitar, and was impressed, not for the first time, at the proficiency of the double kick pedals the drummer was using. Though not her cup of tea, she usually listened to pop or classical music, she appreciated the passion and talent of the band.

Eddie bounced next to her enthusiastically. Too sparse yet to be called a mosh-pit, it certainly had the energy of one already. A couple of times he put a hand on her lower back, sending thrills of excitement up her spine.

The set lasted about forty-five minutes; the audience whooped and clapped their appreciation for the musicians who were all drenched in sweat from the vigour of their performance.

Eddie leaned over to her. 'Let me get you a drink, then I need another smoke.'

'Okay.'

'What are you having?' he asked.

'Whatever you're having is fine.' Chloe was thirsty and would have asked for a soft drink or water if she hadn't been worried he would judge her as uncool and unable to hold her alcohol. Although she usually preferred a subtle white wine, she would be happy with whatever he bought.

She hung back, not wanting to get caught in the crush at the bar. Mel gave her a nod from across the room, where she and Robbo were chatting with the band that had just finished as they packed up.

'Here you go, you had JD last time yeah?' Eddie handed her a small tumbler filled with dark brown liquid, her face heated as their fingers brushed as she took the glass.

'Well done for remembering.' It was more expensive than the beer he held in his other hand.

'I have a few skills; knowing someone's drink is one of them.' Now he had one hand free, he pulled her behind him out to the laneway. As impolite as it was considered to buy drinks during the bands it was worse to go out for a smoke, and the alley was bustling with people getting their nicotine fix.

Eddie found a patch of wall to lean against a little way from the crowd. There was something about the way he stared at her that made her believe she was the only person who mattered; her belly fluttered and her mind seem to work slowly.

'So Chloe, what did you think of the music?' he asked, eyes roving over her.

'I dunno.' She giggled. 'I'm sure they're very good, but I'm not very hard-core when it comes to music.'

'I loved it. I like all kinds of music though.' He sipped his beer. 'What's your go to album these days?'

'I listen to Lady Gaga when I work out. Mostly whatever is on the radio though.'

'I see.' He nodded and seemed about to say something else but decided against it.

'I know it probably... sounds like a cop out... I guess I'm not very musical.' Her words wouldn't flow in his presence.

'I've never been able to play an instrument, my parents never pushed me that way, but I've always thought the music industry was a fantastic business to get into.'

'You work in the industry then?'

A slow smile spread across his face. 'I have my fingers in a few different things. I was a band booker for a while for a place in Brunswick, but that didn't pan out. I mostly work for myself.'

He must be very driven to be self-employed.

'I'm sure you'd do very well at whatever you put your mind to.'

'Are you flirting with me, Miss Chloe?'

'No, I mean … a little.' Despite the cold, her cheeks were burning.

'Glad to hear it.' He leaned his head close to her ear, his breath warm on her neck. 'I think you're hot.' He stood up again and took a long, meaningful drag on his cigarette. 'I'm sure you hear that all the time though.'

Chloe turned away, her heart racing. 'No, not very often.' She turned her eyes back to him to see his hand pressed against his chest in mock surprise.

'I can't believe it. A girl as cute as you who doesn't know it. How did I get so lucky?'

Chloe never had a man as handsome and charming as Eddie interested in her, she wasn't sure what to do with his attention. Mel would tell her to go with the flow, but her mind spun ineffectually. Should she try to kiss him? Or wait until he kissed her, but risk him thinking she wasn't interested. Eddie stubbed out his smoke and flicked it into the tin nearby.

'Sounds like the next band is on.' He cocked his head toward the door and sauntered back inside. She followed, good job making interesting conversation.

It wasn't like her to be flustered by the attention of a handsome man. She prided herself on the ability to connect with people from all walks of life. Perhaps the slow burn in her groin was to blame for her apparent lack of verbal skills.

The next band was a six-piece, with a trumpet and trombone added to the usual guitars and drums. They played a punk ska set with complicated slap-basslines and infectious beats. Chloe finished her drink part-way through their third song and found Eddie standing behind her, his hands on either side of her waist encouraging her hips to sway. Her stomach tensed and she felt out of breath; it wasn't the dancing that took her breath away.

As the set progressed, Eddie's hands moved their way forward, around her waist, lying against her stomach. His lean form was now pressed up against her back, his groin against her buttocks. She might have imagined it, but she thought there was a hint of hardness there.

'This is our last song, you guys have been great,' the singer announced, his jet-black hair stood stiff in a two-inch-high quiff covered in so much hair spray it hadn't moved through the entire performance. The guitarist struck the opening chord just as Eddie moved around to face her.

He stared into her eyes, the music faded away and there was nothing but his gaze holding hers. He kissed her, his lips soft and tender at first, then little by little, more insistent.

She felt like a teenager, making out in front of the stage. Despite being kissed many times before, it was as though this was the first time. Everything was new; sensations threatened to overwhelm her. Her groin was hot, pulsing, and she knew there would be slickness there, her nipples were pert and sensitive where she brushed against him. The warm place under his hand where he held her lower back felt as though it belonged to someone else.

At some point she realised Eddie had pulled away and was applauding the band taking their bow. She stood for a moment, frozen and dazed from the kiss, before managing to clap her hands.

'You're a great kisser, you know,' he said.

'Thanks,' she replied, still a little breathless. 'So are you.'

'I was going to suggest we ditch the last band and go back to your place, but I know you came with them, so that would be very bad form on my part to tempt you away from your friends.'

'You're right.'

'Another drink?'

She nodded, watching him as he walked to the bar for her again.

'You didn't say he was that hot, babe, damn.' Mel had appeared at her elbow without Chloe seeing her approach. She must really be smitten to be so oblivious.

'He's not bad.'

'I saw you two locking lips in that last song.'

Chloe smiled, unsure what to say.

'You absolute slut.' Mel batted her upper arm playfully. 'I don't think any of the band would notice if you snuck off early. Just saying.'

'Don't say that, I don't need any more temptation today.' Chloe shook her head. 'I have a rule about hooking up on the first night.'

'There are always exceptions, and for someone who looks like that, who only has eyes for you by the way … I would.'

Eddie waved to her from the bar and pointed to the door, obviously headed out for a smoke. 'As long as you won't hate me if I disappear. I'll text you to let you know, so you don't worry.'

'Thanks, babe. You know I need to be sure you haven't been murdered.' Mel followed her gaze to the door. 'You better follow; I know your mind is there anyway.'

Chloe smiled, gave her friend's hand a squeeze and bounded after Eddie into the laneway.

'Am I approved then?' he said, holding her drink out for her.

'I don't know what you mean.'

'I know what girls are like, your little debrief there was definitely getting the seal of approval from your wing-woman.'

'Who has been giving you all our secrets?' Chloe took a sip from her drink, this one had a lot more JD in it than the last, she wondered if he was trying to get her drunk, although he didn't need to. 'Mel said the band probably wouldn't miss me if I happened to leave before or during their set.'

'Oh really?' Eddie's eyebrow pulled up. 'You don't seem the type to go home with a stranger.'

'I'm not.'

'But?'

'It seems like a good bet I won't regret it in the morning if that kiss was anything to go by.' Before the kiss, she had been all hormones and nerves, but now she tapped into some hidden confidence. Perhaps she was just the right amount of drunk, or her hormones had kicked in, Chloe didn't want to question it.

'You wouldn't regret it. That's an Eddie Travers guarantee.' He watched her from under half-closed lids. 'I'm going to finish my drink, and then I'm going to get into a cab. I'd love you to join me.'